SERPENT'S WAKE

Cover art by Beth Alvarez

Edited by Savannah Grace Perran

First Edition: November 2020

ISBN-13: 978-1-952145-10-0

SERPENT'S WAKE

BOOK FOUR OF THE SNAKESBLOOD SAGA

BETH ALVAREZ

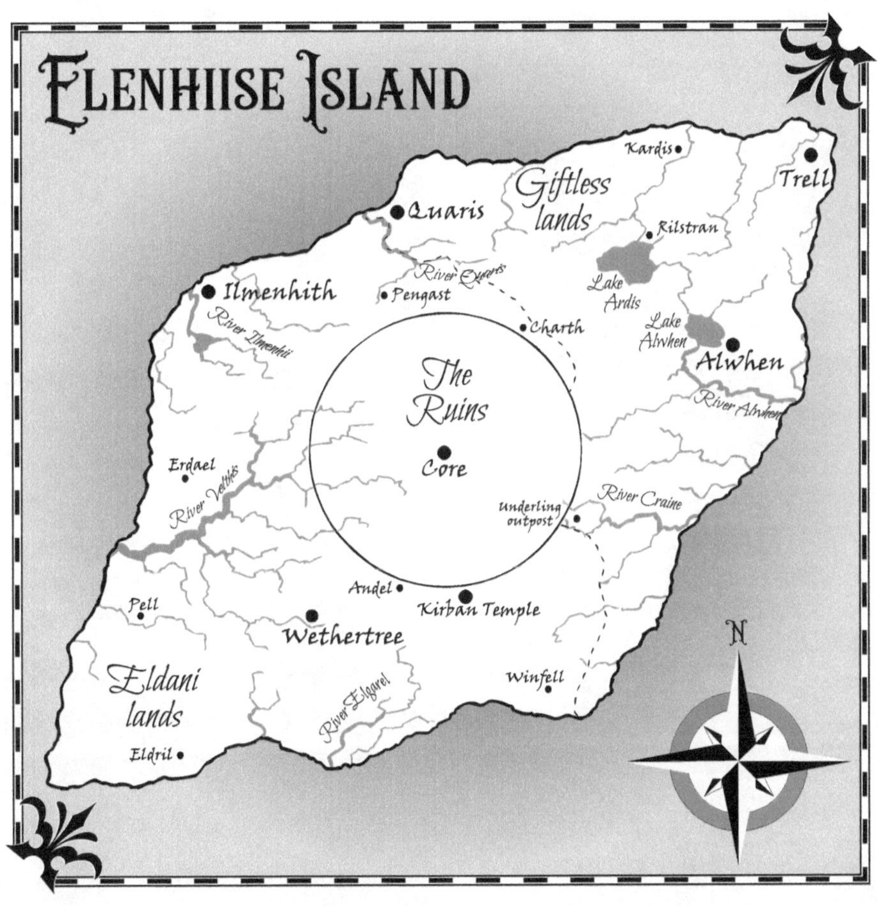
Elenhiise Island
Kardis
Trell
Quaris
Giftless lands
Rilstran
River Quaris
Ilmenhith
Pengast
Lake Ardis
River Ilmenhii
Charth
Lake Alwhen
Alwhen
The Ruins
River Alwhen
Core
Erdael
River Velthis
River Craine
Underling outpost
Andel
Kirban Temple
Pell
Wethertree
N
Eldani lands
River Elgarel
Winfell
Eldril

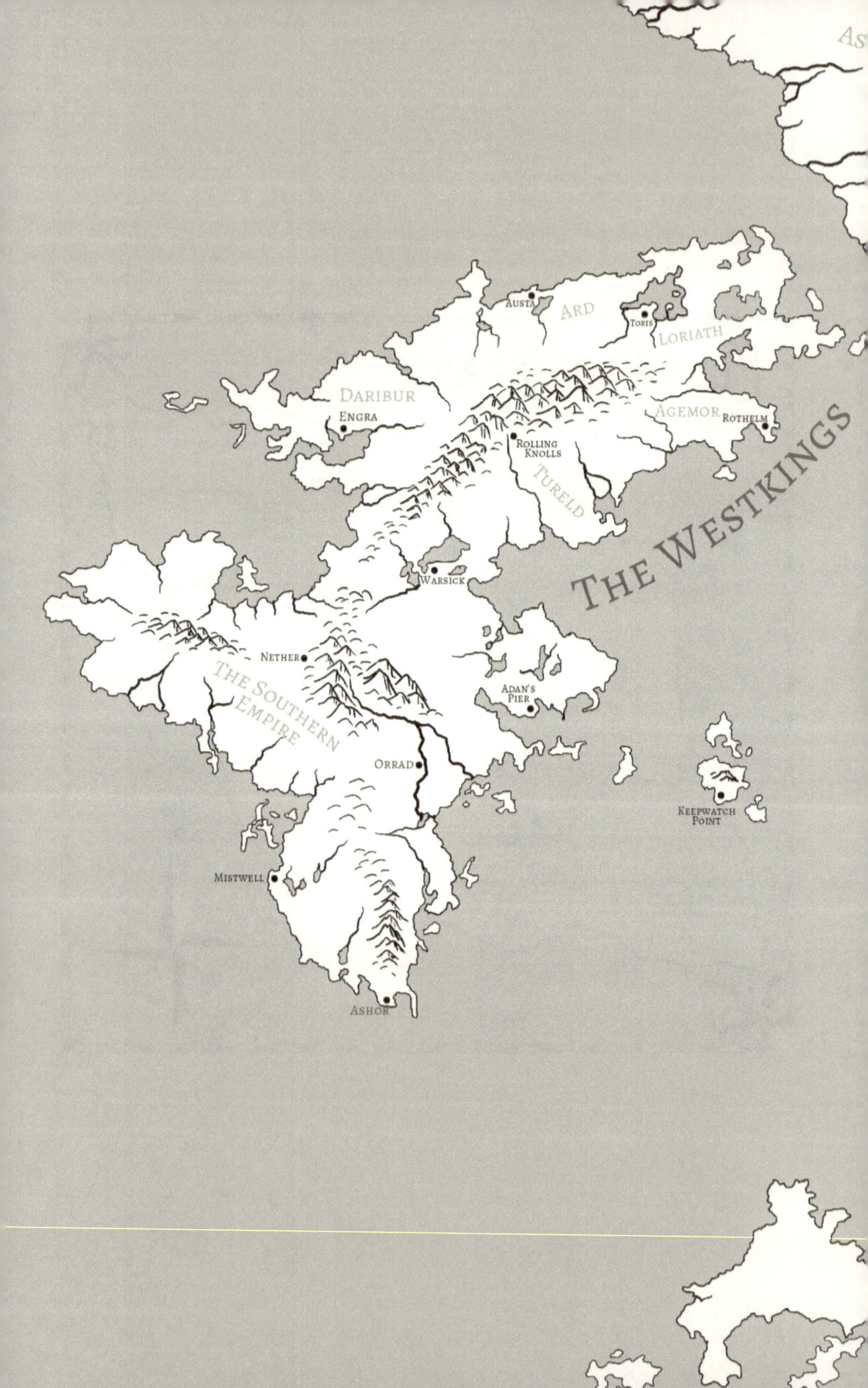

AS
THE WESTKINGS
ARD
AUSTA
TORIS
LORIATH
DARIBUR
ENGRA
AGEMOR
ROTHELM
ROLLING
KNOLLS
TURELD
WARSICK
THE SOUTHERN
EMPIRE
NETHER
ADAN'S
PIER
ORRAD
KEEPWATCH
POINT
MISTWELL
ASHOR

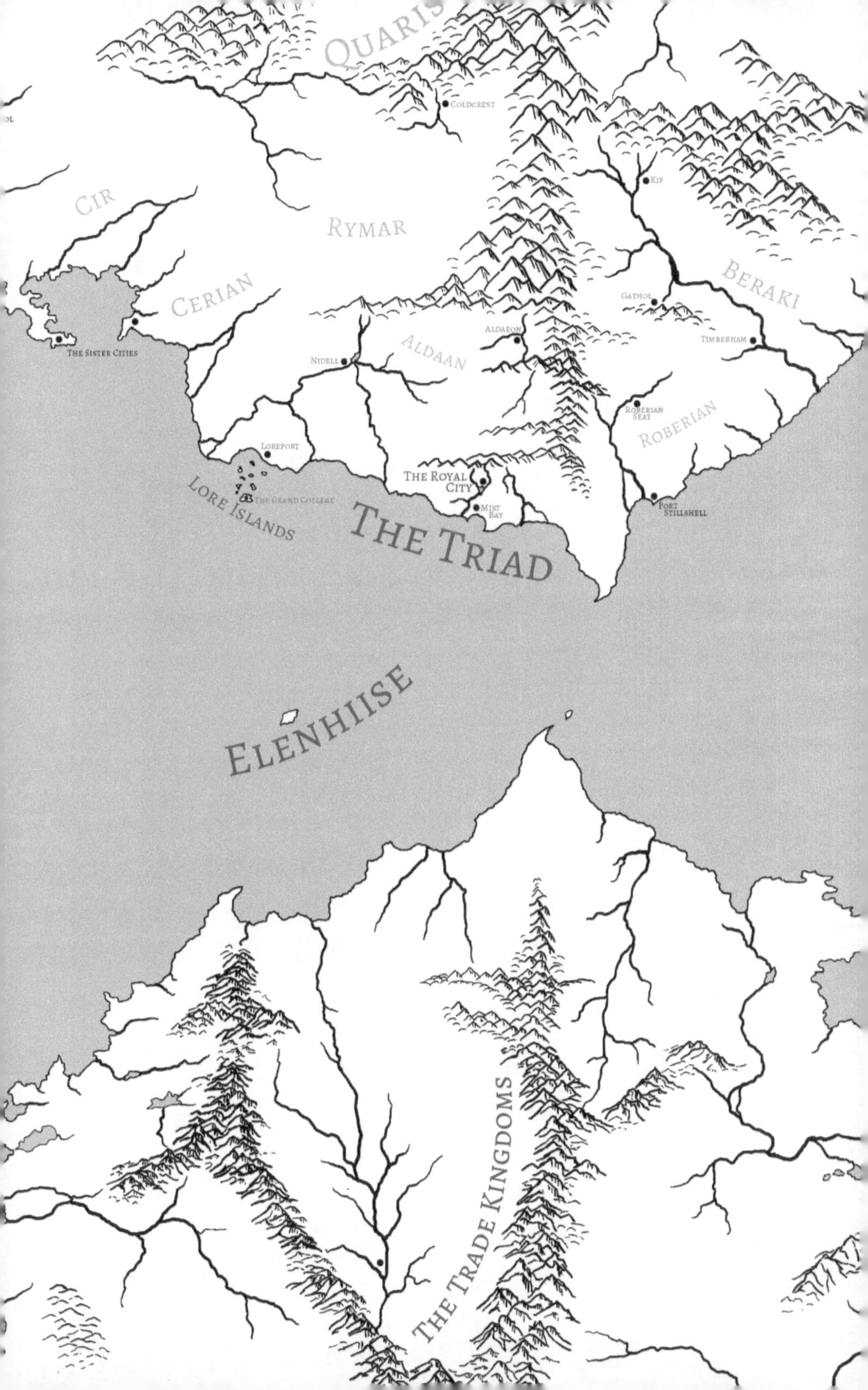

QUARIS
COLDCREST
CIR
RYMAR
KIP
CERIAN
BERAKI
GATHOL
ALDAEON
TIMBERHAM
THE SISTER CITIES
NIDELL
ALDAAN
ROBERIAN SEAT
ROBERIAN
LOREPORT
THE GRAND COLLEGE
LORE ISLANDS
THE ROYAL CITY
MIST BAY
PORT STILLSHELL
THE TRIAD
ELÉNHIISE
THE TRADE KINGDOMS

CONTENTS

1

SISTERS

SHYMIN RUBBED HER FOREHEAD, PUT DOWN HER PEN AND LEANED back in her chair. The candle on the windowsill burned low, down to the last hour-mark notched into its side. A mage-light would have been more effective, but she preferred the flame's warm glow. Nights alone didn't seem so uncomfortable by candlelight, and she spent more nights alone these days than ever before.

Rikka and Kytenia had been avoiding her since their elevation to blue robes. She didn't understand why. That she'd been passed over for promotion stung, but she wasn't angry at them for the decision the Masters had made. She wasn't angry at them for avoiding her, either, but she was hurt. It was one thing for Rikka, a long-time friend, to avoid her. But from Kytenia, it was something else entirely. They were sisters. The least Kytenia could have done was talk to her. Instead, she avoided their shared room until late at night, when Shymin was bound to be asleep. She always had some sort of excuse, claiming Nondar kept her busy with this or that until the small hours of the night, but Shymin didn't believe it.

Shaking her head, Shymin marked her place with a ribbon and closed her book.

There had never been any bitterness between them when Shymin advanced faster, or when she proved stronger and more adept with magecraft. Kytenia had not always been thrilled about being left behind, but Shymin refused to feel guilty for exploring the full potential of her ability. She'd never mistreated Kytenia or done anything to make her feel excluded because she was a lower rank, though a part of her had taken delight in her newfound importance. Kytenia had always been the favored daughter; prettier, more domestically skilled. For once in her life, it had been nice to be better at something. She'd still made an effort to make Kytenia feel valued. Why couldn't Kytenia do the same?

Behind her, the door creaked open. Shymin pushed back her chair and turned, careful to keep her expression impassive.

Kytenia looked surprised. "It's so late. I didn't think you'd still be awake."

"Close to three," Shymin agreed. She rose and left the candle burning as her sister stepped in and closed the door. Her cotton nightgown waited on her bed. Shymin changed out of her green mageling's robes, fingering the coarse fabric for longer than it deserved. Then she folded her robes and left them atop the chest at the foot of her bed. She had expected a scolding for staying up late, or even just the question of why. But Kytenia didn't speak, and Shymin felt the chill ache in her heart grow a little sharper.

It wasn't as if she had no reason to stay awake. She had chosen to push herself harder in her studies when Kytenia and Rikka were promoted and she was not. So long as her studies took precedence, she was allowed to stay up however late she pleased.

Though Shymin had explored other possibilities for how she might have fallen short, her studies were the only thing she thought she could improve. She wasn't a bad student; she'd always made acceptable marks. But there was always room for improvement, and though she was stronger, she supposed Kytenia might have developed more finesse in use of her Gift.

Finesse, not strength, was what they looked for in Master mages. Perhaps that was why she'd been passed over. Shymin paused, watching her sister fold her own robes and fetch her hairbrush.

"How is Master Nondar?" Shymin asked as she peeled back the blankets and slid into bed.

Kytenia glanced over her shoulder. Her eyes were weary and her mouth pinched. "Well enough. He's recovered a great deal, but it will be a while before he's back to himself."

Shymin nodded. "I'm surprised he's well enough to keep you studying so late." That the Archmage had decided to tutor Kytenia was no surprise, given how skilled she was in healing. But healing was her affinity too, and Shymin did not know how to compete. The position of Master of Healing had not been filled after Nondar's ascent to Archmage. There were no mentors left.

Kytenia shrugged and worked the tangles out of her hair. "Sometimes you do what you have to. Mastering the arts he can teach me is important. Should I put out the candle?"

Instead of answering, Shymin used her magic to extinguish the flame.

"Oh," Kytenia said. "Good night, then."

Shymin drew the blankets to her chin, listening as her sister climbed into bed and settled for the night. Squeezing her eyes shut, she willed herself to sleep. She didn't want to be jealous, but she couldn't help it. Once again, just like home, Kytenia outshone her in every way.

———

EDAGAN GRUMBLED to herself as she shuffled papers into order and tucked them into her desk. "Come in," she barked. She'd barely had a moment to rest, never mind address business. Neither she nor Anaide thought Nondar ready to resume his regular duties, which meant much of his work landed on their desks. Keeping it out of his hands only generated more work. She half expected her door to open for another messenger bringing her more bad news, and she narrowed her eyes when a green-robed mageling entered instead.

"Good morning, Master Edagan." Shymin dipped in a bow and trained her eyes on the floor as she presented herself in front of the large desk.

Edagan pursed her lips and leaned back in her chair. "Well," she started, then paused to clear her throat. "I've not spoken to any magelings yet today. What could you possibly need?" She struggled to keep her tone soft despite the edge in her words and the severity of her expression. She didn't mean to belittle the needs of the mages in her charge, but she couldn't think of anything someone might have sent a mageling to address.

The girl hesitated, shifting on her feet. "I was told you were overseeing staff and housing, since the Master in charge of those fields defected and has not returned." She faltered over the last word. Edagan couldn't blame her; no one in the temple liked to talk about that mess.

"That's correct." The aged woman laced her fingers together and rested her elbows atop her desk.

"In that case," Shymin said, fiddling with the cuff of her sleeve, "I'd like permission to move quarters. I share a room with my sister and I fear the schedule of our studies is different enough now that we disrupt each other."

It was such a minor request that Edagan almost laughed. Only a nagging doubt in the back of her head stopped her. The girl looked familiar, though Edagan couldn't place her name. She saw so many magelings about the temple that she couldn't possibly know them all. One of Nondar's old students, she thought. And not really a girl; a young woman, possibly several years older than their young queen. She leaned forward. "You share a room?" That was uncommon, especially now. They'd had few enough magelings before the temple's divide. Now their numbers were smaller than ever, and the stream of people who sought admittance to study magic dwindled further as the months dragged on. "What is your name, girl?"

"Shymin."

"Your full name."

"Shymin Silaron, Master."

Edagan's white brows lifted. "Your sister is one of the Archmage's apprentices, isn't she?"

The young woman flinched. "Yes, Master."

Taking the role of Master's apprentice did mean more work, but there was no reason it should mean complete disruption of a mageling's normal schedule. Even for an Archmage's apprentice. Edagan shifted and chewed the inside of her lip as she turned the information over in her mind. She knew there was something odd about Nondar's request to raise magelings to blue, but it was such a trivial matter she wasn't sure why it had stuck in her mind. On its own, she hadn't had reason to give it second thought. Now this mageling stood in front of her, citing trouble stemming from her sister's studies. Perhaps granting the old man his request had been a mistake.

"I wouldn't have thought a mere apprenticeship would change things to that extent," Edagan said at last. "What are your schedules like? Perhaps we can also rearrange your classes to make recovery easier for both of you."

"Well, my class schedule is normal enough," Shymin said slowly. "But Kytenia rarely attends her regular classes anymore. She's so busy studying with Archmage Nondar. Running errands for him, too. Last night it was halfway to dawn before she came to our quarters. It isn't unusual for her to be out that late now. Sometimes it wakes me, which is why I'd like a new room, Master."

"I see," Edagan murmured. Even learning trade secrets from the former head of an affinity wouldn't account for so much time spent in studies, and the heavy realization something was amiss fell on her shoulders like a weight.

She and Anaide had thought nothing of the old man taking an apprentice. They'd thought little more of him raising his apprentice to the blue, or that he wished to teach her healing methods he'd never shared with anyone else. Clearly, they'd been foolish. And Nondar had been clever, pulling the wool right over their eyes. With that in mind, students and their lodgings were the last things she wanted to concern herself with, but there were appearances to keep.

Edagan sighed and forced herself to speak. "I trust you know which rooms are empty? Select one for yourself and if anyone takes issue with it, you may send them to speak to me. Once you've chosen your new quarters, make sure your teachers are informed, and bring a written note of your new location to me so I may add it to the books."

"Thank you, Master." The young woman's shoulders sagged with relief, indicating she'd expected her proposal to be met with resistance. Another curious thing, given how few magelings they hosted in the temple's dormitory.

"Think nothing of it. If that's all, you may leave. I have a great deal of work to do. I cannot afford to spend time in idle chatter." Pulling her desk drawer open again, Edagan pretended to be busy while the girl excused herself.

As soon as her office door clicked shut, Edagan's frown deepened.

Fooled, all of them. The thought made her blood boil. What Nondar was playing at, she didn't know, but she suspected there was little time to waste. Edagan pushed herself from her chair, smoothed her white hair and straightened her matching robes. Only when she was as stern and pristine as her reputation did she send a sharp Calling to Anaide. She hurried into the hallway and made it only a handful of paces before Anaide stepped from her own office.

"Good morning," Anaide murmured. The Master of Water didn't look pleased at being disturbed, but there was a troubled shadow in her expression as well. As there should be, Edagan thought. She wouldn't have used the Calling if it weren't urgent.

"Ah, Anaide. I was just about to step out for a breath of fresh air. Sitting behind a desk all day puts cramps in my legs. Would you care to walk with me?" Edagan kept her tone casual, her expression bland. She didn't have to say anything else. They'd established polite phrases as signals in the wake of the temple's fracture; a walk indicated she was uncomfortable speaking in the Archmage's tower.

"Of course," Anaide replied cordially, tucking her hands into the wide sleeves of her robes. "I had the same notion, myself. It's a pleasant day outside."

The two women descended the tower in silence. Magelings and Masters alike scattered as they approached, leaving the way clear. Edagan was sure their expressions were forbidding. She didn't know what the other woman had been working on, but Anaide's mood seemed no better than her own. It wasn't until they reached the temple courtyard that Edagan spoke. "A seat in the gardens," she suggested. Anaide nodded in agreement.

The trees bore thick scars from the fire that had ravaged the temple a year prior, but new, vibrant foliage promised most of the garden had recovered. Though she wouldn't admit it, Edagan was glad. She was fond of the flowers, although she spent little time among them.

She led the way to a stone bench beneath the leafy boughs, spinning an invisible ward around them without so much as a gesture. It wasn't strange for them to want to speak of business in the gardens on a pleasant day. It made more sense to ward against prying ears outdoors than in the middle of the tower, in any case. Warding around other Masters, instead of magelings, would have been suspicious.

"I've just dismissed the sister of Nondar's apprentice from my office," Edagan started without preamble. She'd never been one for pleasantries, but the blunt beginning still made Anaide grimace. Uncaring, Edagan sat and continued. "She requested new quarters, as the unusual schedule Nondar has set for his apprentice has disrupted her studies."

Anaide's expression darkened as she settled on the other end of the bench. "What do I care if a mageling's schedule is disrupted?"

"You ought to care quite a bit, since apprenticeship alone isn't enough to keep a mageling in the Archmage's office or private quarters past the middle of the night."

Anaide started to speak, then paused and pursed her lips. Edagan saw the reflection of her own thoughts in the woman's eyes. A shadow of disgust, then thoughtful consideration, followed by suspicion.

"What manner of things would take so much time to teach?" Anaide murmured at last.

Edagan snorted. "We're warded, no sense in being vague. Nondar takes a proficient healer under his wing, raises her to blue, and seeks approval to teach her trade secrets all in short succession. It's obvious he means to begin manipulating ranks in the temple."

"His post as Master of the House of Healing still hasn't been filled." Anaide rubbed her brow. "The other magelings he raised, what about them? One was another with a healing affinity, but the other was air, wasn't she?"

"Yes, air." Edagan scowled as the word left her tongue. They should have realized it earlier, should have thought to check the affinities of those magelings sooner. "Melora's post, too, is vacant. That leaves a mageling with a fire affinity yet unaccounted for, but I don't imagine it's coincidence that he selected the magelings he did, either."

Anaide's brows lifted. "His apprentice—Kytenia—she was one of the magelings close with our queen, wasn't she?" A note of contempt colored her tone when she spoke of Firal.

Edagan regarded her with a frown. Anaide was not often reckless, but she'd do well to mind her opinions did not seep out through her voice. A conversation for another time, she decided.

"She was. I don't make a practice of paying attention to the friends magelings keep, but I remember seeing both her and the air mageling in the palace often, right after Firal took the throne." Again, Edagan cursed herself for not noticing sooner.

"So," Anaide sighed. "That was why he didn't raise the other Silaron girl. The three of them together might have been too remarkable. So he chose the sister closest to the queen. What of Ellaith, then? The other girl with a healing affinity?"

Edagan shrugged. "We had little reason to be suspicious of an unknown mageling with a healing affinity put in his charge. Two to seek power, one to throw off the trail."

"Crafty old man," Anaide growled. She gripped her knees through her robes until her knuckles grew almost as white as the fabric. "I knew he was chosen because of his relationship with the queen, but I never would have thought he'd try to put the whole temple in her power."

"He is Archmage. The temple might as well be in her power as long as that's the case." Edagan caught the inside of her lip between her teeth. It was not too late to take action of their own, though it was difficult to focus on the positive when she was angry. They'd found him out soon enough to change things. Now they only had to do it. "But who can we raise to rival his choices? They're still magelings, which works to our benefit, but I'm sure he'll push to appoint them to white before long."

"So we need to choose Masters to squeeze into the positions before his magelings are eligible." Anaide sighed, turning her eyes toward the temple's central tower.

Edagan understood her dismay. In years before, it wouldn't have been difficult to find candidates. Now it was nigh impossible. After the rift in the temple the last Archmage caused, they couldn't trust many of their mages. The group they'd taken with them was too likely to side with Firal over the temple's leadership, and the group they'd parted from was too likely to side with Nondar for the simple fact he was Archmage. Between the two groups, still only tentatively reunited beneath a half-blood with failing health, they would be hard pressed to find mages that understood they had the temple's best interests at heart.

"I'm afraid I haven't any Masters to suggest either," Edagan said.

Anaide threw up her hands in defeat. "Then we have to start elsewhere. First, we find what he's teaching them. Then we pick our candidates. We can begin with a mage to lead the House of Fire, since with them in our hand, we'll still have control of the majority of the houses. Then we can look for options for wind and healing."

"There's always the other Silaron girl." Edagan flicked a hand toward the dormitories. "Shymin."

Anaide snorted and gave her a skeptical look. "And what good will she do us?"

A grim smile twisted Edagan's mouth. "We know she's strong in her healing affinity, which makes her a reasonable choice. But since Nondar passed over her for a promotion to the blue, there's already a wedge between the Silaron girls. If we happen to see something in her that the Archmage didn't, it would make her more likely to play into our hands. And if she stands with us but retains her connection to Firal, she may be quite useful."

A thoughtful look drifted across Anaide's face. She tapped her chin with a forefinger and nodded. "Yes," she murmured. "I believe you may be right."

Edagan pushed herself from the bench and smoothed her robes. "Then that's settled. You start worrying about a candidate for fire. This evening, we'll check Nondar's records to see if they mention what he's covered with his choices. I'll start with the girl."

"Right now?" Anaide asked, surprised.

"She'll be returning to speak to me, so I might as well." Edagan dismissed the ward around them with a flick of her fingers and started back to the tower. Anaide lingered in the garden.

Many times since the temple's fracture, Edagan found herself grateful she and the Master of Water worked well together. She rested easy in the knowledge the other woman would manage her part without further input. But they would have to meet again before long. If Nondar could think clearly enough to deceive the two of them, there were other worrisome matters to discuss.

They had been careful to hide correspondence from the palace regarding the trade Firal wanted to open with the mainland. Thus far, they'd kept all of it from Nondar's hands, but they were forced to count on the assumption he'd forgotten the plan in his failing health. It wasn't that they didn't want trade; they did. Trade simply needed to be arranged between the temple and the college on the mainland, instead of between kingdom capitals, and that would take time and skill to navigate. An alliance between the college and temple could be powerful, but it carried the risk the ever-shrinking college might try and pick the island clean of mages.

Mage blood ran stronger on Elenhiise than it did on the mainland, but the island needed its mages. As a native of the island, Edagan had only the stories shared by the previous Archmage and her original team—Nondar included—to go by. Those stories were frightening enough. Corruption ran deep in the mages on the mainland. Corruption that had, Edagan reminded herself, seeped into the island with Envesi.

It was safer for everyone if trade began with the Grand College recognizing the temple as an equal. If Nondar moved too hastily, they risked the weakened temple being swallowed by the college. With Firal holding the reins, Edagan had no doubt they would be hasty.

When she reached her office, Edagan sat at her desk and fished out the next stack of papers she had to process. She couldn't rest easy with the new knowledge she faced, but there was little she could do but wait for the mageling's return and be grateful she wouldn't have to wait long.

In late afternoon, a knock at her door pulled her attention from her work.

"Come in," she called, sliding the last papers into her desk drawer as the door opened.

"I've brought the note you asked for, Master," Shymin said as she slipped inside. She clutched a small scrap to her chest and lingered at the doorway.

"Of course, thank you." Edagan beckoned her with a finger. "Bring it here, girl, and sit. I'd like to speak with you a moment."

The mageling hesitated and a flicker of concern crossed her face. But she obeyed, closing the door and creeping forward to seat herself in one of the small chairs before the desk.

Edagan drew a large volume from a stack on the floor. "I pulled up your record so I would have it handy to update." The Master mage opened the thick logbook to a marked page. "I noticed a remarkable improvement in your grades of late. It's contrary to what I expected, given what you said about your schedule being disrupted."

Shymin's concern grew to plain worry, her brow furrowed. "I don't mean for you to think I'm trying to trick you. The two are related, but not how you might think. It's just that I've worn green for almost two years, and after my sister graduated ahead of me, I thought maybe it was because I'd been lacking in my studies."

"Lacking? Certainly not." Edagan reached for her pen. Her other hand stretched out across the desk. "Give me your room number, child. Let me write it down, then we'll speak."

The girl passed her the scrap of paper and sat back. Her hands clutched at her skirts with pale fingers. The number written indicated her new quarters weren't far from the room she'd shared with her sister since admittance. Edagan supposed it was a sensical choice. It would be easy to move her belongings to her new quarters. The Master of Earth scratched the old room number out of her book with the butt of her pen and wrote in the new one.

"Your grades have never been lacking," she said at last, laying her pen aside. "But improvement is always welcome. I've yet to lay it before the Archmage, but I would like to see you raised to the blue before the week is out. That is, if you don't think the change of rank is too much to handle while you are moving rooms?"

Shymin gaped for a moment before she tried to speak. "N-no, Master. Of course not."

"Good!" Edagan folded her hands atop the record book and offered a smile. "Because I have a proposition for training I'd like you to undertake as soon as you're in blue."

"What is it, Master?" the mageling asked, nervous hope painting her face.

Edagan leaned against her desk. "The records indicate you're a skilled healer. That being your affinity, I'm sure you are aware the House of Healing is still in need of a new Master to lead it."

Shymin's eyes widened.

Despite herself, Edagan cracked a smile. It seemed speed would not be such a difficulty after all.

2

THE WINDS OF WAR

SNOW DRIFTED ON THE WIND IN SUCH LARGE FLAKES, SERA HEARD the soft patter of their landing. They obscured her view and confused her magic, but not the rest of her senses. The hills that surrounded her hummed in her awareness. Her pointed ears trapped every sound, and the sharp scent of ice that stung her nostrils promised a stronger storm to come.

She squinted as a snowflake blew against her face and caught on her eyelashes. A shake of her head was all it took to dislodge it, but she hated to move at all.

Only a sliver of her dark skin showed around her eyes. The rest of her was swathed in mottled gray and white to let her blend in with the rocky, snow-covered terrain. Behind her, a handful of scouts waited for a signal. She wished she could give it. The rocky trail ahead was undisturbed. Frustrated, she rose and turned. Her hand flicked in a silent signal. *Nothing here.*

A half-dozen scouts popped up across the landscape, their shoulders slumped with disappointment. Sera spread her arms and shrugged as she trudged to rejoin them.

"Nothing at all?" one of the scouts asked as they converged.

"The snow works in their favor. Severe weather skews my

perceptions and the clouds that are coming bring worse than this." She motioned overhead.

The scouting party exchanged looks. Sera tried not to be offended. They didn't have to like her answer. Not liking it didn't change it. With the way the weather interfered with her Gift, there was nothing they could do but keep looking.

"Should one of us report?" another scout asked.

She shook her head. "Not until we have something worth reporting. If the gryphons saw mages in the pass, they're here. Somewhere."

"Are you sure you'll feel them?"

Tempting as it was to snap at the man's tone, she let it slide. "My perception of magic may be limited by the weather, but limiting is all it does. When we get close, I'll feel them. Come." Sera straightened her cowl and marched past the other scouts. The rest of the group followed.

The officers leading their party wouldn't be happy, but there was no point in pushing onward. There were more trails to check, and no reason to continue forward on a path that bore undisturbed snow.

Despite being called a pass, the path through the mountains was not a single clear roadway. It branched and forked in at least a dozen places. All of them led to the Aldaanan capital, eventually.

From another vantage point, she might have paused to look down at the city and mull over everything that had transpired to put her feet on that path. Or she might have if she had *time*. Garam was counting on her ability to find the enemy mages. They couldn't have anticipated the snow, and anything that gave Garam's army an advantage had to be used.

The Aldaanan mages had admitted to tampering with the weather. Sera could only assume that was why the clouds that piled ever higher in the sky resembled thunderheads, instead of the soft blanket of gray that usually accompanied snow. The storm would be wild, fierce. Hard on their soldiers, but hard on the enemy mages, too.

Despite the interference snow and rain caused with her senses, their presence was not without benefits. With that much water close at hand, her strength would be much greater. She feared her strength would be needed now more than ever.

Though she had spoken with the gryphon Ria at length, Sera still did not understand what had transpired at the top of Aldaeon's tower. Before that event, Sera had been torn on whether or not they could trust the Aldaanan. Now, she was certain they couldn't. Being one of only two mages in her brother's army had made their assistance appealing, and while they could offer her nothing, their promise to assist Rune in honing his power had swayed her in their favor. She still didn't know what they'd done to him, but when she'd left the camp, he'd been too weak to speak.

Anger simmered inside her. Standing against the rogue mages of Lore was madness enough without losing their best fighter. She had rued him for that title early on, when Garam had ordered her to oversee his training. That she'd been put over a free mage had been an exercise in both frustration and humiliation. She'd never wanted to be a teacher, never wanted to be snared by her brother's political aspirations or his army. She hadn't even wanted to stay in the Royal City, but he'd claimed she was the only person he could trust, so she'd stayed. There had been nothing she could do to teach him, and her power so paled in comparison to his that she wondered how Garam ever thought she could help at all.

Yet when it came to Rune himself, she simply couldn't dislike him. He was strange, no doubt, but there was a strength in him she had come to admire. No one had escaped the Royal City Arena before. He was their first Champion and the people of the Royal City had come to adore him, whether or not he acknowledged as much. A lesser man might have used such fame to his advantage. Instead, all Rune seemed to care about was finding a way to purify his magic. A task the Aldaanan had promised to assist him with, she reminded herself. Instead, they'd abandoned the city in their hour of need—and left Rune atop the tower to die.

Her foot broke through a crust of ice and she stumbled. Growling, she righted herself before the other scouts could offer help. She'd had enough of the army to last her a lifetime. Garam —her own brother—hated magic and held her at arm's length because of her Gift, yet found her power too useful to let her go free. Yet Rune had accepted her so easily, and the moment he'd taken her to dance on the night King Vicamros declared war, she knew she'd finally found a friend.

Sera understood if the Aldaanan mages did not want to face conflict with Lore. She understood their penchant for pacifism. But she could not forgive what they'd done to him.

Until Rune recovered, she was the only mage in the army that sought to stand against the Grand College.

Which meant she was the only one who could find the mages in the pass.

Keep moving, Sera reminded herself. She gritted her teeth and adjusted her cowl again. The fabric was wet from her breath and the rough-spun wool threatened to rub her face raw in the cold. She'd grown used to the bitter winters of the northern continent, but that didn't make them pleasant.

If not for her brother, she could have gone south already. She could have returned to her homeland, reclaimed her family's land and been basking in the balmy summertime. Instead, the only two people she cared about were in Aldaeon. All the more reason to defend the city, she supposed.

The platoon Garam had sent to establish a barricade in the pass waited ahead. A lieutenant strode to meet her.

"No one's here," she called over the wind. "They must have taken a different path."

"We've changed direction three times already," the lieutenant protested.

"And we'll change direction thirty more, if we must," Sera replied. "You know what Garam said as well as I do."

The lieutenant's brows twitched with displeasure, but he turned back to issue the order. Sera lifted her chin as she watched him go. She bore no true authority over the soldiers before her, but in the eyes of many, the fact she was Garam's sister made her an unofficial second-in-command. She did not envy her brother's rank—or his lackluster title as Captain of the Royal City Guard, or his responsibility over all the king's armies—but there were times the respect was useful.

"Which direction should we head?" the lieutenant called from where he clustered with the other officers.

Sera let her mage-blue eyes wander the mountain peaks and rolling hills. They had to move fast, before the snow obliterated any signs the mage army may have left behind.

"We move south," she declared.

The lieutenant's mouth twisted, but the officers scattered and began barking orders at the soldiers huddled before them.

"South?" one of the scouts behind her asked. "We shouldn't travel any farther from the camp. Not in this weather."

She shook her head and cast a glance toward the ever-thickening clouds. "The weather is precisely why we should. It'll hinder our movement, but not theirs. Or did you forget we're marching against mages?"

Flustered, the scout turned away.

"That's what I thought," Sera muttered. "Now come on, all of you. We scout south."

With luck, they wouldn't have to scout far.

THE SNOW OFFERED a harsh reminder Rune had forgotten his spats. His clawed toes turned numb as he stared Garam in the eye. The captain was the only soldier in the camp who appeared ready for battle. The rest scrambled about, half-armed and half-armored.

"Whatever the Aldaanan did to you, it couldn't have come at a worse time," Garam muttered. "Where's your gear?"

"Whatever the Aldaanan did," Rune repeated with an edge in his voice, "I haven't recovered enough to use magic at all. If I move against college-trained mages, I—"

"You'll fight the same as anyone else," Garam said. "We are without mages because of you, and you are bloody lucky I didn't just kill you myself when I found out. I ordered you to the southern company, and you're going to move. I'm sure you'll find your strength comes back real fast when there's someone trying to kill you."

Rune bit his tongue as the captain moved on. If the company expected a mage to shield them, they would be sorely disappointed. If he didn't have an opportunity to speak to the officers before they marched, his presence alone could put their lives at risk, fooling the men into believing they had a competent mage on their side. He didn't want to mislead them, but he didn't know how to explain he didn't have the strength to defend himself, much less shield an entire company. Swearing beneath his breath, he turned back to his tent to retrieve the rest of his gear.

His armor proved a burden in the fresh powder. Still weakened, he stumbled often. Each time, he staggered upright and cursed the snow. The ground was icy where men had trod, though his claws gave him traction where boots would have none. The soldiers had gone farther than he expected. He arrived at the rear edge of the company breathless and fatigued. He braced his hands against his knees and tried to find enough air to speak before moving into the cluster of men. The officer leading the group didn't give him a chance.

"Where have you been?" The man stormed toward him, scowling. "The men are ready to move. Get to the front and—"

"We can't face them," Rune interrupted, glowering back. He

couldn't tell what the emblem on the man's uniform signified. Despite the long march from the Royal City to Aldaeon, he hadn't been part of the army long enough to memorize their insignia. "I can't hold back an army of mages on my own."

The officer's face reddened and his eyes bulged. Clearly, the man wasn't used to having orders protested. He opened his mouth to speak, only to be interrupted by a warning bugle at the front of the army.

Massive mage-lights flared to life over the trees, illuminating the mountainside as the sun fell beyond the horizon. Rune's stomach lurched and he scanned the trees. He should have been able to sense them. Instead, he felt nothing. He didn't realize he'd stepped back until the officer grabbed him by the neck of his breastplate and hauled him forward again.

"Shield the men, now!" the officer bellowed.

Rune didn't have a chance to try.

Shrieking bolts of energy arced overhead and fell over the army like arrows of light. Dozens of white-robed mages spilled from the mountains, resembling ghosts against the snow. In unison they paused, drew their arms back, and thrust them forward to send another volley of bolts into the army.

The soldiers fell out of formation, racing for cover or charging ahead as they laid eyes on their enemy. Rune tore himself free of the officer's grasp. He staggered away and reached for the energy flows around him. Again he felt the build of pressure, an aching strain, an again the power slipped beyond his grasp. He gritted his teeth and struggled to reach just a little farther.

Magic snagged against his will. Desperate, he laced his own strength around it and struggled to bring the power to heel. It resisted. He forced it to obey and flung his hand toward the mages ahead. Pure, raw energy lanced through the air, streaked past the soldiers and crashed into the hillside. Mages screamed as the earth exploded beneath their feet.

Pain overtook him. It shot through his limbs and rang in his head, stabbed behind his eyes and chased the air from his lungs. Rune fell to the snow and gasped for breath. He trembled, unable to find the strength to seize magic again. A glance ahead showed the mages still coming. But at least now they knew there was a mage with Garam's men. They didn't waste their time with distanced attacks now, uncertain of who might be shielded, unwilling to waste their energy. It was the best he could have done for his company.

A relief, since it was all he could do.

He had to move. He knew it, but getting to his feet still took everything he had. Rune almost fell with the first step he took, wasted precious moments in trying to find his balance. A handful of soldiers moved to meet the mages head on. Bursts of light and sound made him grimace and turn away. He couldn't fight with magic and he didn't have the strength to hold a sword.

There were no options left. Though he ached, and his body screamed in protest, he ran.

There had to be a way out of this. He wouldn't die in the snow, not after everything he'd been through.

A massive shadow passed over the army as something moved between the floating mage-lights and the ground. Rune looked up and his heart leaped with hope.

Overhead, a gryphon wheeled and bore down on the mage-light that hovered in midair. The enormous stone crashed to the ground in the middle of the mage army and panicked cries rose all around it. The light was blinding, forcing the mages to a standstill. Another gryphon struck down another light, and Rune's hope became relief as the sky filled with wings.

The gryphons screeched at their enemies and to one another, falling into a V formation as they swept over the battlefield. Sparks flashed bright against the dark sky and the gryphons dropped tiny globes into the cluster of mages. Rune barely had time to wonder what they were before a series of deafening explosions rocked the night.

Banking smoothly, the gryphons swept low between the trees

and sailed overhead. Gouts of flame poured after them and Rune spat a curse. Dozens of mages still moved toward them. Battered and bloodied, but still moving forward, racing toward him in pursuit of the gryphons. He turned and ran, his pain and exhaustion forgotten.

Again the gryphons turned. Explosives dropped too close behind him, urging him to move faster. He wasn't alone. On every side, soldiers scrambled to escape. They ran north, toward the camp. They slipped and skidded in the hard-packed ice. Rune threw a glance over his shoulder. The mages loomed ever closer, in spite of the explosions that shook snow off the trees and rattled his already aching skull.

He slammed into another armored body and they tumbled to the snow.

Rune caught the man by the shoulder and hauled him up, startled by how light he seemed. Fire and explosions boomed behind them. A gryphon screamed and crashed into the snow only feet away, flames devouring its feathers. The soldier lingered, frozen.

"Move!" Rune snarled, dragging him forward. Snapped back to himself, the man obeyed.

They ran until their breath burned and every muscle threatened to fail. Just when Rune thought he could run no more, he spotted an outcropping of stone with a sheltered alcove on the northern side. He shoved the soldier that direction. The man didn't need a second order. With sounds of war echoing behind them, they both pressed into the hollow and collapsed to the frozen ground.

Rune gasped and leaned back against the stone, uncertain he'd ever find his breath.

The soldier shook so hard his armor rattled. Frantic, he clawed his helmet off over his head and threw it aside. He fell to his hands and knees and vomited into the snow.

Rune's eyes darted from the helmet to the soldier's face, and his stomach plummeted to his knees.

3

UNREST

"Sɪᴛ ᴜᴘ sᴛʀᴀɪɢʜᴛ."

Vahn grimaced and lifted his head as his father stepped into the office. Firal was normally the one to look over the morning reports, but she had taken a Gate to the temple to meet with the mages. For what, he didn't know. He hadn't thought it his place to ask. All of her friends still resided in the temple, and her mentors as well. She had plenty of reasons to visit.

Shifting upright in his chair made him grimace again. He hadn't realized how stiff he'd become, hunched over the desk all morning. "You expect me to act like a king, but you still talk to me like I'm a child."

Ennil laughed and pushed the door closed with his boot. "You are a child. Mine. You may be grown and married, but you're never too old for your mother to turn you over her knee, either." Despite the gruff way he spoke, his expression softened as he crossed the room. "I want you to present yourself in a dignified manner. Sit up straight. There's a throne for you on that dais downstairs, and it's the same size as your wife's. Carry yourself like you deserve it."

Holding back a frown, Vahn looked away. He didn't deserve that throne, but he wasn't about to begin that argument with his father. That their marriage had not been planned was family knowledge, but aside from Archmage Nondar, Medreal, and Firal's few friends from the temple, no one knew the real reason they'd married. He didn't regret his promise to look after and protect Firal, but there were some days he wished protecting her hadn't required so much sacrifice.

"I'm trying," he said at last. He put aside the reports and rolled his shoulders, willing the stiffness in his muscles to abate. "I'm doing my best. I know you want me to call myself king, but how can I? We're nobles, but not royals. I can be king-regent when Firal is ill, but otherwise, I'd be king-consort at best, or—"

"I know it's not the norm." Ennil stopped in front of the desk and gave the papers a disinterested glance. "But the kingdom needs strong leadership, rulers they believe are powerful enough to bring things under control. A reasonable man would know the troubles he faces are a result of things that happened beneath King Kifelethelas, but most of your subjects are not reasonable."

Vahn raked his fingers through his cornsilk-blond hair. "Then how am I supposed to convince them? I can't even convince myself that we can manage this. Even with your help."

"Because you are seizing power!" Ennil made a fist and raised his arm in a gesture of might. "Don't think of this as Firal's inheritance. The two of you aren't yet proven. You're new rulers taking over a fallen kingdom, seeing the window of opportunity to make something of yourselves and moving through it. Once things are settled, she can grant you the Crown Matrimonial and you can officially share the burden."

Vahn glanced away, tight-lipped. This conversation was nothing new; these were things they'd been over a dozen times already. He appreciated that his father tried to support them, but one retired military officer was nothing compared to an entire city in a state of unrest.

Ennil was quiet for a time, though his eyes never left his son. Eventually he sighed and dropped his hand to his side. "I know you're trying, Vahnil. But let's be honest, we both know you never wanted this. I appreciate that you decided to stand by Firal and your child, but I know if you thought you had a choice, you never would have put yourself in a position like this."

The mention of Lumia—Lulu, as he called the girl—made him grimace, but Vahn couldn't disagree. He hadn't felt he had a choice, trapped between a promise and Kytenia's insistence. "We do what we must," he murmured, trying to push Kytenia out of his head. He still saw the hurt on her face from the last time they'd spoken. He wasn't sure he'd ever replace that vision with anything else.

"And we must make the best of it," Ennil agreed. "So why aren't you?"

Vahn frowned. "I'm not sure what you mean."

"You aren't happy with Firal. There's no affection, no spark between you. You're both unhappy with this situation, but you decided to get married, so it's not a situation that's going to change. It may not be a passionate marriage, or a very romantic one, but it can still be happy." Ennil paced around the desk to stare out the windows. He opened his mouth to speak again, then stopped. His brow furrowed and he paused a few paces from the glass.

"What?" Vahn pushed himself from his chair. His eyes skimmed the sky and rooftops before his gaze dropped to the streets, where a crowd milled between buildings. No, it didn't mill; it boiled. The crowd moved like waves in the sea, spitting rocks at buildings and the figures in gleaming armor that stood in their way.

"Get your sword," Ennil barked as he spun toward the door. "And your armor. It's time for a lesson in leadership." He made it no more than a step before someone knocked. Before either of them could respond, the door flew open to reveal a guard on the other side.

"We've seen it," Vahn said, hurrying into the hallway before the man could speak. "We're coming."

Ennil moved alongside him. "Call whatever officers aren't

already out there fighting. His Majesty wants them to meet us at the gate."

"Yes, sir," the soldier said. He bobbed to Ennil, then looked flustered and bowed to Vahn before he hurried back the way he'd come.

Vahn half-ran toward his quarters. "Someone needs to tell Firal. She's in a meeting at the temple."

His father stayed right on his heels. "The baby is with her?"

"Yes."

Ennil nodded. "They're safer there, at least until this is contained. We can send a court mage to notify her."

The mages. Vahn had almost forgotten them. "Go, tell them I said to Gate one mage to the temple and then have the rest meet with us and the guard in the courtyard. They can help with defenses."

"Good thinking." Ennil nodded again, then turned to race toward the office where the mages would be awaiting the queen's return.

Vahn burst into his rooms and scrambled for his sword and armor. His hands shook so he could hardly fasten it on. He'd only been in one battle, something he didn't want to think of again. He had known more fighting would come in his lifetime, but he'd never expected it to happen in his own home city. He belted his sword at his side with trembling fingers and almost left without grabbing his helm.

More guards ran down the hallways ahead of him, flocking to the courtyard where his father and eleven mages waited alongside two dozen men in armor. Their rank as officers was evident by the colored half-capes and plumed helmets they wore. More men in plain armor waited just beyond the palace gates.

Ennil met him a short distance from the guardsmen and mages to help him right his armor. "I can't lead for you. Not any more. I've been retired from my post for too long. I'll stay beside you and advise you where I can, but you're the king and you're calling the shots."

"How am I supposed to lead? I have no idea what to do!" Vahn kept his voice low, too aware of the guardsmen watching him. Angry voices carried on the wind from somewhere beyond the palace walls. His hands already felt clammy in his gauntlets. He wasn't sure how he'd hold his sword.

"Ilmenhith is built in a wagon wheel pattern for a reason. Easy to shut off and isolate problems in any street from the main hub without sacrificing mobility in the city." Ennil spoke quickly, adjusting Vahn's cape and buckling the strap on his helm. "The riot is isolated to one street right now, which works to our advantage. Split your force into three groups. One primary force to press them back so they can't approach the palace. Two smaller groups to move down the streets to the left and right, catching any strays and then closing in on the mob from the other end of the street."

Vahn moved toward the waiting officers with his hand on the hilt of his sword. "And where should I be?"

"With the main press. Remember, we're not trying to kill anyone, just subdue them." Ennil strode ahead, his shoulders squared and head held high. Though retired, he was still powerful. From the way the officers straightened when he approached, they knew it, too. "Listen well, His Majesty brings orders!"

The title gave him a chill, but Vahn tried to ignore it. "Divide the guard into three groups." His voice cracked halfway through the last word. He drew a deep breath and steadied himself before he spoke again. "Half will press from the front. One quarter will move there," he pointed left, "and the last quarter there." He pointed right and paused to wet his lips before he went on. "Come together to press the mob from the other side. Move fast, lest anyone try to escape."

"What are we to do with them?" one of the officers asked.

Vahn hesitated.

"Arrest them, fool!" Ennil snapped. "The law hasn't changed since your new rulers were crowned."

Sending his father a grateful glance, Vahn nodded. "If they won't settle, take them by force, but don't kill any of them unless absolutely necessary." He paused again as he caught sight of the mages in their own small group behind Ennil. He tried to catch their eyes. "Send one mage with each small group and two with the main group. Offer shielding against thrown objects and tend anyone injured. The rest of you mages are to stay here and defend the palace gates if necessary."

Temar, leading the mages, dipped in a bow. "Of course, my king." Her bow was mimicked by the others. She turned, calling names and ordering four mages from her group to their new places. She remained with the rest, assigning herself to defending the palace. Vahn felt a pang of guilt; they served unerringly, and aside from Temar, he didn't even know their names.

"Let's move out!" Ennil roared.

Vahn shook himself from his thoughts and moved ahead alongside his father, through the gates and into the wide avenue that ringed the palace walls.

The officers split the guard without needing further direction. The two smaller groups fell into order and advanced into the streets.

"You'll need to be at the front with the officers," his father said in a low tone. "Don't worry, they'll do everything in their power to ensure your safety. But if you're going to bring this city under control, you have to be present. Right in the thick of things, not afraid to show your face."

"Will they know my face?" Vahn asked miserably.

"They'll know your armor. Only the king wears something that ornate." Ennil chuckled and tapped a knuckle against the etched silver breastplate Vahn wore.

"Shields up!" one of the officers shouted as they reached the front. The men fell into ranks alongside them and lifted shields to form a defensive barrier, broken only by the king and his father, who carried none.

"Swords!"

In a single motion, every soldier drew a blade. A chorus of metallic rasps filled the air. Vahn readied his sword and watched his father do the same. He didn't want to fight. He wanted to retreat to the temple, find Firal and hold his daughter.

"This is nothing," Ennil said beside him, his words soft and reassuring, meant for Vahn's ears alone. It wasn't much, but it was all the reassurance he needed.

The officer said nothing more. The noise of the crowd in the street ahead of them seemed suddenly dim as Vahn realized the guardsmen looked to him for the order. Him, the inexperienced and uncertain message boy from the army's bottom ranks, who had been in one battle and only narrowly escaped death. His mouth dried as he lifted his sword, the single word hoarse as it escaped his throat. "Forward!"

He took the first step a moment late, then lengthened his stride to keep cadence with the wave of guardsmen that heaved forward and flooded the street with shields ready and weapons bared. Shoulder to shoulder, they filled the walkway, armor brushing buildings on either side.

The mob saw them and people turned toward the soldiers. Rocks pinged off shields as they advanced. Vahn resisted the urge to duck when a stone hurtled past his head. A woman shouted behind him and he caught a ripple in the air as the two mages spun a barrier over their heads. He had just enough time to suck in a deep breath. Then the groups collided.

Angry shouts and frightened screams filled his ears as the guards tore into the side of the mob, driving people back or clubbing them down with the broad side of their swords. Guardsmen moved in front of Vahn and Ennil unprompted, bearing their shields ahead of them.

Helpless, Vahn stared as everything moved around him. Why was he there? He didn't want to fight, but he didn't want to be a figurehead, either. He had to do something, help somehow, protect his family. Gritting his teeth, he tightened his grip on his sword and pushed forward.

"Wait!" Ennil caught his shoulder. Angry, Vahn shrugged away and continued onward.

He broke through the front line, ahead of the shields. People around him grew still, staring at him in surprise and disbelief.

Then the moment passed. Guardsmen battered those who stopped, while others in the mob turned to flee. Armor glittered at the other end of the street as the two smaller groups of guardsmen converged and moved to meet them.

Someone came at Vahn with a cudgel and he barely brought his sword up in time. He caught the weapon and twisted his blade as he repelled it, throwing the man off balance. A guard struck the man down and the army moved over the top of him. There were men at the rear to collect the fallen and escort them to the prisons, though Vahn didn't even know if the palace dungeons were large enough to contain the mob. How many could they arrest? How many could they hold? What if all of Ilmenhith began to rebel? He struck down another man.

This is nothing, he reminded himself, repeating his father's words. He focused on his breath, willed the noise to fade to a hum in his ears. He struck down another.

This is nothing.

They pushed forward and crowded the hordes together until they began to collapse. Turmoil lay ahead of them, urging them onward, begging them to act. The city had to be brought to order.

This is nothing.

Vaguely, Vahn realized he didn't even know why the uprising began.

4

AN UNEXPECTED SOLDIER

SERA GLANCED BACK THE WAY SHE'D COME AND SILENTLY HOPED THE company had remained on its toes. She'd been gone a long time, and the longer she was gone, the more likely they were to think her absence meant something. Either they'd think she hadn't found anything, or they'd think she had—and been captured, or worse. She winced at the idea.

The farther they scouted, the more she'd come to feel like the other scouts slowed her down. She'd insisted on pushing ahead by herself, continuing the search for enemy mages. There was no sense moving all the soldiers until they knew where they were going. Though the gryphons had been the first to spot the mages in the pass, the creatures dared not fly over the encampment again. Given their vulnerability to magic, she couldn't fault them for that.

Magic was one reason she thought it best that she scout ahead. Even if Garam's soldiers were not Gifted, their existence —their very life—would stand out to any mages with a healing affinity. Traveling in a group would only make their presence more obvious. She was just one person. Gifted or not, she would be harder to detect alone. The company was vulnerable without her there to shield them, but she was the only scout who could defend herself against the mages.

The farther she went, the less she thought she would have to.

The pass was empty. Since parting from the rest of her group, she had seen plenty of places where mages had been, marked by broken underbrush and trampled paths they hadn't bothered to cover or conceal after their retreat. There were no options for hiding places aside from a handful of scraggly pines, and everything she saw and sensed indicated they'd simply gone back the way they'd come. Sera couldn't think of a reason for them to retreat, unless they'd grown intimidated by the company Garam had sent to meet them.

Yet they hadn't come near enough for her to catch their presence. How would they have known a force had been sent to meet them? If she hadn't sensed them, they shouldn't have detected her. Unsettled, she followed the path until there was no sense in going farther, then continued for a moment more.

The tracks separated abruptly. The mages had veered off into a narrow, craggy trail that led due south.

Mingled vindication and panic churned in her stomach. Abandoning stealth, Sera spun and raced back to the company. She burst from the trees and waved her arms to get the attention of the officers at the front of the formation. They were on their toes, she saw. Ready and waiting, their weapons drawn.

"They've gone farther than I imagined," she called. "They've split us off as a distraction while they hit the camp from the south." She was furious at herself for not thinking of the possibility sooner. Their scouts had scoured the mountains for vantage points before the mages arrived. Garam and his officers knew of the narrow trails that wound all through the ranges, but they hadn't stopped to consider their enemy might know them, too.

The officer at the forefront cursed as he turned toward the troops. "Back to the camp! We'll need to bolster defenses. Scouts—"

Sera didn't stay to hear his orders.

Fleet-footed, she ran ahead, skidded down rough hillsides and bounded through the trees. Poor planning, she decided. Poor planning with poor luck on top. Everything had come apart after the Aldaanan disappeared, and it had been no more than a day.

Then there was Rune. Concern for her fellow mage tightened her throat. Garam would have roused him and sent him to fight, regardless of how weak he was or whether he'd recovered. Without her there, he was the only hope for defense against magic the army still had. Silently, she prayed he would be able to hold out.

Trees gave way to the clearing that surrounded Aldaeon and Sera skidded to a stop at the top of a hill. The camp below seethed with activity. Rumbles like thunder echoed to the south. She could only assume it was the mages. The icy air scorched her lungs and her limbs felt like lead weights, but she forced herself to press on.

Every soldier in the camp seemed to be in her way. They ducked left and right in front of her as they scrambled for weapons and armor and ran to join their officers.

A flash of familiar armor in the crowd caught her eye and she jumped on her toes. "Garam!"

He didn't hear her.

Growling, Sera shoved her way forward and raised a hand overhead as she shouted for him again.

Her brother's head turned and he froze in place when he saw her. She slid between armored bodies to join him. His expression grew dark as she neared. "Why are you—"

"A ruse," she said before he could finish. "Their forces never meant to strike from two sides, they meant to split us. The eastern force took a narrow trail to the south to merge with the greater group. All mages are to the south, not east."

Garam swore. "I just sent another group east." He shoved a soldier out of his way and hurried toward the edge of the camp.

"Mine will catch them and redirect them." Sera trotted to keep up beside him. She was a tall woman, but even she could not match her brother's long-legged stride. "Everyone else needs to go south. I need to join them. Even if Rune were at full strength, he wouldn't be able to protect the army against that many mages on his own." She hadn't realized how out of breath she was until she tried to speak. Her chest and throat burned. "We need a different strategy, or else—"

"The gryphons are taking care of that," Garam interrupted. "Seems they weren't as eager to abandon the aerie as the Aldaanan were."

Startled, she stumbled in the snow. "But magic is so deadly to them! The college mages could kill them with a thought. What can the gryphons do?"

Her question was answered as they crested a hill and she saw the small encampment on the other side. Gryphons milled about on the ground, a steady stream of them coming and going, staying just long enough to fill the satchels slung around their necks. A handful of gryphons worked at a makeshift table, filling dark ceramic spheres with something scooped from barrels.

"Blast powder. An Aldaanan invention," Garam said. "The gryphons know how to make it from a certain mix of minerals. It explodes when exposed to flame."

"They're fighting the mages with these?" Sera asked in disbelief.

He shrugged. "It's the best we've..." He trailed off as flashes of magic, fire and mage-lights illuminated the horizon. His mouth tightened and he started forward, not running, but walking briskly enough she knew he was unsettled.

She hurried after him and trained her eyes on the meeting of land and mage-lit sky.

Two soldiers staggered over the crest of the next hill. One supported the other, though neither appeared steady on their feet. Even from a distance, Sera could sense him, and when Rune fell to his knees and took the shorter man with him, she resisted the urge to throttle her brother.

The battlefield was the last place Rune needed to be. She'd known Garam would send him, but some small sliver of her had still hoped he'd have the sense to let the man rest. He'd been more dead than alive when the gryphon carried him down the tower. How could he be expected to fight only a day later?

She sprinted ahead, slid to a stop in the snow, and knelt beside them. Threads of magic answered her the instant she reached for them and she gathered them close, prepared to heal the men. She reached for Rune, but he batted her hands away before she could touch him.

"I'm fine," he managed between breaths. "Just weak. Can't fight. Can't move."

She turned to the second soldier to ask if he needed healing, but when she saw his face, her heart skipped a beat.

He was shorter than her and pale with fear, but she still shrank into a bow before Vicamros II, crown prince and heir to the Triad's throne.

Garam held no such respect. He grabbed the youth by the collar and hauled him to his feet. "Why are you here?" he demanded. His expression grew darker when the prince didn't immediately reply. He shook him, as if to jar an answer loose.

"Garam!" Sera scrambled to her feet, grabbed his arm, and wrenched his hand free. The prince stumbled backwards, his mouth working wordlessly.

The captain glared at her and jabbed a finger toward the boy. "He is the last person who should be here! When I find out who helped him sneak into the army, I'll—"

"I did," Vicamros interrupted, voice shaky. He flinched when Garam turned back toward him, but drew himself up and tried to meet the captain's stare. "I got in by myself."

"Garam, now isn't the time for this." Sera gestured toward the horizon, where the sounds of men mingled with those of magic and gryphons.

With a grimace and sigh, Garam let his shoulders drop. "You're right," he agreed, though bitterness seeped from his words. "Take them back to the camp. Wait for me to return."

Sera took a half step forward and reached for his arm again. "You're not going out there without me."

He shrugged away. "What would you do?" He scowled at her and pointed at Rune. "If he can't hold them off, neither can you."

She snorted. "He's too weak to fight after what happened with the Aldaanan. I'm still at full strength and—"

"And I am entrusting you with the well-being of not only our other mage, but the life of the heir to the Triad's throne." Garam's voice softened and he laid a hand on her shoulder. "You're the only person I would trust with this. We'll discuss what to do with the two of them once I come back. Right now, my men need clear orders and strong leadership. And I need you to keep Prince Vicamros safe."

Sera bit her tongue, warring with herself and silently cursing him for being right. If the prince were to be seen on the battlefield, he'd become the mages' highest priority. They'd do everything in their power to capture him and ransom him back to the king—if they didn't kill him, first. The camp was the safest place for him, and a mage the best guard. She pushed Garam's hand away. "Stay safe, Captain."

The corner of his mouth pulled upward with the faintest of lopsided smiles. Garam drew his sword and moved south.

Uneasiness welled in her chest. Sera tamped it down and tore her eyes away from her brother's back. "On your feet, lizard," she muttered as she reached for Rune's arm. He tried to push her away but didn't have the strength. Vicamros took his other arm and the two of them pulled him up.

The trip back to the camp was slow and difficult. All three of them stumbled along through the snow, tripping over their own feet and each other's. Sera tried to stifle her agitation, but couldn't help grumbling. "Stupid beast, you never should have left your tent. Who decided you were well enough to fight, anyway? You?"

"Your brother." Rune gave her a sidewise glance and seemed amused when she bristled.

She elbowed him in the ribs and regretted it immediately when he lost his balance and fell again.

"Careful," Vicamros prompted.

Sera bit her tongue to hold back a retort.

A steady stream of soldiers moved past them, headed south. They paid no mind to the three of them, or to any of the other injured soldiers that staggered back toward the campsite. Sera, on the other hand, frowned at sight of how many soldiers she'd have to heal.

Healing wasn't her affinity. She'd grown adept with it, being part of the army, but she had assumed she would have the help of the Aldaanan once the battles began. She could only hope that after a good night's rest, Rune would be recovered enough to assist her. Though now that she thought of it, she didn't know if he had any skill with healing. She knew very little about his power, other than that he was a free mage, but his glowing eyes were enough to tell her that. Everything else was a mystery.

Rune's tent sat near the southern edge of the camp—a small blessing, given how heavy the man was. The closest campfire had been extinguished, but she cut toward it anyway. Both she and Vicamros were short of breath and perspiring by the time they helped ease Rune to a seat beside the ashes. There was still enough wood in the fire pit that Sera only had to look at it and tug the lingering energies to bring the flames back to life. Vicamros jumped back a step and looked at her in surprise. Rune slouched forward and cradled his head in his hands.

"Head hurt?" Sera asked. She'd left the brandy in his tent that morning. It was hard to wrap her mind around the fact it had only been that morning. It felt like an eternity since they'd sat together and she told him the Aldaanan had left. The way that message affected him still weighed on her heart. The news had crushed his spirits, so soon after their spark began to return.

She retrieved the bottle and pushed it into his hand. "Take a couple swallows and let it sit, it'll help the pain. I'll see what I can do for you after I make a round and check for other injuries." She paused, eyeing Vicamros. "You come with me."

The young man swallowed, but nodded. Vicamros stayed close at her heels, kept his head down and stayed quiet. She was surprised no one seemed to recognize him, but perhaps in his uniform with dirt smudged on his face, he didn't look so much like the prince they knew.

It didn't take long for her to tour the camp. Most injuries were minor and did not need more than a moment to mend. Frustrated as she was, providing healing services offered some solace. It wasn't where her Gift lay, but at least it was closer to aligning with her own desires.

She'd grown to resent her brother's insistence she remain part of his army, she realized as she tended a fracture in a young man's leg. It should have been her own children she tended, instead of soldiers. She struggled to focus on her work instead of the desire to heal scraped knees or elbows for children that didn't yet exist, rather than bloodied skulls and battered limbs for men who might not survive the war. There would be time for a family, Garam had promised.

The longer she waited, the less certain she felt there was.

Within the span of an hour, she'd circled back to the beginning. When they reached the fire, Rune still sat beside it, holding his head.

Sera worried her lower lip. The liquor should have done something by now. She signaled for Vicamros and pointed at a tent across the fire pit. "I don't know where you've been sleeping that you've gone unnoticed, but stay there tonight. I want both of you close. Get up, lizard. Let's get you into your bedroll and I'll see what I can do for your head."

Vicamros offered an arm to help Rune rise and received a

glare in return. He flinched and pulled back. "All right, suit yourself. Call for me if you need me, ma'am." The prince stepped around the fire and slid into the tent she'd assigned to him.

Slowly, Rune dragged himself up from his seat, still gripping the bottle she'd given him. He swayed on his feet and broadened his stance until his balance returned.

Sera crossed her arms. "How much of that did you drink?"

"None of your concern." He pushed past her and staggered into his tent. The corked bottle slipped from his hand and landed in the blankets with a clink. His hands went to the straps of his armor, but his clawed fingers were clumsy and he pried at them to no avail.

"It is too my concern. You're in my care, remember?" She followed and caught him by the arm to make him hold still. One by one, she unfastened the straps, helped him take off his armor, and stacked each piece beside the tent's opening.

"There's nothing you can do for me."

She huffed. "You could let me try."

He turned his head, his snake-slitted eyes glowing faintly in the dark. Compared to the brilliance they'd borne before, they might as well not have glowed at all. "Don't you understand? I have no power! I'm not weak because of fighting, or because I haven't slept. I'm weak because all my life, my strength came from the magic I had access to. I didn't even realize I was using it, and now I can't. They've bound me, Sera. The Aldaanan bound my powers."

"Not possible." She watched him sit, then sat beside him. "If your magic was bound like mine, your eyes wouldn't still be glowing." She held out her hand. "Let me see? I might not be able to fix it, but if you let me tie power with you, I might be able to tell you what they've done." If he really was as weak as he claimed, it would likely be the only time she'd ever be able to twine her magic with that of a free mage and not be harmed.

He regarded her silently for a long time before he reached to touch her hand. The contact was unnecessary, but made the process easier. She laced her fingers with his and gave his scaly hand a gentle squeeze, then closed her eyes and reached for his energies. Their magic meshed easily, as easily as their linked hands.

It wasn't like before, when she'd touched his energy and felt she might be seared away. All around them, she sensed energy flows she hadn't been aware of. His untamed Gift should have awakened them. The power should have raced toward them, as it had before. Instead, when she tried to call the flows, nothing answered. All she felt was the pulse of his life force. It seemed strong and steady to her, but if he was used to being connected to the ebb and flow of everything around him, it was no wonder he found himself weakened.

Curious, she twisted her energy around his and reached for a flow in the air. She caught it, but it didn't bend to her. Puzzled, she released it and reached for a flow beyond the tent instead, where the essence of water hung heavy in the snow. Despite her water affinity, it resisted their joined contact. She gritted her teeth and strained to move it. Instead of the flow shifting to her will, it was as if their joined power snared on something, pulled tight, and could not move. Her heart sank and she let go of his energies.

He looked at her questioningly.

She shook her head. "You aren't bound. I can feel everything through you, power I didn't even know could be manipulated. But that catch when we try to move things... I think it's a seal. Cutting you off from being able to use anything but your own life force."

She could tell he understood from the way his face fell. It was worse than being bound.

"So I truly have nothing left." he murmured, looking down.

Sera swallowed. "Why do you say this?"

His eyes slid closed. "I lost my family. I lost my home. I lost my sword. I lost my freedom. Now I've lost my power. I've lost everything."

"You still have your life."

"And what good does it do me if I have to spend it living like this?" He flexed his clawed fingers, then curled them into his palms. "Power was the only consolation I had. I might have been born a beast, but at least I was strong. Now I've lost even that. I'm... weakened, worthless—"

"Shh!" She pressed her fingers to his lips. He looked at her, his eyes glazed and sorrowful. It wrenched her heart. "You are not worthless. Do you understand me? You're still clever, a skilled fighter—"

"I'm just a monster," he interrupted.

"No." She cradled his face in her hands and forced him to look at her. Softly, tenderly, she caressed his cheeks. "You're a man."

His eyes closed again. She leaned forward and brushed her lips against his. The brandy was thick on his breath, but she didn't care. He responded as if hopeless, clinging to the last scrap of life he had. Her chest ached with sympathy for his hurt.

She kissed him harder and his hopelessness became desperation. She straddled his hips and pushed him down into the blankets, forgetting the war outside.

5

COUNCIL

It had been a long time since Redoram Parthanus had attended a formal council meeting, but he supposed it didn't matter. The meetings never really changed. There were those who opposed his return to council, given his time in prison, but he paid them little mind; they were the ones who'd put him there in the first place.

He was a man of some virtues, and unlike some councilors, he was able to boast of the fact he had never broken the law—not that lawfulness was difficult in the Royal City. King Vicamros had few and fair laws.

Illicit dealings aside, Redoram simply didn't like the subtle games and plays for power the other councilors made. He was there to advise the king, nothing more. Wealth and comfort were gifts his family had provided and he saw no need to seek more than what he already had. Food on the table and good books to read was enough. For that matter, even in prison, he hadn't been discontent. If only as much could be said for the rest of the kingdom.

Discontent was what brought the council together today, and what caused the war to begin at all. The mages were discontent.

The Aldaanan were discontent. Between the two of them, they made sure the rest of the people Vicamros ruled were discontent, as well. Redoram had a hard time finding sympathy for the mages, despite being one of them. He'd always thought the Grand College a little too desperate for power and had never liked comparing himself to them. The college was useful for those who sought training, like he had at a young age, but the organization bore little worth beyond that.

Yet they still thought they deserved the right to lead Lore and lashed out against anyone who disagreed. The thought made Redoram smile, though wryly. Disagreement was what had gotten him in trouble before. With that in mind, a part of him expected to be escorted back to the dungeons after the council meeting adjourned.

Pausing outside the council chamber, he smoothed his robes and adjusted the cap on his head. It had been some time since he'd worn the dark blue velvet befitting a man of his station, and it felt odd. The many rings and heavy jeweled necklaces felt odder still, but he wouldn't show himself before the king looking like a pauper. If he was to speak in opposition of mages today, he needed to look like his word carried enough weight to make it worth listening to. He drew himself up, pushed the doors open and stepped inside.

It wasn't Redoram's first visit to the council chamber since his release, but with King Vicamros in attendance, the room had been transformed. Normally set a short distance apart for councilors to meet in small groups to discuss specific business, the half-dozen square tables had been pushed together to form a long line down the middle of the room. A throne sat at the head of the row, the flags of all three kingdoms draped over its back. Redoram had expected the room to be full to bursting, but instead, six people sat at the tables and only one empty chair remained. Had he thought he'd be the last to arrive, he would have left home sooner.

No one spoke and everyone looked uncomfortable. Redoram took his place with his head held high. He laced his fingers together as he settled at the table and looked at the others in attendance.

For a small council, it was about what he might have guessed. He was there to represent the scholars throughout the city—a compliment, given that he knew Survas had taken his place on the scholar's council—and the others were three women and three men, all familiar. Redoram skimmed their faces, curious to see what he could glean from their expressions alone.

Dark-eyed and pretty-faced Thelia was there to represent Roberian. She twirled her hair around one finger, the way she often did when nervous.

Gillan, a mage of strong Eldani descent who sometimes removed her nose from her book long enough to represent Lore, stared at the table with a furrowed brow, perhaps wishing she had a book with her.

Solas, a young Aldaanan man who was to represent his home country, gave away nothing. Or at least he looked young, Redoram thought with a grim smile. The lad had represented Aldaan for as long as he could recall and was probably several centuries his senior, despite not looking a day over sixteen.

The others were Nielan, the weasely man in charge of the royal treasury, Landus, the master of docks, and Bryndis.

Bryndis met his gaze with a slight smile, though her eyes remained as shrewd as ever. She was not a noble, but she was a crafty woman. It was no wonder she'd found her way onto King Vicamros's council. But Redoram doubted that knowledge was all she offered the king. While she was a handful of years older than Vicamros, she had aged gracefully, and the way she carried her plump and womanly form made it clear she knew how to use her wiles. She had set herself at the far end of the row of tables, directly opposite the empty throne. That alone was telling, but a man infatuated was often blind. Redoram wouldn't cast the first stone; he'd had lovers in his prime, too, though perhaps none as cunning as she, and he made a mental note to speak of it with the king later.

Satisfied by his assessment of the room, he settled deeper into his chair. He barely had time to make himself comfortable before the door swung open again. A cacophony of rattling armor and booted feet announced the king's arrival. Redoram stood, as did the rest of the councilors, and all of them turned toward the doorway.

A half dozen men moved in ahead of Vicamros, another half dozen behind. A pair walked at the king's side as he swept across the council chamber to take his throne.. The rest assumed defensive positions around the room.

"Majesty," Bryndis said, dipping in greeting. Her bow was mimicked by the others, though Redoram watched her from the corner of his eye as he bowed. There was a snide twist to the corner of her mouth. He didn't like that at all.

Vicamros waved a hand and dropped into his throne with a scowl. "Be seated."

His sharp tone wiped the smile from Bryndis's face.

Redoram expected her to comment, but to his surprise, Gillan was the first to clear her throat and speak after everyone sat. "Your Majesty, as representative of Lore, I am honored to be present despite the ongoing war—"

"We aren't meeting about the war," the king interrupted, his expression even darker than before. "Your blasted war has caused me more trouble than you realize. I have called you together because you are the heads of the most important factions, and I want this to go no further than it must. Do I make myself clear?"

"Perfectly," Gillan murmured. No one else spoke.

Leaning back into the thick cushions of his throne, Vicamros sighed and rubbed his eyes. "My son is missing." His shoulders sagged and he looked suddenly weary. "And with Captain Kaith in the field in Aldaan, there's no one in the city guard competent enough to be told."

Redoram blinked in surprise. "When did this happen?"

"I don't know." The king frowned. "Trying to find him in the city has been like chasing a ghost. Everyone claims to have seen him. Councilor Survas of the scholars insists he was in the library yesterday, and yet the maids tell me his bed has been made for at least a week. It's unsettling to think the maids are the only ones in my city being honest with me." His eyes fell on Gillan and the mage shifted uncomfortably.

Bryndis laughed, earning herself several startled looks. "A boy playing games. He's still a child, my king. Where could he have gone?"

"I don't think he's worried about the prince having gone somewhere on his own," Thelia said, casting a shadowed glance toward Gillan as well. "The mages of Lore's Grand College are in open rebellion against the Triad, but they are still allowed free movement within the three provinces and the Royal City. Why is that?"

Gillan sputtered and thrust herself from her chair. "How dare you? Not every mage in the city stands with the Grand College. If I were a puppet on Headmaster Tolmarni's strings, I wouldn't be a part of this council."

"But you are part of the college's affairs in the city," Solas said. The young Aldaanan's eyes narrowed and he leaned forward in his chair. "Lore stands to gain a considerable amount of power if King Vicamros pulls his forces out from between your country and mine. How do you suppose they would accomplish that?"

"I haven't called this council for the lot of you to point fingers," Vicamros snapped. "You are here to tell me what you know. You are to draw information from your own sources so I can find my heir."

A long silence passed before Landus finally coughed, shrugged, and folded his arms over his chest. "Well he's not been to the ships, so if someone has taken him, it'll have to have been by land."

"Or by magic," Thelia said, leering at Gillan again. Flustered, the mage glared back.

Redoram stroked his beard and frowned deeply. "Gillan has already said she doesn't support Headmaster Tolmarni in his push against the Triad. Pointing fingers at her isn't going to help."

"You would take her side." Nielan sneered, tilting his head back to look down his nose. "We haven't forgotten that you are a mage, Parthanus."

Gillan snorted a laugh. "Yes, a mage who has been in prison for how long?"

Bryndis rapped her knuckles against the table, her face stony. "The lot of you are getting off track. If the king is concerned about the whereabouts of his heir, you should be falling over each other in your rush to find where he's gone. Or do none of you care about the future of the Triad?"

Nielan met her gaze with a hard stare. "Wars are expensive, civil wars especially so. If the prince is missing, chances are it's related to the war. And the blame for the war lies solely on Lore."

Redoram shook his head. "Now, you know that isn't true. The Aldaanan are as much to blame for the fighting in the capital city that set off the—"

"The Aldaanan can't be blamed for college mages picking fights in the streets," Solas protested.

"Enough!" Vicamros roared, slamming a fist against the table. The room fell silent, though the mages still eyed each other like unfriendly cats.

When no one else spoke, Redoram licked his lips and went on. "Regardless," he started cautiously, studying the king. "I do not believe any one party is at fault for anything that's happened. But we are at war, like it or not. I cannot say what the best course of action is, but whether or not the war is ended, His Majesty wishes his son to be safe."

"And what do you say should be done about these circumstances?" Thelia asked, her dark eyes shadowed with suspicion.

Redoram shrugged. "His Majesty mentioned Captain Kaith. I say we begin there, with sending a message to the army in Aldaan. Kaith is a trustworthy man, and if he can do anything from his location, he will."

"Do it," the king said. He rubbed his chin as if to soothe his nerves. "If nothing else, it will let him know the mages may have a hostage. If the college mages have my son, the deployed armies need to be prepared for that situation."

"Shall I notify the naval fleet?" Landus asked.

Vicamros nodded. "Yes. And Thelia, you are to notify the retainers stationed in Roberian."

"Of course, Majesty," Thelia murmured.

Nielan shook his head. "The news will spread like wildfire. It could damage the stability of the Triad in a number of ways."

Bryndis lifted her chin. "Do you have a better suggestion?"

The treasurer said nothing, shifting awkwardly in his seat.

"Then we have a starting point." Vicamros turned to Redoram and gestured toward the door. "Go. Send a message to Kaith and let me know the moment there is a response."

Redoram pushed himself from his chair and dipped in a bow. It was better not to speak; there was nothing left to say that wouldn't ruffle feathers. He slipped into the hall and closed the door on the sound of Vicamros giving orders. Once he was alone, he released a quiet sigh. When he'd set foot in the council chamber, he hadn't fathomed anything could get worse. Already, he dreaded what sort of response he might receive from the captain, but he would not shirk that responsibility.

He only made it a handful of steps before he realized he was being followed.

"Do you think it unusual the scholars have seen the prince when he obviously isn't there?" Bryndis called.

He turned to face her as she walked down the hall, her full hips telling just why the king found her so enchanting.

She stopped an arm's reach away, her eyes narrowed. "Perhaps I'm the only one who finds it odd, but you would be the best person to ask."

Redoram fought back a frown. His hands slid down over his velvet robes before he caught himself and pretended to flick dust from the fabric instead. The unconscious gesture was born out of appreciation for the fabric that had not graced his skin in years, but it would be easy to misinterpret as nervousness. "It is odd, but who can say what games the councilors play? I am not the only scholar on Vicamros's council, if I might remind you. I don't know why I was chosen to represent them today."

"Especially given that your time away from council kept you separated from the Triad's affairs. Then again," she murmured, touching a finger to her chin. "Perhaps that's why he chose you. You haven't had enough time to scheme since your release."

His brows lifted before he could catch himself. Who was she to speak of scheming? Bryndis meddled in affairs for the simple entertainment of it. "Strange to hear you accuse me of involvement. I mean the prince no ill. I was not the one who sent the young man into the arena, after all."

Her gray eyes widened and she retreated a step. He'd meant to keep that tidbit to himself, but the effect it had on her dashed any regret from his head.

It had been curiosity that drove him to ask how the prince had managed to enter the arena for combat, but once he began following the trail, he knew where it would lead. It hadn't been difficult to convince the other councilors to reveal the knowledge. Redoram was a man of authority and power in the city, after all, even after his time in prison. It hadn't been surprising to learn the woman had been involved, though it was concerning, given how close she was to their king.

"That isn't the same, Parthanus," Bryndis said at last. She bridled her surprise and brought it to heel. Her gaze hardened, steely and shrewd. Yet he would not be cowed.

"No, you're right," Redoram agreed. He kept his tone so pleasant, he knew it would nettle her. "This might have nothing to do with the war. For all we know, he could have chosen to slip out of the palace to pursue a girl. Until we know more, we can't assume the prince is at risk. Not at all like sending him to the arena, knowing his opponent has been proven as a skilled fighter. I can't imagine what the king would think of that."

She gritted her teeth. "Putting him in the arena was not what you think. And I have every intention of explaining the matter to the king, but on my own terms." Her voice dropped and she moved closer. A hint of worry flitted across her face. "You won't tell him before then, will you? I didn't mean to imply—"

"You certainly meant to imply I was involved," he said before she could finish, his tone still infuriatingly calm. "But you are right, it is too soon after my release from prison to know what is going on in this city. All I know is that my king has given me an order, and if you will excuse me, I have a message I must send to Garam Kaith." He straightened the cap on his head and turned to leave.

She took a hurried step after him. "If you are sending word to Kaith, I must beg a favor."

Redoram paused mid-stride and turned his head to look at her.

Bryndis glanced over her shoulder before she spoke. "Before the conflict with Lore erupted, I asked Captain Kaith to take care of a small problem. One he should be able to solve without being in the city. Please send him my regards, and ask if he has dealt with the issue."

Strange as the request was, Redoram nodded and gave her a disarming smile. "Of course, Lady Bryndis."

She smiled back, though a shadow remained in her eyes as she returned to the council chamber. He couldn't blame her;

none of the councilors really trusted one another. He turned her request over in his mind, working it into the planned correspondence in his head. It was too vague to tell him much, but if he worded the request right, a response from Captain Kaith would tell him everything he needed to know.

6

BONDS TO TIE

"I WISH WE COULD DO THIS MORE OFTEN. YOU WOULDN'T BELIEVE how much I've missed our time together." Firal cradled her teacup in both hands and blew away the steam. The morning was still cool enough for the warm drink to be a comfort in both her hands and her belly, reminding her of tranquil mornings in Core. She tried not to think of those days, and instead looked at the flowers outside Kytenia's window.

The temple gardens were as beautiful as ever; one would never know the temple had burned a year before. Everything felt just as it had in the days she'd been a student. Or it almost did, she thought as she cast a rueful glance to the soldier beside the door. They never let her go anywhere alone if they could help it.

"I've missed it, too." Kytenia grinned at her from the other side of the table. She scooted her chair closer. "I've missed company in general, really. It's not like I've had much time to spend with anyone since I began helping Nondar, but after Shymin moved to her own room, even sleeping feels lonely. Though I'm sure you don't have that problem."

Firal flushed and put her cup down. "Kytenia, I don't—I mean—"

Her friend lifted a finger to silence her and surprised her

with a laugh. "I meant the baby." Kytenia glanced to the floor, where Lumia lay on a blanket, kicking her feet and cooing at her nursemaid. Medreal returned her glance with a look of amusement.

Firal blushed brighter. "Yes, well she doesn't sleep the whole night yet, so that means none of us do. Medreal and I are both up all hours of the night. I don't know what I would do without her help."

"With how precious Lulu is, I'm sure you'd have no shortage of people willing to help. I'd say I could have pictured myself helping you, but that isn't really true. I mean, I would help you, of course," Kytenia added hastily, "I just never pictured any of us as mothers, is all."

"Stranger for you to imagine Ran as a father, I'm sure." Firal smirked and sipped her tea.

Kytenia's laughter rang sweet through the room again. "No, I never imagined that one. But oh, this morning has been wonderful. Just like old times, sharing stories at a table and talking about what trouble he's gotten you into. Would that Rikka or Shymin were free to join us."

"Where are they, anyway?" Firal asked. "I know you and Rikka must be busier now that you wear the blue, but you're here. What keeps Shymin busy, these days?"

"I'm not sure what Shymin is doing. We don't speak often. I think she's jealous that I was raised before her, to be honest." A shadow of sorrow clouded Kytenia's eyes and Firal almost regretted asking. But then she shrugged, drained the last of her tea, and refilled her cup. "As for Rikka, she and I are both attending special studies under Archmage Nondar. I spend more time with him, since I am his assistant and apprentice both, but Rikka takes many of her studies with him. Since a Master hasn't yet been raised to replace Melora as Master of the House of Wind, I mean."

Firal pursed her lips and stared at the teapot. "I suppose they haven't raised anyone to replace Alira or Nondar yet, either.

You're a healer, perhaps..." She trailed off and touched a finger to her mouth.

Kytenia's face grew solemn. "I think we oughtn't talk about that any more. I know you're the queen now, but temple business is still temple business, and I've seen enough of the unrest between Masters to know we'd best not discuss their actions—or lack thereof—until the Archmage is ready to speak of everything going on in their formal meetings."

Firal gave her a curious look, but said nothing. It was obvious Kyt knew more, but if she was Nondar's assistant now, that was no surprise. She decided to let it go and reached for the teapot to refill her cup. "Well, what shall we talk about then?"

"How about you?" Kytenia pushed the teapot across the table so Firal wouldn't have to reach as far. "You're the queen, you can talk about anything happening in Ilmenhith you want. It's not like anyone will hush you. How are things in the city?"

Firal couldn't help a groan. "The city is a disaster. With all the harvests being washed out last year, there's not enough for anyone to eat. Ilmenhith was unsettled when I was crowned, but to make matters worse, all of Core uprooted and moved to join me."

"I'd heard that," Kytenia said, frowning. "What will you do? Is there anything I can do from here? I know I'm only a mageling, but—"

Firal blinked when her friend stopped short. She put down the teapot without refilling her cup. "But what?"

Kytenia half rose from the table and leaned toward the window. "A Gate just opened in the courtyard, and a Master wearing blue-banded robes came through. Oh! She's coming into the dormitory. There are guards with her, too, what in the world?"

Firal shot to her feet and turned toward the window in alarm. The courtyard was empty by the time she looked, the Gate closed. She looked over her shoulder at Medreal and Lumia on the floor. Voices in the hallway preceded the sound of footsteps and armor, and Kytenia slipped close enough to take Firal's hand before the knock.

Medreal scooped the baby from the floor and stepped back toward the bed.

"Come in," Kytenia called.

A mageling in green opened the door, her face white as a sheet. "A Master of Ilmenhith is here to speak with Her Majesty."

Firal moved forward. "Well, let her in!"

Cringing, the mageling bowed and backed away as the white-robed court Master and her entourage crowded into Kytenia's small room. The Master mage bowed, but Firal scowled at her. "What is the meaning of this, Ceda?"

Ceda bowed deeper. "Temar sent me, Majesty."

Firal straightened. Despite leading the court mages, Temar involved herself in little, unless it was important. "What for?"

Ceda shifted and rubbed at her ear. "Something has incited an... event. A riot in the streets of Ilmenhith. His Highness, King-consort Vahnil requested before he went to confront the uprising that you be notified."

"What?" Kytenia squeaked, clapping a hand to her heart.

A bitter chill rolled through Firal. The skin on her arms prickled with the imaginary cold. She let go of Kytenia's hand and stepped forward. "Then I must return to Ilmenhith at once."

Ceda flinched. "I... I beg your pardon, Your Majesty, but it was suggested you may wish to remain in the safety of the temple until things settle."

"I will do no such thing," Firal protested.

Medreal cleared her throat, earning herself startled glances from the mages. "If I may say so, my queen, it might be for the best. Do not forget that you have business to take care of in the temple before you return home."

Firal bit the inside of her lower lip to keep her expression neutral. She wanted to be serene, regal, but her heart fought her. She was the queen; if the city faced turmoil, she would be there.

But her visit with Kytenia was only a small part of why she'd traveled to the temple, and she wasn't certain she should depart before she had addressed the real issue. Though she enjoyed the time she'd spent with Kytenia, it had merely been a way to wait for Nondar to finish his morning meeting with Edagan and Anaide. Firal mentally scolded herself for putting that meeting off so long. Had she brought it up sooner, perhaps it wouldn't have come to this. Everything she did seemed to come just a little too late.

That the mages wouldn't put their business aside to convene with their ruler said volumes about what they thought of her, but she wasn't ready to begin that battle.

"What do you need to do?" Kytenia's voice was soft and steady, but her hands trembled, betraying her fear.

Firal glanced to Ceda and tried to look stern. "Wait in the hallway. I must finish here."

The court mage bowed and retreated into the hall with her retainer. Firal waited until the door was closed to sigh and bury her face in her hands. She willed herself to remain steady. There was nothing to do now but continue what she'd started. "I came to speak to Nondar. I asked him for help, and he promised to give it to me. But nothing has come of it and I've begun to fear that in the midst of everything, he's forgotten."

Kytenia's face fell and she reached to touch Firal's arm. "Oh, Firal... What have the mages told you about him?"

"They told me nothing." Firal moved back to her chair, sank into it and leaned against the table for support. "They deliberately kept his condition from me. I know he's failing, Kytenia, I know he's been all but bedridden since his stroke. The mages didn't tell me, but I heard. I know I should have come sooner, but..." She swallowed hard and blinked harder. "I couldn't bring myself to come. I've been afraid to see him, to see his condition for myself. So I stayed in Ilmenhith, hoping he'd recover and surprise everyone. Instead, I think I may have lost the only chance we had for help."

Just like she'd lost the chance to call Rune back to her. It had been a handful of days since she'd tried to reach him, though the lack of response made it feel like an eternity. Her throat tightened, and she squeezed her eyes closed to keep the tears from welling up.

"I am apprentice to the Archmage now, Firal." Kytenia eased herself into her chair and reached to take her hand once more. "I can't make any promises as to when I will be able to speak to him in depth, but you can tell me what he promised. If it's at all within my power to help it happen, you know I'll do whatever I can."

Firal squeezed her friend's fingers and tried to smile. "We were going to send a message to the mainland. A petition to open trade. There's a corundum mine beneath the ruins, down in the heart of Core. The Underlings never had much use for the gems, so it's a resource that's mostly untapped. There's gold in the river, too. More than enough to feed the island and bring us stability again. If we can end the hunger, we'll end the unrest. Nondar said he was familiar with a school of magic on the northern continent. He said he would contact them."

"And he hasn't yet," Kytenia said with a thoughtful nod. "I would have heard of it if he had, or else received an incoming response on his behalf."

"Do you think there's anything you can do? I don't know who else could help me. I don't trust the other Masters." Though she dared not say it, Firal had begun to suspect Anaide and Edagan believed the famine would be the end of her rule. Lulu was an infant, and there were no others in Kifel's bloodline. Should something happen to her, it would be up to a council to rule until Lumia came of age—a council the two Masters already helped lead.

Kytenia nodded. "It may be several days before I have a reply for you, but I will bring it to his attention as soon as I have it. I will make it happen, Firal. Even if I have to seize power as Archmage myself to do it, I will make it happen."

Firal laughed, despite herself. "I hope it doesn't take that long."

"You never know," Kytenia said with a nervous smile. "It could happen sooner than you think."

"Given the way things are going, I might find myself wishing that's the case." Firal made herself rise, though she wanted to linger. "Come, Medreal. We have to go home."

The stewardess bowed her head in acknowledgement.

Kytenia leaned forward to clasp Firal in a hug. "Please make sure Vahn is all right for me."

"I will." Firal squeezed her tight. She trusted Kytenia to keep her word, more than she trusted anyone else, but she hated to leave the company of her best friend. Letting go gave her a strange heartache, as if every moment threatened to bring change that would drive them farther apart. But she couldn't linger, and she tore her eyes from her friend's face.

Medreal followed with the baby as Firal led the way into the hall. Ceda jumped when they appeared and immediately set to wringing her hands. It wasn't like the court mages to be so unsettled, but Ceda was the only one who wasn't in Ilmenhith. Just like Firal, the mage had no way of knowing what was happening, or whether her friends and family were safe.

"Most of the Masters will be in the tower library. We will need them for a Gate." Firal swept past the mage and soldiers with her own guards at her heels. "We shall return to Ilmenhith at once."

Ceda paled and hastened to keep up with Firal's quick pace. "But His Highness said—"

Firal stopped dead in her tracks and wheeled to glare at the white-robed woman. "I don't care what he said. He may be my husband, but Vahnil is not my king. I am the ruler of this country and I will not be treated as some child who needs looking after."

Ceda clapped her hands to her mouth and bowed so deep she looked like she might fall to the floor. "O-of course, my queen. My humblest apologies. I only meant to share King-consort Vahnil's concerns, not to imply—"

"King-consort Vahnil can express his concerns by himself," Firal interrupted. "After I see that he's brought back to the castle in one piece. Now move along." She spun on her heel and marched through the quiet dormitory. Behind her, she thought she heard Medreal chuckle.

CEDA WAS the first to step through the crackling portal that led back to the Gate room in Ilmenhith, though Firal had only reluctantly agreed to let her go ahead of the group. It wasn't as if they were walking into a trap. The Gate was held open in both the temple and the stone archway in the palace, which meant people could move through it in either direction. Had they been using a Gate that was not anchored on both sides, it might have made sense to send someone ahead to be sure it was safe, since there would be nowhere to retreat. Instead, the court mage looked silly, peering into the hallway and looking back and forth before motioning the others through.

A pair of guards preceded Firal. Medreal came through with Lumia just after her, and the rest of the guards followed. The men pushed ahead of the group to enter the hall first, then framed the doorway to create a better organized escort. Firal smoothed her dress and strode from the tiny Gating parlor beside the mages' office with her head up and her shoulders squared. "Half of you are to escort Lumia and my stewardess to my quarters and remain there to protect her. Ceda, you will accompany them."

The mage opened her mouth as if to protest, but thought better of it and merely nodded.

"Where will you be, my queen?" Medreal asked, a touch of worry in her face.

Firal snorted. "Dragging my fool husband back in from the

streets by the collar, if I have to." She bent to kiss the baby's forehead, smoothed the girl's dark curls, and gave the older woman a warm smile. "Wish me luck. Perhaps it won't take long."

"We will be here when you return, my queen," Medreal said.

Firal nodded and watched, anxious, as half her guards peeled off to form Lulu's escort. It took some effort to turn and take the first step toward the guards who remained in the hall. They took their positions around her with practiced ease as she hurried onward, their pace an easy match for her quick strides.

She hadn't noticed it at the temple, but now that she was alone with her guard, her stomach churned. While she understood what reasoning might have sent him out the palace gates, the last place Vahn needed to be was with the guardsmen who faced a riot. She'd already lost one husband to violence and misunderstanding, and she was startled to realize she was afraid. She cared for Vahn; he was a dear friend. But the depth of her fear surprised her and made her stomach turn all that much harder.

The roar of the fighting was audible even before she opened the doors to the courtyard. She tried not to cringe as she hurried down the palace steps. A handful of court mages stood at the gate, peering out through the portcullis and shifting uneasily. Firal was relieved to see Temar among them. The court mage was one of few Masters she felt respected her.

Beyond the gate's iron bars, the street roiled like a sea of people, held at bay by a thick line of men in glistening armor. Another long line of guards filed back toward the castle walls, leading captives to one of the small side entries. A pair of mages let them in and out of the palace as the guards escorted dozens of people to the dungeons. Another problem to sort later. Firal rubbed her brow as she joined Temar's group. "How long since this began?"

The mages gave her worried looks. Only Temar appeared unruffled, though she always bore the sort of tranquility Firal strove to achieve, herself. The longer she held the title of queen, the more Firal suspected there was more to it than attitude. Though fine lines skirted her mouth and the corners of her eyes, it was impossible to discern Temar's age. She bore same white hair and too-blue eyes as all Masters, and with them, that peculiar sense of serenity followed her wherever she went. Fitting, then, that she should have one of the most stressful jobs in the palace.

Temar tapped her chin with a finger and glanced to the turmoil in the street. "Half an hour, perhaps more."

Firal didn't like the sound of that. "And it hasn't been calmed yet?"

Temar shrugged. "A problem is always fast to emerge and slow to resolve, my queen."

"What sparked the conflict?"

The mage hesitated to answer. Her eyes drifted to her peers and the whole group shifted. Some shook their heads.

Firal glanced between them. "You don't know?"

No one answered.

Such a simple piece of information might have helped them calm things sooner. Firal huffed, picked up her skirts and turned away.

"Your Majesty, where are you going?" Temar asked.

"To find out." Firal glowered at the court Master over her shoulder. She was surprised to see the woman break away from the mages to join her circle of guards. But Firal didn't protest, taking comfort in the presence of Temar's Gift. She was still most comfortable around other mages and often wished she hadn't had to leave the temple so soon.

They crossed the courtyard at a brisk pace and reached the narrow door to the dungeons at the same time as a guard who led a man in irons. "Stop there," Firal ordered, feeling a twinge of satisfaction when both the guard and his prisoner gaped at sight of her. She didn't wear her crown, reserving it for special occasions, but she still carried herself imperiously and dressed the part of queen. With jewels pinned in her cascading ebony curls and studding her midnight blue silk gown, she made a stunning contrast to the stark blue-trimmed white worn by Temar. If anything, the plain robe of the mage beside her emphasized Firal's importance.

Belatedly, the guard bowed. The prisoner fell to his knees.

Firal let go of her skirts and stared at the man in irons. He cowered at her feet, his head down. "What has he done?"

"Our orders were to arrest everyone involved, Your Majesty," the guard said. He met her eyes when she looked at him, but he didn't hold that contact for long. "He was a part of the mob."

She lifted her chin. "Did you see him attack any of the city guard?"

"No, Your Majesty, but—"

"Other citizens?"

"No, but—"

Firal snorted. "Then why was he arrested?"

The guard stared at the ground. "He was in the mob, Your Majesty. Everyone involved was to be arrested. T'was our orders, Majesty, from His Highness."

From whatever officer was able to bend his ear, more likely. Vahn was too gentle to order any such thing. Firal shook her head. She didn't know why he'd joined the army at all, other than that it might have met some expectation his father had.

Another guard with another prisoner approached. She moved back as they drew near. "Step aside and let them through. I wish to speak with your prisoner."

The guard hauled the man up from his knees and pushed him away from the dungeon door, clearing the way. The captive still didn't lift his head.

"Do you wish to go free?" Firal asked.

"My queen," Temar protested. She blinked and fell silent when Firal raised a hand.

The prisoner looked up, fearful, but with the faintest spark of hope in his eyes.

"Answer my questions truthfully and you may be found fit for release." Firal paused and tried to look purposeful as she scrambled for something to ask. If she chose her words carefully, she might learn a great deal. "Were you present when the fighting began?"

The man nodded. It was a poor question. It told her nothing valuable.

"So you must know what started it." She softened her tone as she spoke, mindful to keep it from sounding like an accusation. "Tell me, what incited this?"

"I was working, Your Majesty," the captive said. He shook his head and dropped his eyes. "I wasn't involved."

She raised a brow. "I didn't say you were. Did you see or hear what began the riot? Did you see how it started?"

He flinched as if he expected to be struck. "A man with a food cart and one of those filthy churls from the camp outside the city. They were already arguing when I passed by, heading back to my master's shop after making a delivery. I shouldn't have stopped, but they were mighty loud about it, Your Majesty. I didn't think it would go to fisticuffs, but it did."

Anger stirred in Firal's chest, but she tamped it down. The citizens of Ilmenhith were her people, too. She couldn't favor the Underlings, no matter how she despised the way they were treated by Ilmenhians. "Go on."

The man heaved a sigh, frustration crossing his face. "Well, Your Majesty, there we all were, hungry as anyone, listening to the man with the cart shouting about having to feed that lot as well as city folk, and the churl from the camp says something about paying fairly. But there's none of us left who can afford to eat, see? So the vendor laughs and says it'd take a whole fist of gold to make it worth his while. And that camp wretch, filthy thief, pulls a whole handful of gold right out of his pocket and says all right! There we are, all us proper folk without a penny to put food in a family's mouth, and that wicked little—"

"What makes you think he stole it?" Firal asked sharply.

The prisoner blinked in surprise and met her eye. "How else would he have gotten it? They're no good, any of them!" His lip curled. "Killing our king in open rebellion and then expecting the crown to feed them! I don't blame that vendor for hitting him. I just wish there hadn't been so many others close to jump in and defend him. And I wish I'd moved on, before the fighting started."

Firal looked to the guard who still held the man's arms. "I've heard enough. Put this man in a holding cell for now. Check his story against what others tell you. If their stories match his, let him free tomorrow morning. And if you arrest any of the people from the camp outside the city limits, put them together in a cell separate from anyone else. For protection of both sides."

"Yes, Majesty." The guard dipped his head and drew the prisoner back toward the door.

She lifted a hand and rubbed her temples with her forefinger and thumb. Her head ached all of a sudden, new facets to the problem making things more difficult than she'd hoped. Neither side was blameless. Resolving things fairly wouldn't be easy.

"What will we do with the Underlings?" Temar asked in a murmur.

Firal gave her a hard look. "Change their name, first of all. They've not called themselves Underlings since before I became queen. We shouldn't keep calling them that." She was as guilty of it as anyone else, but what else was there to call them? They no longer lived in the ruins, so ruin-folk didn't work either. She frowned and put the thought aside. "And we will call for a formal meeting with their leader. Take however many guards you think necessary for your protection and go to the camp. Find Davan, and tell him he is to come to the palace to speak with me once the city is settled. Tomorrow morning, perhaps. If things are calm by then."

The mage nodded. "What will you do now?"

To that, Firal only gave a grim smile. "Wait."

"THAT'S THE LAST OF THEM."

Vahn barely lifted his head at his father's announcement. The last of the city guard filed into the courtyard with captives and wound their way past his seat at the foot of the palace walls. He leaned back against the cool stone and tilted his face toward the sky. It was barely midday, but the hours they'd spent in the street felt like days. Both the street and palace courtyard were silent, though he could still hear the echoes of fighting in his head. It warred with thoughts of Firal and a desperate hope she'd remained somewhere safe.

It had taken more strength than he'd anticipated to quell the crowd, and he'd fought to the point of exhaustion. It was entirely different from his experience on the battlefield. In some ways, he thought it more difficult. No one had been killed, as far as he knew, but subduing what might as well have been an enemy army in close quarters without severely injuring anyone had been a challenge. It had taken a great deal of effort and control to strike with the flat side of a sword rather than the edge, and even more to keep from accidentally stabbing those who tried to move within the fray.

The crowd had dwindled rapidly, according to his father. The past half-hour had been nothing but cleanup, while a number of the guard took time to rest and breathe. Though no one had been killed, their side wasn't without injury. Vahn had insisted no one strike to kill, but the peasantry didn't have the same sort of reserve in fighting the guard. Quite a few men clustered in the courtyard nursed open wounds or broken bones. White-robed court mages moved between them, offering healing. Vahn didn't expect assistance; his bloodied nose and swollen lip would heal fine on their own.

"You did well," Ennil said, shifting on his feet and looking across the courtyard as the last of the prisoners disappeared into the dungeons. Even in retirement, Ennil hadn't softened at all.

Dust and sweat streaked his face, but he still managed to look so composed that Vahn couldn't imagine the man had ever been ruffled at all. "You may not realize it, but you've done yourself a great favor. You've made yourself noteworthy by not only refusing to tolerate violence in your city, but taking matters into your own hands to quell it. You'll have earned a lot of respect from the guardsmen, and a lot of fear from the rest of the city."

"I don't want to be feared." Vahn grimaced at the hoarseness of his voice. He swallowed, his tongue dry as sand in his mouth.

"A king should be feared. You don't have to like it, but you must understand its necessity. Kifelethelas was loved, but he was loved for the things that made him weak. Those things led to his downfall and, ultimately, what led to you taking residency in that palace." Ennil shook his head. "Fear is what keeps a king safe. Remember that."

Given what Vahn knew about Kifel's death, he wasn't sure he agreed, but now was not the time to argue with his father. He pushed himself up from the ground. Every muscle protested movement, his legs shaky beneath him. He put a hand against the wall for support and sucked in a deep breath to steady himself. "I have to speak to the mages. To have them retrieve Firal and Lumia from the temple. Will you see to it the men are cared for?"

Ennil's mouth tightened, but he nodded. "Of course. Go fetch your woman, I'm sure she'll have worried herself ill by now."

Vahn imagined his father was right. He crept toward the nearest mage. His feet felt like lead weights in his armor and he longed to remove it. "When you're finished, mage, I need to speak with you."

The woman in white dusted her hands together as she turned from the soldier she tended. "I've just finished, Your Highness. Do you need healing?"

He shook his head. "I need a mage to go to the temple and retrieve Queen Firal."

Her brows lifted. "Ceda has already returned with the queen

and has just come to assist us with healing. Her Majesty has been here for some time."

"Of course she has," Vahn grumbled, rubbing at the itching crust of blood on his upper lip. "Thank you, please continue."

The mage nodded and he turned on his heel, resting a hand against the pommel of his sword as he made his way to the palace stairs. Of course she'd already returned. It would have been foolish to think she'd stay away. Had she remained in the palace, or had she tried to post herself with the mages to aid their efforts? Anxiety stirred in his stomach, but he couldn't move any faster. As it was, he thought the stairs might be the death of him before he finally reached the top.

The hallways were strangely empty. Most of the palace guard was still in the courtyard, and he assumed most of the serving staff had collected somewhere to gossip. He checked the queen's office first and was disappointed to find it empty. Eager to find his family, he moved on to the private quarters he shared with Firal.

He heard voices from the other side of the door, felt a catch in his throat when they went silent as he turned the knob. The door swung open soundlessly and when he saw Firal sitting at the foot of the bed with the baby and her nursemaid, his heart leaped so that he thought he might fall to his knees.

Relief washed over Firal's face. She thrust the baby into Medreal's arms, jumped from the bed and raced across the room.

Smiling, he opened his arms to receive her.

She slapped him.

"You scared me to death!" Firal's amber eyes flashed fire as she glared up at him.

Vahn grimaced, lifted a hand to rub his cheek and flushed to the tips of his pointed ears. "I don't think I deserved that."

"You most certainly did!" She raised her hand as if to strike him again and satisfaction lit her eyes when he flinched. "Heading off into a riot without so much as coming to tell me goodbye? What if something had happened to you?"

"Your husband was in most capable hands, my queen," Medreal said, a smile of amusement twisting her features. "The city guard is very good at what they do."

"Not good enough to keep this from happening in the first place," Firal said sullenly.

"We can discuss that another time." Vahn stepped around her, closed the door and made his way to the bed. Why couldn't she have been happy to see him? "Medreal, would you leave us for a while?"

"Of course, my lord. I'm sure you're eager for a moment of peace." Medreal cast a sidewise glance toward Firal as she stood and passed the baby to him.

He cradled the girl to his armored chest and released a sigh that seemed to carry the burden of his worries with his breath. He sank to the foot of the wide bed, nestled his face in the dark curls atop the baby's head, and closed his eyes.

"Don't hesitate to call if you need me, my queen." Medreal curtsied as she slipped past Firal and disappeared from their room.

The door no more than closed before Firal folded her arms over her chest and shot him a dark look. "You aren't even sorry, are you?"

He shook his head and she scowled at him, though the expression was short lived. She crossed the room and reached for his face. "Let me have a look at you."

"It isn't as bad as it looks." He lifted his head as she cradled his chin and inspected his nose and mouth.

"No, but I'm sure the councilors and Captain of the Guard will want to speak with us about what happened, and you can't attend a council meeting looking like that."

An uncomfortable chill rolled through him, making him shout and shiver. Lulu squalled in response. Vahn grimaced and returned to his feet as he patted her back and hushed her, bouncing her against his chest. A tingle replaced the throbbing ache in his face. The swelling faded all but immediately, and when he touched his tongue to his lip, he found the split in it was gone.

"Healing is what I'm best at," Firal said with a small smile. She took Lumia from him and settled the infant against her shoulder to soothe her.

The sight made his throat tighten. Without thought, he pulled them both into his arms.

Firal blinked and pulled back. "Vahn, what in the world?"

"You have no idea how glad I am to see you," he murmured, leaning closer. He pressed a kiss to the top of Lumia's head and lifted a hand to touch Firal's cheek. She looked at him in surprise, but all he could do was smile. "It was all I could think about. My father said this fight was nothing, but it was worse than the war. When I rode to battle, I rode a full day from Ilmenhith. There were people I cared about with me, but my home was safe. But this happened here, right in the city streets, right where we could see it from our windows. The only comfort I had was knowing you'd gone to the temple. If I'd known you returned, I don't think I could have managed."

She stared at him, her mouth working to form words. He pressed a gauntleted finger to her lips before he cradled her cheek.

"I learned so much today," he continued. "Not what I expected to, not what I think my father meant me to. All I could think of was keeping you safe, you and Lulu both. You're my family now, my responsibility."

"Of course we are." Firal touched his hand, searching his eyes.

"You don't understand." Vahn shook his head, his brow knit with a wash of emotions. His heart hammered in his chest. Anxiety threatened to make him ill. He cupped her face in both hands and kissed her.

Her eyes widened, but she didn't fight him, frozen in place. Then, ever so slowly, she softened into his touch and his kiss and let her eyes slide shut.

He held it for what felt an eternity. When he finally broke away, he rested his forehead against hers.

"I love you, Firal," he said, and the sound of his own voice made his head spin with the revelation. The fear, the worry, the relief of having her close beside him. He closed his eyes, wrapped his arms around her and Lumia, and held them both to his chest. "I love you."

7

TAKING SIDES

MORNING BROKE LIKE A HAMMER BLOW TO HIS HEAD. RUNE grimaced and turned his face away from the blinding sunlight that peeked in through a crack between the tent's flaps. He pulled the blankets closer and nestled against the warm body curled beside him. The sweet scent of her hair filled his nostrils and he breathed deeply, savoring the feeling of her skin against his, a feeling he'd sorely missed. She stirred and a moan escaped her as she stretched. The sound of her voice made his eyes snap open.

It was not Firal.

Spitting a curse, he jerked backwards and took the blankets with him as he shoved her from his bedroll.

Sera squealed as the cold air hit her skin. She wrapped her arms around herself and shot him a dirty look.

"Get out." He winced at the pain his own voice rendered in his head. Slumping forward, he buried his face in his hands.

"Well good morning to you too," she muttered.

"*GET OUT!*" he roared, thrusting a clawed finger toward the door as crimson light flooded his eyes.

Sera's blue eyes grew frosty as she picked up her clothes from the floor and slid into them without a word. She flung open the tent flaps and left them that way as she stepped outside.

Rune cursed again, jerked the blankets up around his naked shoulders, and squeezed his eyes closed against the light that bored into his skull. He slipped from his makeshift bed with the blankets close, inched toward the tent flaps, and groped for them with his eyes closed. The fabric snagged on his scales and he pulled the flaps closed. The dark eased his headache, and he allowed himself a sigh of relief. He needed water. But first, he needed clothes.

Rune turned back toward the bedroll and paused when the claws on his toes clinked against something. He knelt to pick up the bottle of brandy he only sort of recalled from the night before. It was empty.

Casting the bottle back to the ground, he dropped back onto his bedding and groaned. His memory was hazy. He tried to make it focus. He remembered returning to the camp with Sera and Prince Vicamros, remembered drinking to dull the hurt in his head, remembered deciding not to stop when it dulled his thoughts as well. Everything beyond that was a blur, a strange mix of dream and reality he couldn't seem to separate. He remembered anguish, then comfort and relief.

There was no relief now, he thought bitterly, staring down at the empty liquor bottle.

Why had he done such a thing? He had no head for alcohol. The wine he'd had on rare formal occasions was enough to make his head buzz. And what had he done because of it? His fogged recollection, Sera's presence in his tent, and their mutual nudity was enough to tell him, but he couldn't fathom why he'd done it. Or had he? Firal was all he could think of, all he cared about, all he wanted.

Rune reached for the rings he always wore on their strap around his neck and was startled to find them missing. A stroke of panic shot through him and his eyes flew open to dart across the floor.

He found the rings beside his bedroll, still on their strap. He didn't recall if he'd removed them or if Sera had. Angry, he pulled them on, wondering if she had any idea of their significance. Then he let go of the blankets, dressed, and strapped his sword to his side. He left his armor on the ground. Bracing himself, he pushed out into the daylight.

The camp was quiet, but not empty. Gryphons walked among the tents, hobbling on lame legs or nursing splinted wings. Soldiers moved around them with somber faces, some injured, most exhausted. Theirs weren't the faces of an army that had emerged victorious, though Rune no longer heard sounds of battle. The quiet was a small blessing with the pounding in his head, and he moved to the nearby fire with a hand shielding his eyes.

He'd have preferred to stay in his tent until his headache subsided, but his mouth felt dry and tasted sour, and the barrels near the fire were the closest place to get water.

Most mornings, the smell of the stew pot was welcome. This morning it made his stomach turn. He tried to ignore it as he took a wooden bowl from beside the campfire and used it to dip water from one of the barrels. He would have preferred a cup, but the bowl would do.

The space around the fire was vacant, and with his water in hand, he tested one of the cut logs that served as benches with his foot. It hadn't sat long enough to sink into the earth, and it rolled easily when he pushed. He shoved it closer to the fire and sat. After the first swallow of water sent a shock of cold through his middle, he was grateful for the warmth of the flames.

He didn't have long to rest before the sound of someone approaching made him lift his head. When he saw Garam, he flinched and looked back to his bowl.

"Care to explain yourself?" The captain's voice was always booming and powerful, but it seemed particularly so now.

Rune groaned. She hadn't wasted any time. "I know she's your sister, but—"

"I'm not talking about that," Garam snapped. "We'll get to that in a minute. What I'm concerned with is that we're in the middle of a war, and you're hung over."

"What is there to explain?" Rune rubbed his eyes and tried to take another swallow of water. His stomach churned, but it helped his head. "Went to battle, nearly got myself killed, came back and drank a bottle of brandy. That's how this happens, right?"

The captain scowled and crossed his arms. "There is to be no drinking in my army."

"Maybe your healer shouldn't be handing out liquor, then."

A muscle in Garam's jaw twitched. "It wasn't her best decision. Neither was bedding you, if you ask me."

Rune grimaced.

Garam raised a brow. "You agree?"

How was he supposed to answer that? Anything he said could be taken as an affront. Rune grimaced again and looked away. "It's not about her."

The captain stared at him, the weight of his eyes an unwelcome burden.

Rune squeezed his eyes closed and felt his hands tighten involuntarily on the water bowl. The thump in his head was no better, but felt distant now. "I... broke a vow."

This time, both Garam's brows rose. "With Sera?"

Rune nodded.

Garam continued to stare at him for an uncomfortably long time, a thoughtful look hazing his eyes. Then he shifted on his feet, and his expression softened. "Didn't have you pegged as married."

"Didn't have you pegged as caring." Rune made room on the log for Garam to sit beside him.

"My men are important to me. Understanding them means understanding their needs, and understanding their needs means understanding their lives." Shrugging, Garam sank to the log with a quiet groan. He adjusted his armor as he settled and nodded toward Rune's hands. "She like you? Your partner?"

Rune shook his head. "There's nobody like me, I'm the only one. She's Eldani. A mage."

"One we're fighting?"

"No."

Garam nodded. "Good. I'd hate to have that used against us. This war is enough of a mess already." He paused and pursed his lips. "Kids?"

"We weren't married that long before I—" Rune stopped short and changed what he was going to say. "Before I left." Garam needed to know no more than that.

The captain's eyes narrowed. "Where is she?"

"Across the sea." Rune drained the last of his water and tossed the empty bowl to the ground. His hands curled to fists. "Where I should be."

Garam frowned, and that thoughtful look returned to his eyes. Eventually, he pushed himself up from the log. He took the discarded bowl from the ground beside the fire and strode to the water barrels to refill it. "Sera told me about you. Told me you committed treason in your homeland."

Rune's eyes narrowed. "Are you afraid of traitors?"

"I am. But I'm not afraid of you." Shrugging, Garam offered the bowl back to Rune as he sat again. "Keep drinking, it'll help your head."

Cradling the bowl in both hands, Rune stared at the water. He wasn't sure he could stomach any more. "Not afraid of me? Why?"

"From the time we first set foot outside the Royal City, you could have killed me. You could have killed half the army. You were powerful enough. After our go-round before departure, no one would have been surprised if you did." The captain leaned forward to rest his elbows on his knees. He stared into the fire, his expression growing distant. "But you didn't. You've kept our bargain. I bested you, and here you are. Still in my army, after any number of chances to kill me or just escape."

"You have my sword." Rune took a small sip, just enough to wet his mouth. "If I want it back, what choice do I have?"

"You really expect me to believe you're here because of a sword?" Garam raised a brow. "Weapons can be replaced."

Rune shook his head. "Not that one." But the captain was right; the sword wasn't the only reason he'd stayed. He flexed his hands and dropped his eyes to the claws that still tipped his fingers.

He'd been foolish to think his body could be repaired. He should have left when he first thought the possibility absurd, disregarded what Ria said and headed back to the Royal City. He could have recovered his sword, could have been on his way. But he'd thought he had nothing to lose in trying.

He'd been wrong.

After the previous night, he didn't even have his dignity.

"Sera also told me about your magic," Garam said, jarring him from his thoughts. "I should have had her look you over before I sent you onto the battlefield. I owe you an apology. It wasn't reasonable to expect you to fight off an entire group of mages when I knew you weren't at your peak. Even if I didn't know the extent of your condition."

Rune scowled. What else had Sera told him? At this rate, he'd have no privacy left. He took another drink. "What happened to the mages? Is the fighting over?"

"For now." Garam frowned. "Don't know what happened. All of a sudden, they just turned tail and ran. Retreated, but they were winning. We couldn't even get close enough to touch them. The gryphons did more damage than my men did, but they took losses of their own. Half of them are injured. Quite a few dead."

"And Prince Vicamros?" Rune asked.

The captain snorted. "Alive and well, though walking on eggshells around me. As well he should. I'll have his hide before the day's over. I just have to deal with my officers first. The prince wanted to speak to you, actually, but I asked Sera to watch him and let me go first."

Rune's brow furrowed. "He wants to speak to me?"

"That's what he said." Garam stood and rested a hand against the hilt of his sword, a habit most of the soldiers seemed to have picked up. "I'll send him your way. You stay put, drink your water. I'll have more to say to both of you after this meeting with my men is over."

Rune grunted in response and looked back to the fire as the captain walked away, grateful for a moment of peace while he nursed his drink. He had most of it down before Vicamros arrived.

The prince was by himself. Rune was surprised Garam let him cross the camp without a guard. He thought the captain's concern over the boy was unnecessary, but he wasn't fool enough to say it to the man's face. Vicamros was young, but he handled himself and his weapon well. Their fight in the arena had been one of the closest. Despite being inexperienced in real battle, the prince was skilled and could surely protect himself. Had he been anyone but the heir, he might have been an asset.

Vicamros lingered several paces away, looking at the logs laid around the fire as if he wasn't sure what he should do. He wore his armor and sword, and he held himself as if he expected a battle at any moment. With the way Garam spoke, he likely did. After casting a nervous glance over his shoulder, the prince finally seated himself on the next log over. Close enough for comfortable conversation, but distanced enough to be polite.

"The captain told me you were coming," Rune said, trying not to shiver as he gulped the last of the cold water. That was enough. He didn't think he could get another swallow down.

Vicamros said nothing, though he shifted.

Rune put the bowl by his feet and stretched. His head was better, at least, even if his conscience and his pride were still sore. He'd never thought himself suited to idle chatter, but the silence made him uncomfortable. In silence, there was nothing to drown out his regret. "Last night was your first real battle, wasn't it?"

The prince cringed and turned his eyes to the muddy ground beneath his boots. "I threw up."

Rune couldn't resist a smirk. "So did I, after my first."

Embarrassment made color bloom in the boy's cheeks. "I find that hard to believe. I fought you in the arena, and I watched you before that. You're so skilled. And not much older than me."

"How old are you?"

"Fifteen, sir." Vicamros offered a smile. "I wouldn't think you're much older than that, are you?"

Rune shook his head. "You'd be right, if I aged like you. Though I suppose it makes no difference. Aging more slowly means maturing more slowly, too."

The prince eyed him uncertainly. "What do you mean?"

"I grew up with the Eldani. I age like they do." Rune shrugged. "They still count years, but a year to them gives no more growth and maturity than a few months. We count our ages in pents. Five years at a time, and it's close enough to accurate. If you were like us, fifteen pents, that would make you seventy-five."

Vicamros stared, his mouth falling open. "Most men don't live to be seventy-five."

Rune chuckled. "I know. So you can see why it makes it hard for us. Most Eldani don't bother to keep track of how old they are. Birthdays are less important when you might have hundreds of them."

"So you don't know how old you really are?"

"I didn't say that. In my culture, we determine someone's age by maturity of both body and mind." Rune paused, working numbers in his head. "Were I human, I suppose your people would figure me close to twenty-one. Twenty-two, perhaps."

The prince cracked a smile. "So I wasn't far off in my guess, really."

"Not at all," Rune agreed.

"So your first battle must have been a long time ago, for my people." Vicamros frowned thoughtfully, rubbing his chin.

"Two years."

The youth's mouth fell open again. "That's all? Impossible! In the arena, you—"

"In the arena, people were trying to kill me," Rune interrupted, his expression darkening. "Things change when your life hangs in the balance. I had a great deal of practice under my belt, yes, but not so many battles. I was fortunate in the arena, because the men who came to fight were soft from years of slaughtering prisoners who had never picked up a weapon in their lives. I had. That was the only difference between me and every combatant that came before me."

Vicamros studied him for a long while, his face shadowed with disbelief. Eventually, he turned his eyes to the fire. "May I ask you something?"

"That's why you came to see me, isn't it?" Rune lifted a brow.

"In the arena, when you had the chance, why didn't you kill me?" The young man's face was etched with concern. It was clear he'd contemplated that question for a long time, likely believing he'd never have a chance to ask it.

Rune's expression softened. "Because I knew why you were there. Like I know why you're here. Because I know what it's like to feel you have something to prove."

Vicamros started to speak, but Rune held up a scaly hand to stop him.

"You have nothing to prove to your father," he continued. "You have nothing to prove to anyone."

"It doesn't feel like that," the prince murmured. "I'm to be the next ruler. There's just so much pressure to be clever, to be strong, to succeed. My father expects the most of me, but he won't give me any opportunities to show I can be what he wants."

Rune shrugged. "Your father expressed his gratitude to me

for not killing you. He could have had my head. Now I am a part of his army. What do you gather from that?"

Vicamros hesitated.

Rune went on. "He sees value where others find none. If he does not test you, it's because he already knows your worth. I..." He trailed off, lifted his head and stared into the woods. Something tingled at the edge of his senses. He stood and his hand went to his sword.

"What is it?" Vicamros shot to his feet, looking toward the trees.

"Get the captain." Rune gripped the sword's hilt in one hand and its scabbard in the other. "And Sera." He slid away from the campfire and moved toward the woods. Behind him, he heard the prince scramble from his seat and take off running.

The sensation grew stronger as he moved toward it. The presence of a mage. Two mages, he decided, though both felt odd. One was like being near the Aldaanan when they unleashed their power; wild, untamed. The other was a bound mage, he thought, though the power's signature was strangely familiar. Alone against a single college mage, he might have stood a chance. But if a free mage was with them, the whole army was at risk. He couldn't fight free magic and neither could Sera.

He lingered in place, unsure of what to do. If he could feel them, surely they knew he was there, too. Yet it couldn't be one of the Aldaanan. They masked their power when it wasn't in use. He moved behind a tree, peered into the forest and waited.

Footsteps and rattling armor behind him signaled the captain's approach. Sera reached his location first and ducked behind another tree nearby. "I feel them," she said softly, squinting against the snow.

"Mages?" Garam asked, voice low.

Rune nodded. He started to speak, then froze as a figure emerged from the underbrush. He blinked hard, shook his head, and looked again.

Anger swelled within him and reason left his head. He thrust himself from the tree and stormed toward the woman with his jaw clenched. He was faintly aware of Garam shouting behind him, but he couldn't make out the words.

Her dirty gray robes were the wrong color, but her face and hair hadn't changed. She stared at him, and her mouth fell open. She'd never seen him this way, never seen him for what he really was, but she knew him. Rune grabbed her by the hair and hauled her off balance.

Alira shrieked, clawing at his arm as she fell to her knees. He drew his sword. Shock and panic sprawled across her face as he pressed the edge of his blade to her throat.

"Kirban's mages sentenced me to death," he snarled. "Did you help them?"

"Ran!" she cried. "Lomithrandel, please—"

His eyes flared red as he shook her. Pressure rose in his head as his anger tried to draw power past the seal on his magic. "Did you help them?"

Alira clutched his wrist, unable to free her hair from his grasp. "I wasn't with them! They turned against me, too. I was with the Archmage—"

"Archmage! Where is she?"

"I don't know!" Tears rolled down her cheeks. "She might be following me, or she might be at the college, I don't know!"

Garam struck him full-force from behind. The captain's arm around his neck threatened to choke the life out of him, and Rune dropped his sword. He gasped for air as his taloned fingers scrabbled helplessly against Garam's armored forearm. Sera darted between him and Alira, dragged the woman backwards and pinned her arms.

Rune caught hold of Garam's wrist and heaved forward in effort to pitch him over his shoulder, but Garam struck his knee from behind and sent him to the ground instead.

Sera glared at him and pulled Alira farther away. "Settle down, lizard. She's more useful to us alive."

Again, Rune tried to loose Garam's arm from around his neck. The captain did not budge. Rune grimaced, squeezed his eyes closed, and forced himself to be still. His anger did not fade, but he bridled it and shut himself off from the magic that tempted him, just beyond the seal. Slowly, the pressure in his head abated.

Garam dropped him when his resistance faded and Rune fell to his hands and knees, coughing.

"The other mage," he croaked. The cold air burned in his throat. He couldn't manage anything else before he coughed again.

"He won't hurt you," Alira said hastily. Her eyes darted fearfully between her captors. "Please, don't hurt him. He's just a boy. He can't use his Gift at all yet."

"Where is he?" Garam asked.

Sera jerked her head to the right. "Over there."

Garam put his hand on his sword as he pushed past the mages and moved farther into the pine trees. He stopped only a few paces later. "What in Brant's name..."

Sera stood and hauled Alira up with her. The gray-robed woman did not resist. Sera pushed her toward the captain and she went without complaint. Rune picked up his sword, pushed himself to his feet and rubbed his throat before he joined them.

"Thought you said there was no one like you," Garam said dryly.

Rune stepped past a snow-covered bough to see what they stared at and almost dropped his sword again.

The boy pressed his small frame against the tree he used as shelter. He peered out at them with luminescent blue eyes, their centers slitted like those of a snake. His feet were wrapped in cloth, but his four-fingered hands bore drab olive scales and clawed fingertips that dug at the bark of the tree.

Slowly, Rune sheathed his weapon. He crouched and met the boy's stare at his own level. The boy flinched as if he expected to be struck, then shifted in uncertainty when no blow came. Rune's brow furrowed.

A lifetime spent alone, trying to hide what he was, knowing there were no others like him. Rune almost couldn't believe his eyes, but when he blinked, the boy was still there, peering at him in curiosity and wonder. Rune swallowed hard and spoke in his mother tongue, his words meant for Alira alone. "What have you done?"

"Envesi is with the headmaster of the Grand College," Alira replied in the same language, her voice shaky. "They mean to unbind the magic of the college mages so they can take power over the Triad." She paused and he turned to look at her. The tears in her eyes were so foreign, so jarring, all he could do was stare.

"I didn't want to," she continued, twisting her arms in Sera's grasp. "I wasn't involved in what they did to you. I didn't want it to happen to anyone else, but she threatened me—she made me—and then she left, and I... I ran. I took him. I killed Melora, and I ran."

His brows knit. "You killed Melora?"

Teardrops left glistening trails on her cheeks. "I had to. She wouldn't let us go. She was going to kill him."

Rune frowned. This was not the Alira he recalled, the haughty and spiteful Master of the House of Fire. But then, he wasn't who he had been, either. The thought struck him with a hint of chagrin.

"Why are you here?" he asked, switching back to the local tongue.

"I made a mistake, but it's not too late to change it." Alira met his gaze evenly, her expression earnest. "To join you. I've come to switch sides."

"Why join us?" Garam crossed his arms. "Why not just run away from the college instead of risking your life trying to get here?"

Lines of worry creased Alira's face. "Running away won't

stop the fighting. As long as the college mages are leading a rebellion, mages won't be welcome anywhere. They're a threat to the integrity of the Triad and a threat to any other countries they might choose to invade."

Sera nodded thoughtfully. Her grip on the mage eased, but she did not let go. "The only way to make this part of the world safe for mages is to stop the war."

"Exactly," Alira said. "And while I can't claim to know anything you don't, I can tell you everything I've heard in the college and everything I know Headmaster Tolmarni is planning. I can offer my Gift where you need it, as well."

Garam snorted. "You think one mage is going to make a difference in a war?"

"One might," Sera said, turning toward Rune and the boy behind the tree. "Just not her."

The boy shrank back.

Rune shook his head and stood. "A battlefield is no place for children."

"We have one too many children out there already," Garam agreed.

"That could change." Sera leered at her brother. "If they could scrounge up a free mage once, they can do it again. Better that he be on our side in case that happens."

Alira winced. "He's too young. Trying to access his Gift is too dangerous."

"But it is possible," Rune murmured, looking at the former Master of Fire over his shoulder. His eyes narrowed.

The weighted glance didn't go unnoticed. "How do you two know each other?" Garam asked.

Rune studied the captain for a moment, unsure how to answer without inviting more questions.

Alira held no such reservations. "I was a teacher of magic before I joined the Grand College," she said. "He was a student at the temple where I taught."

Rune shot her a glare. "Her colleagues tried to kill me."

"Something I had nothing to do with," she snapped, a hint of fire returning to her voice. Perhaps she wasn't so changed after all.

The captain rubbed his chin and hid a frown behind his hand. "So you don't trust her?"

"Not half as far as I could throw her," Rune replied.

Sera laughed and gave Alira a small shake. "Considering how frail she feels, you could probably pitch her pretty far. So you'd have to trust her a little ways, eh?"

Garam sent her a reprimanding look. "I can't say I fault his judgment. I don't trust mages either. But I need them, and it's convenient that the number of mages available to me just doubled. That gives me two bound mages and two free mages who can't use their power, but I have to take what I can get." The sarcastic look he gave Rune made him bristle.

"What are we supposed to do with these two?" Sera asked.

"Take them back to the camp. You with the woman, him with the boy. Warm them up, give them something to eat. We'll discuss the rest later." Garam turned on his heel but paused after a step. "And find the army's other child, while you're at it. Might as well take care of two problems at once."

Rune tried not to frown at the mention of Vicamros. He refused to see the prince as a problem, but convincing Garam otherwise seemed unlikely. He shook thoughts of the prince from his head and motioned for the strange child behind the tree to follow him. "Come on."

The boy leaned forward, seeking Alira. She nodded and he crept forward, twisting his small fingers together like he expected punishment.

Unsettled, Rune laid a gentle hand on his shoulder and guided him along the path Sera and Alira cut through undisturbed snow.

8

NEW TACTICS

"MORE BAD NEWS." GARAM TOSSED THE ROLL OF PARCHMENT TO the table, sighed, and rubbed his eyes. Weariness made them burn, but the ache behind them never went away. He'd hardly slept since they left the Royal City. He'd looked forward to bed after the night's meeting, but seemed there was no hope of rest on the horizon, either.

Sera reached for the parchment and he didn't try to stop her. "What is it?" she asked.

"The king is ready to turn the Triad inside out looking for his boy. He's in our army, and we still haven't done a bloody thing about it." He gritted his teeth and bit his tongue to keep from cursing further.

She shrugged and put the note back after only a cursory glance. "We've hardly known about him being here, Garam. It's not like we've been hiding him on purpose. Between the battle, finding our new mages, and preparing to face the college mages again, we haven't had anyone to spare as a messenger."

The mention of the college mages made him grimace. He'd thought that news would be the worst part of his day. He should have known better.

It was strange how fast the college's army had disappeared

after the last fight, but with how many dead mages he'd counted on the hillside afterward, it was no wonder they'd chosen to retreat. They hadn't expected to fight the gryphons and hadn't been prepared. According to Garam's scouts, they had returned and waited in the same mountain pass.

That the mages planned to strike from the same location twice made him uncomfortable. He didn't understand their tactics. He didn't understand mages. For the first time since he'd accepted his position as Captain of the Royal City Guard, he had no clue what to do.

"We still can't spare a messenger," he said at last. "And we still don't have enough mages to Gate him back to the Royal City. But we can't keep him here, he's a liability. He's nervous, useless—"

"He's untried, not useless," Rune said from his seat on the floor. He didn't look up from the book in his hands.

Garam had almost forgotten he was there. "And what do you suggest we do with him?" Though he was loath to admit it, the man had a number of good ideas. Rune's prior experience with military matters showed through his suggestions. Garam wasn't one to pry, but he still wondered what other sort of useful knowledge might lurk in the lizard-man's head. He frowned at the book in Rune's hands. That was a surprise, too.

Rune licked a finger and turned the page. "Make him a part of these meetings, for one. He's young, but not foolish. He's spent his entire life studying military tactics as part of his training to become king. Those studies might be useful. More useful than these books you brought, in any case."

Garam raised a brow and turned to his sister. She shrugged.

"It can't hurt," she murmured.

"It would be doing him a favor," Rune said. "Bolster his confidence and give him a chance to help in a controlled environment. If you don't want him on the battlefield, keep him in this tent and make him part of the planning. You might even give him a chance to issue a few orders. It would be hard for his father to be displeased with us when he learns we have been helping his son become a better leader."

It seemed reasonable, and a valid point. The captain almost cursed again. He didn't want the boy in his tent, didn't want him in Aldaan at all. He had enough worries without the heir's wellbeing resting on his shoulders. But his options were slim and whether he liked it or not, anything that kept Prince Vicamros off the battlefield was a safe choice. "I still don't want him here," he grumbled.

Rune clapped the book shut and tossed it aside. "He has every right to be here. More right than you and certainly more than I. The three provinces are his inheritance. He has every reason to be invested in ending this war."

Garam's face crumpled into a shadowed scowl. "Don't forget who you're talking to, soldier."

The lizard-man didn't even blink. "I haven't."

"What about the other mages?" Sera asked. She reclined against the table where Garam's maps lay spread. A few markers rocked, and she touched a fingertip to the top of one to still it. "Alira and the boy, I mean. What are we supposed to do with them?"

Another thing Garam didn't want to think about. He sighed and rubbed his jaw. The uneven stubble there startled him and he tried to recall how many days it had been since he'd had a chance to shave. It wasn't like him to neglect his grooming; any other time, his beard was as meticulously kept as the rest of him. "Bring them to me. Bring the prince, too. If we have to deal with them, we might as well deal with all of them at once."

Sera pushed herself off the table's edge, eager to leave. "Give me just a minute, then. I'll find them." She paused at the tent flaps and smirked. "Don't plan too much without us."

Garam's expression didn't change after she slipped outside. Silence fell within the tent, and the atmosphere grew as cold as the winter air.

Rune stared at the stack of books on the floor beside the table, his head cocked sideways to let him read titles that were upside down.

Garam watched, frowning. "Did Councilor Parthanus teach you to read?"

"No."

"Where did you learn?"

The eerie light that flashed in Rune's eyes when he looked up made him regret asking. "The same place I learned to dance. And to write. I have excellent spelling. And penmanship, though you might not guess it, with my hands."

"So you're a learned man." Garam crossed his arms. It wasn't surprising, given the way Rune spoke, and he found himself recalling their first encounter. Lord Survas had said he didn't think the strange creature a peasant, but Garam hadn't expected more than a clever commoner. "How does an educated man end up in a prison for stealing food?"

Rune snorted a laugh. "He gets hungry in a strange place." He pushed himself up from the floor and straightened until he was at perfect eye level with the captain. The way he stood—the way he always carried himself, for that matter—irritated Garam more than it should have. It was clear the lizard-man considered himself an equal.

Garam pushed the thought aside. "You were in a position of leadership, weren't you? Before whatever brought you here?"

"You could say that," Rune said.

"And the group of mages this Alira was in, they were part of why you left?"

Rune didn't reply, but a twitch at the corners of his eyes said enough.

Garam rubbed his chin again. Part of him knew he shouldn't needle the man, but a handful questions had repeated in his thoughts since they'd recovered the mages from the forest. "What did she call you when we met in the woods?"

Rune growled. "It's not my name."

"Lomithrandel?"

"It's not my name," Rune snapped, his snake-slitted eyes flashing. "I've given you my name. I've told you what you need to know."

"Is your history with her going to be a problem in this fight?" Garam asked. With the way the two had eyed each other in the woods and considering how hard they worked to avoid crossing paths in the camp, he almost thought a misstep from either side would end with magic leveling half the city.

Rune didn't respond right away. His attention returned to the books, though he studied them with a haze of thoughtful deliberation in his eyes. Not for the first time, Garam wished the man hadn't been born a mage or a monster. He seemed to know how to use the head on his shoulders. Had things been different, he might have made a good officer.

"I don't enjoy her company," Rune said at last, "but I won't be the one to start a problem. Whether or not we're able to work together until the war is over is her choice to make, not mine."

Garam nodded. It was as good an answer as he could hope for. He left it at that and turned to clear notes from the table and readjust the maps.

Before he finished standing up all the markers Sera had knocked over, voices outside announced the approach of his sister and the others. Rune left the books to retreat into the rear corner of the tent, where he stood with his arms folded over his chest. When the others pushed inside, he was as far away from them—and Garam—as possible.

Sera held the tent flaps open and Vicamros stepped in with his head bowed. Alira and the curious reptilian boy were just a step behind. Garam didn't know where the mage had found a white robe, but how strongly she now resembled their enemy left him unsettled.

"Wait for me!" Ria called. Sera paused, looking to Garam for approval.

He waved her in. "Yes, the gryphon too. We'll need everyone

to be prepared, and I don't know if we'll be able to hold off the mages again without their help."

The gryphon huffed and ruffled her feathers as she joined them. "Of course you need my help. Why else would I have come?"

Sera slipped in behind the beast. The tent was large, but with a half dozen people and a gryphon inside, there was little room to move. Ria tucked her wings close and reared up to sit on her haunches. It helped a little, and the mages shifted until they were no longer pressed elbow to elbow around the table.

"All right," Garam said, moving carved pieces across the map to represent the army and their opponents. "We have a lot to go over and not a lot of time. It's already late. The college mages are preparing to attack us again and they'll likely try another night strike. We need to figure out what we're doing and how we're going to do it. The mages we have present are the only mages we've got, and we still have to face down an army."

"Worse, they've tested us and now know what we're capable of." Sera leaned forward to inspect the positions of the markers. One by one, she turned them to line up square.

"Rhyllyn is too young to be involved in this," Alira protested. "Why was I told to bring him?"

"He should be excused," Rune added, though he gave the white-robed mage a sidewise glance from the corner, obviously displeased that he agreed with her. "He's just a boy. He should be behind the lines where no one can find him."

The child shrank against Alira's side and she rested a protective hand on his shoulder.

Garam gripped the edge of the table until his dark knuckles turned pale. His patience was rapidly wearing thin, and the meeting had only just begun. "And Vicamros should be in the Royal City, where there's no chance of any harm befalling him."

"That's different," Rune said. "He's here of his own choosing."

"So two mages are supposed to face an army alone?" Ria

asked. Her golden eyes settled on Alira and Sera, her ear-tufts pinned back in what Garam assumed was fear.

Sera rubbed her arms to ward off a chill. "What other choices do we have? The boy cannot control his power and Rune cannot reach his."

"Why can't they work together?" Vicamros asked, earning himself hard looks from the women.

Garam lifted a hand before they could speak, though he frowned at the youth. "What do you mean?"

The prince bit his lip and bowed his head again, reluctant to meet Garam's eyes. "I mean, I'm not a mage, but I've been listening to them all day." He gestured toward Rhyllyn, who turned his face toward Alira's robes as if it would help him disappear. "Mages can link with one another and share power, can't they?"

The captain pinned Rune with a stare. "Can you share power with the boy?"

"It's possible," Alira said slowly. "It would be foolhardy for anyone else to try to connect to that much power, but if the two of them are the same..."

"Then he might be able to bypass the seal the Aldaanan put on his power," Sera murmured.

"Then he needs to do it," Garam said.

Rune's eyes darkened and displeasure twisted his mouth. "Garam—"

"Captain," Garam snapped. Then he drew a breath to soothe the prickle of irritation that stole up the back of his neck. "And that wasn't a request."

The lizard-man gritted his teeth and fell silent.

Garam allowed himself to exhale before he nodded to Vicamros. "Good job," he murmured. "Glad I had you brought in here."

"You?" Sera raised a brow.

He frowned at her and she averted her eyes. The furrow between his brows deepened. It wasn't like her to back down;

she was often the only one who challenged him. But he didn't have time to fish for whatever was bothering her. He'd have to speak with her later.

"Prince Vicamros being here is the next subject on the table," Garam said. "The king wishes for you to return to the Royal City at once, Your Highness, but we don't have enough mages to Gate you there, and it would be foolish to send you with a small escort when half the college is staring us down." He tried to temper his voice with patience and respect. One useful suggestion did not change that Vicamros was little more than a disobedient child, looking for trouble and finding enough to keep all of them busy, but he was still the prince.

"So what am I supposed to do?" Vicamros asked, anxiety creasing his brow.

"If you're going to be here, I'd like to turn this into a learning opportunity. Your father has a good head for battle tactics and military strategy, like his father before him. We'll see if you share the gift." Garam motioned to the figurines on the map. "But while we do that, I want Rune and the boy outside, testing to see if they'll be able to make themselves useful or not. Every moment matters right now."

"I will go with them." Alira put her hands on Rhyllyn's shoulders. "He is my ward and I am undoubtedly the most experienced mage here. They will need me to oversee the matter."

Rune snorted in irritation.

Garam ignored him. "Fine. The three of you, outside. The rest of you, stay here. We've got to have a solid plan before anyone else leaves this tent."

Alira dipped in a stiff bow and led Rhyllyn outside.

The captain watched them go, then glanced up. Rune hadn't moved. "Are we going to have a problem?" he asked, drumming his fingertips on the edge of the table.

With a sound of exasperation, Rune shoved his way past the gryphon and stormed outside.

"It seems you are," Ria said.

Garam sighed. "It seems I am."

Sera bit her lip and gazed at the floor.

They had never been on what Garam considered good terms, but he and Rune had an understanding. They spoke the same language—not verbal, but the language of war. Yet in their short time occupying the same camp, that connection had atrophied. Garam did not know if it was his distrust for mages or Rune's connection to the Aldaanan that caused it. There was no need for his men to like him, but he did demand loyalty. He did not know how to wring cooperation out of a man as stubborn as Rune.

"You best not prod him, Captain," the gryphon said quietly, as if reading his thoughts. "If you want him to cooperate, that is."

The captain grunted.

Sensing she would get no reply, Ria wiggled until a satchel slid forward against her shoulder. Garam hadn't noticed the strap buried among her feathers. Sera helped her free the bag and slide it to her breast. The gryphon offered an open-beaked grin as she flipped the bag open and drew a handful of rolled papers from inside.

"I brought the latest reports from the last wing to fly over the mountains," she said. "They'll be the last of the scouts to venture over the mage encampment. We were noticed, so it's no longer safe for our scouts."

"How recent was that flight?" Garam leaned across the map to take the papers when she offered them. Each was tied with a colored string. He chose one at random and slid the string off the end so the paper could be unrolled.

Vicamros watched as he spread the paper atop the map and pinned its corners down with stones. "Amazing," he murmured. He inched closer to study the small addition. "It's like a map of its own."

"And its lines match the captain's map near-perfectly," Ria said with a hint of pride.

The prince brushed a hand over the other rolls. "Where did you get these?"

Whatever pride the gryphon felt evaporated and her feathers went flat. "I beg your pardon?"

Vicamros gave her a blank stare.

"I'm surprised you don't know," Sera said as Ria started to bristle. "Your father's best cartographers are gryphons."

"They're probably the best in the world," Garam added.

The gryphon trilled, the shine coming back to her eyes. "High praise coming from you, Captain."

"I don't have to be comfortable around your kind to respect what you can do," Garam replied dryly. He ran a finger across the new map, tracing the lines of movement the scouts had depicted in colored inks. "You've got a literal bird's-eye view of the world. No way anyone can do better than that."

Vicamros frowned. "If my father employs gryphons as cartographers, how is it I've never seen any at work?"

Ria's cheer vanished almost as swiftly as it had returned. "It's no safer for us to fly over the Royal City than to fly over the mage army. We used to visit quite often. Now our meetings must take place beyond the city's walls."

"The mage-barrier keeps them out," Sera added before the prince could ask.

"It soul-blights us, is what it does." Ria's voice dropped to the hushed reverence that came with fear. "Eats us from the inside out, chews away at us until there's nothing left but husks. Too dangerous. Can't risk it. There are so few of us now, as it is."

Vicamros's brow furrowed. "I thought the soul-blight was a myth."

"If only we were so lucky," Garam grumbled under his breath.

The prince blinked twice. "I'm surprised to hear that from you, Captain. I thought you were a man of reason."

"I'm a man of facts. I've seen firsthand what the blight can do. Men are lucky. In our kind, it stays on the inside."

"In your kind, you have to bring it upon yourselves," Ria said.

Garam grunted. "That, too. Suffice to say, Highness, magic is poison for our feathered friends here. A single direct exposure is enough to kill them. If the gryphon scouts say it's too dangerous to fly over the mage encampment, the best thing we can do is listen."

"Which is why the only scouting from this point forward will be done by me and the other soldiers," Sera added. She leaned over her brother's shoulder to study the small paper map that amended the mountains. "There are more trails through this part than I thought."

"Lots of opportunities for the mages to sneak up on us," Garam murmured. He leaned back, crossed an arm over his chest and braced his elbow against it as he stroked his beard. The uneven edges bothered him. His fingertips traced the bumps and patches over and over, until he reminded himself of a dog that couldn't leave a sore spot alone.

Sera tilted her head to view the map from another angle. As if that changed anything. Still, she relocated a few stone markers based on what she saw. "I'm guessing no more scouts means we'll have no more aerial support during battle?"

The gryphon let out a small, uncertain whistle. "Ah, I can't say. The wings are divided on the matter. They won't take any unnecessary risks, but who knows what will be necessary? The aerie is our home. We're not as willing to leave as the Aldaanan were."

"I don't understand," Vicamros said, earning himself some curious looks. He ducked his head. "About the Aldaanan, I mean. They were willing to help us before. They had the power to crush Lore's mages and didn't seem afraid to use it. Why would they abandon us? What changed?"

Sera spread her hands in a helpless gesture and shrugged. "Your guess is as good as mine."

A flick of the gryphon's feathers caught Garam's eye. It was small, a subtle ruffling of her breast and a flattening of her ears, but her eyes darted away, too. She knew something, it seemed. As soon as he could speak to her in private, he'd have to find out what. He tucked the thought away for later.

"It doesn't matter now." He reached for another one of the gryphon's small maps. "We're still here and we're on our own. That's what we need to focus on."

Ria nodded and clacked her beak in approval. "Agreed. I can't guess as to what aerial support you'll have, Captain, but I will report as soon as I'm able."

"Good. You're dismissed." Garam loosened the strings that held the tiny map closed. It curled more severely than the previous one. Older, he assumed. Were it not for the numbered grids the gryphons placed on their maps, he wouldn't have known what to do with it. He laid the paper flat and slid a finger along the edge of the large map on the table until he found the corresponding location.

The gryphon released another whistle and gave the table and its large map a single wistful look, obviously longing to stay. Then her feathers ruffled, and she excused herself from the tent.

Whether or not he liked the gryphons, Garam had to admit they were beneficial teammates—and reasonable ones, at that.

Vicamros watched her depart. "If the Aldaanan left, why did the gryphons stay?"

"Eggs," Sera said.

Garam's head twitched up.

Sera raised a brow. "Didn't you know?"

He didn't.

She heaved a sigh. "The Aldaanan had no children. The only little ones in Aldaeon belong to the humans, who have no way to flee. The gryphon nests are here, too, and their eggs take a full year to hatch. The current clutch is due to hatch in the spring. This far into their nesting cycle, the eggshells are too delicate to risk moving them."

Another complication. Garam struggled not to curse. "Where are the nests?"

"I don't know, but we can find out."

His eyes narrowed. "We?"

Sera nudged the prince with her elbow. "We."

Vicamros stepped aside and rubbed his ribs as if injured. "Do you think the nests will be a target for the mages?"

"If they weren't before, they are now," Sera said. "Those explosives the gryphons made did a lot of damage to the mage forces."

"Then we owe it to the gryphons to protect them," the prince concluded. "If they hadn't been dropping those spheres, I don't think I would have made it out of there alive." He drew himself up like a man with a purpose, a new light in his eyes.

Garam wished he shared the sentiment. "One more thing to defend," he muttered. "Just what we needed."

9

——————————————

NEW TALENTS

ALIRA STOOD WAITING SOME SHORT DISTANCE FROM THE CAPTAIN'S tent when Rune stepped out into the frigid evening. He eyed her and the boy at her side and considered walking on, leaving her to face the captain's wrath and fend for herself. But there were few places he could go, and none of them would have kept him hidden for long.

He regretted not leaving sooner. He regretted his own stubbornness and refusal to give up his father's sword. He should have abandoned it and fled the Royal City as soon as he'd been freed from the arena. Not that he knew where he would have gone, but he could have been free.

Rune clenched his jaw. It wasn't too late, but the weeks of effort he'd put into trying to earn his sword back the fair way would have been wasted, placing him farther behind than ever before. He felt a fool for ever falling into this situation to begin with. Again, he worked over the idea of ignoring Alira and his orders and returning to his tent.

He waited too long. Alira closed the distance between them with Rhyllyn trailing at her heels.

"May I speak to you?" she asked.

"A pointless question," Rune growled, "since you're doing it right now."

Her expression shifted and he thought she looked pained. "I realize you aren't happy with the temple mages, and I don't blame you. I never knew of your circumstances until after the temple divided. I thought I was doing the right thing, making the right choice, joining the side that had the temple's best interests at heart. It wasn't until we were in the college that I realized I had chosen wrong. I learned about what they did to you, and I was appalled."

"And yet here you are, with another they've made just like me." He gave her a cold, forced smile.

Alira reached for the boy, drew him close and hovered over him like a protective mother hen. A spark of irritation lit in her eyes and, for a moment, she looked more like the Alira he'd known on Elenhiise. Then she exhaled, and the light of anger faded.

"I don't expect forgiveness," she said. "I know I've made horrible mistakes. But I was not involved in anything that happened to you, Ran. I knew you were to be executed, but I wasn't a part of that decision, nor was I there to see what kept you from the gallows. To see you here was the last thing I expected. I was pushed into exile before you were to hang. I thought you were dead."

There was a sincerity in her words that made him uncomfortable. Rune knew he had no reason to be angry at her; he'd been a child in gray mageling robes when she'd been raised to the position of Master of Fire. But she'd donned white again as soon as she'd joined Garam's army, making it clear she still thought of herself as a Master of Elenhiise. Those ties were less easy to forgive.

Had the Archmage not fanned the flames, everything could have been different. He could have been sharing a comfortable bed with his wife instead of standing in the frigid wind with snow around his feet. But he saw the way Alira hovered over the child and it gave him pause. She cared for the boy, and the boy trusted her. That much was clear. And despite all the hate for the temple and its mages that burned within him, he couldn't help seeing himself reflected in the child's serpentine eyes.

"If you are going to speak to me," he said finally, "you will call me Rune."

Alira smiled sadly. "And if you are going to channel power through Rhyllyn, you are going to let me make sure you can do it without both of you being killed."

The child's shoulders bunched up at her words, but he didn't speak. It seemed he rarely did.

Rune gave an exasperated sigh. "I don't want to channel power through him."

The mage shrugged. "I don't know what kind of relationship you have with these people, but listening to Captain Kaith speak, it doesn't sound like you have much of a choice."

She was right, though he wasn't about to let her know it. Still, a small voice nagged in the back of his head, encouraging him to run. He quashed it, looking at the boy. "My tent is at the other end of the camp. We'll practice in the field there, far enough away that we won't distract Sera or keep her from sensing any of the college mages if they approach."

Alira nodded and gestured for him to lead the way.

It wasn't a long walk from one end of the camp to the other, but no one spoke along the way. Now and then, Rune glanced over his shoulder and fought the desire to study the white-robed mage through narrowed eyes. He wasn't comfortable with her walking at his heels, knowing he was powerless to stop her if she decided to strike him with magic. But she did nothing, walking in silence with a serene look on her face, and again he found himself wondering at how little she resembled the Alira he'd known.

She'd been an angry woman, hot-headed and sour of disposition, always quick to brandish her sharp tongue. Now she seemed calm and strong, and she treated the boy beside her with a tender, motherly gentleness. He watched her pause when Rhyllyn stumbled and fell in the snow. She righted him and murmured soft reassurances as she brushed ice from his knees. They were both worn, but they worked together well, obviously having overcome a number of trials together in their trip north.

Trials he knew nothing about, he realized. He knew nothing of what they'd been through, other than what Alira had told him in haste. That whatever she'd suffered had driven the woman to kill Melora should have told him enough to know she'd changed. It was unfair to assume she couldn't become something other than the hateful Master he'd known. He had changed a great deal, after all, and their new lives had begun at the same time.

Rune paused at the campfire and lingered a moment before he pointed her toward the empty space beyond the last row of tents. "We'll practice there, just in case something goes wrong."

"Do you expect something will?" she asked.

"Best to assume something will always go wrong," he muttered as he made his way to the open field.

The untouched snow glowed blue under the moon. Rune gazed at it for some time before he turned to face the others. "He should come closer. And you should stay where you are."

Alira tensed at the suggestion.

Rune rolled his eyes. "I'm not going to hurt him. If he's going to be on the battlefield with me, he needs to be comfortable being alone with me. You and Sera will have your hands full."

Her jaw tightened, and for a moment, he thought she would refuse. But eventually, she nudged Rhyllyn forward.

The boy moved a few paces, paused, and looked over his shoulder. His lip trembled and his tiny hands quivered. He brought them together in front of his chest and picked at the scales around his claws. Alira nodded, and he carried on.

Rune crouched as he came near. Still several paces away, the child clutched the hem of his shirt and froze in place with his eyes fixed on the snow at his feet.

Rune raised a brow. "Are you afraid of me?"

Rhyllyn nodded.

"Why?"

"You tried to kill Miss Alira," the boy whispered.

"I did," Rune admitted with a frown. "I don't expect you to understand why. It's a very long story. A sad one."

Twisting his shirt between his small clawed hands, Rhyllyn did not lift his head.

"But that part of the story is over. It won't happen again," Alira said.

Rune glanced at her and was surprised to see her smile. Her face was reassuring, but her eyes reflected worry. At a loss for words, he dropped his gaze to the boy in front of him.

"Go on, Rhyllyn," Alira urged. "We have to do this."

Rhyllyn kept his head bowed and shuffled forward through the snow until he was within arm's reach.

Rune held out his hand. "Let me have a look at you." When the boy didn't move, he inched forward and tipped Rhyllyn's chin up with a finger. They locked eyes.

It was more like looking in a mirror than looking at a stranger. The child's eyes shimmered with fear and glowed with power he couldn't contain, yet did not know how to wield. He held himself stiffly, as if he wasn't comfortable in his own skin, as if he feared the way others might react. Yet there was something else there, too. Something foreign, something Rune never had.

A tiny glimmer of hope, as he looked up at a stranger who was just like him. A small sliver of desperation, eagerness, a desire to hear a word of approval.

Rune smiled despite himself. "I'm not going to hurt you. Alira's right. We have to do this, and that means learning to work together. All of us."

Alira released a sigh of relief and the worry faded from her eyes.

The boy sniffed once and inched forward in the snow. He

wobbled, and Rune put out a hand to steady him. Nothing looked amiss, but the child still grasped his arm as if fearful.

"He's adjusted considerably," Alira said, "but he's still unsteady on his feet."

"Is he?" Rune leaned back to look the boy up and down. "How long has it been?"

The mage considered the question for a time before she spread her hands, palms up in defeat. "If I'm being honest, I don't know. The days all blended together as we fled. We didn't keep normal hours and hardly rested."

"How is a child supposed to manage that?" Skeptical, Rune peered at her from the corner of his eye.

Alira seemed unperturbed. "When he could not walk anymore, I carried him until I couldn't, either. My Gift kept me moving. The strength that kept us alive was not mine."

Under any other circumstances, that might have been an alarming admission. Borrowing strength through magic was dangerous, but at times it was all too necessary. He'd lived through instances like those. Replenishing his own strength from outside sources could keep him going for days with no sleep, but always left him feeling odd, weak, like the person he was had become washed out.

Rune frowned and returned his attention to Rhyllyn. "Stand up straight, let me see your legs."

The boy obliged and Rune nudged him with his knuckles to adjust his stance. "Bend your knees a little. Your center is different, now. Standing on your toes all the time changes your balance. There, good. Now move your feet out to the sides. Don't keep them close, you want them right under your hips, good and square. Good. Now spread your toes. Good?"

Rhyllyn nodded.

Rune nodded back. "It'll make the tops of your thighs tired if you're still too long. If you're going to be standing a while, rock your hips forward like this, straighten out, and lock your knees. But keep things soft when you walk and it'll be easier."

"Walk with him," Alira urged.

Little fingers grasped at Rune's hand for support and he clasped them firmly. The child's hand was warm, but thin, too bony for a boy his age. He turned and guided the boy in a small circle around the clearing. "Better?"

Rhyllyn nodded again.

"If I hadn't already heard him, I'd think he was mute," Rune said.

Alira chuckled. "Given what he's been through, can you blame him for being timid?"

"I never said I did." He led the boy back to the center of the clearing and crouched before him again. There was a little more light in his eyes, now; a hint of confidence. Rune allowed himself a small twinge of satisfaction. He rested his elbows on his knees and cocked his head to the side. "What's your name?"

"Rhyllyn," the boy all but whispered.

Rune knew it already, having heard it from Alira, but there was something to be said for proper introductions. "I'm glad to meet you, Rhyllyn. And a little jealous, too."

The boy's brow furrowed. "Why?"

"Because I spent my whole life thinking I was the only one like me, and here you are, no higher than my hip and you already know you're not alone." Rune shifted in the snow. "Now, are you ready to practice?"

Rhyllyn's face fell. "I don't want to fight," he murmured. His luminescent blue eyes shimmered with unshed tears.

"You don't have to." Rune rested his hand on Rhyllyn's shoulder. "I can fight for both of us, but I need you to help me. You and I have the same power, the same kind of magic. But I can't reach mine, so I need you to let me borrow yours. Can we try?"

Rhyllyn nodded and rubbed his eyes with a sniffle.

"All right. Let's see what we can do." Rune let him go and sat back on his heels. He dropped his eyes to the snow underfoot, gaze unfocused as he tried to feel the current of power in the child before him. It wasn't refined like that of the Aldaanan, or even Alira or Sera. Trying to find it was like looking at a dim star and hoping it didn't vanish once it had his attention, and trying to catch it was like trying to grasp a plume of smoke.

Alira pushed against the edge of his awareness, probed the two of them without interfering. "Push back when you feel him reach for you, Rhyllyn. It'll help him find you faster."

"I don't know how," the boy protested, his voice cracking.

"You can do it," she reassured him. "Just concentrate on him in front of you and imagine pushing forward to meet him. Push with your heart and your mind together."

To Rune's surprise, he felt a small pinpoint of power come together in the boy, a tiny beacon to his senses. He met it with his own energy and merged the two as Filadiel had taught him. It wasn't the same as sharing a link with a bound mage, which felt like holding hands. Linking with Rhyllyn felt like weaving a tapestry of threads, working them together until it created a blanket of power that flowed between them like the tide. Raw power that flowed freely toward him, unfettered by whatever bonds restrained his Gift. Rune seized it.

Rhyllyn yelped and recoiled. The threads of shared energy snapped and lashed back against them both. Rune stifled a shout as pain surged in his head, but the stray magic struck the boy so powerfully that he fell.

Alira darted forward and dropped to her knees beside him.

"He's all right." Rune put a hand to his temple. He hadn't fallen, but the backlash was stronger than he'd expected. The sting reminded him too much of a whip. If he hadn't known better, he might have thought his scalp was bleeding. He growled and shook his head. "He's got to stay with me or this isn't going to work."

"Can you try again?" Alira helped Rhyllyn back to his feet.

The boy grunted as he dug his clawed toes into the snow and tried to balance on his own, but he nodded.

Rune sighed. "Again," he murmured.

Alira stayed beside the child and offered directions in a quiet voice. It made their connection easier to forge, though Rhyllyn broke the bond several times more before their link was strong enough for Rune to pull any real power through it.

He started with a trickle, just enough to magnify his senses and reacquaint himself with the energies he hadn't immersed himself in since the day at the aerie's peak. Then he drew more, marveling at the sensation. It felt like breathing deeply in spring, finally filling his lungs without coughing on the frigid winter air. Hope fluttered in his chest and he thought of the tiny, fingertip-sized patch of pale new skin on his arm. If he could just meditate, let the magic surge through him as it had before...

The connection that tied him to Rhyllyn wavered and he caught himself with a wince. No, it was too early for that. He still hadn't learned how to put himself back into that state, with or without magic. He couldn't expect to do it and maintain the connection he held with the boy at the same time.

So he practiced, instead. He made mage-lights and scattered them across the snow like fallen stars. He stirred the campfires, watched them brighten in the dark of night. He roused the breezes and woke the earth; both shifted subtly at his call. And Rhyllyn fed him power, all the power he could hold, until the stars began to disappear in the gray of predawn.

When the boy began to rock on his feet, Alira scooped him into her arms. The tether between them severed without warning and snapped back just as hard as before. Rune clutched his head and growled against the pain again. "We're not finished," he said through clenched teeth.

Alira shot him a dark look. "He needs to sleep. He's just a boy. Look at him, he's exhausted."

"And if the college mages decide to attack us—"

"If the college mages attack us now, you'd not be able to do anything anyway," Alira interrupted. "He's too tired to keep practicing. Let him rest, for Lifetree's sake." She turned away and moved toward the tents as Rhyllyn nestled his head against her breast.

Rune watched her retreat, protests dying on his lips. The boy looked small in her arms, smaller than his years should have accounted for. The former Master had bathed the child since their arrival, but the absence of dirt only made it easier to see how thin he was. It was obvious the boy had come from a hard life and had no reserves to keep him going through trying times.

Slowly, Rune followed her. "There's room in my tent, I have the space to myself. We can lay him there."

"And me?" Alira asked, raising a brow.

He'd hoped she wouldn't ask. Instead of answering, he changed the subject. "I want to speak to you."

She pursed her lips. "Then we'll speak."

He stopped beside the fire and motioned her toward his tent as he settled near the flames. He was tired too, he realized; working the flows had taken more out of him than he expected. It was different, working with energy funneled to him from someone else. If he was tired, the boy must be exhausted. It was no wonder Rhyllyn had trouble staying on his feet.

Minutes passed before Alira emerged from the tent again. She smoothed her white robes as she glided past Rune to sit on the other side of the fire. She tucked in her feet and sat up straight, proper and authoritative like any Master mage. But when he looked at her, he couldn't see the harsh and sullen Master of Fire any longer. He saw the child's feet, so like his own, dangling as she carried the boy to bed, and the kiss she'd put atop the boy's head as she slid inside the tent.

"He's very fond of you," Rune said at last.

Alira shrugged. "I'm all he has."

The words he'd meant to share fled, leaving a tangle of frustration and emotion he doubted he could unravel in one sitting. Unsure what was left for him to say, he laced his fingers together and rested elbows on his knees. "You're not the person I remember."

"We've both changed. You aren't as I remember, either. But then, what I remember was you in the guise of what everyone wanted you to be. Smiling and laughing, making a nuisance of yourself around the temple." A sad smile tugged at the corners of her mouth. "Now I wonder how much of it was real."

It was strange to think back to his time at the temple. It seemed so distant, his year on the mainland longer than any other he'd lived. "I was happy then. I just didn't realize it. The problems I had then seem so trivial compared to now."

"I know," Alira murmured. "And it pains me to see what's come from the temple's mistakes. Not just for you. But there used to be a light in your eyes. Now you look like you're hollow."

It was an apt description, though he snorted in amusement. "I wouldn't have figured you for the motherly sort."

"You never knew me very well. Though I don't blame you. The way I was in my time at the temple was trying. I was someone special. But I wasn't myself." She motioned to the fire between them. The flames stirred. "I was Master of the House of Fire. One of the youngest Masters ever raised, before you, and the youngest to ever lead a House of element. I was proud, but the other Masters always treated me as a child. I always felt I had to prove myself to them. It made me bitter."

"And now that you have nothing to prove?"

"I'm happier." She smiled, an expression that seemed to come easily to her now. "But I've learned a great deal about myself and my Gift since being forced to leave Elenhiise. It's easy to think that fire only burns, consumes, destroys. But it can also nurture, sustain. Its warmth helps the world grow. Fire helps temper strength. It burns away impurities and leaves only the best behind. Fire gives life."

He saw the sense in her explanation and nodded, staring at his feet. He didn't know how to reply.

Alira spoke again, eliminating the need. "May I ask you something?"

Rune looked at her again.

She wet her lips and avoided his eyes. "I know the dangers of what we're facing. I'm not afraid, not for me, but... if something should happen to me, will you look after Rhyllyn?"

His brows lifted. "Me?"

"You understand him in ways no one else can. You know the struggles he'll face in life. You know how his magic works."

"I don't think I'd make a very good father."

"You don't have to. Just be a brother to him." Worry mixed with fear on her face. "I just don't want him to be alone."

"Then we'd better not let you die." Rune cast a glance to the sky. Soft pinks and yellows illuminated the horizon. "You should sleep. I'm sure you're as tired as he is."

She eyed him. "And you?"

He shrugged. "I know you'll want to be close to the boy. I can sleep elsewhere. Don't really want to share my tent with a woman who isn't my wife."

Alira pushed herself up with a quiet chuckle. "It seems you have your father's sense of honor. Suit yourself. Just make sure you're rested. Magic is hard on the body, you know. I'm surprised your hair isn't already white from the strain."

"Is that why it turns white? I thought you were just old."

She paused mid-stride and shot an acid glare over her shoulder.

Rune tried not to smile and dropped his gaze to the flames. A little bit of the old Master Alira, it seemed, was still there.

10

OLD POWER

FIRAL SPUN TOWARD HER OFFICE DOOR THE MOMENT MEDREAL HAD it open. "He said he loves me!"

The stewardess shut the door with her foot. "I suppose I ought to have brought coffee." She balanced the tea tray on one arm. A thin plume of steam wafted from the teapot's spout.

Medreal rarely made an appearance without her tray these days; there always seemed to be someone with nerves in need of soothing. Firal never knew whether to expect chamomile, mint, or the regular black tea she smelled as the stewardess approached.

Placid as ever, the old woman put down her tray and turned a cup right side up to fill it. "Your daughter is asleep now. I've asked one of the nursemaids to sit with her until you are free. We'll have plenty of time to speak. It seems we'll need it." She cast a knowing glance toward the morning's paperwork, untouched on the desk.

Firal tried to still her feet long enough to join her, but they did not obey. Spacious as the office was, she felt like a caged animal, distressed and anxious.

"Come," Medreal said. She let the teapot hover above the cup until the last quivering droplet fell from its spout. "Sit. You clearly have a lot on your mind. You act like this is a terrible thing."

"It is a terrible thing. This was a marriage of convenience. He wasn't supposed to love me!"

"Convenience for whom, my queen?"

Firal stopped pacing and stared at her in surprise.

Medreal poured cream and spooned honey into the cup and then held it up in invitation. "It seems to me that it isn't convenient for anyone."

Thoughts of all the nights Vahn had spent sleeping on the floor flitted through Firal's mind. She pitied him sometimes and felt guilty at others, but his continued understanding—both toward her personal convictions and the need for outward appearances—had earned him respect. He was honorable, whether or not his reputation said so.

"You know why we married, Medreal." Firal stared at the tea, unsure if she wanted it. Part of her hungered for comfort and soothing. Another part was feral, unable to rest, driven by a desire to escape. She turned away and returned to pacing. "And you are not helping. You've done nothing of late but try to push Vahn and I together."

"You are together, my queen."

"Well, I was married to someone else first." Firal stopped to look at the teacups a second time. Sighing, she tried to smooth her wild hair as she moved to her desk and sat down.

Medreal placed a cup before her and filled one for herself. When she sank into one of the small chairs in front of the desk, teacup cradled in her gnarled hands, she sat straight and proper.

The display made Firal glower and slouch in her seat. She snatched her cup from her saucer and planted her elbows on the arm rests. "I don't understand, Medreal. Before he vanished, it seemed like you supported the relationship I had with Rune. Ran, I mean. You spoke of hope. I don't understand why your opinion has changed."

Medreal stopped before her teacup touched her lips. It

hovered there for a long time without her taking a sip. Then she lowered it, and her gaze fell to the floor. Almost imperceptibly, her shoulders sagged.

Firal took it in with a frown. For the first time she could recall, the stewardess looked burdened, worried. Not wanting her to feel her efforts were wasted, Firal lifted her cup and took the smallest of sips. "What haven't you told me, Medreal?" she asked in a murmur.

Smiling sadly, the old woman closed her eyes. "A great deal, I'm afraid."

Firal's face fell, but she said nothing.

Medreal's throat fluttered as she swallowed her obvious nerves. The corners of her mouth twitched with emotion she couldn't quite suppress. "I hardly know where to begin. There's so much to say."

"You could start with answering my question," Firal suggested, willing herself not to grow frustrated.

"It's a complicated question." The stewardess rubbed her teacup with both hands, as if to soak up its warmth. "There are facets to the situation I'm not sure you understand. You're in a precarious situation, my queen, and I've feared trying to address it because I haven't the words. Words do not escape me often, I'm sure you understand. But with Lord Tanrys, they do."

Firal's brow furrowed. She knew Medreal didn't like the man, but Ennil was her father-in-law and a member of her cabinet both. She couldn't avoid him any more than she could avoid her own shadow. "What do you mean?"

"I realize I am only a stewardess and nursemaid. Confidant or otherwise, there is only so much value in my opinion. But Ennil Tanrys is a dangerous man. A powerful ally and a formidable enemy." The old woman raised a hand before Firal could say anything. "I respect him for his capability, but I fear what he could do if he knew what I know."

Not a day passed that the truth of Lumia's parentage did not weigh heavy on Firal's mind. It sprang to the forefront of her thoughts easily now. The girl's looks were a blessing, her round cheeks and raven curls connecting her easily to her mother. Yet the vibrance of her eyes was an undeniable link to her father. Firal hesitated to call them violet; they lacked any subtlety. A brilliant purple shone in the girl's wide eyes, the unusual color enough to catch everyone's attention.

"I understand the need to pretend," Medreal went on. "I agree it's best and safest for all of you. I had not entertained the idea you might do anything other than pretend until I saw the king-regent in your bed."

Heat rose in Firal's cheeks and she blushed to the tips of her ears. "It isn't what you think," she blurted.

"Oh, no, it's precisely what I think," the stewardess said. "I do not question your fidelity, my queen, and it would not be my place to do so even if there were reason to question. But you cannot forget that by the laws of Ilmenhith, you are wed to Vahnil. And as far as they know, he is the only husband that could possibly exist."

Firal had told herself as much dozens of times. "That may be, but I can't forget the truth so easily."

"I did not suggest you should." Medreal turned her cup in her hands and traced the rim with her thumbs. "However, this is a truth, if not the one you find ideal. For your own safety, my queen, it may be best to embrace it."

The warm teacup in Firal's hands no longer offered comfort. She huffed softly and made herself take a sip. "So much for a marriage of convenience."

"Not very convenient for anyone at all," the stewardess said.

"What do you suggest I do, then? I can't just choose to love somebody." A twinge of guilt tugged at Firal's heart. She had tried to allow herself to feel something in the moment Vahn kissed her. His lips had been soft and inviting, his kiss both impassioned and tender. It had startled her, and though she'd closed her eyes and let it happen, it was nothing like when Rune had seized her and kissed her the same way. There had been fire then, her heartbeat like wild wings against her ribs.

With Vahn, she felt nothing.

No, that wasn't true. She rubbed lines of worry from her forehead as she thought the moment through. She had felt *something*. Just nothing like she what she expected, or like she thought there ought to be. A flicker of wrongness, betrayal, followed by a soft wash of acceptance and peace. No heat. No passion. Nothing that left her wanting more. Only the understanding that this was simply the way things were—and perhaps the best things could be.

"I don't suppose you can," Medreal said. "But if you believe you can tolerate things remaining as they are, perhaps it would be best. No fervor is needed. Only acceptance."

"Vahn deserves better than that."

The stewardess inclined her head. "I have no doubt of that. But he made his promises, as have you, and for better or for worse, the two of you have sworn an oath. In desperate times, we do what we must. You never set out to trespass against the oath you made before."

Firal squeezed her eyes closed. How different the weddings had been. One simple, firelit and performed at a moment's notice. The other lavish, filling the city with celebration that lasted days on end. Yet only one was genuine, the other a hollow shell of what could have been.

"Kifel would have blessed us," she murmured. "He wanted us together. Ran and I."

Medreal put her teacup aside. "I don't doubt that you loved Lomithrandel, my queen." She leaned forward and rested a hand on Firal's arm. "Even I was charmed by his vigor, his passion for life despite the struggles he faced. Perhaps things could have been different, but we only hurt ourselves by clinging to that which did not come to pass. You know, though, how hard things would have been. How hard he worked to hide himself.

Ilmenhith was his home, but when he was here, he was never free."

Prickling tears burned her eyes, but Firal nodded. *Free* was precisely how she would have described him within the shelter of the ruins. Once she had removed his mask, that freedom had grown. The ruin-folk accepted him in ways Ilmenhith never had. In the wake of all that had happened, they now never would.

The old woman's hand rubbed up and down her arm, stroking the same way she soothed Lulu when the baby fussed. "My heart always ached for him," Medreal said. "Not for the trials he faced then, but for those I knew he would encounter later in life. I did him no services by keeping secrets from him. I see that now."

"You couldn't have protected him from what he is," Firal said.

Medreal's lips twitched. "Perhaps, my queen. Or perhaps not. There are things you don't know, don't understand, about free mages like Ran."

"Free mages?" Firal's brow furrowed. The words rolled from her tongue as if they were foreign. "I'm not certain what you mean."

The old woman swallowed hard before she found her voice again. "Have I permission to tell you a story, Majesty?"

Firal motioned for her to go on.

A shadow of sorrow darkened Medreal's face. "It was a great number of years ago, I don't recall how many, when people first came to Elenhiise from the northern reaches of the world. Humans, most of them, though there were a few of what you now call Eldani. They came seeking refuge and chose Elenhiise because of its seclusion. They were in rebellion, not for sake of power, but for sake of love. The leader was a man like any other. Like Kifelethelas, or Vahnil. And his bride was Eldani."

"Kifel and Vahn are Eldani, not human" Firal protested.

Medreal raised a hand to quiet her. "Things were different in those times. The difference was clear, Eldani ears so tall that mankind called them rabbits in mockery. Magic, too, was different. The Eldani—Alda'anan, as they were known then—were practitioners of magic before the bonds of affinity existed. Their power was unlike yours, but very much like Ran's. The Alda'anan on the mainland avoided humankind, and because humankind was Giftless, the Alda'anan in the rebellion mistakenly believed their kind looked down upon man because of their lack of power. In reality, they didn't look down on them at all, but avoided them to spare the hurt that came from outliving them. Free mages never die of old age. Or at least, they haven't yet. Death only reaches them through sickness or strife."

Firal eyed her sullenly. "I've never read anything about this."

"It isn't in the temple's history books, my queen. The Archmage did her very best to stamp out knowledge of the mages that lived here before the temple's founding." Medreal sighed. "But it is referenced in journals you may read, if you'd like. There are a handful of them hidden in the palace."

"Perhaps," Firal murmured. "Go on."

"Among these rebel Alda'anan was the first Queen of Elenhiise. She left her family because of infatuation, knowing she would outlive her Giftless husband and thinking she was prepared for it. She was wrong. But it wasn't until after their new kingdom was established and her husband passed that she realized it was a road the Eldani mages had walked before. Grief, loss, an eternity of loneliness." A tiny quiver shook the old woman's voice.

Wary, Firal eyed her. "What happened then?"

Medreal did not meet her gaze. "She sought her family for help. They could offer little, but she begged them to spare her children the same fate. No one should suffer the loneliness of eternity. They visited the island and bound the magic of the half-mages, as they had done on the mainland before secluding themselves from mankind. The half-mages and their descendants would live long, but not forever. So they could pass on. The queen lived for her children. Once they were gone, she faded away."

Firal studied her for a time. The woman's presence tingled in her senses, the same muted, mild way as always. For a moment, she wondered why she had never paid it any attention. There was something familiar in it; something wild, like what she had always felt in Rune. Yet Firal had never thought to question it. Her stewardess had never so much as touched magic. "Medreal," she said slowly. "How old are you?"

"I don't know," the old woman admitted with a weak smile. "Time means less to us than it does to you humans." Firal opened her mouth to protest, but Medreal raised a hand. "No, don't look at me that way. There was more Eldani blood in what they cut from my ears than in your entire body."

Firal put down her cup and leaned forward over her desk. Obligingly, Medreal swept back the hair from her ears to let her young queen see the scarred edges clearly for the first time.

"Oh, Medreal." Firal slid from her chair and stepped around the desk to gather the stewardess into her arms. "You never told me!"

"It was better that no one know," Medreal said, though tears shone in her eyes. "It's easier for everyone that way."

Firal sank to her knees at the foot of the old woman's chair. Her mind reeled and she didn't know what else to do. "It was you," she whispered.

Her stewardess gave a single nod. Firal's throat tightened. Before her sat the first queen—the rightful queen, and her ancestor. Disbelief and sweet relief danced into tangles within her, and words spilled out in a rush. "Why did you stay? Why didn't you return home? You wouldn't have had to be alone, and—"

"I was never alone. I'm still not alone. I have you, and I have Lulu. Like I had Lomithrandel, and Kifel, and so many before them." Medreal smiled and warmth seeped back into her face, though tears still brimmed on her white eyelashes. She cradled Firal's face in her hands, gently and lovingly.

Firal stared up at her as if seeing the woman for the first time. It made her heart swell in unfamiliar ways. Kifel had been torn away from her before she'd had a chance to know a father. She'd never had a mother, or even so much as a family. Now the sweet, motherly figure who oversaw her palace and brought her tea on silver trays filled every empty role. She had already, Firal realized; she simply hadn't known they were blood.

She hugged her, and they cried.

Eventually, Medreal brushed Firal's hair back from her face and dried the tears from her cheeks with the palms of her hands. "You bring me such joy," the stewardess said. "But this is why I changed my mind, dear heart. I realize it's difficult to understand, but Lomithrandel is like me. Aging, but eternal. I wish you to be with one of your own kind, so you can be happy. So you can grow old together. So he can be spared the pain I've already felt."

"But I don't understand," Firal said. She sniffed hard and dried her eyes with her sleeve. "Why didn't you bind his power, too?"

"Because, dear child," Medreal said with a mirthless smile. "I couldn't do it alone. A free mage's power is great, but not so great as to manipulate magic itself. To do such a thing to my own children, my sisters had to help. It crossed my mind a thousand times while I helped raise him, but I was powerless to do anything. So I sent him north, hoping he would find my family. If there's anyone left in this world who can help him, they can."

Firal's jaw slackened. She'd suspected a number of her allies had been involved, but she hadn't suspected her own stewardess. The look on her face must have betrayed her surprise, for the old woman nodded.

"Yes," Medreal admitted. "I helped free him. He was like a son to me, like his father before him. I couldn't..." she trailed off and averted her eyes. "I had to," she finished weakly.

"Do you know where he is? If he's all right?" Firal asked, a note of desperation in her voice. But Medreal shook her head and Firal's hope faded as quickly as it had sprung to life.

"I don't know. And I may never know, my queen. I'm not even certain if he made it to the harbor to escape. But if he did, it may change nothing. There's nothing to say any other free mages still live."

Firal's brow knit with confusion. "But you said you were eternal."

"Eternal, not immortal. We can be killed like any other." Medreal frowned, stroking Firal's hair and letting her eyes wander to the windows. "For all I know, I may be the last. Well, no," she corrected herself. "There is, after all, Lumia."

Firal's eyes widened. "What?"

The stewardess brushed her cheek with one hand, gentle and comforting. "Yes, your child is a mage. A free mage, like me. Like her father."

"How can that be?" Firal choked, confused. "How could you know?" The girl had been born a scarce handful of months before. It was not until an Eldani child had eight pents or more behind them that a Gift became evident. Or what she knew to be an Eldani child, she thought with a touch of chagrin. How had the name been carried down through such a diluted bloodline? How many generations had it been?

"I thought there might be a chance, however slim, that her father would pass his Gift on to her. It wasn't until recently that I was sure. Free magic is different, but it calls to like power. I sense it in her, as I sensed it in Ran. As I fought to keep him from sensing in me." Regret flitted across Medreal's face. "It will take time for her power to become evident to you, longer for her eyes to glow. I can teach her to hide it. As I should have taught Ran."

Firal shifted back and sat flat on the floor. Every new piece of information added to what already overwhelmed her, and she was no closer to solving her first problem. "Why didn't you teach him, then? If you could have helped him—"

The stewardess shook her head, forestalling the rest of the question. "I could have aided him in gaining control of his Gift, but there was nothing I could have done to aid him in his struggle against what the mages had done. To teach him anything would have meant revealing myself, as well. Make no mistake, Majesty. I am strong, but even my power has limits. The Archmage was a dangerous woman who sought magic for treacherous purposes. Having Ran under her thumb would have been treacherous enough, and he was a wild . Imagine if she had been able to capture a free mage whose power was already under control?"

The thought was enough to make Firal shiver. Envesi had proven herself unscrupulous and power hungry on her own. To imagine her with unfettered magic was terrifying.

Resisting the urge to groan, Firal rubbed her face with both hands. "I don't know that I feel any better after this conversation. Politics, history, magic and mages..." Her daughter sat in the forefront of her mind, a tiny, innocent thing who was just discovering her hands, hiding the burden of magic so powerful it had twisted her father's form. "What will I tell Vahn?" she asked weakly, laying her head in Medreal's lap.

The old stewardess chuckled and threaded fingers through the queen's hair. "Well, I suppose you could start with whether or not you love him, too."

ORDERS

A WHITE PIGEON STRUTTED ON THE WINDOW LEDGE. IT PAUSED NOW and then to peck at the glass. Arrick Ortath heaved a sigh of relief. A bird from the college. There were few things he hated more than the ugly corvids that carried messages from other mage outposts. The college was the only organization that seemed to prefer pigeons. The birds were not as fast, but they were reliable and docile, in addition to being more pleasant to look at.

The Master mage smoothed his white robes as he stood. A bone-deep weariness had settled over him, long council meetings and sleepless nights robbing him of comfort, but it felt good to move. It reminded him he was still alive. A messenger pigeon on the ledge meant the army was still alive, too.

The correspondence office was not his usual station, but he had taken it upon himself to monitor it anyway. Seeing information come and go helped his nerves, which had grown more and more frayed since the war began.

He still could not wrap his mind around that word. War was for hardened soldiers and stoic kings, not for mages, scholars, and teachers. Their entanglement in this situation was pure foolishness, a feud gone too far. And for what? Even if they could strike down the Aldaanan, there was still the king to face. Reason, it seemed, had escaped the council.

Arrick opened the window and gathered the bird in his hands. It made all manner of curious clicking and clucking noises, reminding him of his general discomfort around animals. They were worse than small children. At least with infants, someone was always nearby to correct how you were holding them. He shifted the bird in his fingers until he could open the tiny canister on its leg and retrieve the message inside, then carried the creature to the adjacent dovecote, where its fellows waited. He stuck the bird inside and gave it a few awkward pats before he closed the door. It wasn't that he disliked living things; they were delightful to look at and listen to, but he always felt as if a wrong touch would cause them harm. He was better with gardens, where any unfortunate pruning mistakes would eventually grow back.

The birds did not seem to mind how awkward he was in working with them, at least. None had ever pecked him. At least, not yet.

"Now, let's see what you've brought me," he muttered as he fastened the dovecote's latch. He unfurled the scrap of paper as he crept back to the chair he'd occupied most of the morning. As his eyes swept the short message a second time, he abandoned the thought of the chair. Instead, he swept out the door and down the hall.

Headmaster Tolmarni's office was not far from the correspondence office, but the emptiness of the hallways magnified his echoing footsteps and made the walk seem longer. Arrick was used to the bustle of busy students and mages between assignments. Magelings were never assigned to the field, not even for apprenticeships. That they had been assigned to the battlefield, of all places, did not sit well with him.

"Lambs to the slaughter," Arrick muttered to himself as he stopped before the headmaster's door. His hand hovered before the wood for a time before he knocked. Eyrion would know it was him, his Gift's signature unique even among the college's numbers. That, he thought with a frown, and because next to no one remained within the college halls. Only the councilors and a handful of attendants had stayed behind.

"Enter," the headmaster barked.

Arrick put on his most stoic expression and strode into the office. Diplomacy had always been one of his strengths. He was skilled at hiding his opinions and talking in circles, but never afraid to make himself heard. His outburst in council over the declaration of war had been the talk of Lore for weeks. A shame it had not convinced anyone else to stand against such madness.

"A message has just arrived from the mages in Aldaan," he announced as he approached Eyrion's desk.

The headmaster's eyes drifted up from the papers strewn across his desk. "Important, for you to bring it directly to me."

"Indeed," Arrick said.

Eyrion sighed and put down the sheet of notes in his hand. The man loved his papers. Most of what lay across the desk was probably useless, but Arrick let his eyes wander, nonetheless. Now and then, snippets of powerful information lay among the headmaster's scribblings.

The office door creaked open a crack and a scribe peered inside. "You Called, sir?"

"Yes. Summon the councilors for a formal meeting," Eyrion said with a flick of his hand.

The scribe bobbed her head and disappeared again.

Arrick frowned. "Where did she come from? I saw no one in the hall."

"I Called her several minutes ago. I had intended to request coffee, but this, unfortunately, changes things. I suppose she can bring refreshments to the lecture hall while the letter is read." The headmaster pushed himself up with another sigh. "Inconveniences."

"I hardly think you have the right to call a situation you willfully created an inconvenience," Arrick said.

Eyrion waved a hand as if to brush away his concerns. "The affair is mine to oversee, but the minutiae are beneath me."

"Minutiae are what sustains your army." The last word felt and tasted foul as it left Arrick's mouth. He rubbed his tongue against the roof of his mouth as if to cleanse it. "Minutiae are all that keep our mages from crumbling in fear. No one dares go against your word, Headmaster, but that doesn't mean they have any level of confidence in your decisions. You've condemned them, Eyrion, and they know it."

"Pah!" Eyrion waved his hand again. "Our standing within the Triad is of little consequence. You're a learned man, do you really believe one school in Lore is all the world has to offer us? The Aldaanan cause strife, dissent, turn the Giftless against us. Our reputation here was ruined long before this war began. We stand only to profit. For those white robes to mean something again." He cast Arrick a glance from the corner of his eye as they strode into the hall together.

Unconsciously, Arrick smoothed his robes. "I don't think it will be so easy to crawl out from under the shadow of conflict."

"Then you don't know the state of magic in the world," Eyrion said dismissively. "Even in the southern continent, where they've distrusted magic for centuries, schools have begun to flourish again. Desperation overpowers many things, even fear. Attitudes were quick to change when they realized mages could free them from the drought and starvation they've suffered for longer than the Giftless can recall."

That was news Arrick had not heard. The corners of his mouth twitched with uncertainty. "I find that hard to believe. Magic has been outlawed in the south for—what—thirty pents? More? Healing takes much longer than injury. How soon could we possibly expect to see growth?"

Eyrion flicked his fingers as if counting. "Time for two generations of the Giftless to grow old and die out. The young embrace new ideologies more readily than the experienced. Four pents is all we need to change everything."

"You presume to overextend your reach," Arrick murmured. "The south will raise its own schools, with its own beliefs. The Grand College will carry its blemished reputation everywhere."

"Then we will dissolve and become a new school. Really, Arrick. I expect more open-mindedness and forward thinking from my Masters."

Arrick said nothing.

It was easy for Eyrion to consider abandoning the college. He was young, as far as headmasters went, and did not hail from Lore. Few Masters from outside the college's tradition ever rose so high. Arrick, however, had a legacy behind him—numerous generations of ancestral mages who had served the college. He, himself, had served since before the Triad's founding. He was not so eager to go.

When they arrived at the council chamber, the rest of the councilors already waited at the table. Arrick left the headmaster's side the moment he was able and joined the others. Eyrion seemed in no hurry.

The other councilors shifted as Arrick joined them, their faces ranging from amusement to concern.

"What's this about?" one asked in a murmur.

Arrick shook his head and did not answer. They would all hear, soon enough.

"A message has come," Eyrion announced as he took his place at the head of the table, "from the mages outside Aldaeon." His eyes settled on Arrick, cold and expectant.

Arrick stared back as he presented the scrap of paper he still held. "The mages have the city surrounded, but they are unsure how to progress."

The headmaster's eye twitched. Evidently, he'd expected different news. "They sent word by pigeon for that?"

A soft rustle of fabric filled the air as the councilors shifted and looked between themselves.

"Their orders were to strike the Aldaanan," Arrick said. He held Eyrion's gaze, not firmly enough to challenge the man, but enough that the others knew he was serious. "They cannot. The Aldaanan have abandoned the city and disappeared."

Voices burst into the silence, angry, confused, and dismayed. A half-dozen arguments warred for attention and in the center of it all, Eyrion stood, his face grim.

"The mages request direction," Arrick continued, raising his voice, "because only the Royal City's army remains."

The headmaster lifted a hand and an uncomfortable pressure filled the room, a small manipulation of air that silenced the arguing councilors. When all was still, he released the magic and leaned against the table's edge. "How many mages remain with the army? Did they say?"

Arrick extended the tiny message across the table. "They are uncertain, but they believe the number is three. One may be injured."

Scowling, Eyrion snatched the paper from his fingertips. He unrolled it and studied the scant few lines of writing.

"They should pursue the Aldaanan," one of the councilors said.

Another shot her a glare. "How could they? The message says they disappeared. Our mages would not ask guidance if it was as simple as following them."

"They must have Gated elsewhere," a third put in.

The second scoffed. "All of them?"

"Enough," Eyrion barked.

They fell silent, their faces like those of scolded children.

"The army is to continue," the headmaster said. "There are events at play that I am not yet ready to disclose. The disappearance of the Aldaanan is temporary. They will be found. For the moment, the war shall go on, until the distraction is no longer necessary."

"Distraction!" Arrick roared. He shot to his feet and slammed his palms against the tabletop. "The lives of mages are at stake! Magelings, even! You would have children killed for the sake of a distraction?"

"The mages on that battlefield were ready to lay down their lives for the college and all it stands for," Eyrion said, his tone as placid as if he were discussing lesson plans and not sending innocent mages to their deaths.

A man across the table drew himself up in anger. "The mages on that battlefield shouldn't have to! Our quarrel was with the Aldaanan. The only reason we push against the Royal City is because they stand in our way!"

"We never should have pushed against the Royal City to begin with," Arrick said. He pressed his hands against the table until his nails turned white. "It was a fool's errand. There are mages on the Royal City's council who would have sided with us, who would have worked to give us more leverage in the capital. We are here for the preservation and expansion of knowledge. We are better than war. Our battles take place in council chambers."

All around the table, mages answered with emphatic nods. Arrick suppressed a humorless smile. If only they had supported his protests at the beginning.

Eyrion glared at them. "My word shall not be contested. I am headmaster. If you cannot abide by my order, you may leave this council."

"You honestly believe our mages should continue when our target is gone?" A woman on Eyrion's other side leaned forward until Arrick could just see her face, her expression pinched with worry. Minet had been a loud supporter of the attack before. That even she questioned the wisdom in continuing was vindicating, but Arrick found no pleasure in being right.

The headmaster raised a brow, unamused. "Now is the best time to strike the Royal City's army. The only risk to our numbers was the strength of the Aldaanan. If they are gone and we surround Aldaeon already, this is a valuable chance to strike and remind the world what mages can do."

"Not all the mages on the field will be able to take a life," someone else objected.

"Not all mages will be willing, you mean," Eyrion said. "Magic being used to kill is nigh unheard of, but not impossible. If we were not dangerous, why would the Aldaanan have wished to silence us? To remove our power?"

The councilors did not seem to know how to reply. They glanced between themselves, unsettled and shaken. Were he a man of less emotional fortitude, Arrick might have wept. They were scholars, not killers. How could this be the vision the headmaster bore for the college?

"Go," Eyrion commanded. "Issue the order. The moment they receive it, our forces are to strike." He crumpled the note in his hand and turned to leave.

"But Headmaster," Minet said, stepping after him. "What of the residents of Aldaeon? The Giftless who support the army?"

The headmaster's blue eyes narrowed, as empty and soulless as the ice they resembled, and Arrick shuddered even before Eyrion spoke.

"Crush them."

1 2

NEW BONDS

RUNE GAVE THE LACES ONE LAST TUG. "HOW'S THAT?"

Rhyllyn wriggled his toes. Despite how bony and slender he was, his fingers and toes maintained the pudgy roundness of any other child. His tiny claws peeked from the leather and Rune reconsidered his instructions. He'd asked for a set of the spatterdash-like foot coverings similar to what Sera had commissioned for him, but the boy's feet were so small. Perhaps closed toes would have been better.

"Too tight," Rhyllyn said.

Rune untied the knot and wiggled the laces loose at the ankle. A few careful tugs evened them out. "Better?"

The boy nodded and Rune knotted the laces again.

After they'd arrived, Rune had wondered how Alira and the child had trekked through the mountains without the boy sustaining frostbite. Then he'd recalled Alira's fire affinity. Even after years around mages, he couldn't wrap his mind around everything they used their magic for.

Like all the temple's students, his power had been all but forbidden, but he'd also lacked the knowledge necessary to integrate his Gift into his life the way the Masters did. Magic was a constant in Alira's life. Sera's, too. Everything he'd learned

137

from the Aldaanan mages should have made it that constant for him, as well. Instead, his power was sealed, and he found himself envious of the small comforts that power provided. Even in the frigid winter air, Alira's food never grew cold.

"Do I get a coat, too?" Rhyllyn asked, snapping him out of thought.

Rune pushed himself up and started toward the trail that led from the camp to the town at the foot of the tower. "Yes."

The boy's eyes widened.

"Why wouldn't they give you a coat? It's cold." Rune had a mind to get one for himself. His uniform was thicker than what he was used to wearing, but still not enough. He assumed he would acclimate to the cold eventually, but another layer couldn't hurt. Had he access to his magic, he might have tried to mimic Alira and project warmth into his surroundings.

The child didn't answer. Instead, he caught Rune's fingers with his tiny hand and held fast.

Startled, Rune glanced down. That the two of them spend time together had been Alira's suggestion. She believed a bond between them would make it easier to combine their power in the future. Whether or not she was right, Rune didn't know, but he wasn't opposed to trying. With the mages lurking in the mountains, finding something to aid that connection had become vital.

He wiggled his fingers free and wrapped the boy's cold hand in his. Rhyllyn offered a timid smile in return.

In Core, Rune had never had difficulty getting the children to like him. Ironic, given that he'd always hidden his face. But he'd been happier then. Leaving the island had changed him, and he admitted his disposition was not what it had been. The first several days, Rhyllyn had hidden behind Alira's skirts and tried not to look him in the eye. This was their first outing together. For the child to have warmed up enough to touch him was impressive progress.

The army's cobbler had provided the footwear, as he had

with Rune's, but the supply wagons did not have the means to clothe a child. A handful of coins jingled in his pocket to pay for clean, proper garments. Rune didn't know where Alira had gotten them, being that she'd left Lore with nothing, but he suspected she'd conned them out of Garam or Sera somehow.

"Can I..." Rhyllyn started, then promptly clamped his mouth shut.

Rune raised a brow. "Can you what?"

"Could..." A brighter red tinged the boy's already rosy cheeks. "Could I have a hat, too?"

The request was so simple that Rune snorted a laugh. "Yes, you can have a hat."

A brilliant grin split Rhyllyn's face. "I never had a hat."

"I am surprised. It's so cold here." Come to think of it, a hat sounded like a good idea. Rune wondered if anyone would protest if he tried to stretch the coins a little farther.

"Papa said they were too expensive." The boy lowered his voice as if relating something he wasn't supposed to repeat.

Rune frowned. "Papa?" Alira had indicated the boy was an orphan.

Again, Rhyllyn shut his mouth. He tucked in his chin and looked sullenly ahead.

An odd sense of discomfort stole up Rune's spine. "How long have you been alone?"

Silence.

He changed the question. "You were alone?"

Rhyllyn scuffed a foot against the snow as they continued toward Aldaeon's main street. "Papa died."

A soft, low ache grew in Rune's chest. "Mine, too."

The child glanced up, his blue eyes wet with unshed tears.

Gently, Rune squeezed his hand.

"My uncle didn't have a hat, either. But maybe he has enough money now?"

They stopped and Rune cocked his head to the side. "Your uncle, he lives?"

Rhyllyn hesitated and then nodded once. "The mage gave him money."

The discomfort returned, this time twisting into a cold lump of uneasiness that sat in Rune's stomach like a weight. "Money for what?" And what mage? Surely not Alira. He didn't trust her, but she'd risked a great deal in bringing the boy to Aldaeon, and he knew the mages well enough to be sure the Masters would never do anything to incriminate themselves.

The boy did not answer.

Rune grunted softly. He didn't need to hear anything else. Bitter heat swelled in his chest until a twinge in his head made him wince and gather his senses. He'd spent years unconsciously touching magic when his emotions flared. According to Filadiel, that was part of what changed the color in his eyes. A deep breath settled his nerves, his long exhale filling the air with white frost.

He tugged Rhyllyn's arm and the two of them started down the street again. "You can have two hats," Rune said.

Rhyllyn almost glowed.

Most of Aldaeon's important businesses sat along the main street. Charming houses stood along branching avenues, but every business of note followed the straight cobblestone path that ran from the tower toward a long structure he'd been told was a communal dinner hall. Beyond it sat jumbles of stones that looked like building projects that had been abandoned. More houses, he'd heard, set to be continued in the spring. With the Aldaanan now gone, he wondered if construction would still resume.

Other soldiers walked the streets, running errands or just killing time. Most seemed worn or wary. Rune was the only one who walked with a practiced ease. A number of soldiers cast him irritated looks, which he ignored. It wasn't that he was not concerned. He knew the mages waited just beyond the city and could crush them at any second—and that he was powerless to stop them when they did. But the calm face he put forward was as useful in politics as it was on the battlefield. So long as no one knew you were scared, they had no power over you.

The human residents of the city roamed the main street, too, but they saw his outward confidence differently. They stared at him in awe and curiosity, sometimes respect, occasionally disdain. At first, he'd assumed their reactions were simply because he was different. It hadn't taken long to discover it was because his reputation preceded him.

Little bells jingled when Rune pushed open the door to a tailor's shop. He tugged Rhyllyn inside and motioned for the boy to wipe his feet on the stiff straw mat. The boy held Rune's arm with both hands as he did.

A woman behind a large cutting table put aside her sewing and stood to greet them. Her eyes widened with recognition.

"My lord Champion," she breathed as she dipped in a curtsy. "What can I do for you?"

Rhyllyn tilted his head to give Rune a curious look.

"The boy needs clothes," Rune said as he dried his own feet. "Soon. Something ready-made."

The woman nodded. "I haven't much for the little ones, but a few things may fit."

"A coat, too. And hats." He glanced at the boy from the corner of his eye and Rhyllyn grinned up at him.

"The hatter is a ways down, a squat building with a glass window. Coats I can do, but you'll have to wait. I know I haven't anything to fit him today." The woman pulled a pair of large trunks from under her table, opened the lids, and dusted her hands together. "Can you wait for a coat, or...?"

"He needs it soon, but we will wait if we must." Rune nudged Rhyllyn's back and the boy trotted forward to peer into the trunks. Colorful clothing sat heaped inside, though each garment was neatly folded.

"There are bolts of wool behind the table, far to the right." She pointed, then bent to wiggle a few pieces of clothing free from their stacks. "I oughtn't push things aside, but he can't be bounding around with no coat this time of year. I could have it done by tomorrow evening."

Rune nodded. "We would appreciate it." He left Rhyllyn with the seamstress and paced around the table to look at the cloth.

The woman shook out a tunic and held it up to Rhyllyn's shoulders. "You're such a slight thing," she murmured. "I think everything I've pulled will be too—oh! Your hands!"

Rune turned his head. The woman cradled Rhyllyn's hands in hers, inspecting his tiny claws and drab olive scales. She shook her head, closed her hands over his, and rubbed his fingers.

"I beg your pardon, my lord Champion, I didn't realize..." She trailed off and swallowed. A stern look drifted across her face. "You can't have your little one out like this, his fingers are chilled to the bone. The glover is in with the hatter. He'll lose his little fingers if you don't wrap him up."

Rhyllyn wiggled one hand free and patted her arm, as if to offer comfort. "It's not his fault, don't be mad. It's warmer at the college. Miss Alira didn't bring me anything warm."

"I don't care whose fault it is. Even the gryphons don't let their young strut around with their limbs uncovered when it's this cold outside."

Again, Rune gave the woman a sidewise glance. Somehow, the suggestion he *let* Rhyllyn go without bothered him more than the implication the boy was his. "That's why we're here," he said, a hint of a bite in his words. His claws drifted over the bolts of brushed wool fabric. "Rhyllyn. What color?"

The boy's eyes widened and he strained to see over the table. "Orange?"

Rune frowned and let his hand hover above the material. The closet thing he saw was a deep rust. "This?"

Rhyllyn nodded with a grin.

Beside him, the woman returned a handful of tunics to the trunks and pulled out others in a smaller size. "Lay the bolt on the table. I'll measure him for his coat before you go. Here, these two tunics will fit. I think I've one more, somewhere, then we'll find you some trousers."

The bolt the boy had chosen was snug between the others and took some effort to dislodge. When Rune had it free, he carried it to the table and ran a hand over its surface. The nuances of the texture were lost beneath his scales, but he could tell it was cushiony and thick, and the friction of his hand slipping across it caused a glow of warmth against his palm.

"There," the woman said as she pulled one more tunic free.

Rhyllyn eyed it with a small, sad frown. "Are there any gray ones?"

"Gray?" she exclaimed. "Why ever would you want—" She stopped short and turned to look at Rune.

He blinked and followed her gaze. His uniform, like everyone else's, was a dull, uninspired gray.

The woman laughed aloud.

Sheepish, Rhyllyn scuffed his foot against the floor. "Miss Alira said he'll be my brother. So we should look like each other, right?"

"I don't think you need to worry about that, little one." The woman ruffled his hair and turned back to the trunk. "Here, look. This one's ivory, but I can dye it gray and have it ready with your coat. How's that sound?"

"Expensive," Rune said.

"We'll make it work," the seamstress replied. "Here, these trousers ought to fit you. Lifetree's mercy, child, but you're filthy. The tower's good and warm, with or without the mages here. You ought to go over there and have a good wash." The shift in her voice was subtle, but Rune caught it.

"How does the city fare?" he asked. He kept his words low, as close to sympathetic as he could manage.

The woman shrugged. "No one is happy, but I cannot say we are surprised. The Alda'anan were with us, but they were not part of us. They have always done things their own way."

Rune frowned. "What did you call them?" He'd heard that before, the slight break in the middle of the name that changed the way the vowels sounded. Filadiel, the leader of the Aldaanan, had used it once, when there were only free mages present.

Her brows lifted. "Alda'anan?"

"Yes. Why... why do you say it that way?"

She shrugged. "It's their name. What they call themselves. I know others slur it, change it a bit—everyone outside Aldaeon calls them Aldaanan—but we know them for what they are."

"Yes," Rune said slowly. He didn't know how much she understood, but the difference in sound meant something to him. Recollection of the years he'd spent half-heartedly listening in linguistic studies tickled the back of his mind. Old words, older than the archaic tongue Redoram said he spoke, words that had evolved into something else. He didn't know how he hadn't noticed before.

Alda'anan.

Elder Ones.

He gave his head a shake. "Did they speak with the people of Aldaeon often? Did anyone know them well enough to guess where they have gone?"

The seamstress hesitated. She plucked a stray thread from a pair of trousers as she refolded them. "They were friendly and kind, but most of the time they kept to themselves. I'm sorry. I don't know."

Rune exhaled in quiet disappointment.

"Will these fit?" Rhyllyn asked as he pulled another pair from the trunk. They fell short on his legs and the woman took them back. The boy leaned forward to look for more, unaware of his interruption.

"There are some in the city who may know," the woman added. "I couldn't tell you who, but there are plenty who had close ties with the mages. If you spend time asking, someone is bound to have heard something." She put two pairs of trousers on Rhyllyn's pile of clothes and patted the top. "There. Come over here, now, little one. We'll get you measured for that coat."

Rhyllyn followed her to the table, where she posed him and turned him to take measurements. Rune crossed his arms and leaned against the wall.

He wanted nothing more than to delve into the city in search of answers, but he doubted it would be easy, and there was little chance he'd have any more opportunities to ask questions soon.

And even if he did find a lead, what good did it do? Until he was more practiced in sharing power with Rhyllyn, it wasn't as if he could Gate anywhere. It wasn't likely the Aldaanan would have gone anywhere he could follow, anyway. Returning to the Royal City was one thing, but he knew little of the rest of the Triad.

Rune rubbed his brow to chase away the lines of thought that nestled there. Thinking of the Royal City brought his father's sword to mind, too. Were he able to open a Gate, he could return to the captain's quarters and locate the blade, the last scrap of his shattered life that still seemed within his grasp. There was no doubt Garam was an honorable man, and Rune had no reason to think he couldn't convince the captain to return the sword when all was said and done, but that meant waiting for the war to end when there was no guarantee any of them would make it through alive.

It did not take long before the seamstress patted Rhyllyn on the head and put his stack of folded clothing on the table. Her cheery voice pulled Rune back from his dismal thoughts.

"Well, that will do. You'll have to pay for his coat up front, but if you come back tomorrow evening, it'll be ready. His tunic, too." She shifted the ivory tunic off to the side.

"Will you write the cost for me?" Rune reached for his pocket. "I will need to return it to my superior." At least, he assumed he would have to give proof of the spending to Garam.

The woman nodded and crossed to her inventory books, a haphazard pile on a table near the door.

Rhyllyn rocked forward to stretch an arm across the table and stroke the rust-colored wool. His legs wobbled beneath him and he gripped the table for support. "I don't like this," he muttered.

Rune raised a brow. "The fabric?"

"My feet." The boy extended one leg and flexed his ankle. "I can't stand on my toes anymore."

A hint of a smirk tugged at the corners of Rune's mouth. "That's not true, you're standing on your toes right now. You're on them all the time. You'll get used to it." He uncurled his fingers to count the coins in his palm. He returned a few to his pocket when the seamstress returned with his note, then poured the rest into her hand.

"Thank you, my lord Champion," the woman said with a small smile. "I'll see you tomorrow eve."

Rune nodded and ushered Rhyllyn out the door.

"Why did she call you that?" the boy asked as soon as they were outside. He clasped Rune's hand without being prompted.

"Call me what?"

"Cham-pi-on." Rhyllyn drew out the syllables in a singsong way as he kicked a clod of snow.

"Hm. Word from the arena must not travel as quickly as I thought," Rune said.

Rhyllyn dug his feet into the ground and jerked them to a halt. "That's *you*?" he cried, his blue eyes wide and shining. "The Arena Champion?"

"The only one there's ever been, I'm told." Rune tugged the boy's hand. "Come. We still need your hat. Hats."

"Champion," Rhyllyn whispered to himself. He hopped along at Rune's side, a new bounce in his step.

They received a few fleeting, curious looks from passersby. Rune ignored them all and remained silent for the rest of their walk.

It was not far to the hatter's shop, and when they slipped inside, Rune found it was warmer than the seamstress's building. He closed his eyes and allowed himself to bask for a moment as he closed the door.

From the other side of the shop, a small warble lifted to greet them. Rune's eyes flew open.

"Look who it is!" Ria trilled in delight and rose onto her hindquarters behind a high counter. "I never would have thought to see you here. Oh, and the little one!"

Rhyllyn's eyes widened. "A gryphon," he breathed, a hint of wonder in his tiny voice.

Rune's brow furrowed. "Haven't you seen them in the camp already?"

"Not close," the boy whispered.

"Well, you're about to get closer." Rune steered the child toward the counter, where Ria sat alongside a woman with dark hair. "What are you doing here?"

The gryphon snorted, an odd, nasally whisk of a sound. "What do you suppose I'm doing?" She lifted a hat with a broad, floppy brim in her awkward forepaws. "I'm making a hat."

Rune raised a brow.

"I'm an apprentice milliner," Ria said with a hint of pride. "Each hat has turned out better than the last. I think the next one should be a deep burgundy, maybe with silk flowers. Can you show me how to make the silk flowers, Etta?"

The woman at the gryphon's side nodded in silence, though her lips took an amused twist.

The gryphon's enthusiasm was infectious and Rune felt himself crack a smile, too. "I thought you were a cartographer," he said.

"I am." Ria's feathers ruffled in annoyance. "Cartography is my passion! But this is my vocation."

"I wasn't aware gryphons wore hats."

"Well, we don't. Not particularly." She lowered the hat to its stand. "But people like you do. Imagine flying the world to sell my hats anywhere I went. A traveling hat shop!" Her feathers smoothed and she trilled again.

Rhyllyn giggled.

"Ah, but you're here for a reason! Do you want a hat?" She lifted her work in progress again, hopefully, while the brim drooped like the petals of a wilted flower.

Rune motioned to the boy. "For him. Something to keep his ears warm, protect him from the elements. And then something for fun."

"Oh! Well, I'm sure we have something for that." The gryphon clicked her beak as she returned the hat to its stand once more. Her paws looked massive beside the little hat, but she picked bits of dust from its brim with delicate precision. Then she pushed past Etta to beckon Rhyllyn to the far end of the counter.

"Gloves, too," Rune added.

Ria ruffled her wings. "Gloves may have to wait, but we'll make sure you get them. Come here, little one, let me have a look at you." She grasped Rhyllyn's shoulders and inspected him with a critical golden eye, then cast Rune a distinct frown. "You'll need to speak with Captain Kaith. The boy needs double rations, he's too thin."

Rune fought a prickle of irritation. "Alira will take care of it." It wasn't his fault the boy lacked what he needed, but everyone seemed to think he was to blame.

The gryphon shrugged and stepped aside as Etta pushed herself from her stool behind the counter and brought a thin cord with her. She wrapped it around Rhyllyn's head and inspected the colored marks that decorated its length.

"We don't make things for children often," Etta said as she took down notes. "Their mothers usually see to that."

Rhyllyn's face fell, and Rune felt his hackles rise.

"Which is why we're here," he said, crossing his arms. "We're making him family."

Ria's feathered ear-tufts lifted. "Are we, now?"

"We have to," Rune said simply.

The gryphon's hips wiggled, like a kitten ready to pounce.

"Birds of a feather flock together, as it's said. We gryphons like the saying," she added to Rhyllyn. "But don't call us birds, little one. It's a rude thing to say. We all fit together, though. Not just gryphons, but all of us misfits in the army."

"Speaking of the army…" Rune flicked a hand toward the rows and shelves of hats that lined the room. "With everything going on, is there time for all this?"

Ria tucked her chin into her chest as if offended. "We must have time for the things that bring us joy, especially in war. We can't let ourselves sink into a mire. Even you must have something that makes you happy."

He hesitated.

"A hobby?" She tipped her head to the side.

His jaw tightened.

"Something you enjoy doing?"

"Just make the hats," Rune snapped.

"Enough, Ria," Etta said as she pulled bins of supplies from underneath the counter. "You've no need to agitate him."

The gryphon flicked her feathers and feigned indifference as she turned back to the task at hand. "He'll forgive me, so long as he still wants to sleep in the aerie."

Rune stalked to the window to stare outside. Beyond the displays of strange, brushed felt headgear that was the norm in Aldaeon, a deep shroud of gray storm clouds loomed over the mountains.

More storms. More cover for the mages who waited in the mountains. The skies had not settled after the Aldaanan departed, but he didn't know what they had done to alter the weather. Filadiel had confessed to bringing the snow, but he hadn't shared how long the effect would remain. Rune couldn't fathom they'd give the college mages such an advantage on purpose, but he also hadn't imagined they would leave.

"Finding the Aldaanan," he murmured.

Ria's ears perked. "Hmm?"

"Something I would enjoy doing. Finding the free mages."

He'd enjoyed their lessons together, however brief they'd been, and the moment he'd seen progress—and felt the kindling of a tiny spark of hope—had been the first time in ages he'd known any sort of happiness. It had been quashed atop Aldaeon's tower, when they sealed his power. More than anything, now, he wanted answers.

The gryphon considered for a moment, then flicked her tail. "Travel, then," she said. "That seems a fair hobby to me."

"Travel?" Rune almost laughed, leaning forward to peer up at the dark clouds that drifted ever higher into the sky. "I don't know about you, but I get the feeling we're trapped."

13

HARD LESSONS

SERA WATCHED THE SKY CHANGE COLORS FROM HER SEAT IN FRONT of the tent she shared with her brother and Prince Vicamros. She hadn't slept, but she didn't think anyone had.

The snowstorm had arrived in the evening, crackling thunderheads piling so high they'd blotted out the light long before the sun set. Howling winds had scoured the camp while lightning crawled on the underbellies of the clouds and gave the driving snow an unearthly glow.

The camp had been restless throughout the storm. Soldiers milled about and took shifts to steal what rest they could. Though the night proved uneventful, everyone had kept a watchful eye on the mountain ranges that surrounded the valley. Sera couldn't blame them, though she didn't know how long they hoped to last in a fight while a blizzard raged and nobody slept.

Her own mind still buzzed with too many questions for her to rest, though she ached with weariness. With or without the storm, she couldn't have slept with men coming and going from her quarters at all hours of the night. That was the greatest disadvantage of sharing a tent with the men in charge, she'd decided. The stream of officers who filtered through the tent

151

with plans and orders never ceased, regardless of whether or not the rest of the camp slept. Sometimes they lingered to argue over the broad map that filled most of the tent. And Garam, as far as she knew, never slept.

Another wave of energy from the eastern edge of the camp interrupted her thoughts.

She had already tried to shut them out of her senses to keep her focus clear, just in case the college mages moved, but the exchange of power between the two free mages on the other side of the encampment was too much to ignore.

Stifling a groan, Sera shifted on her stool and rubbed her face with both hands as the soft pink of the sky shifted to a warm, golden tone. Most of the snow had been cleared from the camp itself, but it sat in shoulder-deep mounds beyond the campsite's edge. If not for the snow, one wouldn't know the storm had come at all. The fields beyond were not as bad, but the drifts were as deep as Sera's hips in some places. Garam had not mentioned the storm or how it would affect their plans, but she didn't need him to say anything. Without the Aldaanan on their side, the army was already crippled.

Wild magic flared again and she grimaced. That she could differentiate their magic from that of the college mages should have been a comfort, but having that much power teeter on the edge of her awareness made her sick. Well, she admitted, not the power. Just what it meant.

She didn't know how they were supposed to survive this. More than once she'd considered suggesting they abandon Aldaeon. The Aldaanan had been their enemy's target, and the Aldaanan were gone. Yet if the Aldaanan were all the college mages were after, why hadn't they abandoned their attack when the free mages disappeared? It seemed as if they were waiting for something, but what, Sera did not know. As long as the rest of Aldaeon's people remained, though, the army at the city's edge was their only defense.

"Are they still at it?" Garam's voice made her jump. She

craned her neck to look up at her brother. Behind him, the officers left their tent in a single cluster and filtered into the rest of the camp.

"It's getting slower. I think they'll finish soon. They've got to be tired by now." She shrugged and looked to the east again. Rune and Rhyllyn had begun their practice the moment the storm ended. Under Garam's instruction, they were supposed to melt as much of the snow around the camp as possible. As long as the soldiers were buried, they had no hope against mages. Not that they had much hope on even ground, either. She couldn't keep her brow from furrowing.

Garam folded his arms over his chest and watched the officers disappear among the tents. Once they were out of sight, he spoke again in a lower voice. "What's the matter?"

"I don't think he should fight," Sera murmured. It was a thought that had run through her head a hundred times over the course of the night. "It's bad enough to ask him to enter battle when his magic is crippled, but the boy... It's just wrong to involve a child. If he cannot wield power without the child there, how can we expect him to defend the army?"

His sable eyes settled on her, a weight as heavy as her thoughts. Sera's shoulders bunched and she bowed her head to stare at the dirty snow underfoot.

"Have you spoken to him?" His question was surprisingly gentle, considering how angry he'd been when she told him what she'd done.

Sera raised one shoulder in a halfhearted shrug. "He'll let me know when he's ready to speak. It's not my place." She hadn't stopped kicking herself for what happened. Even before she'd learned he was married, it hadn't been right. Rune had been drunk, and she hadn't let the decision be his. She'd misinterpreted the sarcastic, playful demeanor he had around her as interest, and she wasn't certain she would live that down.

"If it hurts you, then it is your place." He laid a hand on her shoulder, an unusual display of brotherly affection. Garam was a stern and stoic man. The last thing she'd expected him to offer was comfort.

Sullen, she pushed her booted toes at a chunk of ice.

Her brother sank into a crouch beside her chair. "You always were good at picking the ones you couldn't have."

She grimaced and turned her face away. "I don't need you to lecture me."

"I'm not lecturing," Garam said. "I trying to tell you I understand."

"How could you? The only love you've ever had is for your job."

He smiled, a soft, sympathetic expression she rarely saw him wear. "That's what you think. There have been women in my life, though not many, and not often." He glanced to the horizon as the first golden sliver of the sun peeked over the mountaintops. "But this is the problem with having a big heart. The bigger it is, the more easily it's broken."

The muscles in her back and shoulders tightened, and she fought the urge to curl in on herself and disappear. She wasn't a meek child and shouldn't be ashamed of her feelings. Instead of shrinking, she rubbed her arms against the cold. "I just... I thought things were different. He seemed so comfortable with me. We work well together. After that dance in the palace, I..." Her throat grew tight and she swallowed hard. Vulnerable as she felt, she would not cry. "I thought he understood."

"You need to talk to him. You never know what battle might bring, you shouldn't leave anything unsaid."

"I made him break a sacred vow."

His eyes narrowed. "You didn't make him do anything. What he did is on him. But you did give him the alcohol, so you probably should apologize for that."

Indignant heat surged within her. She gasped and smacked his shoulder. "And here I thought you were trying to make me feel better!"

Again, he gave her one of his rare smiles. "Not trying to

make you feel better. Just trying to make sure my army is functioning the best it can."

Rolling her eyes, Sera pushed herself up from the rough wooden stool she'd taken from the tent. "Do you ever think about anything other than your army?"

"I think about the city." Garam shrugged. "And food, sometimes. Which I think I'll get now. You should go find him, maybe have breakfast and work things out."

"Maybe," she grumbled, watching sunlight spill down the mountainside as he left.

She tried to focus on the presence of the other mages, but the surging sense of power was no longer there. Had they ceased practice? She didn't want to cross the camp and interrupt if they were still busy, nor did she want to disturb them if they had returned to their tents to collapse in exhaustion.

But she could find a hundred reasons not to cross the camp and speak to him, and while she didn't like it, Garam was right. She could only blame herself for misunderstanding their connection, reading it so terribly wrong. All she'd meant to offer was comfort and reassurance. Rune's reaction the following morning had wounded her, but it was the marriage he'd told Garam about afterward that had burdened her mind and heart.

Stilling her thoughts, she crossed her arms tight over her chest to keep out the cold and started across the camp.

When she didn't sense any magic at work on her walk, Sera expected to find Rune asleep, but he sat at the fire nearest his tent with his elbows on his thighs, gazing pensively at the flames.

Sera hesitated. There was a sullenness to his expression, which wasn't unusual; it was the air of serenity around him that gave her pause. She lingered outside that sense of peace for some time, just watching. But he never stirred, and eventually she cleared her throat.

He started and sat up straight, looking at her in chagrined surprise.

"I thought you'd be sleeping, what with how hard you've worked all morning." She inched forward and paused on the other side of the logs that ringed the fire.

He jerked his head toward his tent. "Kid's borrowing my bed. Don't think I could sleep, anyway. Too much on my mind."

"I suppose there would be. It must be difficult for you to work with that mage from the college, given how you felt about her in the woods." She meant only to tease, but he still flinched.

"I think we're past that," he said. "I think we're all right now."

She sat down, crossing her ankles and making herself comfortable. The warmth of the fire felt good after sitting so long in the cold outside her tent. "How did you say you met her?"

Rune shrugged. "She was one of my teachers, once. If you can believe that."

"But you wanted to kill her. Why the sudden change of heart?"

He hesitated. "I realized I can't hold her responsible for the things that happened to me. I didn't know where she was, didn't know if she was involved. I assumed she was part of it because of her position in the temple where I trained. I was wrong."

"I suppose you're glad, then. Better to learn the truth from her. If you'd killed her and then learned she was innocent... I imagine you'd regret something like that." She tried to smile, but the expression wouldn't come.

He glanced at her as if he had something to say, then seemed to change his mind. His eyes fell back to the fire.

Sera found herself less comfortable in the silence. She climbed back to her feet as she tested words several times over in her head. They caught in her throat and she struggled to push them past her lips. He spoke before she could make a sound.

"I owe you an apology." He laced his clawed fingers together and rested his mouth against them as he planted his elbows on his knees.

She stared at him in surprise.

"I'm sure Garam spoke to you, after..." Rune trailed off, his brow furrowed. His eyes glazed, no longer seeing the flames.

Her heart stuck in her throat like a lump. She swallowed against it and winced when it sank instead. "Yes," she managed. Again, she swallowed, and the words came easier. "Garam told me... well, everything you told him, I suppose. I didn't mean to let things sit, but I didn't know how to come talk to you again. I didn't know how to apologize."

His face remained unchanged, as still as if carved of stone. "Why should you?"

Sera hugged her arms to herself and stared at him in uncertainty. No matter how she felt about him, she realized he was not always predictable in his reactions. She'd expected anger. Instead, she wasn't sure he felt anything. Fine, then. It was for her benefit, not his. To ease the ache in her chest and the weight on her mind. "I led you astray. For that, I'm sorry. I never would have thought you had someone."

He scoffed. "Is it that hard to believe? Because your brother said the same thing."

"I didn't mean it like that," she muttered. "It's just that with you being here, and the arena, and the prison before that..."

"I had to leave her behind. It doesn't mean she stopped existing." He paused, then shook his his head as if inwardly scolding himself. There. There was that anger. He'd bridled it, though, put it in its place. A frustrated sigh escaped him. "But you didn't know. I didn't tell anyone, so how could you?"

"I still shouldn't have." Sera shifted her weight to her other heel and twisted one of her white braids around a finger. It grew harder to look at him. She turned away. "You were inebriated."

Rune snorted, his mouth twisting with a humorless smile. "Not your fault I can't hold my liquor, either. I never was much for alcohol. I should have known better."

"That doesn't change anything," she protested.

He raised a hand before she could say more. "I'm angry enough with myself. I don't need to be angry at you, too."

Sera closed her mouth and stood in silence for a long time. The soft crackle of the fire filled the air. Her hands inched higher up her arms to rub her shoulders and she crept closer to the fire. It warmed her skin, but ice lingered in the pit of her stomach.

Eventually, Rune stirred. "I don't fault you for what happened. I don't remember it, but that's my fault. I do remember drinking, but everything after that is..."

"Hazy?" she suggested.

"If that. I don't have any idea what I did. I just know that I didn't think I was that kind of person."

She shifted on her feet, unsure what to say.

"I don't want you to think I was avoiding you." He gave her an earnest look. "I've had so much to think about. To sort out in my head. I didn't understand why I would do this. I was angry, at first. I wanted it to be someone else's fault. But in the end, there's only me, and I realize that this happened because out here, in the snow, the war... a part of me has given up."

"I know you don't want to be here," Sera murmured. "I don't think any of us want to be here."

"I came because I thought the Aldaanan mages could help me. Because they *could* help me." He turned his hand, palm up, and flexed his fingers. The glossy green scales that covered his hands glinted in the morning light. "They had the power to fix this, to fix me. And if that happened, I thought I could go home. Now, I don't know. I don't know what I'm supposed to do. I have less than I started with. Now, I don't even have hope."

She took a single step closer. "How long has it been? Since you left your homeland?"

"I don't know. A year? It was spring when I arrived. Still cold in the night. I don't know how long it took to cross the sea."

"That's a long time to be away from the people you love." The bite in the air grew to be too much. She shoved a cut log closer to the fire and sat down again, her hands out to absorb warmth.

"It is," he agreed. "I imagine it will be much longer before I can return." He traced the strange scar on the back of his left hand with his thumb.

Sera made a soft sound of understanding. With the snow that surrounded the camp and filled the mountain passes, she imagined none of them would go home soon. She longed for the comforts of the Royal City. Her warm bed and the tall fireplace in her quarters. Proper meals, warm baths, and oils for her hair. Just thinking about that made her scalp itch. She resisted the urge to scratch.

"I know Garam wants the army to work smoothly," Rune said.

It took great effort to keep from rolling her eyes. "That does seem to be his biggest concern."

"I will try not to let my mistakes hinder the army."

"I'm sure Garam will appreciate that." She turned her hands to warm their backs. She didn't mention herself being one of those mistakes, and from the way his eyes fell on her, she knew he'd noticed.

It didn't matter. Sera repeated those three words in her head. She'd done what she'd set out to do, eased her conscience and said what she was ready to say. A small, fragile part of her longed to say more, to voice the feelings that had twisted her heart, to acknowledge the misunderstanding that had encouraged them to grow, but she'd already decided it wouldn't be fruitful.

"Tell me about her," she said after a time.

Rune glanced up. "What?"

"Your wife."

His brow furrowed. "Why?"

"So I can understand you better. I'm still the senior mage in this army. You still answer to me. It's important for your superiors to understand your situation." She gave a lofty sniff and peered down her nose.

"Garam said something like that, too." He hunched forward

to rest his elbows on his knees once more. "There isn't much to tell. She's a mage. Her mother was a mage, too."

"Were you married long?"

"No. Not long enough." The corners of his mouth twitched and he hid his small smile behind his hand. "I still suspect she married me out of pity."

"I can't imagine any other reasons. You seem short on redeeming qualities."

He snorted. "I am sure she would agree with you. She hated me for many years. I admit it was my fault. It was hard to make her hate me, but I didn't think there was anything else I could do. As I am, who could feel anything else?" He ran his hand up his arm and his brow furrowed. "And yet in the end, it didn't matter to her at all."

Sera forced a smile. It hadn't mattered to her, either. She'd been startled at first, then curious, but as off-putting as his scales had been in the first moment, they had faded into simply part of the way he was. "She was not like you, then?"

He shook his head. "Until Rhyllyn, I didn't think there were any like me. No. She is Eldani. Dark hair. Shorter than you, fairer than me. Her mother was from the north. Her legs were pale as a pitcher of cream."

A snort of a laugh escaped her and she cupped her hands over her mouth and nose. "Somehow I don't think she would appreciate that."

"No," he agreed with a chuckle, "but it's true. She would be angry at me for mentioning the width of her hips, too, but I liked it."

"She sounds like my exact opposite," Sera remarked.

Rune raised his head to study her. "I suppose so. Even your eyes... They're so blue. Hers hadn't changed yet, last I saw her. She was a mageling when we married. When I left the island, her eyes were still like honey lit by fire. Like all her spirit set them aflame."

She couldn't help but smile at the way his expression softened and his eyes unfocused. "The star in your sky?"

"No," he murmured, smiling at the fire. "She wasn't a star. The stars are fleeting glimmers that change with the seasons. They move on, burn out. She was vibrant. Constant. She was the moon. Bright enough to illuminate all the shadows around you, make you see things you never knew were there." His smile faded, the fleeting light in his eyes replaced with melancholy. "The moonrise makes the night more brilliant. Sometimes it's so big in your sky that you think you can reach out and take it. So you follow it to the end of the earth, but then it meets the horizon and slips just beyond your grasp. And when the last light fades from your life, you realize that all along, you were afraid of the dark."

Sera's heart wrenched and she looked away, blinking against the sting in her eyes. "You would be a poet, wouldn't you? Garam wouldn't even be surprised."

"I think I surprise the captain a lot more than he would like."

She had to agree. Everything about Rune had been a surprise. It was no wonder she'd grown fond of him; between their early lessons, the night at the Spiral Palace, the march to Aldaan, and every conversation they'd shared beside the campfires, she'd learned something unexpected at every turn.

"What will you do now?" She allowed herself to wipe her wet eyelashes. The tears were already cold. She rubbed the side of her hand against her thigh to dry it.

"Rest, I suppose." Rune frowned at his tent and then stood to scan the rest of the camp. "I'm sure I can find somewhere in the aerie to catch a little sleep."

"That's not what I meant." She shook her head. "Your wife, your home... I'm as uncertain as you are about what will happen here, but you can't give up."

"If only it were that easy," he murmured. "Look around us. Even with Rhyllyn's help—even if I had my own power back— I'm not strong enough to Gate the whole army out of here. And even if I could, then what? What about the gryphons? What about the rest of Aldaeon? I never would have imagined the mages would linger. They will crush us. You know that as well as I do."

Sera breathed deep, the cold air burning her chest. The back of her neck prickled and she suppressed a shudder. "I don't know that," she said. "I have no idea what to expect. And between the mages and the snow, I don't know what hope we have to escape. But I promise you, if we survive, I'll do anything I can to help. I may not have it, lizard, but I believe in love. Don't sacrifice what you've already fought so hard for. The soldier moon sets, but it will rise. It always rises."

His expression remained unchanged, but a soft light returned to his eyes, a hint of the otherworldly glow he'd lost the moment the Aldaanan stripped him of his power. "Then," he said slowly, "I guess I have to believe it will rise again."

14

LETTING GO

DAYS CREPT BY AND FIRAL'S HEART SANK FURTHER WITH EACH HOUR that passed. A thousand different reasons why Rune wouldn't answer her Calling ran through her head. None of them were pleasant. All of them made her regret that she hadn't tried to reach him sooner.

Yet she couldn't fault herself. The Masters had cautioned her against the use of magic during her pregnancy and her recovery afterward. It was too dangerous to expose an unborn child to the flux of power, and too risky for her to try to control it in a weakened state. She'd only just begun to feel like herself again, able to walk without feeling short of breath, able to work without feeling exhausted after only a few hours. Now had been the soonest it was safe for her to try to find him.

It just wasn't soon enough.

She knew a small change would have been enough to keep her from opening a Gate directly to him; it could have been a difference as simple as a fresh injury or a new scar. But the only two reasons he wouldn't have replied to her Call were that he couldn't, or that he simply didn't want to.

All it meant was there was nothing more she could try. She'd kept herself awake at night, wondering if she could have done something differently. The only other mages who knew Rune well enough to open a Gate directly to him were the three Masters who led the temple, and as far as she knew, two of them wanted him dead. There was no use in having anyone else attempt contact, either. If any other mage had tried the Calling, he wouldn't have had a reason to respond. But in the end, it didn't matter. If she'd made a mistake, there was nothing to be done about it now. She had tried and she had hoped, but the silence told her everything she needed to know.

Checking her boot laces again, Firal deemed herself prepared. She smoothed her skirts and crossed to the table. Her private quarters were quiet. Lulu slept and Vahn had taken his leave some time ago.

He objected to her taking the infant with her, but he wasn't going to stop her, either. The ruins were empty. There was nothing left to fear. And Firal had made it clear that she meant to make the trip alone. She didn't expect him to understand her need for privacy, just that he respect it.

Firal went through the things on the table one last time and tucked everything into her satchel. Her journal and sticks of graphite went first, followed by food and a water skin. Last of all she added two small pouches, things she didn't think she could bear to look at again. Then she slung the satchel's strap over her shoulder and retrieved the baby from her cradle. The girl stirred, then nestled into her chest and settled.

"We won't be there long, my love," Firal murmured as she made her way to the door. "It's just a small thing we have to do."

A wide half-circle of court mages waited in the Gating parlor when Firal arrived, though they were not alone. She had expected Medreal and Davan to be present, but a third figure stepped forward.

"Minna!" Firal cried, throwing an arm around the Underling woman. She clasped her tightly and then stepped back to look her over.

Minna smiled, though like her husband, she looked more

careworn than Firal remembered. "I had hoped to see you before now, Majesty, but Davan here says you've been busy. I thought it best if I come see you instead of waiting for you to be free. I've brought something for you, thought it best if you have it before going." She looked over her shoulder and Davan stepped forward, a bundle of cloth in his arms.

"What is it?" Firal asked, watching curiously as Minna shook out the long piece of plain fabric.

Smiling sadly, Minna nodded toward the baby. "Things would be a bit different if you were with us, Majesty. But I thought I'd bring a bit of the underground to you, since you're going back that way. Davan, love, would you take the little one?"

Davan started forward, but Medreal stepped between him and Firal and took Lulu into her arms instead. Minna's mouth tightened, but she said nothing. She wrapped the cloth around Firal, crisscrossing it over her shoulders in a way that was difficult for Firal to follow. "In the underground, women can't afford to have their hands full all the time, so they wrap themselves up like this and tuck the baby inside. It's tradition for a woman's mother to weave a wrap for her after she marries, but you came to us alone and I haven't a daughter. After the wedding, I thought I ought..." she trailed off, swallowed and blinked hard.

An ache stirred in Firal's heart. She reached for the older woman and drew her into a warm embrace. "Thank you, Minna," she murmured, tears stinging her eyes. She couldn't tell the woman who Lulu's father truly was, though the desire to made her heartache worse.

Minna patted her back, then pulled away. She wiped her eyes and motioned Medreal close. The stewardess seemed reluctant to let her take the baby, but the expectant look on Firal's face made Medreal comply. Minna cradled the drowsy infant close for a long, tender moment, then laid the baby against Firal's breast and showed her how to pull up the cloth wrappings to hold the girl in place.

Firal shifted, her hands hovering under the baby in the wrap. Movement came easily and nothing pulled loose. "It's perfect. Thank you, truly."

The Underling woman nodded once. "Now it'll be easier to take care of business." She moved back and clasped her hands together.

Davan cleared his throat. "I drew a map for you, Your Majesty, showing the way to, ah... the old leader's quarters." He held out a roll of parchment.

Firal took it and unrolled the scroll for a quick look. The old queen's rooms hadn't been far from the throne room. It would be easy enough to get there. "Excellent. Thank you, Davan. With luck, it won't be long before I return."

"Shall we initiate the Gate, my queen?" Temar inclined her head as she spoke, though she glanced to the other mages in the parlor.

Firal nodded. Aside from Temar, more than a dozen mages had come for this. She hoped they would be enough. "Remember, it should take no more than three hours. Don't seek me before then. I'll Call once when I'm back at the meeting point and ready for the return Gate. Two Calls for emergencies. I don't expect anything should happen to me, but I don't want to take chances, since I have Lumia with me."

Minna's eyebrows shot up at the name.

Trying not to look at her, Firal went on. "If I haven't returned in three hours, notify Vahnil and send Davan in with however many men he feels necessary."

"We shall pray they aren't needed, my queen," Medreal said.

Giving another, stiffer nod, Firal strode closer to the stone archway in the center of the room. She rested a hand against Lulu's back and waited for the linked mages to seek her energies. She felt the invitation and threw herself to it, closing her eyes and focusing on the image she wanted—the one part of the underground city she knew wouldn't have changed.

The other mages directed the flow of magic; she only guided

it. Opening a Gate was beyond her skill, and had the temple's Masters been involved, she wouldn't have been allowed to guide the opening, either. She tried not to think of them, retraining her thoughts on where she wanted to go before she opened her eyes.

Crackling lines of energy wove together within the arch, white-hot and blinding, then flashed and faded as the image became clear. Firal's throat constricted. The Gate stabilized and the white-robed mages bowed their heads. Temar moved closer and pressed a coin into Firal's hand before she motioned her forward.

They released her energies and she drew a breath, funneling magic into the coin to create a mage-light. It flickered to life as she stepped through the Gate into the darkened room she'd once called home.

Everything was just as she'd left it, from the neat stack of firewood beside the hearth to the cozy bed in the corner. The sight stirred fond memories and sorrow at the same time. She wondered at how long it had been since she'd lain there, nestled in the arms of her first love. Then she shook her head, scattering the thoughts and trying not to let herself become distracted again. The Gate behind her was still open. She couldn't see it, but she could feel it, and everyone in the parlor could see her through the stone archway. The notion of unseen eyes on her gave her a chill.

She still didn't understand exactly how Gates worked, and now she realized she may never learn. Nondar had been open to continuing to teach her. He had promised to help her refine her abilities now that she'd reached a plateau in strength. The Archmage's failing health changed matters. Anaide and Edagan clung to the old reasoning that a ruler shouldn't have more than basic training, as mages were meant to serve both halves of the island. With all mages now back within her territory and Relythes building a wall between the two kingdoms, that was no longer the case, but Firal still doubted she could change the minds of the two women.

She lifted the mage-light a little higher. Something glittered beside the bed. Her brow furrowed and she crept closer. An amulet hung from the bedpost by a silver chain, the stone shining black and blue. She recognized it as Rune's, as the pendant that altered his appearance, but she didn't know how long it had been there. He'd never donned it again after their wedding, never needing to disguise himself again. Somehow, she'd never noticed it there. She took it from the bedpost without stopping to consider why.

Behind her, the power of the invisible Gate wavered and dissipated. Firal allowed herself a sigh of relief. The mages, like Vahn, had not wanted her to venture into the underground alone, but at least they hadn't fussed when she said no. Temar's displeasure had been clear in her eyes, but she had bowed her head and assented. The woman heeded her better than the temple mages, but Firal suspected it had more to do with Temar liking her than simply that she was the queen. She turned that thought over in her head. If Nondar couldn't help her progress with her magic, perhaps Temar could.

The pendant flashed blue in Firal's hand. The light startled her, but the movement made it flash again. Now that she was older and a more experienced mage, its magic simmered in her senses. It hadn't, before she'd touched it. Had she sensed it without touch, she supposed Rune's disguise would have been found out long ago.

Memories of him flooded her head and she turned to sit on the edge of the bed, her free hand resting on the baby. She slid her thumb over the gemstone in the amulet and contemplated the magic that hummed against her skin. Such little movement was needed to change its color, and she tilted it back and forth to watch the iridescent blue fire slide across its surface.

The lines between Rune's identities blurred now, whenever she looked back. She'd lost count of the days since she'd Called him. At first, she'd wondered if he'd gotten her Call at all. If the magic that went into that beckoning sensation functioned in the same way as Gates, it would have explained the problem. But Temar had assured her the two were very different. Gates were bound to a physical destination, which was why Gating parlors were so important, built with simple shapes that were easy to remember. Some, the woman had explained, even bore a location's insignia on the wall to provide a simple, clear image to remember. Before that, Firal had never noticed Ilmenhith's seven-pointed star etched on the wall of her own palace's Gating parlor.

The Calling, on the other hand, had nothing to do with appearance. Where Gates relied on the body, the Calling relied on the soul, the known essence of the person one sought to summon. That presented its own problem, by Firal's reasoning. What happened if the person you tried to contact had changed? If they were no longer the person you'd known?

"I suppose all we can do is hope that's not the case," she whispered to the baby on her chest.

Clutching Rune's pendant in her fist, Firal closed her eyes. One more try, she'd promised herself. It was not a large window of time, but it was all she could offer. She filled her thoughts with memories that made her chest ache.

The playful spark that always lit his eyes. The pensive way he'd stare at the blank wall as he sat at the desk to work through missives and plans. The halting, hesitant movement of his fingers when he reached to touch her skin. The stunning smile he shared so rarely, that filled her heart with warmth. So many little moments had formed her vision of who he was. Courage and fear mingled in everything he did.

She drew a breath and Called for him again, sending a long, tender pulse of emotion that begged for his response. Then, returning her thoughts to the task ahead, she pushed the pendant into her satchel and crossed to the door. She lingered for just a moment before she pulled it open.

Now, she'd done all she could.

The hallway beyond the door was dark and eerie, lacking the

warm comfort she'd associated with it when the hallway led home. Familiar doors lined the walls along the way to the inverted tower, each marked with unique symbols she'd learned to recognize, but never learned to read. Her pace slowed as she strode past Minna and Davan's old home. She still could hardly believe they had convinced all of Core to uproot and move, leaving behind who knew how many centuries of life. She could not say she would have been willing to do what the ruin-folk had done. Their loyalty deserved more than she could offer.

Beside the river in Core's main cavern, the market still stood. As she walked, the mage-light in her hand populated the stalls with shadows. Every stall was empty, though that was no surprise. The ruin-folk would have needed every resource at their disposal to move so many people all the way to Ilmenhith.

The winding hallways between the market and the palace were where she lost her bearings. Firal pulled Davan's map from the top of her satchel and rested a hand on the sleeping baby's back. She counted doorways and branching paths to find her way to the throne room. Before long, she grew grateful for the cloth wrap that held Lulu to her chest. The baby fussed in the oppressive silence, but stayed still, comforted by the sound of her mother's heartbeat beneath her ear.

"I don't know how I'll know when three hours are up," she murmured, rubbing Lulu's back through the cloth. "I forgot how dark it is down here."

When she reached the end of the hallway, she pushed aside a tapestry to slip into the throne room beyond. The darkness was oppressive. Her mage-light seemed too small as she moved between the columns of black stone. Her footsteps echoed and she found herself struggling to keep from clutching the light. Willing her fingers to relax, she lifted her hand a little higher. She rounded one of the columns and came face to face with a man.

Firal shrieked and recoiled, dropping the mage-light and clutching the baby to her chest. But only the infant's frightened wail answered her cry, and she wrenched her eyes open.

The mage-light on the floor cast a ruddy glow onto a statue's features, lighting them from underneath and making his snarl seem even more frightful. A statue, not a man. Breathing a sigh of relief, Firal hushed the baby and rocked on her feet until the girl quieted. Then she looked at the statue again.

There were carvings and reliefs everywhere in the underground, but she couldn't recall ever seeing statues. Certainly not in the throne room. She picked up the mage-light and crept forward to take a better look. When she saw the stone face clearly, her heart skipped a beat.

It was Tren.

Firal had wondered what happened to the man, knowing he would have presented a strong opposition to moving anyone out of Core. Especially to answer the summons of a new queen. For a moment, she thought it only a statue, but she couldn't imagine someone capturing his features so flawlessly, each and every hair defined. His face was frozen in a snarl, his posture a lunge. His hands still clutched his sword which, even more strangely, remained steel.

She circled him, brow furrowed in wonder. The hair on the back of her neck prickled uncomfortably. Even his clothes were stone, but she couldn't fathom what could have done such a thing.

No, that wasn't true; there was no residue of magic present that she could feel, but she knew it had to be the result of magecraft. She didn't know how it could have been brought to pass, but the underground had been home to two powerful mages. Who knew what they could have done? She shivered and tore herself away from the sight. There was little time to spare, and she left the stone man behind.

Davan's map led her to a tapestry directly behind the throne. Firal put the map back into her satchel, stroked Lulu's hair with one hand and held the mage-light with the other. The hallway behind the tapestry stretched straight ahead for a time before two other corridors converged with it, just ahead of a simple door. She expected the door to be locked, but it swung open at the slightest touch. The hinges groaned, low and mournful.

The room beyond was lavish, but Firal hadn't expected anything else from the former ruler's chambers. Plush carpets underfoot muted her footsteps as she slipped inside. The bed was unmade, red satin sheets spilling off the side and across the floor. She shuddered as the sight of the woman's bed stirred unpleasant memories. Willing herself not to look that direction again, she instead turned toward the desk that stood against the far wall. Books cluttered the desktop and a small stack of volumes sat on the floor beside it. A glance around the room showed there were no other books, and she assumed the one she was after would be in the pile.

Firal pulled back the chair, sat at the desk and took the first book she could reach. Its cover was worn, as if from years of reference. She flipped it open and blinked in surprise. Empty. She leafed through it, frowning. Every page was blank. Even as a queen, she couldn't fathom the waste of an empty hard-bound book. She slid it into her bag.

The next book was a history of the island; the one after that was a volume of bawdy poetry. She tossed both to the floor, working her way through the stacks with growing frustration. None of the books were labeled and some were in languages she didn't understand. Davan had been certain when he said the book she needed was full of diagrams and illustrations that showed how to work the lifts. Not a single book fit the description.

"Perhaps she had a library," Firal murmured, wincing at the way her quiet voice echoed in the empty room. Or perhaps a library was too much to ask. Books had been a precious commodity in the underground. If there was a library, she didn't know where to look. Davan hadn't mapped anything other than what he thought she might need. She consulted the parchment again, nibbling her lower lip. There was another room sketched out, not far from the chamber she stood in. Hurrying back into the hallway, she studied the map again before following one of the branching paths that twisted away and moved deeper into the earth.

Lulu wiggled, forcing Firal to pause. "I should have brought a candle," she murmured as she adjusted the fabric that crisscrossed around her body and resumed exploration. "At least a candle would tell me how long we've been here."

The corridor leveled out eventually, the right side of it lined with doors. Davan's map didn't show more than one room and Firal grimaced, wondering if she'd taken a wrong turn. One by one, she tested the doors. Each swung open easily and she was surprised to see there were no locking mechanisms on any of them. Though the rooms on the other side of the door were furnished, each was so cold and sterile she couldn't imagine anyone had ever slept there. Guest rooms, she decided at last, though she couldn't fathom they ever had guests.

She started to turn back after the fourth door, but paused when a glance over her shoulder showed the fifth stood open by an inch. Firal slid toward it and nudged the door open with her foot. The door bumped into something and stopped. She pushed harder and the resistance gave way.

It was another guest room, though from the mess of papers overflowing from the desk and table, it appeared to have hosted a scholar for quite some time. Piles of books sat beside the bed and on the floor, one of the toppled stacks having been what impeded the door. Curious, she inched toward the table and peered down at the papers strewn across it.

Complex diagrams and illustrations filled countless pages, some as wrinkled as if they'd been crumpled and smoothed a dozen times over. Sheets of notes were numbered in the corners to match them to drawings.

"The Underlings have a fascination with mechanical things," Firal murmured, recalling the conversation from long ago. She picked up a page of notes, tears stinging her eyes. She recognized the handwriting and it changed the meaning of the words in her head. The Underlings as a whole had forgotten the gears and their workings. Only one had been interested in them. The memories of him were everywhere here. It made it hard to think. Forcing herself to drop the paper, she turned her attention to the books.

Several matched the description Davan had given; unlabeled volumes with illustrations of what looked to be the lifts and their mechanisms. She fit them into her satchel, knowing she didn't have the time to sift through them to find which was the right one. There would be plenty of opportunities for that later, and she was running out of time.

With the books in hand, that meant there was only one thing left to do. Firal followed the map in reverse and wove her way back to the market.

Instead of returning to the designated meeting point, she wound her way up the spiral pathway at the end of the river, keeping close to the wall. She'd never gotten over her fear of the gaping chasm in the middle of the strange corkscrew path. Carrying her baby beside it only made things worse. Fighting her nerves, she climbed to the top, stepped out into the sunshine and fresh breeze, and walked into the gardens.

Once carefully tended, the herb garden was now all but overgrown. It pained her to see it, knowing how hard she'd worked to cultivate the plants. But she walked on, stopping only when she reached the grassy field and serpent's-tongue trees at the back of the garden. White blossoms clustered along the branches and falling flowers danced on the wind. Firal caught one as it fell and tucked it behind Lulu's tiny ear. Then she took a second blossom from the grass and twirled it between her fingers.

Hugging the baby in her wrappings, she stood and listened to the rustling branches and birdsong overhead. For a moment, she felt as if she were home. She closed her eyes and waited, savoring the sunshine and the tranquility she had not known since she'd taken the crown.

Lulu drowsed for a while and woke hungry. Firal checked the sun's position to guess at the time, then sat in the grass to feed the girl and rock until she felt she could linger no longer. She made herself move back toward the path into the underground, thinking of her unanswered Call.

Firal stopped beside the yawning chasm, staring at the flower in her hand. "You can't hear this," she murmured, "but it needs to be said. Would that I could speak to you instead of the wind." Her throat tightened and the baby fussed. She stroked the girl's dark hair as she knelt and reached into her satchel. "I've written a letter for you. I'll leave it on the table, just in case you ever find your way home."

Her fingers slid past the letter to find the pair of pouches she'd packed. She pulled them free. It had been a silly choice, she realized now; the island's climate was inhospitable to aspens. They never would have grown in the tropical heat. Still, she ran her fingers over the bulging pouch of catkins fondly and blinked back tears. "Just remember I loved you," she whispered.

Squeezing her eyes closed, she upended both pouches and spilled the seeds into the abyss.

15

THE ATTACK

A DIM WHINE PULLED RUNE FROM SLEEP. GROGGY AND DISORIENTED, he lifted his head and listened as the sound intensified. The mass of warm feathers above him shifted and he drew a breath. A booming impact rocked the tower and stole the question before he could speak.

Ria screeched, clapping her birdlike forepaws to her ears. A second explosion against the side of the tower knocked her off balance. She spilled into the floor in a tangle of legs and lashing wings. Spitting a curse, Rune clawed his way from the nest of cushions. He caught the gryphon's leg and rolled her over on his way to the door.

Whistles and warning calls echoed through the open central shaft of the aerie. Gryphons emerged from their nesting chambers, some blinking in sleepy confusion, others raising panicked cries. Far below, the shouts of men on the ground floor of the tower were all but lost beneath the whistling trills and wing beats.

Ria skittered against the stone floor, slipping in her haste to make it to the center of the tower.

"What's happening?" Rune asked, his words husky from sleep. The whine returned. He tilted his head, trying to determine where it came from. It wasn't a sound, he realized; it was power buzzing in his senses.

Magic struck the tower in a blast. He staggered as dust and pebbles rained down from the walls.

"The mages! They know we're nested here. They're after us now. We were the reason they lost the last battle, remember?" Ria shoved past him, her golden eyes wide with fright. "There are hens sitting clutches, babies who can't fly—"

Rune cursed again. *Rhyllyn.* He couldn't sense the boy in the camp below. He turned to run, but didn't make it farther than a step before the mages struck the tower again. Ria lurched against him and they both slipped over the edge of the walkway. The gryphon shrieked and caught his legs. Blood rushed to his head as he swung upside down in the chasm. Panic exploded in his chest and everything in him went cold as the ground raced up to meet them.

The gryphon's wings snapped open, slowing their descent. She flipped him in her grasp to seize one of his arms. He swung backwards until his shoulder creaked with pain. Then Ria rocked him forward and released his arm just as she pulled upward into an aerial ascent. He hit the ground rolling and crashed into the wall of the tower as she spiraled back into the frenzy of wings above.

A soldier Rune didn't recognize came to his aid, pulling him upright and crouching beside him to ask questions Rune was too dizzy to answer. He managed a sound of affirmation and rubbed his head with one clawed hand, as if that would stop the spinning. The man slapped his back and turned away.

The ground floor of the tower churned with activity. Much like the inverted tower in Core, the lower floors were residences. He'd thought the tower had only been occupied by the Aldaanan, but the place still brimmed with people. The soldiers were evacuating the tower residents, aiding women and carrying children, pushing everyone out the door. Grimacing, Rune thrust himself to his feet and followed.

The snow outside was blinding in the midday light. He squeezed his eyes shut and focused on the energies around him, trying to locate the army's other mages. Even when he tried, he couldn't feel them, power too thick in the air. Stifling the urge to curse more, he caught a soldier by the shoulder and raised his voice to be heard. "Where is Captain Kaith?"

The soldier gestured wordlessly before he pulled away to rush back into the tower.

Rune turned toward the south and shaded his eyes against the brilliance of the clear sky. A small cluster of men made a dark shadow against the white ground. He moved toward them, the cold kiss of winter air through his thin shirt reminding him he'd left his uniform's dress coat beside Ria's nest. He ignored the cold and pressed on, breaking into a run as soon as he was clear of the crowd beneath the tower. "Garam!" His voice felt rough. The bitter air made him cough.

The captain turned, his face stone but his eyes burning with intensity. "Where have you been?"

"Where is Rhyllyn?"

"With Sera and Alira. They're shielding part of the village. The tower is too big to protect."

Rune bit back an oath. "The gryphons have young in the aerie."

"I know." Garam's face was grim. The fire in his eyes faltered with emotion. Regret, Rune thought. Realization they could not protect the gryphons, or their young.

"Where are the college mages?" Rune asked, scanning the skies. Bursts of power rippled through the air from every direction to explode against the tower's sides. He turned, trying to follow one streak of energy and then another.

"They're everywhere. Came from the south, split their forces to surround us while the main group began an assault on the village. As soon as we were scrambling to aid the civilians, the mages turned their attention to the tower to keep the gryphons from coming to our aid." The captain spat at the ground. "I don't know how we didn't see them coming, Sera and Alira were both feeling for mages the whole time—"

"They're college-trained," Rune interrupted. "They can mask their power. Just like Lumia could."

Garam blinked. "Lumia?"

Rune shook his head and spun toward the thatched roofs.

If the other mages were defending, it wouldn't be hard to find them, and it only took a moment to form a guess. Civilians hurried toward the long, two-storied dinner hall, while men removed furniture from it to make room. The numerous tables began to form barricades in the streets. Men piled behind them to strategize. Rune sprinted toward the makeshift fortress without waiting for orders. He didn't notice the mage-barrier until he ran into it.

A thousand pins and needles stabbed beneath his skin before the barrier repulsed him with a sharp crackle. Rune staggered backwards and looked up in surprise. The barrier's surface rippled and then grew still, invisible once more. Just like the mage-barrier that had always surrounded Kirban Temple. Only this time, it didn't let him through.

He put a hand forward, flexing his fingers before he touched a claw to the barrier again. It sizzled and snapped, electric sparks shooting out to bite him. He jerked his hand away. People moved past him on either side, passing through the shield without difficulty. He watched for a moment before he understood. He was a mage, held outside like any other.

For now, at least. Rune cringed at the thought. Barriers were powerful, but not impregnable. An organized strike could break through. His eyes swept up the tower as understanding washed over him. That was why they attacked the tower—not because of the gryphons, but because it would take too much power to penetrate the force field. Why sacrifice energy by wielding their magic against the barrier directly? The tower shuddered under the assault, but the blows came from no more than four locations. It was the best strategy they had. If the tower fell against the barrier, three mages wouldn't be enough to hold it.

Gritting his teeth, Rune hammered a fist against the barrier and winced at the sparks. "I need Sera!"

The soldiers on the other side of the mage-barrier said something—to each other, he assumed, their voices too low for him to hear. Then one hurried toward the dinner hall and the others moved back toward the tower.

The barrage of magic against the aerie hadn't ceased. Rune gritted his teeth and made himself breathe. He couldn't do anything but watch and wait, trapped outside with no power, no weapons and no armor. Gryphons wheeled above the tower, spinning like a cyclone, darting to and fro to avoid the bolts of magic college mages hurled at them. Rune's eyes narrowed. It wasn't any defined element, just raw bursts of power. The result of mages tied together without a shared affinity. They had to be linked in groups; a single mage wouldn't have been strong enough to create the sort of explosions that knocked stones from the tower and punched holes in its walls.

"Where have you been?" Sera's voice snapped his attention back to the ground.

Rune gave her a dark look. "Can you say anything without repeating your brother?"

She raised a brow, unamused.

He gave an exasperated sigh. "Never mind, just let me in!"

"I can't." Sera gestured to a line in the snow he hadn't noticed, a narrow, icy streak where the magic had melted the top crust of snow. "The mages caught us off guard. We had to put the shield up without you. It's all or nothing, now. Any mages outside have to stay outside. If we try to make an exception, the entire barrier will fall."

He kicked snow at the mage-barrier and watched with agitation as it passed through without harm. "Then you've got to bring Rhyllyn out here."

She threw up her hands. "He can't pass through the barrier

either! Aren't you listening? Mages on this side stay on this side, mages out there stay out there."

"But if he's right next to me on his side of the barrier, we might be able to find a way to share power through it." He looked to the aerie again. There were gryphons on the ground now, herding clumsy balls of gray fluff toward the mage-barrier. He jerked his head toward them. "Can they get in?" If the barrier repulsed him, he didn't want to think about what it would do to the gryphons.

"They'll be fine. This isn't like the barrier in the Royal City, but we're taking precautions. We're preparing to shield another building for their offspring. We hope to raise it once they're all inside so they won't have to pass through a barrier, but it's testing our limits."

Rune paused to study her. He hadn't noticed how pinched her face was. Her eyes were dull with exhaustion. He cursed himself silently. Rhyllyn couldn't help yet, unable to wield his power by himself. Alira and Sera were holding the barrier alone. How had they managed this long? It took half a dozen mages to hold the barrier at the temple. Even Envesi hadn't been able to support it on her own. He swallowed his frustration. "Bring Rhyllyn."

Her brow knit with concern and she opened her mouth to protest.

"Trust me," he said, voice softening. "I have an idea."

She eyed him, then tore away to lope back to the dinner hall with long-legged strides.

Rune rubbed his arms through the thin cloth of his shirt and stamped his feet in the snow. He was miserably unprepared. Every mist of breath before his face reminded him of the wicked cold.

He didn't have to wait long. Sera returned, pulling the boy along by the sleeve. Rhyllyn couldn't keep up with her and foundered in the snow. She urged him back to his feet and coaxed him to the barrier where Rune waited.

"What are you going to do?" she asked, helping the boy find his balance when they stopped. Rhyllyn shivered in the cold, his small hands jammed into the pockets of his rust-colored wool coat.

"Don't worry about us. You go back to Alira. The two of you need to be close, and the barrier needs all of your concentration right now." Rune glanced to Rhyllyn and did his best to muster a smile for the boy. "We'll take care of everything else."

"If you hurt him, I swear—" Sera started.

He raised a hand to forestall any argument. "Don't forget that my refusal to hurt a boy is what got me out of the arena." A figure in white appeared at the hall's front doors. He spared Alira a single glance. "Besides, he's as much my responsibility now as anyone's."

Sera caught his gaze and held it for a tense moment, her mouth half open with words she couldn't say. Then she closed it and simply nodded before she rushed to rejoin Alira at the door.

Rhyllyn watched her go with a troubled look on his face. When he turned to Rune, his blue eyes were pale. A color representing fright, Rune assumed. Sympathy tugged at his heart.

Sympathy would have to wait.

"Ready?" he asked.

"I can't come across," the boy said. "Miss Alira says we can't share magic across the barrier without breaking it, either."

"We aren't going to share across the barrier," Rune said, though he craned his neck to see the barrier's surface. It rippled where stray energy blasts struck it, but it remained up. "We're going to share through it."

The boy's brow furrowed in consternation. "What do you mean?"

"They can't let us through the barrier because it's anchored. See?" Rune pointed at the ground and swept his claw to the side, as if to trace the line of ice atop the snow. "The snow melted and froze again where they asked the earth to help them hold it down. Since it's anchored, you can help feed energy to the barrier."

"But I don't know how!" Rhyllyn wailed.

Rune dropped to one knee and met the boy's snake-slitted eyes with his own. "You can do it. You have to, or else people here will be hurt. Once your power is flowing into the barrier, I should be able to find it from this side. Once I have hold of it, all you have to do is hang on. Can you do that?"

The boy's face was doubtful, but he nodded.

"All right." Rune sucked in a breath and willed his nerves to settle. "Start just like you did when we practiced. Gather yourself together and push. But instead of pushing toward me, push right here." He reached to touch the ice ring. A spark leaped at him and he winced and jerked his finger back. "There. Where the flows of the barrier join with the flows of the earth. Can you feel it?"

Rhyllyn nodded again, staring at the ice with a single-minded intensity.

Rune glanced up, watching for signs of change in the barrier's all but invisible surface. "Push as hard as you can. You'll feel it when the flows respond, they'll reach out to you just like I did. It's just like taking someone's hand."

The boy lifted his hands and held them out in front of himself, as if reaching for a person. His eyes unfocused, and he moved.

"Wait!"

The boy's hands struck the barrier. Blue electricity burst from its surface, pitching him backwards. Rhyllyn cried out as his back hit the ground. He curled in on himself with his arms to his chest.

Rune leaped forward without thinking and hit the barrier. The shock that rolled through him made his hair stand on end. His heart skipped a beat, then hammered in his chest as he blinked at the sky. He pushed himself up to one elbow, shaking his head to ward off confusion. He didn't remember falling, but the barrier had responded more violently than to his first contact. The shield's edge lay several feet away.

"Rhyllyn!" He struggled to get up. His chest felt strange, his limbs numb. He staggered and fell to his knees in the snow.

Groaning, Rhyllyn rolled to his stomach and pushed himself up. He looked frightened, but his eyes were clear when he turned his head to look at the barrier again.

"Are you all right?"

The boy nodded mutely.

Rune's shoulders sagged with his sigh of relief. "Reach for it with your energy only. The mage-barrier hurts more each time you touch it."

"My head feels fuzzy." Rhyllyn rubbed his eyes and squinted at the ground. There was a patch of ice on either side of the shield now, marking where the magic had lashed out against them.

"I know. Just try again, please." Rune couldn't help the desperation in his voice, or his nervous glance toward the gryphons above the aerie. There were more of them in the air now, but instead of spiraling above the tower, they swept out in patternless loops away from the tower. The booming of explosions against the tower was accented by new explosions elsewhere, as the gryphons retaliated with bombs. He forced himself to focus on Rhyllyn, watching as the boy braced himself to try again.

Color bloomed in the child's cheeks as he pushed himself and struggled until his face crumpled with effort.

"You can do it," Rune urged.

"I can't," the boy panted.

"I know you can." Something rippled where the mage-barrier met the snow. Rune refused to look. "You're the strongest mage here, Rhyllyn. You were born to do this."

"But I wasn't born this way."

"It doesn't matter." Rune scraped a claw along the edge of the ice. Everything would have been easier if he could just touch the child's hand. "It doesn't matter how your Gift woke. Magic doesn't come from nowhere. You have this power for a reason. Maybe this is why."

Rhyllyn's face twisted.

The barrier whined. A wide ripple of blue swept from a point between them and spread over the entire dome as a surge of power reinforced it. The boy gasped and fell to his knees.

Rune jumped to his feet. Twinges of pain pinged inside his skull as he reached for the barrier with his own energy, seeking Rhyllyn's.

It did not reject him. Power rushed into him as he plunged into the flow of magic, drawing strength into himself and funneling some back to the boy. The air around him sang with might, the flows rejoicing at his touch. "You did it!"

"I did it!" Rhyllyn repeated, gasping for breath as a timid smile split his features.

Rune motioned for him to sit and the boy settled on the ground with his hands behind him to prop him upright. Within moments, the strained shade of Rhyllyn's cheeks faded to a healthy pink.

"Just stay connected to the barrier. It's what lets you connect with me." Rune drew more energy and bolstered the shield, thinking of Sera and Alira. He could lighten their load, but he could offer them no other aid. Until he found the college mages, at least. He scanned the horizon and then looked to the sky. A streak of power shot from the west.

"Stay here, where it's safe," Rune said. "As long as we're both close to the mage-barrier, we can share power."

Startled, Rhyllyn started to rise. "Where are you going?"

Holding out a hand to tell the boy to stay put, Rune turned westward. "To take care of some mages."

It was easier to ignore the cutting cold with the power that filled him. It warmed him from the inside out, scoured everything else away. He drew as much of it as he could hold as he ran along the barrier's edge toward the source of that bolt, hanging tight to the awareness of the boy that lingered in the back of his head. He couldn't afford to lose his concentration, couldn't afford to let anyone distract him. Retaining his focus had always been his weak point, though Firal had tried to hammer it out of him. He couldn't let it be a weakness now.

Firal. Every time she crossed his mind, his chest tightened with grief, frustration, and longing.

Not now, he growled at himself.

Shadows swept over him as gryphons circled above. He followed their lead through the village, knowing he had to be close. Moving away from the mage-barrier, he stayed mindful of his connection to it and stopped as soon as he reached the limit of his tether. Mages and Garam's men moved through the trees on the other side of the tower, visible, though barely. Earth, ice, and snow exploded at random, always in the wake of a gryphon's shadow. He grimaced. Even connected to the flows, their explosives would kill him just as easily as they killed the college mages and the few soldiers who were foolish enough to linger when a gryphon passed overhead.

The light-dappled shadow of wing feathers passed over him and for a fleeting instant, it reminded him of the rippling shadows beneath the serpent's-tongue trees back home. The tightness returned to his chest. He could almost smell Firal's hair, sweetly floral as it snagged against his scales.

Emotion hit him so hard it almost drove him to his knees. Sorrow, desperation, need. Memories of everything he'd had with her and lost in exile threatened to drown his senses. Home, underground in Core. Her body molded to his as she hugged him tight. He needed her. They needed each other. He had to go *home.*

Rune faltered in the snow. Pain crept in around the edges of his awareness as his connection to the mage-barrier began to slip away. *Not now!* He gritted his teeth and forced the thoughts away. They clawed at his mind, filled his body with a prickling pins-and-needles sensation as they tried to hold fast. He couldn't risk distraction, couldn't lose himself beneath such powerful feelings. Not now, not with Aldaeon under siege.

Bracing himself, he focused on his link with the barrier and his connection to Rhyllyn through it. Rune drew more energy, testing the load by adding one tiny rivulet of magic at a time. He wasn't linked to the other mages directly, but he couldn't risk overloading Alira and Sera by weaving too much new energy into the shield they all shared. He felt the barrier grow unsteady, a sign he'd reached its limit. It rippled like a bubble about to burst and he released the last trickle he'd tried to seize. Slowly, the barrier stabilized. He could only move so much power through the shield, less than he could move through Rhyllyn directly. It wasn't what he'd hoped for, but it would have to do.

Rune closed his eyes and sought the mages ahead. They dotted the landscape like candles, illuminated in his senses. Small clusters drew his attention and he reached for the ties of magic that linked them. He wasn't sure what he was doing. He'd only done it once, accidentally, but it was the only thing he knew to try to prevent the mages from striking the tower. He brushed the tendrils of their power and set his jaw.

He seized them.

Curling his fist tight, he stared at his hand and struggled to imagine he held the flows they tried to manipulate. The energies strained against his grasp. He pulled.

Mages shrieked somewhere amidst the trees. He couldn't see where, but he felt them. He pulled harder, clenching his teeth as the energies resisted. It wasn't as easy as he'd expected, but he wasn't as strong as he had been then. Tightening his hold, he steeled himself and tried again.

A thread snapped. A mage fell screaming. He felt the nourishing warmth of that flow turned free, struggled to keep it from breaking his concentration. Another thread of energy snapped.

It didn't replenish him as it had when he'd severed Lumia

from her Gift. He didn't understand why, but faintly, in the back of his head, he became aware of the scar in his hand.

Focus. He shook his head and trained his sight on a cluster of mages as they emerged from the forest and moved toward the tower. He didn't know which mage he held, but another thread snapped, and Rune reeled backwards and almost lost his balance. The link between the college mages broke. A handful of the mages fell among the trees, howling in what he could only assume was pain. He hadn't understood Lumia's grief when it happened. Now, with his magic sealed as it was, he knew the agony of being separated from power.

Three down, he thought, though he didn't know how many there were or how many he could stop. He shook his head again. Why couldn't he control his thoughts? Why now, of all times? He struggled to regain his focus as he turned his attention back to the enemy ahead.

Link after link, he picked them apart. No matter how many mages he cut off from power, there seemed no end to the fighting, nor did the mages ever seem to come any closer. It felt as if he'd been there for moments and years at the same time, the flow of power through him both disorienting and intoxicating.

Another tie snapped.

Another mage screamed.

He lost count of how many ties he severed, lost count of the screams of agony and dismay that echoed through the forest. He saw mages fall, clutching their heads, but the soldiers among them never seemed to gain any ground.

A tiny, nagging sensation begged for his attention. Rune tried to shrug it off as he pulled more power for the next strike. Abruptly, the power pulled back. Startled, he paused. He couldn't draw the flows any longer. They drew him.

Rhyllyn.

His heart skipped a beat and his eyes flashed to the skies. The gryphons had moved without him noticing. A cacophony of wing beats and eagles' cries sounded to the south. Cursing at his own carelessness, Rune almost tripped over his own feet in his hurry to return to the boy. He hadn't taught Rhyllyn anything about how to wield magic on his own; the child could do nothing to defend himself if anything went wrong, and a blue ripple that spread across the domed surface of the mage-barrier told him something was about to.

Hang on! Rune pushed the thought across his link to the barrier, hoping it translated into a sense of reassurance that bore more confidence than what he felt. Breath burned icy in his lungs as he ran, forgetting the cold and the fighting behind him.

Rhyllyn came into view, alone at the edge of the mage-barrier with his arms outstretched, as if his hands alone could stop the endless rows of college mages that marched toward him. The boy's head turned and the look of terror on his face sent a lance of fear into Rune's heart.

In unison, the mages struck the tower.

The spire shattered like glass.

16

NEW TACTICS

VISIONS OF EMBERS FILLED ENVESI'S HEAD WHEN SHE CLOSED HER eyes. Though the cinders of the ramshackle little house had been cool for weeks, she still visited daily. She hadn't stirred the ashes, but wind and rain exposed the charred bones in the ruin of her workshop. She should have moved them, taken pity on the woman and given her a proper resting place. To do so would have implied she cared.

She didn't.

It was no surprise Alira decided to turn on them, but Envesi never expected the girl would decide to fight. She'd thought the young mage would simply flee. The loss of the extra hands caused inconvenience, at worst. But when Alira hadn't returned and Melora hadn't either, the former Archmage knew she would return to find a problem. She'd never expected this.

Melora hadn't been a remarkable mage. If she had been, she might have ended up a court mage instead of a Master of a House of element. But she had been loyal and supportive, and that meant something. Envesi shed no tears for the woman, but she was sorry to see her gone.

More sorry, though, to see Melora's bones were the only bones buried in the wreckage and ash. Wherever Alira had gone, she'd taken the child with her, and that was a problem. The last thing Envesi needed was another sign of failure floating around in the world.

The wind stirred her hair and Envesi turned her head to watch ash swirl into the air.

No matter how she approached the problem of the corruption, she couldn't figure out how to fix it. To come so far and be defeated by magic itself was humiliating. For all her experience, she still didn't know how to keep the flows from twisting, and she couldn't afford to keep stalling. She wouldn't dare call Eyrion a friend, though they had known each other long enough that he was lenient with her now. But Eyrion Tolmarni was not a forgiving man, and he was ready for results.

Results she'd have to offer single-handedly, now that Melora was gone. She didn't know if she could do it. Then again, she was working with the Archmage of the Grand College. If Eyrion couldn't lend her enough power to make it happen, no one could. She was not eager to share knowledge after Alira's defection, but she had made greater sacrifices before.

Smoothing her snowy hair, Envesi sighed and turned away from the charred husk of the house. She kept traveling to the house as if she would find it whole. Since she'd made the mistake of leaving the women to work on their own, she'd spent every day trying to figure how to fix the trouble she was in. Eyrion hadn't been happy when she'd stalled. Now she was out of time, and still the ashes told her nothing.

Disgusted, she returned to the college.

Though she remained composed on her way through the college's corridors, Envesi's thoughts were anything but. Before she'd left for Elenhiise, Eyrion had been the only student who could rival her strength. Now he was one of few mages whose power outstripped hers. She wouldn't voice her respect for the man, but it did exist.

The headmaster would be in his office now; she made her

way toward it absently. The office door was ajar. She didn't bother to knock before she slipped inside.

Eyrion barely lifted his head, his pen poised above the paper like a bird about to light. Then his eyes fell back to his work and the steady scratch of the pen against paper filled the room. "You're late."

"I wasn't aware I was supposed to be here at a certain time," Envesi said.

"It's past a matter of hours. You are weeks late." He paused again and gestured with his pen. "Close the door."

She pushed the door closed with her magic instead of her hands. When the Archmage did not react, she drew herself up regally as she moved across the floor. She wore a plain ivory dress instead of her assigned gray robes, but he didn't seem to notice. Nor did he seem to notice her discomfort. Her trek to the desk reminded her too strongly of the way magelings had approached her, when she still led the temple.

He finished writing as she neared his desk and put his pen aside. "You're alone."

She blinked, surprised. She hadn't expected him to notice that, either. "I am."

"Why?"

"Alira has abandoned her studies and left the college. She could not withstand the effort of scaling the ranks again." It was a neat lie, one that rolled off her tongue with ease. The first half was truth, and if he'd heard of the woman's absence by now, the fact she'd disappeared would be all he knew. "Melora is dead."

"Dead?" Eyrion straightened and lifted his eyes to her face for the first time.

"She was many years my senior. Our Gifts help us outlive many of our peers, but it would be foolish to assume it spared us the effects of aging." Her mouth twitched. Melora's attitude and energy had kept most from noting her age, but Envesi had watched the woman too long to see anything but a withered face, knobby fingers and skin that was riddled with age spots.

The hint of truth would make everything easier for the headmaster to accept.

He frowned. "I heard nothing of burial arrangements. We have no cemeteries here."

"A funeral pyre is customary for mages in her homeland," Envesi interrupted smoothly, feigning an expression of sorrow. "She passed just before Alira chose to leave us. Alira's Gift is in fire, of course, so we thought it fitting that she assist. The ashes have been spread in the field north of the coastal village. Were we on Elenhiise, they would have been spread across her family's farmland, but we did the best we could with what we have."

Eyrion regarded her silently for a time. Eventually, he sighed and nodded in grudging approval. "Then to earth she returns."

Envesi bowed her head and stifled her amusement. She hadn't misjudged; he had no room to disagree, not knowing the traditions of the tiny island from which the three mages had been exiled. As far as he knew, she had no reason to lie to him, and enough aspects of her tale could be verified by any number of mages if he decided to press.

Still, he studied her face for a long, uncomfortable moment before he spoke again. "You should have come to me with this news sooner, so I would understand your lack of timeliness in our arrangement."

"I am sorry," she lied. "Melora and I were colleagues for many years. I required privacy and time to myself after her death."

He laced his fingers together. "Then I trust you come to me now because you are ready?"

She drew her tongue over her lips. "Yes, but you should understand there are some intractable effects of the process that cannot be circumvented."

"I don't care," Eyrion snapped, rising halfway from his chair. "Can you free me from the bonds of limitation or not?"

Envesi leveled her eyes with his and gave a single nod.

"Without the two mages you practiced with?"

She nodded again. "It is at the limit of my capability, but it can be done."

A gleam lit his eyes and he stepped out from behind his desk. "Then there is no need to wait any longer. Our war teeters on the verge of victory. The Aldaanan have been driven from the north, leaving only a meager defense to flatten before we can seize their territory."

"Why bother with their territory?" She was reluctant to admit she knew little of mainland affairs these days, but the dispute with the Aldaanan seemed to be over restrictions on magic within the Triad's provinces, not over land.

The headmaster offered a wry smile and stroked his white hair. "Ah yes, you are an outsider now, aren't you? I shouldn't expect you to know how affairs here stand." His cold blue eyes grew unfocused, thoughtful. "We had hoped to eliminate the Aldaanan mages, but forcing them to flee is good enough. If Aldaan falls under our control, then the tower-eared rabbits who call themselves mages of the old ways will have no say in how magic is handled within the Triad. We can lift the ban on power in the Royal City and bring the Grand College back to prosperity."

He clasped his hands behind his back and strode toward the narrow windows to gaze at the sea. "Never in my youth would I have expected to inherit the college in such a state. When we were children, the Grand College of Lore was renowned for its mages. It was only after bloody Vicamros conquered Lore and Aldaan that we began to fall out of favor. Not just here, but across the entire northern continent."

"That's not how I recall it." Envesi trailed her fingers along the edge of his desk as she moved after him. "The mages of Lore were already falling out of favor when I was pulled from the college and sent to Elenhiise. Though I will agree it has gotten worse. What has Vicamros done to sour things so quickly?"

Eyrion's lip curled in a sneer. "I say he conquered Aldaan,

but it isn't the truth. The Aldaanan submitted to his rule willingly, seeing it as an opportunity to spread their influence beyond their borders. Magic is unnecessary, they said. They filled the king's head with false hopes of medicines and machinery that could do the jobs mages have always held. Anyone could become a healer, they said. Anyone could use the wind's power to their advantage. They offered him books. Scrolls and records from their supposed stores of knowledge. He opened an academy in the Royal City and asked scholars to study the texts."

She scoffed. "Mages could never be replaced so easily."

"You'd think that, wouldn't you?" He smiled, though his face grew grim. "But even horses will be rendered useless if they have their way. One of their machines—you should see the thing —is called an iron horse. It uses fire and water to move wheels on guide rails. Vicamros means to see it built before his son takes the throne."

"And you believe taking control of Aldaan will prevent him from doing such a thing?"

"I believe taking control of Aldaan will give us free rein with our craft. So we can bring healers and court mages back to the Royal City and show him what he's been missing." Eyrion shrugged, but his face betrayed determination.

Envesi forced a smile. "Well then, I suppose that's all the more reason to give them better mages."

"Yes." He turned to face her.

She opened her arms. "Lend me your power, Eyrion. Give me access to your Gift, and I shall give you strength beyond what you've ever dreamed."

"Yes," he breathed again, his eyes glazed. "I will restore my college. Whatever the cost."

He seized the energy in the air around him. Envesi shivered at the presence of his intimidating Gift, marveled at the idea of how much stronger he would be once she severed his ties to affinity. She reached for his power and wove it with hers.

"Remember what I have done for you," she whispered. Then, gathering his might into her, she began.

It wasn't the same as the creation of Lomithrandel, or even the same as severing the bonds that held the powers of the boy they'd used for practice. If anything, severing the ties to Eyrion's affinity would be easier. His Gift was fully fledged, letting her sense clearly which flows fed into his power naturally and which he had to bend to his will.

Wind stirred around them as she found his connection to that element. Through him, she felt all the power of the winds that swept in from the sea. She hadn't expected him to be tied to air, though she realized air was just as strong at the coast as water might be. Hurricanes, after all, didn't form above dry land.

Closing her eyes, Envesi focused on the wellspring of power within him. From the flows he grasped, she traced her way to where the threadlike flows seemed to meld with his spirit, the one vivid, pulsating source of energy no mage could touch. Already her head pounded. She breathed deeper, struggled to retain her focus. She concentrated on the point where the flows joined with the essence of his being.

For the first time, she realized that only a mage with a healing affinity could do what she sought to. No other mages could sense the energies within a person clearly enough to find what she had. The tiny, glowing pinpoint of power was all but invisible, even to her. It sparked as he drew the flows into himself and fed them to her, bubbling behind a dam of tiny, woven threads of energy.

She used his power against it. Picking first, digging for a loose tendril, latching onto it when she found it and gathering all her strength. She pulled.

The headmaster groaned. His connection to her wavered, then steadied. She dared a glance at his face, watched him grimace as she pulled harder, drew more from their link, funneled it underneath the loose weft.

The thread of power gave.

Envesi shrieked as energy lashed back against her, knocking her to the floor. The binding that held his Gift unraveled, replacing the pinpoint of light in her senses with a flood.

Eyrion clutched his head and cried out as everything around them erupted into chaos. Wind howled through the narrow windows. The floor trembled underfoot. His cries rose into a scream as the power filled him and his very body began to glow. His flesh rippled, twisted with the might he couldn't contain. Blood stained his white robes as claws sprouted at his fingertips and dug into his scalp.

His hold of his newfound power failed. Magic surged in the room until Envesi's hair stood on end.

"Let go of the flows!" She shielded her eyes as he shone more and more brilliantly.

Screams of pain became those of panic, and the smell of burning flesh scented the air.

"Let go!" she shrieked.

Lost in agony, Eyrion Tolmarni exploded in flame.

INHERITANCE

"WERE YOU PLANNING TO TELL ANYONE YOU MOVED TO A NEW room?" Rikka crossed her arms and leaned against the doorframe, a dour twist to her mouth.

Shymin sat up and tried to find words, but nothing came to mind. Her halfway-unpacked belongings still sat in a ring around her on the floor. She'd never owned much, but the idea of sorting through and organizing everything as she unpacked had been too delightful to refuse. Kytenia had always managed the cleaning and organization. As a result, their shared room had always felt more like Kytenia's than hers. For the first time in her life, Shymin had a space of her own, and she intended to enjoy it.

"Well?" Rikka prompted.

"After I finished unpacking, yes," Shymin said at last. She scooped a handful of papers from the floor and pretended to sort through them. In truth, she'd sorted that stack twice and still hadn't decided where it should go. "The Masters granted me a day off to finish getting things in order. I wanted to have everything put where it belongs before I told you. I knew you'd want to see, and... well, it's hardly appropriate to have guests over when it looks like this." She waved a hand at the mess on the floor.

Rikka snorted, unimpressed. "Did you ever consider we might want to help you?" Without waiting for an invitation, she stepped inside and picked up a stack of folded clothes. "Where do these go?"

A protest sprang to Shymin's lips, but she thought better of letting it free. If Rikka wanted to help, it was better to let her. "The chest at the foot of the bed. Lefthand side."

The redheaded mageling stepped over a pile of books to open the chest. "Kytenia said you moved out days ago. We could have had this all done for you by now."

"I don't think Kytenia's interested in helping. She's so busy with Archmage Nondar." She hadn't asked for help, either. A hint of guilt washed through her, and Shymin put her head down. If she had asked, would her sister have made the time?

"We're all busy, these days. I saw the Masters put up a notice for impending evaluations, and that your name was on it this time. Do you think you'll graduate?" Rikka sorted the clothes into two smaller piles, then arranged them by color and stuffed them into the chest.

"I hope so." The notice of evaluation came so close on the heels of her asking for her own quarters that Shymin couldn't help her suspicion, but she didn't dare question it. If it helped her reach the blue, it didn't matter whether the Masters were only taking pity on her. That was all it could be, she'd convinced herself; even with all her extra study, her performance as a healer hadn't changed.

Rikka dropped onto the bed with a sigh. "Well, good luck. I know it's hard to advance without a Master to oversee your affinity."

That yielded a quiet grunt. "I can't believe they still haven't replaced the Masters who..." Shymin trailed off, unsure how to describe what had happened. It had been a year since the former Archmage and two of her Masters had been exiled, and even most of the mages who had sided with Envesi now referred to the woman with disdain. Shymin couldn't say she felt comfortable doing the same. She'd run messages for that side and she still wasn't sure she regretted it. The former Archmage's methods had been questionable, but that didn't change the fact she'd been devoted to magic—and what was best for the mages.

"I'm sure there's a reason," Rikka said, brushing a speck of dirt off the blankets. "I'm sure they'll see to it soon. You've heard the rumors about Archmage Nondar?"

Shymin wished she hadn't. "You think he'll name replacements?"

"I don't think he'd want to leave it up to the other Masters. Nondar is loyal to the crown, and not all of them like Firal as much as we do."

Unsettled, Shymin picked up her hairbrush from the mess of belongings on the floor. She ran her fingers over the bristles, then leaned to the side to leave it on her desk. "I just hope someone is chosen soon. I know you understand how hard it is without a leader to show the way. Kytenia's so lucky that Nondar's taken her on as his assistant."

"I'm not sure how I advanced to blue, if we're being honest. I've studied hard, but mostly in places I felt I was lacking. But even those are hard to learn with the Houses being leaderless. I wish I'd pushed sooner. That I'd been a better healer when..." Rikka trailed off, a glassy sheen coating her eyes.

"It wasn't your fault." Shymin pushed herself from the floor and joined her friend on the bed. Rikka's shoulders slumped and she turned away.

They had discussed the battle outside Ilmenhith at least a hundred times in the year that followed, but it never seemed to help. Nothing would undo the death of a friend, and nothing kept Rikka from still struggling with Marreli's loss. The subject came up so often, Shymin wasn't certain anything would ever dull the pain.

"You know you couldn't have changed anything," Shymin said, softer. "I was there. Kytenia was there, too. We're both healers, but neither one of us sensed she was failing until it was too late."

"Then I should have just been stronger." The glassiness in Rikka's eyes welled into tears. "I should have been able to protect her. She was my best friend, Shymin. The sister I never had. How could I fail her so badly?"

Shymin wrapped her in a hug, not sure what else to say. Every mage had been needed for the battle, but Marreli had been the youngest of the group, barely more than a girl. She should have been allowed to stay in Ilmenhith, to help bolster the city's defenses, instead of being sent to war. They'd all blamed themselves for the mageling's death, and then they'd blamed the Masters, but blame had gotten them nowhere.

Rikka hiccuped against her shoulder. "I know you want to help, but you don't understand. You've always had Kyt, you've never been alone. After Firal left, and after I graduated to blue, there wasn't anyone left. And now I feel like you have to hate me because you didn't even tell me you'd moved."

"But I was going to," Shymin protested. "I swear I was. It's just... it's hard." The confession escaped before she could stop it, and she winced when Rikka lifted her head to look her in the eye.

Flustered, Shymin turned away, but the weight of her friend's stare demanded an explanation. She picked at the edges of her nails and fixed her eyes on the objects still scattered on the floor. "You're not the only one adrift." Her voice trembled; she swallowed hard to steady it. "After you and Kyt graduated, I didn't know how I fit anymore. I was left behind, and between losing Marreli and Firal leaving us, there wasn't anyone left to keep me company. I've thought of leaving the temple so often, Rikka."

"Leaving?" Rikka's voice cracked and she squeaked the latter half of the word. "But where would you go?"

"I don't know," Shymin admitted. "Home, maybe, if they'd let me in after Relythes ordered all mages to leave. I don't know if I still have a place there, but it's not like I have a place here, either. Yet how can I leave when the temple is all I really know?" She spread a hand and gestured around the sparsely-furnished room.

"But we need you! Not just me and Kyt. The temple needs you. Your Gift is so much more useful than mine. What can I do?" Rikka flicked her fingers toward a mess of papers on the floor. The air answered, shifting them a few inches. "What good is that?"

"It's good for a lot. Your affinity needs Masters, now that Melora is gone. Someone will replace her, and you'll climb the ranks."

A doubtful twist came to Rikka's mouth. "What about you? You don't think you'll climb? They're pushing your evaluation fast and your House doesn't have a leader, either."

Shymin clamped her jaw shut before a retort could escape. She'd redirected her friend's thoughts away from Marreli, if accidentally, and wanted to make the most of it. The last thing she wanted was to send her into a negative space again. "I'm still just a green-rank mageling," she said softly. "But if I had to guess..."

Rikka's brows twitched upward in an invitation to continue.

Though she wanted to go on, it was the first Shymin had dared speak of her suspicions, and she couldn't help but lower her voice as if she feared she'd be overheard. "I think it will be Kytenia."

"What?" Rikka blinked. "That what will be Kytenia?"

"The new Master of Healing," Shymin murmured. "Nondar took her as an apprentice for a reason, I'm sure of it. I'd be willing to bet that's why. I would have thought Firal would reach that point eventually, since she was his favorite, but with Firal no longer part of the temple..."

"He needs the next best choice," Rikka concluded. She lifted a hand and smoothed back her fiery hair, a thoughtful look coming to her face.

Shymin nodded once. "Kyt makes perfect sense. She's closer to Firal than any of us. Picking her means there would always be at least one mage in the temple's leadership who remains fiercely loyal to the crown."

Rikka nodded slowly as she weighed the information. "I suppose that does make sense. But what does that mean for you? None of the Masters leading affinities have ever had family in the temple. Can you even stay part of that House if your sister is put in charge? Would they kick you out?"

"I don't know," Shymin admitted. "I suppose I can always ask to be relocated elsewhere. They could send me to Ilmenhith. Maybe I could apprentice under the court mages until it's time to be stationed elsewhere."

"And what do you think it means for all of us?" Rikka asked softly. "Everything's already changed so much that none of us have anyone left in the temple, and—"

Shymin raised a hand to stop her. "Don't be ridiculous. We've still we've got each other, even if we're busy."

"And feeling lost," Rikka said.

"And lost," Shymin agreed. "But we're still friends, you goose. You and me and Kytenia. And Firal, even if she's not here."

Rikka frowned. She ran her fingers through her hair before she tucked a lock behind her pointed ear. "You think it'll stay that way?"

Reassurance leaped to mind, but something made Shymin rein it back in before it reached her tongue. She hadn't stopped to consider what would happen if Kytenia really did become Master of the House of Healing, and Rikka's concern now weighed heavy on her mind. If Kytenia was raised, would she be allowed to stay, or would their shared affinity bring accusations of favoritism down on her sister? She swallowed and tried to smile.

"I hope so," was all she said.

ARRICK COUGHED and waved a hand before his face. It did little to free him of the acrid smoke that still hung in the air, but at least the smog had thinned enough for him to see. His eyes watered and he paused to wipe them with the sleeve of his robe. A mage behind him stepped forward to offer a damp rag. He accepted gratefully, put the cloth to his mouth and nose, and breathed easier. He didn't know who'd thought to bring them. He'd have to praise someone later.

A fire in the Grand College was worrisome enough. More concerning was how none of the Masters had been able to smother the flames. They'd watched helplessly as people fled the palatial residence where all Lore's mages had rooms. Every Master still in the college had tried to help. All of them had failed. Even Arrick had been unable to stop it, and he had earned his place on the college's council by rivaling Headmaster Tolmarni in strength. In the end, they'd been forced to wait for the fire to burn itself out.

The stone halls of the building were blackened with soot. Ash and charcoal filled many of the college's rooms. Not all of the residence had burned, for which Arrick assumed they should be grateful. The far half of the building, which overlooked the sea, was ruined.

"How do you suppose it started?" a Master murmured behind him, making him frown. He wondered the same thing.

The council had divided, half the Masters remaining in the college courtyard while Arrick led the other half into the residence to investigate the matter. Not everyone at his heels was happy to be there, considering the obvious magical nature of the fire. He couldn't blame them, though he wasn't concerned. A handful of councilors had been quick to suspect a magical attack, but if a mage had caused it, there was little reason to think they'd still be in the building.

Arrick's mage-blue eyes drifted upward as they moved down

the hall. The smoke was thicker here, though the ceiling was gone. Holes in the floor of the third story let him see all the way to the top of the building. That would be easy enough to repair, he decided, thinking of where he would house displaced mages. There were empty classrooms that could be outfitted as temporary lodgings, but he figured it more reasonable to rearrange the assigned rooms to prioritize the mages still present in Lore. His lip curled as he thought of the mages sent to war, and he found himself glad for the cloth against his mouth.

He'd opposed Eyrion and his war most vocally. In fact, he'd been the only Master to stand without being cowed. The thought put a sour taste in his mouth. Of all times to be opinionated, he suspected this was the most inconvenient. More than a few Masters had sent suspicious glances his way.

"This must be where the fire started. Everything is burned two stories up." Arrick turned toward the ruin of a doorway. He hadn't paid attention to where they were going, but now he paused and lowered the rag from his face as he realized where they stood.

"Here?" someone asked.

Arrick raised a hand, gesturing for them to wait. Slowly, he strode into the headmaster's office. The walls and floor were black as a coal bin. Soot stained the hem of his white robe as he moved. Embers still glowed in remnants of furniture along the walls, but the desk and chairs in the center of the room were nothing but ash.

There were a thousand reasons for a fire to have started in Headmaster Tolmarni's office, but Arrick could only think of a single reason for it to have been caused by magic. He looked to the narrow windows in the charred stone wall and considered the sheer drop to the ocean on the other side. If someone had fled, they would have had to walk out the door. "There might be a trail in the soot," he called to the mages in the hall. "Perhaps we can find which way the guilty party went, but there's been no one here since the fire began."

A glint in the cinders caught his eye as he turned to leave. Arrick stared at it for a time before he bent and held a hand above the ash. It was as cool as if it had been there for days, not an ember to be seen or felt. He dug into the ashes with two fingers, lifted a lump and brushed away the soot. Gold gleamed beneath the grime, melted into a shapeless mass. He turned it over in his hand and his stomach dropped. Gemstones dotted the other side. The blue and yellow sapphires of Lore and Aldaan still glittered, whole. The shattered remnants of the emerald of Roberian swam between them. "Headmaster Tolmarni," he breathed in disbelief.

Swallowing hard, Arrick closed his fingers around the remainder of the Headmaster's signet ring. He rose and returned to the hallway to display it flat on his palm. The other councilors stared at it, stunned to silence.

"It must have been a free mage," Arrick said. The cool metal felt heavy in his hand. He didn't know what to do with it. "I can think of no other way for the headmaster to be killed in this fashion."

"An Aldaanan assassin?" Minet asked. She bore little love for Eyrion; she was one of few women on the council and the only one brave enough to take Arrick's side in opposing the war. He saw no anger in her expression, only thought.

Orneld, on the other hand, gave Arrick a dark look. The old man would have supported Eyrion in anything, even if the headmaster had ordered mages to walk off the side of the school and fall into the sea. "Or an assassin hired by someone closer to home."

"Please," Arrick said, meeting Orneld's eye with a neutral expression. "We are all councilors. I did not agree with his decisions, but I didn't hate the man. But this needs to be taken to the council at once. Minet, please gather the others into the lecture hall. The rest of you may speak your opinions there." He tore his gaze from Orneld to glance at the other Masters with them, most of whom merely bowed their heads and turned away.

Only Orneld lingered, staring at him for a long time before he followed the others out of the burned building. Arrick couldn't begrudge the old man for his suspicion. The possibility the council would peg the matter on him didn't escape his consideration. He hadn't been quiet in his opposition, and if something befell Eyrion, there were few mages who could stand as Arrick's rival for the position of Headmaster of the Grand College and Archmage of Lore.

Sighing, Arrick turned the melted ring over in his hand before he slid it into his pocket and moved after the other mages. There was nothing to be done. They would have a long night ahead of them, but if nothing else, at least he was sure of one thing.

The war was over.

18

ALDAEON FALLS

Sera closed her eyes and tried to focus on the mage-barrier, wishing she could shut her ears to the noise of the people crowded close on every side. She and Alira lingered close to the door, just in case Garam needed them. If they'd been any farther back in the building, they would have been trapped by the press of bodies. They came uncomfortably close to being trapped now.

She didn't like having everyone clustered in one spot, but there was no other way for them to shield Aldaeon's people against the college mages. Someone had suggested their communal dinner hall and, while it wasn't the most comfortable arrangement, she had to agree it was easier to defend than the tower.

Sweat beaded her brow despite the cold that blew in through the open doors. The frigid air was a welcome respite from the heat that grew from the crowd that packed the hall from end to end. The cries of children rose above the anxious murmurs of their parents. Some adults cried, too. Sera wished they would be quiet, then berated herself for the thought. Their lives hung in a precarious balance, with only two mages by the doorway to keep all of the Grand College's forces at bay. But she needed to concentrate, and the longer she held the shield, the more the sounds of frightened people around her grated on her nerves.

Alira touched her shoulder, a gentle gesture of comfort and sympathy.

"I should be out there," Prince Vicamros grumbled behind them.

Sera opened her eyes. The prince had made the same complaint a dozen times already. He paced near the door—the only open space—in restless frustration. The constant click of his boot heels on the stone threatened to drive her mad.

"Garam wanted you here," she said, though she didn't know why she bothered. They'd been over it all before.

"I should be helping," Vicamros protested. He spun toward her with a hand pressed to his breastplate. "These are my people. I should be out there protecting them, not hiding under shelter like a coward."

"Hiding?" Alira blinked. "Oh, no, Highness. You must misunderstand Captain Kaith's intentions."

Sera turned to the other woman in surprise. Alira looked worn, but her smile was supportive and serene.

Vicamros paused his pacing. "What do you mean?"

"You aren't the only soldier here." The white-robed Master mage swept a hand toward the crowd. A handful of men in armor remained near the front of the hall. "You aren't cowards. You're the last line of defense. Should the barrier fall, everyone would look for a leader among the panic. Who better than the crown prince? Why do you think Captain Kaith entrusted you with this job?"

His frown of displeasure slowly melted into begrudging acceptance. "I suppose that makes sense."

Resisting a smirk, Sera closed her eyes again.

Something pushed against the mage-barrier. For a moment, she thought the mages had come close enough to try and tear it down. Then the sensation changed, and another thread of energy joined the stream they used to hold the shield. A trickle at first, just enough to let them know someone else was trying to aid them. Then a torrent of power surged into the barrier, lifting such a weight from her that Sera almost collapsed in relief.

Alira caught her by the arms and held her steady. "Clever boy!" she laughed. "Who taught him that, I wonder?"

Whether the woman meant Rune or Rhyllyn, Sera wasn't sure. Her eyes unfocused as she concentrated on the flow of energy through the barrier. "They're pulling power through the shield?" She'd never realized such a thing was possible, but she hadn't thought about it, either. She tried to relax, grateful for the lighter load, but concern filtered into her thoughts. If it was that easy for a mage to join after the barrier was established, how easy would it be for the college mages to unravel it? She knew anchoring it to the earth created a weak point, but they needed the extra support the anchor offered. Without an anchor, she didn't think they'd be able to sustain the barrier at all.

Alira nodded. "So it would seem. Now we just have to hope he can do something useful with it."

Sera said nothing. With the shield reinforced by a free mage, she sank to the floor, seeking rest. As if reading her mind, Alira settled on the floor, too. Sera held tight to her ties to the barrier, just in case, but the burden of keeping it erect and stable was on someone else's shoulders now.

Prince Vicamros lingered beside them, though he stared out beyond the open doors.

The sounds of battle were all but lost in the noise of people. Not for the first time, Sera found herself glad Aldaeon was a small city. Or, small compared to the Royal City, she thought. Aldaan as a whole was isolated, sparsely populated, and home to only a handful of settlements. Giving the territory equal footing in the triad was only formality, and she suspected that if King Vicamros ever expanded his rule, Aldaan would end up being swallowed by another province. But she couldn't deny the benefits the mages of Aldaan had provided as allies. The schools in the Royal City taught strange, useful things because of the free mages.

They had offered useful gifts, too. The magic-nullifying barrier that sheltered the Royal City was one, as were the pendants that allowed mages to defy it. Sera touched the pendant around her neck as it came to mind. She never removed it, though she sometimes wondered how much power was necessary to create such objects. Embedding magic in something lifeless wasn't possible for anyone but the Aldaanan. The mages in the Grand College had spent centuries trying. As far as she knew, they continued to fail.

Her pendant hummed with power between her finger and thumb. Only a handful of mages had been declared trustworthy enough to wield power within the Royal City. The Aldaanan had selected her and crafted her pendant accordingly. She frowned and twisted the chain between her fingers. If she couldn't protect their home, would the Aldaanan still trust her with such a gift? And if they didn't return, did their approval even matter?

Something prickled at the edge of her senses. Sera turned, alarmed. "Alira—"

"I feel them," the other mage said, her voice tight, drawn.

Prince Vicamros muttered an oath.

Sera leaped to her feet and joined him at the door. She shuddered as a chill washed through her, but it had nothing to do with the cold.

Outside, Rhyllyn stood with his back to the hall, his hands raised as if to ward off the endless ranks of college mages spread before him.

The mages moved in unison, swiveled toward the tower and raised their arms. Alira shrieked the boy's name as she shoved Sera aside and burst into a run.

Together, the mages struck.

The mage-barrier shattered and magic struck Sera like a whiplash between the eyes. She cried out and reeled backwards. Someone caught her; she didn't see who. Stars flashed in her field of vision and she blinked hard to clear her eyes. Frightened screams flooded the hall. When her sight returned, her heart threatened to choke her.

Rune and Rhyllyn stood alone between their shelter and the sea of enemy mages. The air around them almost glowed as energy passed from one to the other. They were linked again, without the shield, and Rune drew power without restraint. The upper half of the tower hovered above them, but the air distorted and rippled beneath the stone as the flows Rune wielded to support it threatened to come undone.

Men in armor rushed from every direction and clashed with the wall of mages. Bolts of energy streaked through the sky and knocked gryphons from the air. Feathers wafted from the skies as the pained screams of eagles filled Sera's ears.

"Come on." Alira caught her arm and dragged her out into the snow. "We've got to help them!"

Sera stumbled and grimaced. The snow gleamed in the sun and made her temples throb anew. "I can't," she gasped. "I need a moment."

"You don't have a moment," Garam barked. His voice startled her and she spun to face him. He didn't give her a chance to speak. "They need you. This is our last chance!" He took her free arm and helped her find her feet.

"Sera!" Rune called to her over his shoulder, his face every bit as pleading as her brother's. "The tower!" His knees buckled with exertion. Stones fell around him from the broken spire he couldn't hold.

She thrust Garam and Alira away. The ground swayed beneath her—or perhaps she rocked on her feet—and her head pounded. She tried to ignore it as she pushed herself to a sprint. Halfway between the dinner hall and Rune, she found her balance, stopped to concentrate, and drew a breath.

Magic filled her as air filled her lungs. Her fingers twitched and she curled them into her palms to keep them still. She twisted the energy into threads, more delicate than the wild flows that filled the air around her, and spun them into something tangible.

Alira caught the edge of her power and funneled herself into it to push it farther. Rhyllyn joined a moment later, his raw power refined into something useful by what Sera could only assume was Rune's doing. She shut the other mages out of her thoughts, closed her eyes and focused on the rippling power she tried to control. Cold tore through her, sapping her strength. The new barrier they worked to forge pushed beneath the stones that hung in midair. She couldn't falter now.

A gryphon screamed. Her eyes snapped open as the tawny creature drew a shattered wing close, curled in on itself and plummeted into the crowd of mages.

Ria.

Rune spun to watch her fall. A wordless shout of rage tore from his throat. A surge of power seized the barrier Sera held and twisted the flows into a new form. She started forward, but a strong hand closed on her arm.

"Don't," Garam barked as he pulled her back toward the hall.

She resisted, digging in her heels and staring in horror.

Stone heaved and the shattered tower rolled over like a wave. It crested above the army of mages and crashed down over them. The earth beneath her feet shuddered with every impact. Screams of pain and terror filled the air.

"Don't look," her brother's voice rasped beside her ear.

Something small and cold touched her hand. She started and looked down as Rhyllyn wrapped his small hand around her little finger and hid behind her legs. Power rippled in the air around him, though it flowed through him as easily as water poured through a sieve. His blue eyes were wide with fright and for a moment, she wasn't sure if Garam had spoken to her or the child.

Dust rolled up from the battlefield, creating a merciful veil to hide the fate of the mages and men. Sera choked back tears and sank to her knees as the dust turned the sky red. Garam touched her shoulder, his face growing solemn as the quaking subsided and left deathly silence in its wake. The soft clatter of shifting stones echoed somewhere in the dust cloud, followed by the quiet rattle of pebbles as they rolled to a rest on the bloodstained earth.

She squeezed her eyes closed. "Are they—?"

"Don't look," Garam repeated soberly.

RUNE SCRAMBLED OVER THE STONES, cursing every time he slipped. Rock tumbled and shifted as he moved across the ruin. His claws snagged on white cloth—a mage's robe—and he shook his foot free. Somewhere ahead, he heard a rattle among the tower's remains. He pushed toward it through the dust, his heart in his throat.

Nearby, wounded mages groaned, low and mournful. Ignoring them, he waved the dust away. Wind stirred at his fingertips before he knew he'd summoned it, and the air around him cleared.

Feathers stuck up from the rubble at odd angles. Rune's pulse accelerated and he bounded across the debris to cast chunks of stone aside.

A soft, wheezing rasp escaped the gryphon as he uncovered her.

"Ria," he panted.

She twisted her head to look at him, her golden eyes hazy. "Ah... the Champion."

Rune seized a large slab and strained to move it from her wing. It didn't move. He gritted his teeth and dug in his claws. Somehow, he gathered the strength. The slab flipped over and slid down the incline, atop the rest of the tower's remains.

The gryphon's breath was fast, shallow. Even after she was uncovered, she did not stir.

A bitter chill clawed at his heart. Rune knelt beside her,

spread his hands above her prone form, and hesitated. "Ria, I—I can't heal you, I—"

"No," she agreed in quiet resignation. "And yet, poison as it was, magic always intrigued me." Her beak parted in a weak approximation of a smile.

His hands still hovered above her. Unsure what to do with them, he did the only thing that felt natural. Her eyes brightened as he stroked her ruffled feathers.

He swallowed hard against the too-familiar feeling that lodged itself in his throat. "I'll call for the others. They'll know—"

Ria hissed softly, cutting him short. "It's too late for that." Her good wing lifted to expose her side, where a thick, black substance oozed from a long wound.

Ichor. Black blood. Like his. Rune's eyes flashed to her face.

"I told you," the gryphon mused softly. "The wing... the wing is not so bad, but I can already feel the taint growing in me... making me... cold." Strangely, she chuckled. "Would that all of us were so strong as you."

Fear. That was the name of that lump in his throat. He'd felt it often in the past year, but not like this. Not since he'd held his father. "I'm not," he choked. Grief, still raw, bubbled to the surface and threatened to burst.

"No? You have to be." She grinned at him, though her head sank back against the stone as her third eyelid drifted partway across her eye. "You're the only one who's survived this poison in your soul. You'll have to teach the little one, as well. Ah, his hats... Etta will have to finish..."

Rune's clawed fingers curled in her feathered mane.

Her head lolled, her eyes glazed. "I wondered," she murmured. "To be full of such poison... full of such hate... to be so full of poison, but still you survive. What must you be?"

"Ria—"

She pressed a clawed forefoot to his chest. "The antidote," she whispered with a grin. "That's what you must be."

He caught her foot and held it with both hands. Her eyes grew hazier, her breath a short, shallow pant. The sense of helplessness that washed over him became a crushing weight. Even with everything Firal had taught him, there was nothing he could do. No way to ease her pain, no way to shorten her suffering. All he could do was sit, wait, powerless to do anything but watch as the magic consumed her.

Slowly, Rune leaned forward. He cradled her neck and buried his face in her feathers.

"Here," Garam's booming voice called behind them. The rubble crunched beneath booted feet.

A gentle hand touched Rune's back. He didn't move.

"It's bad," Sera said beside him, soft and sympathetic. "But the wound is worse. I think it will take her before the blight does."

"Small blessings," the captain muttered.

Sera leaned forward and ruffled the gryphon's feathers. They tickled against Rune's neck as they moved. "Thank you, winged one," she whispered. "You honor us with your sacrifice."

"Mages?" Garam asked.

"It's not the time, Garam," she replied, an edge in her voice.

"We don't have the time," the captain said.

She sighed. "They've gone. They'll regroup in the mountains. Those who are still here..." She paused and sighed again. "No one remains." Her hand rubbed across Rune's back, gentle and soothing. It did nothing for the ache that throbbed in his chest.

Garam grunted softly in acceptance. "We need to send word to the king. A Gate would be best—"

"Really, Garam, you're so heartless sometimes." Sera stood and worked her way across the sliding stones, rock clattering in her wake. She said something else, but it was in a harsh whisper, and Rune couldn't make out the words. Their voices faded with their footsteps.

Ria's feathers felt warm against his skin, a comfort she'd shared dozens of times since she'd joined the army's procession and escorted them to the north. It didn't feel like the handful of weeks it had been. Ria was a kindred spirit, a misfit alongside him, a companion who had been warm and welcoming when the rest of the army still eyed him with distrust.

A friend—one of precious few he'd ever known.

Rune's claws curled in the soft, downy fluff against the gryphon's skin as he fought to hold his composure.

His breath steadied as Ria's faded and finally stopped.

19

A PROMISE FULFILLED

THE REMAINING COUNCIL WAS SO SMALL THAT NONDAR DIDN'T understand why they bothered to use the council hall near the top of the tower. Tradition, he supposed, or maybe formality no one was ready to abandon. He would have been happier to hold the meeting in his office, or even at the round table in his private quarters. Despite having his cane at one side and Kytenia at the other, it was still difficult for him to walk. His leg didn't work like it ought to, and though he had his wits about him, his tongue often felt otherwise.

"Are you sure you won't need me in there?" Kytenia asked when they paused outside the door.

Nondar clamped his jaw, sucked in a breath, and reminded himself she was only doing her job. He'd been the one to select her to help. He couldn't criticize her for offering assistance, though he did wish she would accept his answer the first time he gave it. Once was more than enough. "Quite sure. I am more than capable of moving myself from a doorway to a chair. Besides, this is a formal meeting of council and you are not yet a Master. Not that I imagine you would want to be present. I'm sure there will be unpleasant things said about you."

The corners of her mouth twitched, but her expression didn't change otherwise. He patted her arm. Her level head would serve her well. He only wished the mages he was about to confront were as good at keeping their composure.

"I will send for you you when I am finished here," Nondar said as he took hold of the door. "But don't wait for me. This may take some time."

The girl nodded and took a step back, though he knew she would hover beside the door until she was certain he'd reached his seat. He slipped inside and shut the door behind him before she could peek.

Edagan stood beside the council table, but Anaide had already seated herself. A handful of Masters ringed the room, though not as many as he expected, given the nature of what they were to discuss. The only mages with authority to speak on the matter were the two women at the table, but he had believed the rest of the temple's masters would be curious enough about the decisions being made that they would come to listen. Lifetree knew they had opinions on everything, and were very good at ensuring their unwanted opinions were shared. Nondar had not anticipated this meeting would be any different.

Anaide watched him as he made his way to the table, the way a wolf might watch a lame deer. She expected a feast, that much was evident. A part of him almost delighted in knowing she wouldn't have it.

"Fair morning, Archmage," Edagan said, her tone cool. She waited until he reached his chair and made himself comfortable before she sank into her seat. She still recognized him as her superior, which spoke volumes. Their manners made it clear who they thought would take his place.

Nondar grunted as he hung his cane from the edge of the table. "The council hall is emptier every time we sit in it. I will be glad to see the country's unrest over and have our mages prospering again."

A funny, pinched look twisted Anaide's face. She didn't think he would live that long. He hoped she was mistaken.

With the three of them seated, all that remained of the temple's council had gathered. The Masters around the edges of the room shifted in anticipation.

"Bringing the temple's council back to full power will go a long way toward helping us recover, I'm sure. We are overdue to have leadership set over the Houses again." Anaide paused and laced her fingers together. "I hope you will hear out our suggestions, Archmage." Her tone took an unusual tilt back toward respect, as if she remembered herself too late.

Nondar held back a snort, but he arched one bushy eyebrow. "Yes," he said slowly, as his gaze shifted to Edagan. "I trust you both have suggestions."

"It is unorthodox," Edagan said, "but in light of the fracture the temple experienced last year, one of our recommendations for House leadership has been selected from the senior magelings instead of our Masters."

No one spoke, but Nondar saw a number of surprised faces around the edges of the room. No doubt some of the Masters present had come to listen because they thought they stood a chance at gaining rank. One or two even looked offended, but no one said a word.

"We have no reason to doubt the loyalty of magelings," Anaide added hastily. "They have served us unerringly and they have never served as Master beneath another Archmage, so there's no need for them to readjust to new rules or new leadership."

"They have served us unerringly," he agreed. He was not sure he believed they lacked ties to temple's previous leadership, but he had resigned himself to the fact bias would be impossible to escape.

Edagan wet her lips with her tongue in an uncharacteristic display of nervousness. "Which is why we suggest Shymin Silaron for Master of the House of Healing."

Nondar's eyebrows rose, carving furrows of surprise into his tall forehead.

"She has progressed remarkably in the past several weeks," she continued. "She progressed to blue just yesterday, but she's strong in her Gift and well-suited to remaining in the temple, and comfortable with the new queen's rule, besides."

"We realize you likely had another mage in mind," Anaide said, unable to hide a note of anxiety in her voice. "But we feel she is the best option we have."

Leaning back in his chair, Nondar twisted his long beard around one knobby finger. Their reasoning grew suddenly clear. He was mindful of his expression, letting his surprise shift to deep thought as he watched their faces. They thought he was troubled, feared he might reject the proposition. If anything, he was amused. For them to suggest Shymin as Master of Healing could only mean they'd adopted the girl as their new champion. A voice to help them leverage more power in council when, as they believed would happen, one of them became Archmage. The thought made his brows lift again.

"I understand your reasoning," he said as a mask of concern settled on his face. "But I would like to address the other choices before we make a decision regarding the House of Healing. I find myself deeply invested in that selection, since I must take whoever is chosen as an apprentice before they can assume the role. I am sure you understand. However, you raise interesting points regarding the choice of magelings. Therefore, I would like to propose Rikka of the blue robes as Master of Wind."

The two women exchanged glances. Edagan turned her hands upward in place of a shrug.

"I don't see why not," Anaide said.

Edagan nodded. "Rikka is skilled enough, and we are pleased to see you are receptive to our suggestion to consider magelings."

"So it shall be written." Nondar straightened and motioned to one of the other Masters nearby. "Fetch some paper, a quill, and some ink. If none of us object, we might as well make it official."

The Master bowed with a murmur of assent and vanished into one of the adjacent offices. So many of the offices stood empty that Nondar often forgot they existed. He did not speak again until the Master returned to lay the requested supplies on the table. Then he extended a hand toward the two women at the table with him. "Anaide, if you would?"

"Of course, Archmage." She moved to his side and sat, turning the paper so he could read as she wrote. She uncorked the ink bottle and penned the declaration in her best handwriting.

Nondar waited for her to finish before he went on. "Next, the matter of a Master for the House of Fire."

"For fire, our recommendation is Balen of the white," Anaide said without hesitation.

"Balen of Wethertree?" The choice surprised him, but Nondar was not displeased. The man was closer in age to Shymin and Rikka than the women at the table, though he was likely still twice the age of the girls. Surprisingly easygoing for a mage Gifted in fire, Balen had helped screen potential magelings for several years before Kifel's orders had brought all mages back to Ilmenhith and Firal had moved them to Kirban. Nondar glanced up, expecting to see the man among the spectators. He was not.

"We had initially considered Tilla, but she lacks the patience the Master of a House should have with magelings," Edagan explained. "Because of his prior work with them, we feel Balen is the best choice."

Nondar could think of no reason to object. In truth, he hadn't put much consideration into who would take the House of Fire. Training of Rikka, Kytenia, and Ellaith had occupied most of his attention. But the suggestion of Balen caught him off guard. He'd expected them to select mages who already had some connection to the two of them, preparing a council that would weigh favor in their direction.

If they believed Edagan would remain head of Earth and Anaide would hold the House of Water until Nondar's death, they only held authority over two of the five Houses. They needed the third House as leverage to keep control, an advantage Balen would not grant. Although the Archmage was entitled to executive decisions, the five major Houses had a great deal of input. As it stood, Balen was a neutral party.

Nondar twisted his beard and shifted, startled. Ah, but they believed that would give them majority. They thought he meant to seat Kytenia as head of Healing and strove to replace her with Shymin. Anaide—who they clearly believed was to become the next Archmage—would be free to elevate whoever she pleased to lead the House of Water, which left only Rikka and Balen outside their camp. A sense of smug satisfaction drifted over him. They had no way of knowing he'd already named his heir. He lifted his eyes at last. The two women still waited for him to speak. "I believe Balen is an excellent choice and just the sort of leader the House of Fire needs as the temple recovers. I agree; he shall be seated on the council."

Anaide added the decision to the proclamation, but said nothing. If anything, she looked more concerned. Nondar resisted the urge to smile. Now they were back to Shymin, the bet they didn't think they'd win. He had intended Ellaith for the position, but they had no way of knowing. He'd thought Ellaith a good choice, one that allowed him to avoid accusations of favoritism by raising three magelings connected to the queen. Little did Anaide and Edagan know, they'd made his job easier.

"And now we are back to Healing." He watched them closely as he spoke. Edagan's eyes tightened at the corners and Anaide's mouth took the same twist it always did when she was worried.

"For the seat of Master of the House of Healing," he drawled, savoring the way they moved to the edge of their seats, "I name Shymin, as the council recommends."

Edagan's mouth fell open.

Anaide clapped her hands together. "You agree!"

"She is an excellent healer. I will begin compiling materials immediately to ensure she knows all that she must." He inclined his head and motioned for Anaide to write. She did so hastily, her uneven handwriting betraying her elation. They thought it a victory. He struggled not to laugh.

"And now you must name your successor," Edagan said, casting a glance toward Anaide that he dared say was almost excited.

"Oh, I have." Nondar allowed a note of warmth into his voice. "Signed and sealed. The order was sent to Her Majesty, Queen Firal first thing this morning. Initiation into the council as future Archmage will begin immediately after the queen's response. But until then, we shall not speak of it. It was a difficult decision, but I'm certain it was the right one." His eyes settled on Anaide. The two women almost glowed.

"I trust the council will support her unerringly?" he asked, twining his gnarled fingers together.

"Of course, Archmage," Edagan said in a rush.

"Good." He considered saying more, but swallowed the words before they could escape. It was best not to kick the hornet's nest yet. "Now, for the next matter. We should discuss the possibility of reestablishing smaller chapter houses across the island. We cannot gather support until we offer something to the people again, and I would like to formulate a plan to present to Her Majesty." He opened his hands in invitation to the Masters that ringed the room. "All of you are welcome to speak on this matter. Come, sit."

The rest of the mages drew chairs and sat along the empty table, reminding Nondar how little time had passed since the council had been full and the temple thriving.

"We have some suggestions, Archmage." A Master he didn't recognize sat at his elbow.

He gestured for her to continue as he made himself more comfortable in his chair. The Master listed cities and waypoints he'd already considered and he half listened, his thoughts elsewhere.

Firal would be opening his letter any moment, making the announcement within the palace and cementing Kytenia's claim.

KYTENIA STOOD as the doors opened. Masters filed into the hallway and disappeared to lower floors of the tower. Nondar was the last to step out. His brows rose with surprise when she came to the doorway to aid him. She didn't know why. Assisting him was her job.

He laid a hand on her arm and gave her a look that said he was appreciative, though he frowned. "I thought you'd be elsewhere, child."

"I thought you would need me." She didn't dare admit she'd been afraid to leave. He was old and frail, but as stubborn as ever. The last thing she wanted to do was offend him.

Nondar turned his head to watch the Masters depart. "Well, I'm glad to see you. We'll have much to talk about. There are things you are not yet prepared for, and you need to be ready for anything."

Kytenia followed his gaze uncertainly. That he'd declared her his successor had been a heavy secret to keep, and she wasn't sure she was ready for the aftermath of it being revealed.

"Don't worry, child," the old man said. She could only figure he'd guessed her thoughts from her expression. "They don't know. Not yet. The announcement will come from the queen, and once you are named by her, you'll have the crown's protection until I pass." He rested a hand on her shoulder, sympathetic and protective. She bowed her head.

She appreciated the concern, but it troubled her that it was needed. As a mageling, she'd never imagined there would be reason to fear Masters. Now that she was being groomed to become Archmage, she almost wished she could escape. But the thought of the temple and of Firal needing someone to manage it kept her there. Besides, she had little else to look forward to. She hadn't attended her friend's wedding, unable to make herself watch the man she'd hoped to someday wed be bound to someone else. She bit her lip and shook away the thoughts.

"Speaking of the queen," she said, dropping her tone despite the fact there was no one around to hear. "I promised I would speak to you about something on her behalf, Archmage."

He raised one thick white brow and glanced toward the stairs, then into the empty room behind him, as if he expected to find someone eavesdropping. "Why didn't she come to me herself?"

"She was going to." Kyenia fought the nervous flutter in her stomach. "She was called back to the palace before you were available, and I haven't had an opportunity to speak to you in private since." Nor had she been certain he was strong enough to carry out the task. His weakness never ceased to worry her.

Nondar did not speak. Instead, he erected a ward around them to safeguard their words and looked at her expectantly.

"She said you promised to help her," she continued, mindful to keep her tone gentle. If he couldn't remember on his own, she doubted he'd be pleased to be prompted. "That you were going to help her contact someone on the northern mainland."

Something lit in his eyes; recognition, perhaps. "Blood and earth!" His expression dissolved into anger and frustration. "That was the meaning for that look Anaide gave me. The blasted woman could have reminded me. I should have done it ages ago. I knew there was something, it hovered there, just beyond where I could reach it—"

"Who can open a Gate to the mainland, Archmage?" Kytenia interrupted, still minding her tone, nudging him back toward the matter she wasn't sure could wait any longer. Her stomach turned at the thought of Anaide and Edagan hiding information from the Archmage, but there would be time to deal with that later. Eventually, the stubborn mages would be hers to deal with.

"Me," he replied gruffly. "Only me, now. Envesi and Melora were the only other mages who knew the college well enough to

Gate there. We intended to teach others, but... Bah, that doesn't matter." He waved a hand, pulled away from her, and turned toward the stairs. He still hobbled, but his irritation made his stubbornness flare. Kytenia knew better than to assist. He'd make his way to the bottom of the tower by himself one way or another, and having her at his elbow would only make him angrier.

"Come on, girl," he called. "We'll go to the palace. Firal's court mages will escort you to the Grand College of Lore."

"Me?" She blinked in surprise and hurried after him. She fell in step alongside him, her hands curled in the skirt of her robes. "But I'm just a mageling."

"You won't be a mageling forever. Business like this will fall on your shoulders when I'm gone." His expression softened, touched by something she thought was wistful. "Though it would have been nice to visit the mainland again. It was my home, you know. Once. Hurry along, we'll tend this and then we must tend lessons. Your Northern Provincial has come a long way since you began studying with me, but your grasp of the language needs to be better if there will be dealings with that region."

She tried not to wince.

Nondar barked orders to the first cluster of Masters they passed. The group jumped and hurried to gather enough mages to open a Gate, but the Archmage's attention remained on her. "You will need to contact the current king. The college itself does not have the authority to make trade arrangements. Be brief, but clear. You may speak of the failed harvests and famine, but do not paint the country as helpless. Emphasize the value of our trade outposts and our location as a waypoint between continents. If you cannot communicate efficiently, request someone who speaks Old Aldaanan, which is what they call our tongue. And if my cousin happens to still be present on the college council and asks of me, tell him his hat is still ugly."

Kytenia shook her head at the onslaught, uncertain she'd

heard correctly. "Your cousin, Archmage?" And his hat? "Why don't you just come with me?"

"Heavens, child, it's called a joke! I'll explain it to you when you return." He didn't respond to her second question, though his face became grim.

They moved through the Gate that had been opened in the courtyard so swiftly, Kytenia's eyes had no time to adjust. She blinked hard in the dim light of the palace's Gating parlor on the other side. A handful of court Masters in blue-trimmed white leaped upright, startled to see the Archmage.

"Fetch Temar," Nondar ordered, and the mages scattered like dry leaves.

"Nondar—" Kytenia started uncertainly. The Archmage turned toward her with a finger raised, and she closed her mouth.

"I'll tell you as much as I can when you return," he said, a sad smile wreathing itself on his face. "There's still a great deal you need to know, but we will discuss it all in time."

Temar swept into the room with a look of mingled surprise and concern on her face. "Archmage, is everything well?"

Nondar cleared his throat. "Business matters. I need you to accompany my assistant on an errand. While you are there, I expect you will familiarize yourself with the region enough that you will be able to Gate her there for future errands without my assistance."

The court mage pursed her lips. "You plan to assist us now?"

His jaw clenched and one of his thick brows twitched with irritation. "Do as you're told, Temar. I am old, not incompetent."

"Of course, Archmage." Temar snapped her fingers at the mages around the room. "The freshest of you, over here. Prepare a Gate. The Archmage will lead."

Nondar turned back to Kytenia. "Remember, child. Brief, but clear. Temar will lead a Gate to return here when you are finished."

"But I still don't know what I'm doing, or what I'm to say!"

Kytenia protested. Her stomach knotted on itself until she thought she'd be ill.

Nondar patted her cheek. "You'll manage, girl."

She swallowed hard and turned as directed when he pointed to the archway behind her. The mages had already begun. The air hummed with energy and the arch crackled with spiderwebbing lines of power. She squeezed her eyes shut against the brilliance. Temar took hold of her arm and gave her a gentle squeeze of reassurance.

Behind them, one of the mages shouted.

Kytenia's eyes flew open and she wheeled, just in time to see the Archmage fall to his knees.

"Go!" Temar snapped, hauling her forward.

"Nondar!" Kytenia shrieked. She struggled against the Master's grasp, but the woman's hand held her like a vise.

Temar dragged her through the Gate an instant before it collapsed with an ear-splitting boom.

NEW LEADERSHIP

"Headmaster Arrick?"

The title made him feel odd. It had been a single day since he'd been named Eyrion's replacement, so it was no surprise, but Arrick suspected the title would sound strange for a long time. He lifted his head, tapping the end of his lacquered wooden pen against his mouth. "Yes?"

"There's a pair of mages here from..." The messenger paused. "Well, I don't know where. We can't understand them well, their speech is broken. They have asked to see someone who speaks Old Aldaanan."

Alarmed, Arrick dropped his pen. They'd found no conclusive evidence of what had happened to Eyrion, but most of the college assumed the Aldaanan were to blame. Just hearing the name made his mouth go dry.

Yet most of the free mages of Aldaan spoke the regional dialect without difficulty, he reasoned. If mages had arrived speaking the Old Aldaanan language, it was more likely that they were refugees. Come to think of it, the missing magelings— those transferred to the college from some obscure school on an island—had spoken Old Aldaanan when they first arrived. Perhaps two of them had returned. He'd assumed them among the dead. Even with the college all but empty, a handful of mages had been lost in that fire. Their deaths hurt the college dearly.

Arrick pushed his chair back from his desk and stood. His private quarters made for a cramped office, but it wouldn't be long before the headmaster's office overlooking the sea was restored. "Very well. Bring them to the lecture hall and call for..." He touched a finger to his chin, considering. Most of the mages who were fluent in Old Aldaanan had been sent north with the army. He'd sent orders for the mages to return the moment he'd been named headmaster, but with the weather that had plagued Eyrion's army, the bird he'd sent could take days to reach them. He could only think of a few other options. "Call for either Councilor Survas or Councilor Parthanus from the Royal City. Gate them here at once."

The messenger blinked. "There's no one else?"

"They will be easiest to reach." Of the two, Arrick preferred Redoram Parthanus. Survas struck him as a weasel, though the man had gotten on well with the former headmaster. Then again, Eyrion Tolmarni had sometimes struck him as a weasel, too. But it wouldn't do to speak ill of the dead, and thinking it was little better.

Arrick stretched and pressed his knuckles into his back. "Well go on, then. The councilors won't summon themselves."

The messenger bobbed in a shallow bow and left.

After the boy departed, Arrick stared at the empty space where he'd been, frowning in thought. He had a thousand things to tend to. Trying to contact the army to the north was most important, and the college had to be settled. He didn't want to waste time dealing with magelings, if that was who awaited him. But if anyone else was capable of handling the situation, it would have been handled already. His Old Aldaanan was rudimentary at best, and he didn't know why the task had landed on his desk. But if a councilor from the Royal City was going to be involved, it wouldn't do for the headmaster himself to be absent. Especially a headmaster so newly titled.

The college's council held understandable reservations about elevating him to the position. Even after the previous day's meeting and discourse, he imagined some still suspected he was involved in Eyrion's untimely demise. But the headmaster's death had shaken him too, and ultimately the council decided he was faultless. Or the majority had, anyway.

Sighing, Arrick made his way from his quarters. He didn't see any reason to move yet, especially with the former Archmage and headmaster's office burned. His own room worked perfectly well and needed no adjustment.

The noisy peal of hammers greeted him as soon as he stepped into the hall, a faint but present reminder that he still hadn't arranged for new furnishings for the offices. More troubles among the countless number of things that needed his attention. And all to be fit in around his dealings with the aftermath of Eyrion's war.

A pair of women waited in the lecture hall when he arrived. One wore a blue mageling's robe, but the blue-trimmed white of a Master on the other made him pause. Arrick frowned and studied the two from the entryway. They didn't look familiar. Neither one of them resembled the magelings said to be missing, and though the elder wore Master white, he'd never seen white robes trimmed with color before. Nor had he seen the heavy liner that marked her eyes. Visitors from afar, he decided. Though why they spoke Old Aldaanan, he didn't know.

"Good day," he called as he strode down into the lecture hall to join them.

The two women startled and turned. The younger gazed at him with wide eyes. Then she seemed to remember herself, and spread the skirt of her robes in a graceful bow. "Good day." Her accent was thick, but she'd understood him. Perhaps they were visiting from Aldaan after all.

"I've called for a translator," Arrick said, slow and clear. "He should be arriving soon."

The younger woman looked to the elder, seeming troubled, but neither spoke. Instead, their eyes shifted to something behind him.

Arrick glanced over his shoulder and did everything he could to keep from grimacing. The messenger had returned with Lord Survas at his heels. Arrick exhaled and forced himself to smile. "Good afternoon, Survas."

"Councilor Survas," the short man snapped, brushing at his velvet sleeves in irritation. "Or Lord Survas. We are not friends, Master Arrick."

"Headmaster Arrick," he corrected, with a twinge of amusement at the startled look on the small man's face. "Or Archmage, if you prefer."

"Archmage," Survas muttered, a tad more respectfully. At least the man learned fast.

"We seem to have visitors." Arrick gestured to the women. "I've just arrived, myself, but they had already requested a translator. How is your Old Aldaanan, Lord Survas?"

Survas made a sound of displeasure. His lip peeled back. "No worse than the last time I was called to translate. Is this the only purpose scholars have, these days? Translation?"

"Well, it is the reason scholars learn other languages to begin with. I'm sure they will do their best to answer in our tongue if they can, but if they falter, please repeat the question for them and translate their responses." Arrick didn't wait for a reply before he addressed the woman in white. "What are your names?"

"Temar Ergain," she replied. Her hand swept toward the mageling beside her. "Kytenia Silaron."

Arrick touched his chest. "And I am Arrick Ortath, Headmaster of the Grand College of Lore. What business do you have with the college?"

Temar glanced between him and Survas. Sighing, the short

man translated and even attempted to look patient while she replied.

"She says they have been sent to seek audience with the ruler of Lore." Survas sniffed, as if the notion were offensive. "She asks who our reigning monarch is."

Arrick didn't look at the scholar again, lest he snap at the man's rude manner. "King Vicamros rules the Triad, which is the united countries of Lore, Roberian and Aldaan. But I'm afraid an audience with the king may be difficult to obtain right now. Our provinces are just ending a civil war."

"Do they need to know that, Archmage?" Survas asked in a low tone.

The headmaster's smile faltered. "They need to know whatever I deem fit to tell them."

Neither woman batted an eye as the shorter man translated.

"She says she understands, but their need is urgent. Their country faces hardship after poor harvests, and they are in immediate need of new trade options to feed their people."

Arrick's brows rose and the last of his smile evaporated. "Why would Vicamros want to open trade with a starving country?"

"Precisely my thoughts," Survas muttered. He sneered as he related the sentiment, though the younger woman only arched a brow and the elder didn't move at all. This time, the younger of them spoke.

"She says their country is rich in corundum gems, and they would be interested in offering our king rights to a percentage of the mine's production in exchange for a steady supply of food."

The headmaster rubbed his chin. That did sound like something the king would be interested in, especially with the flourishing state of agriculture in Roberian. Access to a gem mine could provide benefit for the college, too, if he could determine a way to involve himself.

He dropped his hand and smiled warmly. "Although it is difficult to gain audience with the king, I may be able to help. As

Archmage of Lore, I am to meet with him soon. If I may loan the two of you my office, you are welcome to pen a formal letter making such an offer to His Majesty. I will gladly present the request during our meeting. I am surprised to see mages wearing the college's colors from a place that speaks such an old language, but it is an honor to help anyone tied to us."

The young woman's face changed, her expression odd. Arrick thought it confusion, though he couldn't imagine why. She asked something of the white-robed woman, who only shrugged before she met the headmaster's eye.

"She says they would be pleased to accept your offer. She requests that after the letter is penned, you grant her enough assistance to open a Gate back to their home country." Survas paused to ask a question. Both women nodded. "They also wish to determine when they should return to hear of the king's decision."

"My meeting with King Vicamros is scheduled to happen within a week. If they return after that, we should have an answer, or at least an idea of whether or not he will meet their ruler for negotiations." Arrick clapped his hands together and smiled again. "Now, have them follow me. You come, too. We shall show them to my quarters so they may write that letter, then find help to Gate them home. Please let them know I have enjoyed this discussion, but I have a great deal of business to tend before the day is out, and we shall have to part ways after their letter is complete." He tilted his head toward the entrance as he turned, rubbing his hands together and breathing a sigh of relief and satisfaction.

If he could convince Vicamros he was involved in finding a new trade source and a mine of reasonable value, obtaining the finances and leverage necessary to repair and refurnish the college might be easier than he thought.

2 1

HOMECOMING

DUST IN THE AIR GAVE SUNRISE A BLOODY CAST. THE LIGHT TAINTED the snow fields, and sunset the night before had looked no different. It was a fitting color, Rune thought, a match for the heavy scent of iron and death.

The night had been still, except for a scant handful of mages who had scraped their way back out of the rubble. They had crawled off to regroup in the mountains, or perhaps to flee, but there were so few of them that Garam declared pursuit a waste of time. The presence of mages still tingled in Rune's senses, but he could no longer puzzle out which lived and which had died, leaving traces of power behind.

Once no more survivors clawed their way to the surface, Garam's men had gone out to search for soldiers missing from the ranks. Few had been found. They could only wonder what happened to the rest.

Garam, Sera, and Alira didn't think the mages would be back in the night. All three were eager to seek their beds, though everyone agreed it was better to stay within the village instead of returning to their camp. Rune alone stayed up, watching the dust and debris settle, unable to sleep.

Killing wasn't new. Rune didn't enjoy it, but it wasn't new.

237

What he'd done should have horrified him. Instead, he wrestled with feelings he couldn't untangle. Discomfort was all he could identify.

Watching people shamble about the wreckage of the tower in the dawn's light made him as uncomfortable as the stillness of night. He rolled the runestone that matched his scar between his fingers again and then made himself put it away. It had tumbled between his fingers all night, as restless as his thoughts.

He'd been unable to keep them from pulling the tower down. He'd dropped it on the mages and on their own men. If the second barrier hadn't held, he would have dropped it on Rhyllyn, Alira, and Sera, too. On himself.

Perhaps that would have been better.

Soft footsteps approached him from behind. Countless people huddled inside the dinner hall, afraid to return to their homes, but Rune didn't need to look to know who joined him. The captain bore a certain steadfast presence that was easy to detect, even without magic involved.

"I understand now," Rune said. He didn't stir from where he sat on the front steps of the hall. He'd expected his companions, knew they wouldn't rest easy, the captain least of all. He stared at nothing and slid a clawed thumb over the scar in the back of his hand as Garam sat at his side. "I didn't understand when they did it. When Filadiel and the others sealed my powers."

"Do you?" The captain watched the sky, too. It glowed yellow, faded slowly to ashen gray.

"I didn't understand how anyone could have so much strength at their fingertips and not want it. I thought they were playing the part of pariah because it made their cause seem that much more noble." Rune rested his elbows on his knees and laced his scaled fingers together, staring at his hands. "But they were right to reject it. And you were right to distrust magic. If no one had this sort of power, it would have been a fair fight. We lost too many men because they had no way to defend themselves against mages."

"But we had you." Garam glanced at him, his face stony, neutral. "You were able to stop them."

Rune shook his head. "You had Rhyllyn. It was his strength that stopped them. Mine no longer exists."

The captain stared at him for a time before his eyes drifted to the ruin of the tower. The lower half still stood, a jagged spear that reached toward the sky. "I suppose we both learned from this."

Rune raised a brow.

"I wish I could say my feelings came from something so noble, but they don't." Garam shrugged and leaned back against his hands. "I've worried about my men facing magic. About the Royal City falling under siege by forces we couldn't stop. But I disliked mages a long time before I was Captain of the Royal City Guard."

"Even though your sister's a mage?"

Garam nodded. "To be honest, there have been times I've resented her. I was young when our mother died. I knew Sera did everything in her power to help, and dozens of mages came to see our mother once her health began to fail. But there are some things magic can't do. It can't fix illness when the problem stems from the mind. I knew it, but I wasn't satisfied with that answer. It felt like no one cared to try." He sighed and rubbed his palms against his thighs. "Then I learned about other treatments. Therapies that came from knowledge and practice instead of magic. Things anyone could learn. Things I could have learned, could have used to help her. Things Sera could have learned, if she hadn't been so focused on magecraft instead."

Rune frowned. "Sera doesn't believe magic is the answer to everything. She's said as much to me, though in different words."

"I know," the captain murmured. "And I know she only did what she thought was best."

"But?"

"But it didn't save our family."

Rune said nothing more. He understood the sentiment; it was one he'd wounded himself with over and over again since he'd fled home. For all the power he'd had, it hadn't made a difference. It hadn't helped him save what mattered most. He stared at his hands for a long time, studying the scales he'd hated so long, the scar whose meaning he didn't yet understand. Perhaps he'd looked at those wrong, too. Perhaps they were lessons he hadn't yet learned.

Garam nudged his arm and rose. "Get your sword."

Rune glanced up and reached for the bare blade he'd left leaning against the stairs.

Across the field, a lone figure in white strode toward them. Rune gritted his teeth and followed the captain toward the mage. The snow crunched underfoot where it had been trodden and refroze.

When she saw the two of them coming, she raised both arms overhead in a gesture of surrender. "Captain Kaith?" She stopped at the line in the snow where the mage-barrier had touched the earth. "I've come to speak."

"You're speaking now," Garam snarled. He hadn't drawn his sword, but Rune knew he wanted to. Could have, but didn't. The captain stopped several paces away from the woman and watched her like a man might watch a rearing viper.

The mage looked at Rune. "Sheath your weapon, please. I come peacefully. The Grand College has sent me to retrieve the mages here."

"Retrieve them from beneath the rocks, then." Rune didn't move, his blade held ready to strike. "No one's going to stop you."

Garam raised a hand, signaling him to be silent. Rune growled beneath his breath. A flicker of color lit his eyes.

The mage's mouth tightened, but she drew a breath and her expression smoothed. "I have collected those I could from the mountain pass. They are working to gather the injured who still live. I don't know what has transpired here, but I have come to request your assistance in finding survivors."

"What happened here was self defense." Garam's face remained as neutral as ever, though a fire flashed in his dark eyes. "Your mages tried to destroy this city and kill its people, attacking them unprovoked. Why should we help you?"

"They are not my mages," she replied calmly. "They are mages of the Grand College of Lore, acting on orders from the former headmaster, Eyrion Tolmarni."

"*Former* headmaster?" Rune asked, earning himself a glare from the captain. He glared back and felt twinge of amusement when Garam's upper lip twitched. It was bad enough he'd spoken after being directed to stay quiet, worse that he'd stolen the question from the tip of the captain's tongue.

The woman inclined her head ever so slightly, just enough for the motion to be taken as a nod. "Headmaster Tolmarni is deceased, perished in an accidental fire. The college is in mourning, but Headmaster Arrick Ortath has wasted no time in addressing college business. It is Headmaster Ortath's opinion that Tolmarni's war against Aldaan serves no purpose. Therefore, the mages are recalled and the war is over."

"Over?" Rune repeated. He knew he'd heard her long-winded explanation correctly; he didn't need her to say it again, but he couldn't wrap his head around it. He stared past her, to where the shattered remnant of the tower lay strewn across the snow. Disbelief and a simmering anger tied themselves in knots within him.

Garam opened his mouth to speak, then closed it again. His silence made Rune's rage boil over.

"Your half-hearted peace is too late," Rune spat. His fingers felt numb from how tight he gripped his sword. He flung the blade to the ground at her feet, but she did not so much as stir. "All the good it does you! You want your mages? Look behind you. Whoever fled, whoever survived, that's all that's left. The rest of them are under that rock, along with good men we lost because they were trying to hold your mages at bay!"

"That's enough," the captain said, lifting a hand in gesture for him to settle.

"No, it isn't!" How could he settle when hundreds lay dead because of the mage in front of them? Because of *him*? Rune clenched his teeth and glowered at her. "One day! That's all the faster you had to get here, to keep this from happening. Just one day sooner!"

"It doesn't matter," Garam barked. "The war is over."

"It is over," Rune agreed. He curled his hands to fists, dug claws into his palms until they drew blood. "I ended it."

Garam caught him as he turned away, but he jerked his arm out of the captain's grasp. Rune didn't feel the cold any longer; anger burned hot in his veins.

He should have been glad for the announcement, that they wouldn't have to fight again, but all he could think of as he walked was battle. The screams of people as they were crushed, the smell of death that was stifled by the icy air. Squeezing his eyes closed, Rune tried to focus on the bite of his claws in his palms and let that pain drive all other thoughts away.

Behind him, he heard Garam giving orders, spreading the news he expected would end in celebration. Rune left the noise behind, seeking solitude to release the heavy emotions that made his chest burn. No one gave him more than fleeting glances as he made his way to the broken base of the aerie.

Despite the pain, the black blood that dripped from his hands to the snow, and his determination to focus on those alone, he couldn't stop the vision of a tawny gryphon falling from the sky.

IN THE LONG day that followed, no one seemed to notice Rune was gone. He watched the camp from the top of what remained of the aerie, perched on a stone wall shattered at knee height.

Several floors of the tower were still intact, though rubble filled some rooms and covered most of the ramp in the tower's central shaft. He doubted anyone would have wanted to climb the tower to find him anyway.

There was music below, though no one celebrated. Instead they played hymns for the dead, the covered bodies of mages laying side-by-side with the soldiers who'd fought them. He'd counted each row and adjusted the tally in his head as more corpses were recovered throughout the day. There were no gryphons among them, but he assumed they had their own traditions, funeral rites they would perform in private for loved ones lost.

A rock tumbled behind him and Rune wheeled, his eyes flashing in the evening light. He didn't want to be bothered, but when he saw Prince Vicamros clumsily making his way over the loose stone, his agitation dulled. The young man gave him an apologetic look and paused to brush dust from his legs before he advanced.

"They're going to build something over the rubble that can't be moved," the prince said, stopping in the middle of the room. He looked hesitant, like a bird ready to take flight. "A monument to the dead. They took each soldier's sword and shield, cleaned them up. The captain had them put the swords into a wagon to send home to the families. The shields will stay here as part of the monument, symbolizing that they fell defending Aldaeon."

Rune listened in silence, then turned his eyes back to the village below. Of all the people who might approach him, he hadn't expected the prince. He had nothing to say to the boy. Instead, he focused on what he could see. Small fires created orderly lights along the streets. People wandering with torches resembled fireflies in the eventide.

"I spoke to one of the gryphons," Vicamros continued, his tone diplomatic. Drilled into him by his father and everyone else who expected him to rule, no doubt. "His name was

Thalden. I think he was one of their elders. He asked me to give you something, and Captain Kaith said you'd probably be here."

"What would a gryphon want me to have?" Rune asked in a murmur.

Vicamros drew a long, linen-wrapped object from the inside of his coat. He stepped closer and offered the object at arm's length. Frowning, Rune took it. It weighed next to nothing and he felt a lump rise in his throat even before he opened the cloth.

Inside lay a single feather, the length of his forearm, tawny brown with dark bars along its front edge. His eyes stung and he folded the linen closed. "Why did he send this?"

"For hope," Vicamros said.

Rune's brows lifted. "Hope," he repeated, almost amused. Even now, the gryphon wouldn't let him be. He turned the wrapped feather over in his hand. Silence weighed heavy between them for a long time before the young prince spoke again.

"I never did thank you. For saving me the night of the first battle, I mean."

"I didn't save you." Rune eased himself back from the edge, then stepped down from the wall into the broken tower's uppermost room.

Vicamros shook his head. "You made me run. Made me go back." He paused, smiling sheepishly, and ducked his blue eyes. "I was trying to go forward when you ran into me. Trying to be brave. I thought I had to go forward and fight. You've saved me twice now, and I won't forget it."

Snorting, Rune pushed past him and made his way toward the ramp. "Saved you from your own stupidity, maybe."

"It still counts. And I still wanted to thank you."

The prince sounded so earnest that Rune bit off a retort and gave the blond-headed boy a thoughtful look instead. Then he tore his eyes away to watch the dark path ahead as they walked. "Don't mention it."

Apparently satisfied, Vicamros said nothing more. The prince followed him from the tower and into the darkening night.

They attended the burial of the mages and soldiers in quiet companionship before they went their separate ways. Rune found an evening meal within the camp and listened to talk among the men. Camp would break at sunrise, they said. The army would cut their way back to the Royal City after the college mages Gated themselves back to Lore. No one complained about the lack of Gates to the Royal City; everyone seemed relieved to be leaving at all. The night passed peacefully and, exhausted, Rune slept.

In the morning, he packed the feather in his bedroll for protection. None of the people of Aldaeon came to bid them farewell, but as they turned toward the mountain pass and the long convoy started off, soldiers whispered about their destination. Home, they said. It meant something else for him, but it lay in the same direction.

Rune thought of Ria's feather and walked with hope.

THOUGH SNOW LAY thick through the mountains and the rolling hills on the other side, the army traveled easier. The frozen ground kept wagon wheels from sinking into the earth, and the snow had been trampled by men afoot until it was little more than a crust of ice that crackled beneath the wagons.

The soldiers laughed and joked during the day, relieved to be headed home, though nighttime was more somber. The battles had been few and fleeting, but the mages had done enough damage. Hundreds of swords with no owners rode in wagons at the back of the procession. Rune was uncertain how they knew which blade should go to which family, but he tried not to dwell on it. He was alive; that was what mattered. Worse off, but alive. And having kept his word and served as part of Garam's army for the duration of the war, he hoped their arrangement could be revisited once they reached the Royal City. At the very least, he hoped to go free. Even the loss of his father's sword stung less after fighting with another weapon.

Rhyllyn and Alira rode with the wagons, and some instinct kept Rune nearby. Now and then, the boy would leave his bundle of blankets behind and deliver some sort of snack he'd conned out of the supply wagons. He chattered about the sights the army passed while they ate, always cheerful, until Alira inevitably called him back to the wagons for fear he would freeze. Somehow, Rune always missed him in the silence that followed.

Prince Vicamros joined him for dinner beside the campfire most nights, sometimes hungry for idle conversation, sometimes silent, but always fresh-faced and eager to reach home. Word of the prince being with the army had been sent to the king before they departed Aldaan. The boy thought the forewarning would spare him from his father's wrath. Whether or not he was right impacted Rune little, but he still wished the young man well.

When the army halted for the night only one day from the Royal City, the weather was warm enough that there was no snow on the ground, though calling it warm would have been a stretch. Still, the night was more pleasant than any since their departure, with a clear sky overhead and the comfort of a real bed to look forward to the next day.

After their usual conversation, Rune watched the prince retreat to his tent for the night, pensive. He couldn't help but feel fond of the young prince. In another time, another place, perhaps they would have been friends. Once they reached the Triad's capital, he doubted they would cross paths again.

"He's a good boy." Sera's voice made Rune blink, and he realized belatedly that he still stared into the empty space between the prince's tent and where he sat beside the fire.

"He is," Rune agreed as he returned his attention to the bowl in his hand. Even the stew seemed to taste better, though it was the same thing he'd eaten for weeks. "He reminds me a little of myself, when I was younger. He's better than me, but we're still something alike."

She chuckled, settling on the dry grass beside him. "I wouldn't know. I didn't know you when you were young."

Rune smiled ruefully as he scraped the bottom of the bowl with his spoon. "I was stupid. Still am, but I was more stupid then."

"You can't be that stupid. You dance well. You know how to read." She studied him, a little too intently for him to be comfortable. "You told me once that you committed treason, but I can't see it. The way you treat other men is too noble. So what's your real story, lizard?"

His smile faded with his appetite and he lowered his bowl without finishing. He'd refused to talk when Ria found his island on that map in the aerie and expressed curiosity, insisted on keeping his life secret. How many more deep conversations could they have had if he hadn't clung to anonymity?

"I was a foundling," Rune said slowly. "Taken in by a king and raised as royalty. Had the entire world at my fingertips, all the riches I wanted and women falling at my feet. It wasn't enough. I wanted something greater, wanted to make a difference in the world. But how could I? I had no crown. I thought I needed power to make change happen, to make a name for myself. So I slept with an enemy queen, and she made me her general. I used her armies to overthrow my father's rule, thinking I could be a better king."

Sera's eyebrows climbed her forehead as he spoke, a look of surprise and bemusement sprawling on her face when he finished and silence fell. Then she slapped his shoulder. "You're a horrible liar!" she laughed, mage-blue eyes sparkling. "No one would ever believe that."

"You asked," he said, putting his bowl aside.

Still laughing, she wiped her eyes. "How long did it take you to make that up?"

He shrugged. "It was all I could think about while I was in prison."

"Well, it'll make a good tavern story for when we're back in the capital."

"Perhaps." Rune rested his elbows on his knees. "Now it's your turn. After everything we've been through, it seems I ought to know a little about you."

Sera grinned, but ducked her eyes as if shy. She was anything but. "Ah, you've probably heard it from Garam already. Our homeland was consumed by war when we were young. I came north to study magecraft because it was forbidden where we lived. People distrusted mages. They thought magic would be used unfairly in the war."

"Can't say I blame them," he murmured.

"I feel the same, after all we've been through," she sighed. "But things have changed, back home. Mages are more welcome now. With fortune, I'll be able to return soon. I want to restore House Kaith to glory. That's what I want, you know? Not this. Not wars. I want to marry, and have children."

Rune stifled a laugh. "Children?"

"What? I do!" She grinned at him. "Half a dozen, at least. There's nothing I love more than children. Garam and I were robbed of the chance to grow up as a family. I want to see what it's like to be a part of that."

"I understand," he said, and he meant it.

Sera nodded, but her gaze dropped to her boots. "I have to admit I've been jealous, watching you with Rhyllyn. He's such a sweet boy. I've hated having him here and loved it at the same time. An army is no place for children, but having him here, having a little one to look after..."

His brow furrowed. "That makes you jealous?"

"He took to you so easily, looked to you for protection and support. I saw the way he beamed after you brought him back from shopping in Aldaeon." She cracked a smile again, though it was wistful this time, distant. "I've always thought that would be nice. There's nothing like the love of a child."

"I see," Rune murmured. He hadn't invested much thought into his growing bond with the boy, or what would happen after they reached their destination. A worry for later, he supposed. They were almost there.

Sera chuckled. "But that's enough about that. I can fret about what I've missed, or I can move forward. I know which I will do. I think that's the biggest difference between us, lizard. You look to the past. I look to the future. Where will you go after this?"

Where would he go? Rune rubbed the back of his neck. Elenhiise was all he'd hoped for, yet he couldn't fathom how he would return and still escape the gallows. The Alda'anan had been his hope for an answer. Had he been able to finish what he'd started in the fields outside Aldaeon, perhaps he could have returned as Ran, resumed his life as the dead king's foundling son. But his scales remained.

"I don't know," he admitted at last. "I want to go home, but... I just don't see how."

A hint of sympathy drifted across her face. "Well, I said I'd help, and I promise I will. You never know. Perhaps the Lifetree will bless you with an answer."

"Brant hasn't been kind to me."

"That doesn't mean you're forgotten." She pushed herself up with a grin. "Get some sleep. We'll have our hero's welcome tomorrow."

Rune nodded and turned his eyes to the fire. Warmer though the weather might be, he was still reluctant to leave its comfort. Uncertainty swirled inside his head, and he lingered beside the campfire until well after the moon passed its peak.

Despite what Sera said, there was no hero's welcome waiting in the Royal City when they arrived the following evening. People lined the streets to watch them return and families cheered at sight of their loved ones still alive. But there was no music, no festivity, no flowers strewn in their path.

Here and there, mournful faces turned away and disappeared in the crowd. Rune watched them the longest. It hurt to find oneself suddenly alone, a lesson he'd learned all too well.

The march continued to the barracks, where Garam ordered the horses be sent to the stables and the men to return to their homes, with the promise of a feast-day in the morning.

"And what about you?" Sera asked as her brother instructed her to retire to her quarters. She lingered outside the barracks as the captain gave orders, one of a handful of misfits. Rune, Vicamros, Alira, and Rhyllyn stood with her.

"I will be escorting Prince Vicamros to his father's palace," Garam said with a frown. "Need to find a place for Alira and the boy to stay for now, too."

"I'm sure Redoram could host them," Rune suggested. The white-robed woman smiled at him, amicable if not friendly. Given their past, amicable was all that could be hoped for. Alira had kept her distance during travel, though more out of responsibility in seeing to the child's needs than anything. They had not spoken often, but Rune found he no longer resented her.

Garam rubbed his chin. "No harm in asking, I suppose. Councilor Parthanus will likely be at council with the king, so Alira, Rhyllyn, you should come along." He turned toward the Spiral palace and paused when Sera and Rune moved to follow. "The two of you should stay here and rest."

"You're escorting the prince across the city with no guard," Sera protested. "I'm the only mage here with an amulet to give me access to my Gift. I'm coming along."

Rune nodded. "And Redoram is a friend. If anyone is going to ask a favor of him, it should be me." He had other favors to ask, besides. If he was to leave the Triad, Redoram was the best person he could ask for help in finding his way.

The captain sighed and waved a hand. "All right, then. All of you come along."

The group moved at his heels, their stroll through the city leisurely and unhindered. Sounds of good cheer flowed from open doors and windows to fill the streets. The few taverns they passed were stuffed to the gills, the smells of food that wafted from inside tantalizing after the dull rations they'd had during their campaign.

Mage-lights illuminated the Spiral Palace, as always. Its three-colored banners rippled in the chilly night winds. The guards at the doors nodded cordial greetings to Garam as they moved aside to let the captain's entourage pass.

The main room ahead was dim, but the halls that branched left and right from the doorway were brightly lit. Compared to his previous visit, Rune found the palace interior forbidding. There was little to no decoration in the curving halls, and the first floor bore no windows.

Garam led them up the stairway to the right, past another pair of guards, and to the second floor. "The councilors will be here this time of night. The king will likely be with them."

"What should we say?" Alira asked, doubtful.

Sera snorted. "Nothing. You let Rune speak to Councilor Parthanus on your behalf. The king will be too busy with his son to even notice you."

"Probably for the best," Garam sighed. He glanced at them over his shoulder before he looked down at himself, an action the rest of the group mirrored. They were travel-worn and dirty, hardly fit to appear before the king. The state of the army was part of the reason the victory feast was to take place in the morning.

Rune resisted the urge to brush dust from his uniform. "We've just come back from war. The king would be a fool to expect us to look otherwise."

"The expectations of kings are not foolish," Garam said.

"You must not know many kings."

"And you do?" The captain stopped in middle of the hall and turned to glower at him.

"He was going to be one," Sera said, nudging Rune's shoulder with a grin. "He said so last night. King of the lizards."

Alira quirked a brow and started to speak, but Rune shot her a warning glance and she closed her mouth again.

"I've met enough," Rune said. "Your Vicamros included."

"King Vicamros is your king, too." Garam shook his head and started down the empty hallway again. "Best remember that."

Rune decided to save his retort for another day.

They walked for some time before they reached a pair of guarded doors. The captain stopped to introduce the party, but the prince stepped forward before he could speak. "Is my father in council?"

"Yes, Your Highness," one of the guards said, peering at the curious group behind him.

Vicamros motioned toward the doors. "Let us in. I will see him at once."

The two guards exchanged looks before the first addressed the prince again. "Council is currently in session—"

"Good, I have business with the councilors as well." The prince waved the men out of his way and pushed open the doors by himself.

Conversation in the room halted the moment Prince Vicamros strode inside. Garam and Rune followed close at his heels, while Sera urged Rhyllyn and Alira through the door. The white-robed woman patted the child's shoulder as if to soothe him, though she looked as if she needed soothing, herself.

The king pushed himself up from the ornate chair at the head of the table, his anger at being interrupted replaced with pure relief and elation at the sight of his son. Beside him, Lady Bryndis put a hand on his arm to keep him still.

"Father," Prince Vicamros said, tone cordial. He strode toward the table, offering slight smiles to the dozen councilors who stared.

The king brushed aside Bryndis's hand and rushed around

the table to sweep his son into a hug. Councilors coughed, cleared their throats, or averted their eyes. Then the king caught the youth's shoulders in his hands, shoved him back, and scowled. "Blasted fool of a boy, always trying to get yourself killed!"

"Be easy, Your Majesty," Bryndis cooed as she joined them. The prince turned and opened an arm to her. She embraced him fondly, patting his cheek.

Prince Vicamros laid a hand on Bryndis's shoulder and drew back, his brow furrowed with concern. "I owe you an apology," he said. "Both you and my father. But especially you, Bryndis. I realize now that I made unfair requests of you."

She chuckled. "Speak easy, my prince. Your father knows what I've done."

"And I've forgiven her for it," the king added, his face stony. "But I've not yet forgiven you."

"I didn't expect as much." The prince turned to Garam, but could not make himself meet the captain's eyes. "And I owe you an apology, as well. Bryndis assisted me in acquiring a uniform and joining your army as you rode out, though only because I begged it of her. I never meant to bring you any trouble."

Startled, Garam glanced to the king as if seeking permission to speak. The king's face betrayed nothing. Garam spoke anyway. "She assisted you?"

"A foolish decision, I know," Bryndis sighed. "I should have drawn the line after I arranged for him to be allowed to fight in the arena. But he's like a son to me, and I cannot bear to see him unhappy. He was so desperate to make a name for himself. If I am to be honest, Captain Kaith, it was because of Prince Vicamros that I pushed to have you lead the effort. I knew he would be safe in your hands."

"So you didn't send us out there to be rid of us?" Sera asked, unable to hide her surprise.

Bryndis cocked her head and peered at the others behind the

prince. "Goodness, Vicamros, what sort of mess have you brought with you?"

Rune raised a brow. He hadn't planned to speak, but the startled look on the woman's face made him reconsider. He drew a breath, but the prince turned to smile at them before he could say a word.

"The best of Captain Kaith's army," Prince Vicamros said. "Sera, his lead scout and chief mage. Alira and Rhyllyn, who joined us along the way. And Rune. The Arena Champion, who saved my life on the battlefield. Again." He ducked his eyes, grinning sheepishly. "Together, they were able to hold all the Grand College's forces at bay."

Someone at the table cleared their throat and the group turned toward the councilors.

"There will be time for accolades in the morning, Your Majesties," Redoram prompted gently, a spark of amusement in his eyes. "We are not yet finished here."

King Vicamros rolled his eyes. "Yes, yes. What else is left on the table?"

Another councilor held up an envelope. Rune didn't recognize the man, but the stamp on the broken wax seal was one he'd seen too many times. Ilmenhith's business. He stiffened at the sight.

"A request to initiate trade. Archmage Arrick Ortath of Lore left this with us just this afternoon, asking that it be brought to your attention. An island nation called Elenhiise wishes to ally with us and open trade Gates from the college. They seek to alleviate famine in their kingdom."

The king snorted. "Why would I bother wasting my resources on an island I've never heard of?"

Rune shifted forward, his eyes trained on the letter in the councilor's hand. "Elenhiise? You're certain?" He didn't need an answer. He'd already seen the seven-pointed star that had haunted him since birth.

The councilors and the king all turned their heads at his interruption, none pleased, but most curious.

"You are familiar with the place?" Redoram asked, leaning against the table's edge.

"Somewhat," Rune lied. "The ship that carried me to the Triad stopped in their capital's port. The island is exactly halfway between the northern and southern continents. A remote island, yes, but a thriving trade destination, and incredibly wealthy because of the business that passes through their harbors. I've never seen anything quite like the capital city there." He paused, glancing between Redoram and the king. "I'd think them leverage worth having, considering their mines. Rubies, if I recall."

The last words lit fires in the eyes of the councilors. King Vicamros studied them with a frown. "Is this true?"

"I would trust his word with my life, Father," the prince put in.

The king held up a hand and looked to his councilors.

"The request did mention mines," the councilor holding the letter said.

"It is quite true, to my knowledge," Redoram said with a nod. "I've a friend who resides there, in fact. He found a more prosperous life on Elenhiise than what I lead here."

"Very well." The king straightened, pleased. "Send a response to their leader, offering to barter food. Wars are expensive, and our coffers could use bolstering. We can address a more permanent trade arrangement once we see what they have to offer. If that is all, then council is dismissed." He paused to study Garam. "I will speak to the rest of you in the morning."

"Of course, Your Majesty," Garam murmured.

The councilors bowed their heads and remained in place as the king departed with Bryndis at his heels. Prince Vicamros lingered in the doorway to flash a nervous grin at the group before he hurried after his father.

Once they were gone, Redoram stood and strode toward

Rune with a chuckle. "And so all of you arrive home, safe and sound. With a few extras in tow, it seems." He nodded toward Alira and Rhyllyn, staring at the latter in puzzlement.

Rune stepped back to stand beside them. "As the prince said, this is Alira, Master mage and scholar. And Rhyllyn." He laid a hand on the boy's shoulder. "My brother."

The child beamed up at him.

"Your brother!" Redoram squinted, rubbing his beard. "Well, I can't say I don't see a certain resemblance."

"They are good people," Sera said, flashing Alira a smile that the Master mage returned with warmth. "We hoped you might be able to host them until we can find them a more permanent situation."

Rune gave her a dirty look. She knew it wasn't her place to ask, but she smirked at him and stuck out her tongue.

"Of course, of course." Redoram rubbed his hands together and then stroked his beard. His eyes flicked to Rune. "I'd be happy to have you, as well. It's been a while since I've had a decent game of runestones."

"Thank you," Rune said as the rest of the councilors departed. "I think I'll take you up on that."

"So everything's settled, then?" Sera planted her hands on her hips.

"Until tomorrow," Garam said.

Rune nodded. "Until tomorrow."

AN ANSWER

It was not the end of her efforts. There were rarely true ends to things, only obstacles to overcome. Envesi reminded herself as much, knowing she would likely repeat the mantra often until she overcame the obstacles before her now.

Escaping the college hadn't been difficult, though she wondered how long it would take for Eyrion Tolmarni's death to be traced back to her. Alira was missing, and both Melora and the headmaster had died in fires. All three gone, all three with ties to her. Her connection to the headmaster was not immediately obvious, but he had kept records of their efforts, of their plans to begin freeing mages from the bonds of affinity. He had written down everything they discussed. Though she had the presence of mind to take one journal from his office before she fled, she suspected there would be more notes in his quarters for the college mages to find.

Envesi scooped a handful of sand from the shore beside her and let it trickle through her fingers. The tide would lap at her toes before long, but she was in no hurry to rise.

She could have stayed, she supposed; she could have told them Eyrion's death was an accident. But explaining how she'd been involved would mean revealing secrets she didn't want to share. The ties that bound magic to affinities were her discovery, and the fewer people who knew about them, the better.

Perhaps sharing that knowledge with Eyrion had been a mistake. He'd been in a position to grant her the resources she needed to bring her goals to fruition, which was why she had turned to him to begin with, but he'd been unable to control his greed—or his power.

When she'd fled the college in the wake of Eyrion's fire, she thought she'd lost her final chance. But as she watched the ships leaving Roberian's harbor and drew her cloak tighter around her shoulders, she reconsidered.

The Grand College of Lore was just one of countless schools of magic in the world, and there was one school in which she wouldn't need to gain standing before there would be mages on her side. There were still mages in Kirban Temple who were loyal to her, who would answer her call and aid her. Melora and Alira had been exiled alongside her due to their rank. Most of the other Masters had been forgiven and welcomed back into the fold. Envesi didn't take her exile lightly, but if anything, it was only an inconvenience.

As was the nature of the unbinding.

She'd thought of that often since she'd been cast from the temple and, though she still had reservations about the way the process warped one's body, the time she spent mulling it over had been enlightening.

Long had she thought Lomithrandel a failed experiment. Seeing his deformation mirrored in the boy she'd changed before Melora's death and again in Eyrion, she was no longer sure. Perhaps it was an error, but it could have been something else. It was not failure if the unbinding worked. And if it caused one's outward appearance to become as frightful as their power, was it truly a mistake? How could one's body make a difference when all the world's power lay at their fingertips?

It didn't, she thought with an ounce of satisfaction. And the realization she had never failed was reassuring.

The only problem left to solve was finding someone she could trust. Someone with enough healing expertise, o they could learn the process of unbinding and assist her in unlocking her own true potential. Envesi smoothed her white hair as she thought, still staring out to sea. There was someone she remembered, just vaguely. The name eluded her. A loyal mage, a spy within Kirban, a mageling who had been—until now—far beneath her attention. Ah, that was it. The answer to her problems. A gift in green robes. She remembered now.

"Shymin," she murmured at last, and pushed herself up from the sand.

———

"My queen, a letter has arrived from the northern Triad's ruler, King Vicamros."

Firal blinked several times and the papers on her desk came back into focus. She hadn't realized she still stared at them, her mind elsewhere. In all the time she'd been in her office, she hadn't written a word. She squinted at her stewardess as her vision adjusted, then laid down her quill. "Bring it here, Medreal. Goodness knows I need some good news."

The city had been quiet since Vahn's participation in quelling the riot, though she thought her declaration that the ruin-folk were to return to Core helped. Not all of them were going, of course; some were more comfortable staying just outside Ilmenhith, breaking ground on new farms. It was harder for Ilmenhith's natives to begrudge their presence when the ruin-folk were working, showing active initiative to earn their keep and better the situation for everyone. When half the ruin-folk worked the mines beneath Core and the other half coaxed food production from nearby land, there would be little reason left for anyone to complain.

Then again, it was only a matter of time before they found something else to complain about.

Medreal passed Firal the letter and clasped her hands before her apron. It wasn't until then that Firal noticed the woman carried no tea tray. She raised a brow but said nothing as she took a slim knife from her desk and popped the wax seal. She read the letter twice, then fell back in her chair with a laugh. "I don't believe it!"

"Is it good news, Majesty?" the stewardess asked.

"Vicamros says Elenhiise is known in his kingdom, renowned for its wealth. Elenhiise, renowned? I never would have expected he'd even heard of us! He wants to initiate trade immediately. Beginning tomorrow!" Her heart felt aflutter. Firal clapped a hand to her chest as if to still it. "We are to work with the mages on the mainland. Should trade prove fruitful, we are to establish a permanent, anchored Gate to make trade easier for both our kingdoms."

Medreal smiled, a hint of mystery in her expression. Had she known the contents of the letter? That would explain why she'd arrived without something to soothe Firal's nerves. "A blessing indeed, my queen," the stewardess said. "Is there anything I can assist with in the meantime?"

"Please arrange to have gold ready for trade in the morning, and see that our mages are prepared to manage the Gate." Firal pushed back her chair and rose. She felt lighter, all of a sudden. As if the last of her troubles had finally lifted. "Thank you, Medreal. I believe I will retire early."

"Of course, Your Majesty. Rest well." The old woman bowed and stepped aside to let Firal pass, then turned to tidy the desk.

Firal had grown used to working late into the night after Lumia settled. As the girl began to wake less often, it became easier to find time to focus after she went to sleep. Firal often finished her work well before the first time Lulu woke to feed, and her evening hours in the office had become her most productive. Or they usually were, when she didn't have quite so much on her mind. But the coming days would be easier, she was sure of it. The message from the mainland eased one problem.

An evening with Vahn would ease the other.

Though Vahn was often the first one back to their shared quarters, his assistance in organizing the ruin-folk for their return to Core promised to keep him late, as it had every night Davan met with him to share knowledge of the mine and its workings. Time alone had been welcome at first, but she'd had enough of quiet thinking and reflection.

Looking back at the months behind them, the troubles they faced suddenly seemed so minuscule, where she'd feared they were life-devouring before. Then again, she hadn't been ready to take the throne, and the weight of the crown required her to grow up faster than before. She was embarrassed to recall the girl she'd been a scant year prior, ill-tempered and selfish, carelessly flouting temple rules. Much had changed since then. Or, some had. Firal winced at the thought as she pushed into her rooms. She was less selfish and more respectful now, and she had a better rein on her temper, but she held little hope that temper would ever go away.

Lulu was still soundly asleep when Firal peered past the maid who waited at the nursery door. She motioned the maid away with a quiet thank-you and waited for her to leave before she changed into a simple nightdress. She still preferred to have the baby's cradle beside her bed, but there would be time to move it later. Besides, if she meant to speak with Vahn when he came in, it wouldn't do for their voices to wake the girl. So she carried on as if it were a normal night, scrubbing her teeth and washing her face. She stood at the mirror when he arrived, brushing her hair.

Vahn walked as if on eggshells, tip-toeing into the room and acting surprised to find Firal still awake. Most nights, she was asleep when he returned. He always apologized profusely for waking her. She didn't turn away from the mirror, but offered a warm smile to his reflection. It never took him long to prepare for sleep and by the time she finished her hundred strokes with the hairbrush, he was done and stripped down to breeches and a thin shirt for bed.

"We received a response from the mainland today," she said as she crept toward the bed. They reached it at the same time.

"What did it say?" he asked, hopeful.

Firal couldn't restrain her smile. "Trade begins tomorrow."

"Couldn't have asked for better news." Vahn sat on the edge of the bed and grinned. "Things have gone well enough on my end, too. There have been some growing pains, but everything should be in order for the Underlings to move back to the ruins within the next week. That'll be easier to manage if we have food and other supplies to send with them."

"Are they eager to go?" She couldn't imagine they were happy to uproot and move again so soon after their arrival, but years of survival in the ruins had given their city a permanency Elenhiise's farmers often lacked. Those who stayed behind would have difficulty adjusting, she was sure.

Vahn rocked a hand back and forth in a gesture of uncertainty. "Some of them. Davan is letting them decide for themselves who will go and who will stay. We still need to determine which tracts of land outside the city can be given to Underlings for farming, but we'll get to that. I suppose the next thing we need to figure out is what to call them. I know they call themselves ruin-folk, and that's fine for those who are headed back to the mines, but we need to find a way to include the others here." He reached for a pillow, then paused. "Should I fetch Lulu's cradle?"

"No." She reached to take his hand. "I wanted a moment to speak with you, first. And it isn't necessary for you to keep sleeping on the floor. It's a big bed."

He studied her, his lips twitching as if he wanted to speak but couldn't find the words. Then he gave her a timid smile and glanced away. "I just want you to be comfortable. I know our situation isn't ideal, but—"

She pressed a finger to his lips to silence him, then cradled his cheek in her hand. "I appreciate that. You've been so kind to me, Vahn. I'm not always sure I deserve it. But our situation can only get better."

A hint of color touched his cheeks. "Well," he laughed as he slid into the bed and fell into the pillows. "The floor does get uncomfortable after a while, so I'd say mine already has."

Swallowing against a knot of nerves in her throat, Firal smiled at him and fought to ignore the heat in her ears. "Believe me," she said, "things will be better than that."

She leaned close and let her lips brush his.

Vahn was a good man. Dependable, reliable, gentle. Kind to her and loving to her daughter. She could fare worse.

"Firal—" He drew back, uncertainty bright in his eyes.

"This is my choice," Firal murmured as she pulled the ribbons at the throat of her nightdress.

His breath caught.

As her gown fell away and left her body bare in the moonlight, there were no longer any words to be shared.

KYTENIA JUMPED to her feet when the Archmage's door opened. She spent too much time waiting beside doors these days, but when Edagan stepped into the hall, her frustration was buried beneath concern.

Edagan didn't shut the door behind her, though she did push it halfway closed. "He wishes to speak to you." Her face might as well have been carved of stone, for all it gave away.

"Thank you, Master." Kytenia bowed her head. She stared at the door and waited in the hall until Edagan left. The room beyond was dark and quiet. She was almost afraid to go in. But she smoothed her skirts and moved slowly, slipping into Nondar's quarters and muting the sound of the door's closing with her hands.

Candles burned near the bed, their light softer and more comforting than mage-light. The Archmage lay against a thick pile of pillows, not quite upright, his face turned toward the tiny, flickering flames. Their ruddy light cast harsh shadows on his face, emphasizing the uneven texture and the many creases of his withered skin. His eyes seemed almost too bright, peering out from beneath heavy lids, as sharp and blue as they'd ever been. Sharper, she thought, than they'd seemed of late.

"It's a shame we don't use candles more often," Nondar murmured. His speech was thick and slurred and his face moved little as he spoke. "They're so much more pleasant than cold mage-light."

Kytenia crept to the side of his bed and sank to her knees beside him. "You shouldn't have led the opening of that Gate."

He chuckled, breath rattling in his chest. "Who else was there? I did what I must. What I should have done sooner. I think part of me remembered what I promised, but everything was gray... hazy. Thoughts, ideas, hanging in a mist. A strange thing. Knowing something and not knowing it at the same time. Like the nagging memory of having a thought and then losing it."

She did not reply. She didn't know what to say.

"I've told Edagan everything I can." Nondar spoke slowly, rolling out each word as if the next would escape him. "She's taken meticulous notes. Much of it is beyond what a mage without a healing affinity can do. You and your sister will both be tasked with learning what you can from what she has written."

"I want you to teach me, Nondar," Kytenia insisted.

Again he chuckled. One frail, gnarled hand swayed toward her. She clasped it firmly and her throat tightened when she felt how cold he was.

"I would like to, my dear," he said, "but there are many things I must tell you now, things the others will not. Things I—we—swore not to speak of. Things I cannot allow Edagan and

Anaide to hold over your head when you rise as Archmage after me."

His fingers tightened on hers, his eyes growing unfocused as he stared at the candles. "We have committed so many sins, we mages who came before. All in the name of power. I came to Elenhiise because there was a great future for mages here. One that could not be found in my homeland. The mages of Kirban Temple shaped this island, this culture, before the temple even existed. When Envesi was young and powerful, betrothed to Kifel, and he was eager to curry her favor before they wed."

Kytenia bit her lower lip. She knew King Kifel and the former Archmage had been wed. Nondar had told her and she had kept it in confidence, though she wasn't certain it was secret. No one asked about their young queen's mother. Firal had never spoken of it. That she was Kifel's heir was all anyone seemed to care about. Then again, Kytenia supposed there was sense in keeping quiet on the matter. Envesi's name was no longer loved, and Firal had enough trouble on her plate. "But what does that mean, Nondar?" she asked at last.

"That mages are vital to society only because we make them so." He frowned and his eyes drifted closed. "Think of all the centuries the Underlings survived beneath the ruins without any hint of magic to help them. That's all our craft is. Magic is helpful, not vital. Not as we've made it seem. But Envesi taught us to be strong, to be leaders among the people, to carry ourselves as if we were above them. It is a ruse. One that isn't carried out on the mainland." His face was grim when he opened his eyes again and fixed his gaze on her face. "The balance that keeps mages in power here is delicate, Kytenia. Were we not desperate to bring things to order beneath Firal, I never would have suggested we turn to the mainland in the north for help. They were the best choice because our business can be filtered through the Grand College in my homeland. But our people won't see that the college is near empty, magic all but abandoned. It will be up to you to preserve the balance and keep them from seeing. If mages lose power on Elenhiise, there will be no hope for the craft to recover anywhere."

Kytenia gaped at the torrent of knowledge. How could magic be abandoned? How could anyone fail to see its value? "How am I supposed to do that? I don't know these mages, I don't know what they expect—"

Nondar shook his head. "You will have to determine a method to manage by yourself. We've had no formal contact with the mages of Lore for centuries, dear girl. But there are things you will need to watch for, and starting with those will give you some idea of what to expect."

The thickness in her throat returned and she blinked hard. "Won't you be here to help me? The mainland's mages are coming tomorrow, surely they—"

"I am helping you now, child," he reprimanded gently as he stroked hair away from her face with a trembling hand. "So listen well. There are mages from the mainland who would seek to harm the temple's standing. They practice magic in the old ways, from a time before mages were limited to our affinities. They are the ones who bound it, and they would destroy it if they could. Envesi sought to combat them by creating unbound mages of our own, but the project failed, thwarted by someone who didn't want us to succeed. Lomithrandel was the first unbound, and by the Lifetree's mercy, he will be the last. You cannot let these mages come in contact with the people of Elenhiise. Or any mages from the mainland, for that matter. Lumia, our first Master of Fire, was one of them. She was the last. You must keep it that way."

"I will try," Kytenia started.

Nondar shook his head and touched her face. "Promise me. Promise you will keep the temple safe."

She leaned into his touch, blinking hard. "I promise."

"And promise you will serve Firal faithfully, and keep her safe, as well."

"I promise."

"Good." A crooked smile twisted his mouth and he settled in the pillows. "Though, I must say we were arrogant. I see that now."

Kytenia stiffened as he moved into her shadow. "Master—Archmage—your eyes!"

"The walls, the boundaries, between affinities are thin. Thinner than we realized. To draw the power of everything that is, to give life and form to magic," he murmured, his eyes glazing as the soft glow of blue light filled them. "Perhaps Lumia was right to oppose us. Perhaps we were wrong. Perhaps..." Nondar's voice, with the light in his eyes, faded to nothing. His gnarled hand went limp in her grasp, and as the last traces of magic drained from his body, Kytenia leaned forward and wept into his robes.

***

"You weren't at the reception."

Rune glanced over his shoulder and frowned at the captain before he turned his eyes back to the bustling scene before him. "Didn't feel much like celebrating." He shifted against the wall, his arms folded over his chest.

The Grand College was impressive enough to live up to its name, he supposed, though he was more interested in the people. The college mages had just finished erecting an archway with a slot in the top when he'd arrived. From studying the dozens of identical arches in the courtyard, he knew the slot was meant for a Gate-stone. When he'd suggested trade be considered, he'd never expected to see a permanent Gate erected. They wouldn't add a Gate-stone until they were sure of the arrangement, of course; it would have been foolish to make a permanent Gate to somewhere you didn't intend to visit often.

A handful of councilors had been assigned to oversee trade. It had taken a full day for the workers to collect the crates of foodstuffs prepared for the morning's session, and Redoram was one of the councilors who had stayed up half the night working out the wording of the contract they would carry in the king's stead. Rune knew King Vicamros delegated most tasks, but he still wondered at the arrogance in refusing to meet new trade partners in person. Especially when the arrangement was being made with royalty.

Garam made a small sound of displeasure in his throat and crossed his arms in mimicry of Rune's stance. He stared at the piled crates and the milling workers who unloaded more of them into the courtyard. The councilors stood in their own cluster, arguing over how things would proceed. Most of the disagreement seemed to be between Redoram and Survas. The two of them had been chosen because of their ability to speak Old Aldaanan, not because they could work together. As far as Rune had seen, they couldn't agree on anything.

"You know," Garam said when he got no further explanation, "when you never showed up, I almost thought you'd tried to leave. Councilor Parthanus said you were at his estate. What were you doing there all day?"

Rune shrugged. "Sleeping. And eating. Food and rest are two things I don't think anyone got enough of, out in the field."

"I suppose you're right about that." The captain scratched his chin with his thumb. He'd already managed to trim his hair and beard. A single day after returning from the battlefield, and he was as neat and polished as ever. As if they'd never been to war. "Nothing quite like sleeping in a real bed, anyway."

"Yeah, but it's more restful when you're sleeping alone." Rune cracked a smile as Garam's eyes widened. The man tried to sputter some sort of explanation, but Rune held up a hand. "Easy. You're Garam Kaith, Captain of the Royal City Guard. It would be foolish to think you didn't have a lady or two vying to be a decoration on your arm." He pushed himself off the wall and slapped the captain's shoulder as he started toward the cluster of councilors. Mages were beginning to form a half-circle around the empty archway, signaling they were ready to begin.

Garam coughed and then cleared his throat, shaking off his discomfort as he strode after him. "I'm assuming you came over here with Councilor Parthanus when they opened the Gate this morning. Why?"

"Business," Rune replied gruffly. "Why did you?"

"I'm Captain of the Royal City Guard," Garam said. "Aside from mages and a navy, Lore doesn't have much in the way of military. And King Vicamros isn't feeling particularly trusting of the mages at the moment. At the king's behest, I have men waiting shoreside, just in case this goes wrong."

Rune nodded. It made sense. If he'd not departed with Redoram before first light that morning, he suspected he would have been made part of the guard detail supervising the transaction. He was glad he wasn't. His plain ivory shirt and worn tan trousers didn't offer as much protection against the chill air as his uniform's coat might, but if everything worked as he hoped, he didn't want to be seen wearing another kingdom's colors.

Survas and Redoram stilled their argument as they approached. The air hummed with energy as the opening of the Gate began. The raw, crackling power was enough to make Rune's hair stand on end, though the arch where the mages wove the Gate together was on the other side of the courtyard.

"The mages request that you bring more guards into the college proper," Redoram said as he stopped before Garam. "They don't anticipate any trouble, but feel it would be wise to display a defensive force on this side and they are uncertain the soldiers currently present are enough."

"Will they be visible?" Garam asked with a frown.

Survas gave a lofty sniff. "Gate-stones are not the only method of anchoring a Gate, Kaith. Our mages are working with theirs to hold it open from both sides. Do remember our people must be able to return."

"Do remember Captain Kaith is your superior," Rune said,

mimicking the councilor's tone. "It would be wise to show the man respect when he has an army waiting on the shore."

Garam shot him a disapproving look, but said nothing.

As if to break the tension, Redoram cleared his throat. "As I was saying, the guards currently present should be enough to supervise the opening, but the mages would appreciate having their numbers bolstered before the transport of goods begins."

"It will be done," Garam said, with far more patience than Rune thought the situation deserved.

Rune stepped toward Redoram before the councilor could turn to leave. "I need you to do me a favor." He drew a small, folded letter from his pocket and brushed a claw over the wax seal. He had no signet. Instead, he had used the runestone he'd taken to carrying, marked the wax with the same emblem that scarred his hand. "Once you're through with the treaty and contract, give this to the queen."

Redoram's white brows rose. He studied the letter with interest as he accepted it, but didn't try to peek beneath its folded edges. "What is it?"

"Something I should have sent a long time ago," Rune murmured.

"Hmm. Very well, then. I'll see to it. And thank you, Captain, for being so accommodating. The signing of this treaty will be a landmark event, an alliance the likes of which the Triad has never pursued. I am sure it will lift the people's spirits a great deal." Redoram grinned and tucked the letter into his pocket. "Wish us luck, will you?"

"Of course." Rune stepped back and offered the councilors a respectful nod as the Gate crackled open and then settled. He knew the courtyard of the palace he'd called home was just on the other side, but he didn't dare look. An uncomfortable sense of anticipation and uncertainty had already taken residence in his chest.

Garam's eyes fell on him like lead weights after the

councilors were gone. "*Somewhat* familiar with the island?" he asked, tone sharp.

Rune paced back to his place beside one of the college's buildings and eased himself to the ground. "Not now, Garam."

The captain stared down at him for a long time before he looked back to the councilors. The group passed through the Gate with a small entourage of guards, all of them the picture of dignity. "One of these days, you're going to have to tell me your real story."

"And until then?"

Garam shrugged. "Same as you, I suppose." A cluster of soldiers began to form a guard ring around the mages and their open Gate. The captain started toward them and then paused mid-stride. "I wait."

THREE COURT MAGES stood on either side of the path, with longer rows of men in armor behind them. Vahn and Firal stood together, though she was a step ahead of him, showing her place as ruler despite his newly-adopted title of king. Just king, not king-regent—as he no longer tended all matters in her place— and not king-consort, because they presented a unified front to the people of Ilmenhith. But despite his title, he still took pains to make it clear he bent to Firal in all matters and respected her power as head of the country. Her choice to add him to the line of succession still made him uncomfortable. It was her country. In his head, it would always be hers.

They waited between the end of the two rows of guards, a short distance from the open Gate, but far enough back that the guardsmen and mages could stand between them and whatever came through the portal. There was little reason to anticipate trouble, but Ennil had been firm. The Gate would be, now and always, heavily guarded. Vahn almost wished his father was present for the welcome, but Ennil was upstairs with the other councilors, working out a list of questions to cover with the visiting dignitaries.

"Stop shifting about," Firal whispered. In contrast to his anxiety and nerves, she appeared perfectly calm. And resplendent in her blue and silver silk gown, he thought. His eye wandered the curve of her back and the swell of her hips before he caught himself. There was time for that later.

Clearing his throat, he straightened and stared dead ahead. "I'm trying. I'm just not as comfortable as you are."

"Comfortable?" Her voice quavered with unvoiced laughter and her smile widened. "I'm wearing a corset laced so tight I can hardly breathe in order to stuff myself into this gown, which was made before anyone knew our daughter was on the way and is now a shade too small. I forgot to eat breakfast. There's a hairpin digging into my head, and I have an itch on my forehead, beneath my crown."

Vahn grinned, sheepish. "I meant comfortable with politics."

"Well I'm not comfortable there, either. We're opening trade with a ruler I've never met, who I won't meet today, working through representatives who may or may not even speak the same language as us." Her expression never faltered. She looked as queenly and serene as a painting. "But we do what we must. I've just grown very good at pretending to be comfortable with these sorts of people, that's all."

He started to reply, but the mages and soldiers both stiffened. Reflexively, he stiffened too. The Gate was anchored by mages on both sides, granting them a glimpse through to the other side. He couldn't see much, just a group of people headed toward the Gate—nobles surrounded by soldiers—and a mountain of crates behind them. The party passed through the arch, and the image within the Gate rippled like water.

"Fair tidings, Queen Firal of Elenhiise," called one of the men. An older gentleman, with long waves of white hair and an equally long beard streaked with gray. He wore deep navy velvet embroidered with gold; not the best fabric choice for the island's weather. The man seemed surprised by the warmth. He looked to the rich blue sky overhead and adjusted the peculiar velvet cap that fit snug against his head.

"At least they speak our language," Vahn murmured, earning himself an elbow in the side.

"Fair tidings to you," Firal replied, lifting her chin. "But I am afraid you have me at a disadvantage, for I do not know your name."

A shorter man moved forward, drew himself up and puffed out his chest like a rooster. "I am Lord Survas, High Councilor to King Vicamros of the Triad."

Firal's brows lifted, but her smile didn't fade. Vahn swallowed hard to hold in a laugh.

The bearded man's brows twitched as he suppressed a frown. A half step forward put him beside Survas again. "I am Redoram Parthanus. This is Gillan, High Councilor and Official Representative of the province of Lore. And Nielan, High Councilor and Overseer of the Division of Royal Treasury and Finance." He gestured to the other two in their group as he spoke. The white-haired woman and the slender, long-nosed man both bobbed their heads in respect.

"Are you not a High Councilor as well?" Vahn asked. The man's lack of title seemed conspicuous after the introduction of the others.

Redoram hesitated, then laughed. "Forgive me. I have only recently resumed my place as part of the High Council. I have not yet become used to bearing the title again. But yes, I am. I represent a faction of scholars in the Royal City, heart of the three kingdoms now united as provinces beneath King Vicamros's rule."

A representative of the province they would do business through, an overseer of finance to wring the most money out of them, and a scholar to translate. Vahn assumed Survas was a scholar as well, since the man offered no other title but spoke their tongue.

"So it seems everyone needed is present," Firal said, echoing his thoughts. "My council awaits us upstairs. Shall we join them?"

Survas smiled, a strained, toothy expression that did not seem to come naturally. "Of course, Your Majesty. Better not to waste a moment, what with the circumstances your kingdom faces." He bowed at the shoulders, a motion mimicked by the other three.

Nodding, Firal turned toward the palace. A handful of guards fell in around them before Vahn turned too, and the two of them strode toward the stairs. Five of the mages remained beside the Gate with most of the guards, where they would remain until the treaty was signed and actual trade began. With the white-robed Gillan among the visitors, Vahn was glad to see Temar join the party destined for the council chamber. The court mage walked between them and the visiting councilors.

Firal poked his ribs as they moved inside, though she disguised the motion by taking his arm. "You didn't introduce yourself," she whispered.

He grimaced. It hadn't even crossed his mind. "I'm not used to being important. Besides, I don't know the first thing about trade."

"You would if you sat in on lessons with the mages and your father." Her tone was sing-song, but so quiet her words were almost hidden beneath the click of his boots on the marble floors.

Vahn resisted the urge to roll his eyes. "You'll have to help teach me later."

They paused at the twin grand staircases behind the thrones to let the councilors catch up. The four visitors studied the palace and murmured between themselves. Vahn didn't understand what they were saying, but their expressions and tonality indicated they were either impressed or pleased. Temar called for their attention in whatever tongue they spoke, snapping them back to the task at hand. Firal waited until they were close to continue onward.

She led the way to the large council hall, where a group of people waited. Those inside were seated when the doors opened, but when Ennil and Davan stood, the rest were short to follow. Vahn had grown somewhat familiar with the others in the room; Ordin had replaced his father as Captain of the Guard, and Mosell managed the ships that weren't part of the navy, which meant he managed the harbors and most trade that came and went, too. There were more councilors, but Firal had only called for those who would be directly involved. Vahn had expected to see Nondar, Edagan, and Anaide present, but the three seats typically reserved for the temple mages stood empty.

"Good morning, Davan. Ennil, Mosell. Ordin." Firal nodded a greeting to each of them before she crossed to her seat at the head of the table. Medreal appeared as if from nowhere to draw out her chair. Vahn shouldn't have been startled to see her. The woman flitted through the palace as if she were a ghost. He wouldn't have been surprised to learn she could walk through walls. The stewardess cast him a small, knowing smile as she drew the chair beside Firal out for him.

"Good morning, Queen Firal. King Vahnil." Ennil bowed deeply, as did the others. "And to our guests."

Vahn took his place at Firal's side. They remained standing while Medreal drew chairs for Temar and each of the dignitaries. Once they positioned themselves, Firal sat and motioned for everyone else to do the same. "Shall we begin?"

"Of course." Ennil said before anyone else could speak, sitting straight and glancing between the visitors. "Allow me to introduce myself. I am Ennil Tanrys, councilor serving Queen Firal, as I first served her father..."

Despite himself, Vahn found his attention wandering as his father made introductions and the visiting councilors offered theirs. He had no mind for politics, he decided. He didn't like trying to puzzle out the games nobles played, and he knew little about alliances or treaties or matters of trade. He didn't understand the terms they used, for that matter. The jumble of speech made him feel as if his eyes were going to cross.

"Sire," Medreal murmured at his ear, making him start. "There's a message from the temple. It's labeled as urgent, but I dare not interrupt Firal."

Vahn breathed a sigh of relief so heavy that the councilor who spoke paused.

All eyes turned toward him.

"Is everything well, my king?" Ennil's eyes narrowed.

"Of course." Vahn forced a smile. "A pressing matter, but one I can tend alone. Firal and I have already discussed what we hope to achieve through trade with the Triad. I am sure she can speak comfortably for both of us." He pushed himself up from the table. His smile softened when his eyes met Firal's. The look she gave him was questioning, but she held her silence.

"If you will excuse me." He bowed away from the table and followed Medreal into the hall.

The stewardess closed the door, her brow knit with worry as she turned and held out the rolled parchment, still sealed with black wax. The sight turned Vahn's stomach. He snatched the parchment from her hand, unrolled it and read the message twice before he grasped the full weight of what it said.

"My king?" Medreal asked softly.

"Nondar," Vahn breathed. "He... The Archmage has passed away."

The old woman's expression didn't change, though she tensed.

"Complications of a stroke, damages they couldn't heal. The temple is in mourning. They request Firal's presence, and that she announce who he named as successor." He scrubbed a hand through his hair and pressed his lips together. Did Firal even know who Nondar had named? A flood of concern for her filled him. Vahn had spent little time interacting with the Archmage, though he respected the man a great deal. But Firal spoke of him often, and he knew how troubled she was by his poor health.

"There was a letter from the temple not long ago. Firal didn't open it because she was busy working out a trade proposal, but I am certain it must contain the name of Nondar's chosen successor." Medreal spoke as if she'd heard his thoughts and he looked at her in alarm. But she didn't seem to notice, tapping her chin as she turned away. "I'll fetch the letter. This shouldn't wait. The Master mages will be at each other's throats like wolves until the new Archmage is named."

"Of course," Vahn said. "Bring it quickly. We'd best be prepared. My father and I can escort the dignitaries back to their Gate once dealings are done, so you can have a moment to speak to Firal."

The stewardess nodded and moved down the hall at a brisk pace. Vahn stared after her until she disappeared around the corner, then sank back against the wall and wiped his face with one hand.

He didn't know what to say. He didn't want to return to the meeting with such ill news on his mind, knowing he'd have to hold it in until business was over, knowing he wouldn't be able to keep it from his face. The last thing Firal needed was new worries in the middle of what he thought might be a delicate trade arrangement. So he lingered in the hallway, waiting for Medreal to return.

She did not return quickly. After what felt an eternity, he considered going to see where the stewardess had vanished to, thinking she might need help. But she reappeared before he gathered the conviction to move from his place beside the council chamber's doors, a tea tray in her hands and the letter from the temple balanced atop one of the upside-down teacups. He should have known she'd gone for tea. Chamomile or mint, most likely, something to soothe Firal's nerves after she received the news.

"They should be finishing now. The councilors will be finicky, but the trade arrangements won't be complicated, not without the foreign king appearing in person." Medreal paused, steadied her tray on one arm, and held out her free hand. "The scroll, if you please. Considering the size and power of the ally we're making today, you'd best see his councilors back to their Gate yourself instead of leaving it to your father."

Vahn hated to admit she was right. He opened the doors without knocking and stepped aside to let Medreal in first. Her timing was impeccable; everyone was standing, handshakes and shoulder-slaps concluding their meeting.

"Congratulations on your new commerce partners," Ennil said when Vahn stepped into the doorway. "You're just in time to see them leave." His tone was a sarcastic jest, but good-humored enough to make one of the visiting councilors chuckle.

Vahn tried to smile. "A pleasure to have them. My apologies, councilors, that I was not able to attend the whole meeting. But I would be honored to escort you home while Firal tends things here. As you know, a monarch's responsibilities never end."

"Our men will be right through with the promised supplies," Redoram said. "Will someone be needed to oversee them on this side of the Gate? I am sure one of us would be happy to volunteer."

"That will not be necessary, thank you. I will see that it's tended." Vahn nodded cordially, though his heart sank at the thought of Firal alone as she grappled with the news of Nondar's passing. He wanted to be with her when she heard, but they couldn't risk offending new allies on the first day, and nothing could wait. He was in a position of power now. It was best that he behave like it.

The visitors joined him at the doorway and he glanced over his shoulder just long enough to see Firal's face fall when Medreal handed her the rolled parchment.

Vahn tore his eyes away. "Shall we?" he asked, leading the way into the hall.

Survas walked at his side, a placid, pleased expression on his face. "If your men can help transport goods through the Gate, it would be appreciated. A show of goodwill from both sides, if you will?"

"Of course," Vahn murmured, almost absently. The councilors behind him chattered, but he didn't understand them and didn't bother listening.

It wasn't until they reached the Gate that one of them addressed him again.

"I almost forgot," Redoram said, digging in the pockets of his too-heavy velvet robes. "I promised to give this to the queen. Will you see that it is given to your wife?" He gave a sheepish smile and held out a folded letter.

Vahn blinked. "Certainly, Councilor." He took it, and when his eyes caught the marking on the wax seal, his heart skipped a beat.

It couldn't be.

Not now, not after everything they'd been through, after everything had changed.

"Good!" The bearded man grinned, rubbing his hands together. "In that case, thank you, Your Majesty, and be well. We must return to our duties, but rest assured, the permanent Gate will be established within a week."

Vahn faltered for a response. He was a king now; he couldn't let visiting dignitaries see how easily his world was turned upside down. He swallowed hard as he bowed his head and touched a hand to his heart. "Very well. Safe travels, councilors. Brant's blessing upon you all." Vahn stepped back to let the councilors pass through the Gate. As they crossed to the other side, he murmured new orders to the guards and mages who surrounded the portal.

Men with crates of food began to come through only a moment later. The soldiers assisted, the mages directed, and Vahn shrank back, staring down at the letter in his hand. He thought of the year behind them, of the words he knew would be inside. He thought of Firal, surely crying, needing comfort. As she had needed from him for the past year. That time had strengthened their friendship, let it deepen into something else. He thought of the promise he'd made to a friend, what now seemed an eternity past. He thought of Firal in his arms, and he swallowed.

He crumpled the letter and stuffed it into his pocket.

THE MOUNTAIN of goods in the college courtyard was slow to shrink, even with the presence of the armored men in Ilmenhith's colors who helped carry crates through the Gate. There was more to commerce than just moving things, though. A slender man Rune recalled from the Royal City's council chamber stood by the mages who maintained the Gate and documented everything that passed his station. The fellow was meticulous about his job. Once, he stopped workers so he could count the gourds in an unmarked wooden bin before it was allowed it through. More shipments arrived throughout the day, keeping workers busy until sundown.

Rune watched it all. He only left his place near the Gate once, when Garam took a moment's break from overseeing his men in the early afternoon, and only then after the captain swore to watch for anyone who didn't seem to be there for trade. The break allowed him to stretch his legs, relieve himself, and find something to quiet his grumbling stomach, but Rune returned and resumed his vigil as soon as he had food in hand.

The last of the supplies passed through the Gate beneath a flame-red sky, an unusually vivid sunset for late winter. Men stood and watched the clouds change color as business concluded. Councilors from both sides of the Gate signed papers and gave handshakes before a coffer changed hands as payment.

In a moment of idleness, Garam split away from his soldiers to join Rune at the wall. "Still here?"

Rune nodded and shifted on the ground. "Still here."

Mages had come and gone through the day, replacing those

who held the Gate. More joined them now, as they prepared to open another Gate to send the Royal City's guardsmen back to the fields just south of the capital. The councilors bowed to each other one last time before those visiting from Elenhiise retreated through the Gate. The mages let it fall, leaving the new stone archway empty. The space before it, after a day of endless bustle, finally cleared.

Rune stared at the archway and the empty plaza. His heart sank and bands of constriction tightened around his chest. He swallowed thickly and let his eyes drop. "Still here."

Garam sank to the ground beside him, rested his elbows on his raised knees, and leaned back against the cool stone. "I'm sorry. I know this meant a lot to you."

Lifting a hand to his throat, Rune grasped the rings on their strap around his neck and squeezed his eyes shut. "She did."

The captain stared at the darkening horizon and pulled a flask from his armor. He took a swig and grimaced at the taste before he held it out in offering. "To freedom?"

Rune snorted softly and took the flask from Garam's hand. He jerked the rings and the cord snapped. "To freedom," he murmured, and drank.

23

FREEDOM

A KNOCK AGAINST THE DOOR BOOMED LIKE THUNDER IN HIS SKULL, jarring Rune's head from the pillow. He groaned and grimaced when a servant opened the door to let light into the room, bright and cheerful and like driving daggers into his eyes.

The maid bobbed a curtsy. "Forgive the interruption, my lord, but there's someone here to see you." Her voice grated like a file. The sound made his skin rise in gooseflesh. He shuddered.

"All right," he croaked, lifting a scaly hand to rub his eyes and relieve the stabbing feeling behind them. "I'll be down."

Bobbing again, the maid closed the door and left his room blessedly dark. The windows glowed a soft blue through thick curtains, casting cool, muted tones across the room. Easier to see by than the blinding brightness of the rest of the house, where daybreak had apparently been welcomed with all curtains opened. Still, he had to wrench his eyes open and blink hard to clear his bleary vision.

Rune only half-remembered returning to Redoram's house. He recalled needing Garam's help to walk, but the rest was muddied by the pain that pulsed in his head. He wanted to complain about early guests, but a glance toward the dim windows reminded him he had no idea of the time. For all he knew, he'd slept half the day.

Groaning again, he pushed himself upright. He was still dressed, his clothing rumpled. His uniform waited on a chair beside the washstand, but he barely spared it a glance before he trudged to the door. He didn't want to wear that uniform again, and didn't plan to. Smoothing the wrinkles in his shirt, he braced himself for the light before he stepped out of the guest quarters and made his way toward the parlor where Redoram received his guests.

"Good morning," Alira said as he reached the doorway. So he hadn't slept half the day; only part of it. Her mouth tightened at the sight of him, though she didn't move from the couch. "What's the matter with you?"

Rune stumbled on the edge of the plush rug and shot it a dirty look. As if the rug could help where its edges were. "Rough night," he grunted. He dropped into one of the chairs on the other side of the table, rubbed his eyes, and squinted at her. "Where's Rhyllyn?"

"In the yard, playing with some of the maids. It's pleasant out today, it feels like the first breath of spring." She shrugged. "Children should be outdoors."

Rune slouched in his seat, regarding her with a frown. "I thought the maid said someone was here for me."

Alira raised a brow. "I moved into a space of my own yesterday, while you were out. Councilor Parthanus has been kind in hosting us, but it's no longer required. So yes, I am here visiting. To see you." Her voice was soft enough it didn't grate on him like the maid's, but it still seemed too loud, echoing in his head. He couldn't help but wince. Her expression cooled and she rose to fill a cup from a porcelain pitcher on the table between them. He hadn't noticed the serving tray.

"Drink," she ordered, pushing the cup into his hand.

He expected to see wine, but it was only water. His mouth was dry, he decided, and he lifted the cup to his lips to wet them.

Because he was thirsty, of course; not because one of his former teachers bade him.

As soon as he took the first swallow, Alira reached across the table and laid a hand against his forehead. An icy jolt of energy flowed through him. Rune stifled a shout and jerked back, water sloshing over the rim of his cup. His headache subsided and his vision cleared, but now his mouth and throat felt as dry as scorched sand.

"If you've any sense at all, you'll not let yourself become so dehydrated again. What did you do, sit in the sun all day?" She gave a lofty sniff and settled back into her seat.

He stared. With his eyes bloodshot and heavy and the smell of alcohol still thick on him, there was no way to mistake what he'd been doing. Belatedly, he realized she was trying to spare his dignity.

Not feeling particularly dignified, he drained his cup in a few swallows and wiped his mouth with the back of his green-scaled hand. "Sort of," he murmured. "Why are you here?"

She motioned to the pitcher as she spoke, encouraging him to refill his cup. "When we were in Aldaan, I asked you to look after Rhyllyn if something were to happen to me. We're no longer in danger, but after careful consideration, I think it best if you still play an active role in the boy's life."

Rune filled his cup to the brim and drank half of it before his throat felt cool enough for him to speak. "I told you before that I don't think I'd be a very good father to him. Besides, he's comfortable with you."

"And I care for him a great deal. He is a good child, and I am partially responsible for his plight. But King Vicamros has graciously offered me a position as one of his new court mages. Once I am well-versed in the Triad's laws, I will be allowed to use my Gift as I please, exempted from the barrier that keeps magic from being used within the city." She paused and licked her lips, as if hesitant to say more. She continued anyway. "Additionally, I have accepted a position within the local guild of scholars, which Councilor Parthanus represents. They have many mages in their midst, and it seems the temple on Elenhiise teaches a number of skills that are all but forgotten by mages here."

"How does that affect Rhyllyn?"

Alira smoothed her skirts across her knees. "I am happy to keep him with me, but I will be busy. And because of his... circumstances, I feel he needs contact with someone who understands what he faces. Someone familiar with his sort of magic, too."

Rune snorted. "Me."

"Yes." She rested her hands in her lap. "I am not asking you to act as his father. Just to continue to be a brother to him. To be active and present and show him that someone understands. That he can still earn recognition and respect, even if he doesn't look like everyone else."

Recognition and respect? He almost laughed. "I'm not sure you know much about my reputation here."

"On the contrary," Alira said with a slight smile. "I don't think you know the impact you've had. You have a way of affecting everything you touch. Everywhere you go, you leave a trail of change in your wake."

He stared at her over the rim of his cup as he finished his water. Then he put down his cup and stared at it instead. "Rhyllyn is a good boy."

"He is."

"I never had support when I was growing up," Rune continued. "I want to give it to him. I mean that. But there's something I need to do first."

"Which is?" She tilted her head, regarding him with curiosity.

"Find Filadiel. Or any of the mages who sealed my magic." He laced his fingers together and studied his scales. "They said they would help me. That I could be repaired. But before they could do it, before they could cleanse me, I had to understand things they didn't have time to teach. I'm beginning to understand. And if the corruption that turned me into a monster really can be undone, I need to know. Not just for me, but for Rhyllyn, too. If I find them, he and I might have a chance to be normal."

"Do you know where to look?" Alira asked.

He nodded. "According to the gryphons, they headed north from Aldaan. I can begin there. I don't know how long it will take me. A year, two years, maybe more. But Rhyllyn's growth will slow, now that his Gift is developing. A handful of years is little time to mages."

"That's true," she conceded.

"And I won't be silent. I'll let you know what I find. Besides," he smirked, "the mages of Aldaan can't be the only free mages left in the world. I might run across someone else who can help us."

She bowed her head. "Very well. But I have a request."

His brow furrowed. "What?"

"Return to the Royal City at least once a year to see Rhyllyn."

"I think I can manage that." Assuming he didn't get himself arrested again. And, he thought with a grimace, assuming he'd be allowed to leave at all.

Alira eyed him with suspicion. "What's the matter?" She sounded more wary than concerned.

Rune pushed himself up from his chair. "Just remembering something I need to do." And couldn't, dressed as he was. He sighed, realizing he'd need his uniform again after all. "But I'll send you word before I leave the city. Did you need anything else?"

"No, that's all." She dusted the skirt of her white robe and then rose, offering her hand. "I'm pleased to have been able to work with you in Aldaan. I hope the years ahead bring us friendship."

He looked at her in surprise. A year before, he never would have imagined himself making peace with one of the mages he'd blamed for his condition. Friendship would have been out of the question. Yet as he looked at her now, it seemed so reasonable. Slowly, he reached out and clasped her hand in his taloned grip.

Her handshake was firm but friendly, and her bright blue eyes softened as she let go. "Fair winds, Rune."

"And deep roots, Alira." He smiled, ever so slightly, then turned away. There was one last matter to attend.

***

"HE WAS the closet thing I had to a father," Firal said as Vahn laced his fingers with hers. She cradled Lulu in her other arm, but couldn't bring herself to tear her eyes from the group of white-robed mages that carried Nondar's litter toward a deep hole in the earth. Burial still struck her as an odd practice, but it made sense for the Archmage. He had been afforded few luxuries from his homeland. That he be laid to rest in the way they favored was the least she could offer.

Vahn squeezed her hand. "He was a good man and a good Archmage. You couldn't have made a better choice."

"I only wish he could have held the position longer." Firal's tears of sorrow had turned into tears of relief when she'd opened Nondar's final letter and discovered her best friend named as his successor, but that had only made her grief that much deeper in the end. Even in his dying moments, he had sought to make her life better.

Every mage on Elenhiise stood in the wide, grassy space between Kirban Temple and the ruins. Firal had not truly grasped what it meant to be Archmage until she saw them all together, a sea of multicolored robes sprinkled with clusters of white that reminded her of foam-capped waves. She could only hope she hadn't brought too great a burden down on Kytenia's shoulders.

Slowly, the Masters lowered Nondar's litter into the pit. The sight gave Firal a chill.

"Davan says the Underlings bury their dead in catacombs," Vahn murmured. "In stone sarcophagi and alcoves carved into the walls."

"They do," Firal said. "I saw it, once." How long had it been since she'd recalled that? Falling into the tunnels beneath the ruins seemed so long ago, it could have been a different life.

Beside her, Vahn shivered.

"It's not that bad," she whispered. "I asked Minna about it once, when I lived there. She said it wasn't always their tradition. Their ancestors used funeral pyres, like the eastern half of the island still does. But after construction of the temple began, they feared the smoke would draw too much attention."

He grunted softly. "Do you think they'll mind? Having Nondar buried here, I mean."

Firal shrugged. "I don't know." In truth, it seemed unlikely. Like so many other things that had come to pass under her fledgling rule, it could serve to unify their people. She swayed softly, rocking the sleeping child that rested against her chest.

The Masters retreated from the open grave and Edagan stepped forward from the crowd. Firal's eyes skirted past her to search the faces of those nearby. Since Shymin and Rikka had been named successors to their respective Houses, they had never strayed far from the temple's leaders. Firal caught sight of them with Anaide, but she'd expected to see Kytenia with them. She found her friend some distance away, alone among hundreds of strangers. They locked eyes and Firal offered a nod of reassurance.

Kytenia nodded in return.

"Nondar chose well," Vahn said, following her gaze. "She'll support you through anything."

"She always has," Firal agreed. Just like he had.

Edagan raised both arms overhead and made a slow, gentle motion. The earth answered, and magic tingled in Firal's senses as the ground folded closed around Nondar's body.

Tears blurred her vision and she tightened her grasp on

Vahn's hand as they escaped over her lashes to roll down her cheeks.

A blush of green touched the disrupted soil as grass sprang forth, called by the Master's power. "May he find favor among the stars," Edagan said. Hundreds of voices echoed her words.

"And among the roots," Firal added softly.

Another group of white-robed Masters stepped forward, carrying a narrow stone pillar between them. They stood it on end and Edagan sank it into the earth with a flick of her fingers. It stayed upright when they moved back, a lone marker in the center of the field to signify where the Archmage lay.

Firal swallowed hard.

Vahn brushed tears from her face with his fingertips and then wrapped her in a hug, mindful not to smother the baby between them. "I'm sorry."

She tried to muster a smile, but the expression wouldn't come. "I am, too." She dried her cheeks with the cuff of her sleeve. For a moment, when they'd arrived, she'd regretted that she'd worn a gown instead of mageling robes. The feeling hadn't lasted long. She no longer belonged in the temple; Nondar's passing had only solidified that.

"Are you all right?" he asked, the gentle light of concern in his eyes enough to make her heart ache.

"I will be." Had he asked that question any sooner, she wouldn't have known how to answer. But now, as she leaned into his shoulder and blinked away the last of her tears, she didn't know how she could answer with anything else. Firal gave her eyes one last swipe, then sniffed hard and straightened where she stood. "Let's go home."

She'd lost her mentor, but with Vahn close by—as he had been, since her life had crumbled a second time—she knew she wasn't alone.

GARAM ANSWERED his office door looking cool and collected, and not at all surprised to see Rune on the other side. He shouldn't have appeared as orderly as he did, Rune thought, but then again, anything else would have been uncharacteristic of the captain. Garam's clothes were perfectly pressed, his hair and beard perfectly edged, and the rest of his face as smooth as if he'd just shaved. "You're late," the captain said gruffly, but he didn't look irritable.

Rune shrugged, adjusting the knapsack slung over his shoulder. "Let's get this over with, shall we?"

Grunting in response, Garam stepped into the hall and closed the door. He started for the stairs at an easy pace, adjusting the cuffs of his dark green coat on the way. "With fortune, we won't have to wait long. The king is a busy man."

"And yet you said he wanted to speak with me." It had struck Rune as odd when Garam told him King Vicamros wished to see him, but that conversation had taken place during their trip back to Redoram's house the night before, after Rune had downed too many drinks. They'd both had too many, but the captain held his liquor better.

Garam shrugged and said nothing.

They walked the familiar path from the barracks to the Spiral Palace without speaking. The palace glinted in the midday light, banners fluttering on the unseasonably warm breeze. The first scents of spring drifted on the air, green and fresh and pleasant. It felt like a new season, a new beginning. Rune tried not to dwell on the coincidence. The palace doors stood open and the guards merely nodded a stiff greeting as they passed; the two of them were expected.

Unlike their previous visit, upon their return from Aldaan, the great hall was now filled with life. A throne sat at the far end of the room, on the dais that had hosted musicians during the banquet. Rune could almost hear the music.

There were no dancers this time, but groups of councilors and nobles chattered and formed vague lines that led toward the king. Vicamros lounged comfortably in his throne, conversing with Bryndis—who stood at his side—as he made his decisions and decrees. She saw the two of them first and laid a hand on the king's arm. He paused in the middle of his sentence. Then she gestured toward them, and King Vicamros waved the noble before him away.

"Captain Kaith! Good man. Come, both of you." Vicamros beckoned them and sat upright.

Garam strode ahead and the crowd parted before him. He bowed deeply when he reached the foot of the dais. Rune stayed a step behind the captain, but did the same. He'd have to grow used to dealing with rulers that way. Royals didn't bow to other royals, but he had to remind himself he was no longer Vicamros's equal. Perhaps he never had been.

"I am sorry he was not present at the reception before," Garam said, as if testing the king's mood. "He had urgent personal matters to tend before—"

"I can speak for myself," Rune interrupted, earning himself a dirty look. He met Garam's dark eyes with a level gaze.

Vicamros chuckled. "Yes, and you ought. Because I have questions Captain Kaith can't answer for you."

Garam shifted back, his expression grim.

Rune couldn't blame the captain for expecting the worst. Considering his stint in the arena, it wasn't as if he had a stellar record.

"My son tells me you rescued him in battle," the king continued, leaning forward and resting an elbow on the arm of his throne. "What sort of reward did you think that would earn you?"

Rune frowned. There was an intensity in the king's eyes— weighing, but not judging. Not the look of a man who was trying to root out problems. Instead, it struck Rune more as the light of curiosity. "I helped him find his feet and run. Anything else is an exaggeration, Majesty. It was an act of cowardice, not courage."

Vicamros's eyes narrowed. "You were outmatched and underprepared. Fighting would have been foolhardy. Retreat isn't always cowardice."

"And rescues aren't always made because reward is expected," Rune said. "I didn't know he was the prince until afterward. Before that, he was just another soldier."

"But you did learn his identity, and he tells me you pushed Captain Kaith to allow him to stay. Why?"

"Because young men need chances to prove themselves, Majesty. Better that he have the chance where friends can protect him than in the arena, where he may lose his head."

Bryndis covered her mouth, flushed, and turned away. The king threw back his head and laughed. "You're an honest man, aren't you?"

Rune gave a wry smile. "Sometimes."

Garam sighed.

"So what do you want?" Vicamros leaned back, grinning. "You're honest sometimes, and I'm generous sometimes. And sometimes, you save my only son's life. Name your reward."

Rune thought he'd been walking the line of imprisonment, helping the prince disregard his father's orders. A reward was better than he had dared hope for. He drew a breath and spared Garam a sidewise glance before he spoke. "If it pleases Your Majesty, I would like to be released from my position in the city guard."

The king tilted his head. "And?"

Rune hesitated. "A house in the city or a small parcel of land, perhaps. If I am released from the guard, I won't have a home to return to."

"Land ownership in the Triad would make you a lord," Vicamros said.

"I don't need the title, Majesty. Just a place to rest my head."

Snorting, the king flicked his fingers and laughed. "A farmer, then! Very well. I grant your independence, and we'll find you a parcel in Roberian. But my army holds drafts to draw soldiers from the country. Be aware that your residency means you're obligated to respond."

Bowing from the shoulders, Rune touched his clawed fingertips to his heart. "I understand, Majesty. You are a generous man. I have nothing to offer but my service and my thanks."

"With fortune, your service won't be needed again. But it's always good to know my Captain of the Guard still chooses such capable men to serve my city. Once the papers for your parcel of land have been drawn, they will be sent to Captain Kaith's office for you to claim. Now go, enjoy your independence!" The king waved them away and turned to beckon the noble who had been next in line. The man looked none too pleased at having been forced to wait.

Garam moved back from the dais and Rune followed him, almost dazed. He'd never imagined so much could transpire in just a handful of minutes, though he understood Vicamros's need for brevity. The man ruled three kingdoms, not one, and his councilors had affiliations that made them unfit to deal with some matters.

Rune and Garam made it halfway across the room before hurried footsteps behind them made them both pause.

"May I speak to you a moment, before you leave?" Bryndis rarely hurried, but even in her rush to catch up with them, she managed to look calm.

Rune glanced to Garam, but the captain only shrugged.

She took it as an invitation to speak. "I owe you an apology," she said, looking at Rune.

He blinked. "Me? For what?"

"Well, both of you, I suppose." Bryndis bowed her head and clasped her hands at her waist. "When you were in the arena, I assumed you were a ruffian, a criminal like anyone else in there. People of status are never sent to the arena, if arrested at all." Her cheeks colored as she spoke and she cleared her throat before she went on. "When you spared the prince in your arena match, all I saw was that you had shamed him by refusing to give him a warrior's defeat. At the time, I didn't think it mercy. I thought it arrogance, something we couldn't allow to breed. And so I asked Captain Kaith to make you disappear."

The weight of the last word gave Rune pause. He raised a brow at Garam.

The captain nodded. "She did. But I don't think she expected I would put you in the guard."

"Why didn't you kill me?" Rune asked. "It's obviously what she meant."

"Captain Kaith isn't in the habit of wasting the lives of good men." Bryndis smiled. "For which I'm glad. If not for his judgment, things may have gone very differently in Aldaan. So for all you've done—both of you—you have my thanks. That is all." She dipped in a graceful bow and paced back toward the dais.

"She doesn't think she's going to see me again," Rune said, watching her retreat.

Garam chuckled softly. "She may not be the only one." He slapped Rune's shoulder, then made his way out to the broad street before the palace.

Rune thought Garam meant himself, but subtleties in his tone made him think again. He followed as the captain wove his way through the crowded, curving street that led to one of the city's main gates.

"How'd you know the king would let you go?" Garam asked with a nod toward the knapsack on Rune's shoulder.

"I didn't. But I figured I could ask for time off, if nothing else."

The captain looked skeptical. "Let's be honest. You would have left whether or not I gave permission."

Rune grimaced, but didn't see any reason to lie. "For a while. A lot has happened to me in the past year. I need some time to clear my head before I'll be of use to anyone. I figured I would take a trip to Lore first, visit the Grand College and see what the mages can tell me about the seal on my magic. They might be able to fix it, or at least point me in the direction of someone who can."

"Your land will be ready for you by the time you come back. Planning to settle down?"

"Or have a house built, at least. I promised Alira I'd look after Rhyllyn once I find what I need to know. He'll need stability in his life. It seems like having a permanent home would be a good place to start." The crowd thinned as they neared the city gate and Rune blinked in surprise when two figures moved toward them.

"Look at that, the lizard met with the king and still kept his head!" Sera grinned at him. She stopped a few paces away and leaned against a staff. She had a satchel slung against her back and another hung against her hip, both bulging with supplies. Redoram stood at her heels with a bundle of his own, but the awkward way he handled it made it seem unlikely he meant to travel.

Rune gave her a dirty look, but the expression was quick to fade. "Going somewhere?"

"Northwest." She shrugged. "The Aldaanan never returned. I plan on going back to Aldaeon and giving them a message to pass to the mages, should they ever reappear. They deserve a piece of my mind."

"But she can't leave without this, which is why we came this way." Garam drew a purse from his coat pocket and bounced it in his palm to make the coins jingle.

Sera snatched it out of his hand with a laugh. "Campaign pay is what always finances my trips. This should last me until the next civil war, eh, Garam?"

Behind her, Redoram coughed. "Our civil wars aren't that frequent."

"The fact that we've had more than one is bad enough, considering the age of the Triad. Just be glad I'm considering coming back. I might meet somebody out there and change my mind." She glanced between the three men a moment before she shrugged and turned to go with a wave. "Nobody die before I make it back to the Royal City, understand? Take care of yourselves."

"You too," Rune murmured.

She paused once more to wave over her shoulder, then vanished past the city gate with a spring in her step.

He felt a twinge of guilt as she disappeared. He hadn't thought to say goodbye to her before starting his own travels. All things considered, they were friends. He should have.

"What have you got for me, Councilor?" Garam's voice snapped him back to the moment.

Redoram cleared his throat and held out the bundle in his arms. "I learned a great deal, but I wish you'd allow me more time to study it. Kingswords are imbued with magic, and artifacts like that are so rare the college has never been able to examine one closely enough to learn how it's done. It's a shame that only free mages are able to weave magic into things, I'm sure there's a way for us to do it, as well."

"Kingsword?" Rune demanded. His eyes darted between the captain and the scholar as anger swelled in his chest. "You had it the entire time?"

Redoram only laughed. "You didn't think tutoring you was the only reason I was let out of prison, did you?" He passed the sword to Garam. A wistful look filled his eyes as the captain unwrapped it and examined the twisted black hilt. "Remember, I am a mage and a scholar. And I must say, seeing such a fine artifact has been a privilege."

"And did you learn which king this one belonged to?" Garam stepped back, gripping the sword in both hands and eyeing Rune as if he no longer trusted him.

Redoram shrugged. "After a fashion. It was made as a wedding gift for a man who sought to found his own kingdom. Whether or not he became a king, it's impossible to say, but had he not married a free mage, he wouldn't have been given such an impressive gift."

"Do you know his name?" Garam asked.

"Oh, yes, it—"

The captain held up a hand to silence the old man. "No, never mind." He gazed thoughtfully at the sword for a moment before he offered the hilt to Rune. "I know who it belongs to now. That's what matters."

Rune drew a breath and stared at the blade. He'd given up on seeing it again. It was a relic of a life he couldn't have, a painful reminder of what he'd lost. But it was his father's sword. His sword. He took it carefully, testing it in his hand. The familiar weight sent a wave of relief through him.

"And something else I owe you." Garam drew something from his coat and held it out. Rune raised a brow at the sight of the purse, identical to the one he'd given Sera.

"Payment owed for your time in the guard," the captain explained.

"Keeps me from stealing food and winding up in the dungeon again, I suppose." Rune grinned at him.

Garam snorted. "I'm not pulling your scaly backside out if that happens again. Keep your nose clean. And come back for your land before I decide to keep it for myself." He took a step back toward the palace, then paused to glance over his shoulder. "I hope you find what you're looking for."

Rune nodded. "Thank you, Garam. You've done me more favors than I deserve."

The captain waved a hand in disregard and walked away.

Redoram gazed after him for a time. A sigh escaped his lips as he turned back to Rune and the sword in his hands. "The man it belonged to was a Lord Penedhionn," the councilor said, his voice low. "I hope you bring it back to me one day, so I might finish studying it."

"I'll let you have a look next time I visit. Just don't die before

I come back." Rune hefted the sword up to lay the broad side against his shoulder.

"You still owe me a game of runes," the old mage complained.

"I'll miss you too, Redoram."

Redoram sniffed and rubbed his nose as if irritated. He turned on his heel. "Well, I've studies waiting for me. Things to learn from that mage friend of yours, too. Alira, was it? Interesting woman."

"She taught at the Kirban Temple, a school founded by the Penedhionn royal family." Rune wasn't surprised to see the councilor stop. "It's tradition for royals to keep the name. I suppose Lord Penedhionn managed to become a king after all."

The old mage smiled, his eyes softening. "So it would seem. Easy roads beneath your feet, my friend. Now that you're free." He straightened his cap before moving on.

Smoothing his satchel's strap, Rune moved past the gate. He took in the sight of everything beyond the city walls, another prison now escaped, and slid his coin purse into his pocket. He *was* free, he realized as he stared down the rolling country roads. He'd not expected to find freedom. And for the first time, with no expectations or obligations, every one of those countless roads was open for travel. Shifting the sword on his shoulder, Rune spared it a glance from the corner of his eye as he began to walk.

Perhaps there was always hope to find lost things.

GLOSSARY

Affinity – One's natural inclination in magic. There are five major affinities: Earth, water, fire, wind, and life. These provide the primary source of power a mage can draw from and manipulate. While there are smaller subcategories affinities may fall into, granting specific talents in narrow fields, they are generally related to one of the five and, as result, only the five major affinities are recognized.

Aldaan – One of three provinces in the Triad.

Aldaanan – A faction of free mages.

Alira – (*uh-LEER-ah*) – Master of the House of Fire.

Alwhen – (*OWL-when*) – The capital of the eastern half of Elenhiise island, a region known as the Giftless Lands.

Anaide – (*uh-NAYD*) – Master of the House of Water.

Archmage – The leader of Kirban Temple, generally recognized as the leader of all mages.

Core – An underground city beneath the ruins, home of the Underlings.

Daemon – (*DAY-mun*) – An Underling soldier. His tainted magic has twisted his body into a monstrous form.

Davan - An officer among the Underlings.

Edagan – (*ED-ah-gan*) – Master of the House of Earth.

Eldani – (*ell-DAN-ee*) – The only inhabitants of Ithilear who are known to be Gifted. Eldani are long-lived, due to their magic, and differ from humans only in their pointed ears. Diluted bloodlines are recognized by the reduced point of an Eldani's ear, which directly corresponds with their prowess as a mage.

Elenhiise – (*ELL-en-heese*) – A small island in the middle of the Lantaaran sea, generally used as a waypoint in trade between the region's northern and southern continents. The island is ruled by two factions, the Gifted Eldani and Giftless men.

Ennil – (*in-ill*) – Full name Ennil Tanrys. Former Captain of the Guard of Ilmenhith. Vahn's father.

Envesi – (*in-VESS-see*) – The Archmage of Kirban Temple.

Eyrion Tolmarni – (*EAR-ee-on toll-MAR-nee*) – Headmaster of the Grand College of Lore.

Filadiel – (*fil-LAD-ee-ell*) – Leader of the Aldaanan mages.

Firal – (*fur-ALL*) – A green-rank mageling at Kirban temple.

Flows – The natural ebb and flow of magic, which mages are able to seize and manipulate.

Garam – Full name Garam Kaith. Captain of the Royal City Guard. Sera's brother.

Gift – The ability to use magic.

House – A subsection of mages, ruled by a particular affinity. Mages within the House of Healing, Fire, etc. may take classes together, but their education is overseen by the Master of their House.

Ileara – (*ill-ee-ARE-ah*) – The second moon. The smaller of the two, Ileara is known as The Mother and is stationary in the sky. As it is only visible in the far western regions of the known world, such as the Westkings and the Chains of Raeldan, some residents of Elenhiise and the other eastern regions do not believe Ileara exists.

Ilmenhith – (*ill-men-HITH*) – The capital of the western half of Elenhiise island, which is under Eldani control.

Ithi – (*ith-EE*) – The first moon. The larger of the two, Ithi is known as The Soldier and circles Ithilear once per day. The thirteen months of the year are framed around Ithi's phases; its cycle is 28 days.

Ithilear – (*ith-ILL-ee-arr*) – The world. The name is derived from the two moons, Ithi and Ileara. In folklore, the moons are lovers. Ithi ventures forth to patrol and protect their child, Ithilear, while Ileara remains in one place to provide a stable home.

Kifel – (*kiff-EL*) – Full name Kifelethelas Penedhionn. The Eldani king and ruler of the western half of Elenhiise island.

Kirban Temple – (*KER-ban*) – Founded by Archmage Envesi, Kirban Temple is the only school of magecraft on Elenhiise

Island. A prestigious college sponsored by the Eldani crown and located near the southern edge of the ruins.

Kytenia – (*kit-teen-yah*) – A yellow-rank mageling at Kirban Temple and Firal's best friend.

Lore - One of three provinces in the Triad.

Lumia – (*loo-MEE-ah*) – Queen of the Underlings.

Mageling – A mage in training. Magelings are divided into five ranks before they graduate to Master and wear robes in corresponding colors. The five ranks are gray, lavender, yellow, green, and blue.

Marreli – (*mah-RELL-ee*) – A gray-rank mageling at Kirban Temple. One of Firal's friends.

Master – A mage recognized as skilled enough to wield magic without supervision. Masters outside the temple act as healers and scholars, and are in charge of scouting Gifted children to send for training. Masters who remain within the temple are generally teachers. Master mages are the only mages allowed to wear white. Court Masters and Masters of an affinity mark their eyes with black ink to distinguish their rank.

Medreal – (*mee-dree-al*) – King Kifel's stewardess.

Melora – (*mel-LOR-ah*) – Master of the House of Wind.

Minna - An Underling woman who befriends Firal.

Nondar – (*non-DAR*) – Master of the House of Healing, also known as the House of Life. Nondar is one of few recognized half-Eldani Masters and is unparalleled as a medic.

Ran – Full name Lomithrandel. A blue-rank mageling at Kirban temple and the only part-time student allowed. He considers Firal a friend, while she considers him a nuisance.

Redoram – (*RED-or-AM*) – Full name Redoram Parthanus. Former councilor in the Triad's Royal City.

Relythes – (*rell-uh-THEEZ*) – The Giftless King, ruler of Alwhen and the eastern half of Elenhiise island.

Rhyllyn – (*rill-in*) – A street urchin from Lore.

Ria – A gryphon messenger and amateur cartographer.

Rikka – (*RIK-kuh*) – A yellow-rank mageling at Kirban Temple. One of Firal's friends.

Roberian – One of three provinces in the Triad.

Royal City – The capital of the Triad.

Ruins – A sprawling labyrinth in the center of the island. The ruins fall entirely on Eldani lands.

Rune - A new name given to Daemon.

Sera – Full name Sera Kaith. A mage in the Royal City and a scout for the guard. Garam's sister.

Shymin – (*SHY-min*) – A green-rank mageling at Kirban Temple. One of Firal's friends and Kytenia's elder sister.

Tren – Full name Tren Achos. Lumia's general.

Triad – An empire in the north, composed of three provinces—

Aldaan, Lore, and Roberian—and ruled by King Vicamros.

Underlings – Giftless people driven into the ruins by war, rumored to be monsters and believed to be legend.

Vahn – Full name Vahnil Tanrys. A low-ranking soldier in Ilmenhith's military.

Vicamros – (*vi-CAM-rows*) – King of the Triad.

Vivenne – (*viv-INN*) – Full name Vivenne Tanrys. Vahn's mother. Ennil's wife.